A single mother of two adult daughters, Alexy Mi is living her best life. Residing in Louisville Kentucky, she enjoys playing poker, attending family gatherings, and dancing. Writing is a true passion for her. She enjoys tackling real-life topics such as infidelity and dysfunctional relationships, whereas, the end will always lead to comedic—yet positive outcomes. Alexy Mi's goal is to empower her readers to remain strong through stressful situations, and to encourage laughter and patience while enduring a storm.

I dedicate *Perhaps It Was Fate* to my beloved mother, Wanda A Perkins. Forever in my heart, Momma, I miss you!

Alexy Mi

PERHAPS IT WAS FATE

AUSTIN MACAULEY PUBLISHERS™

LONDON * CAMBRIDGE * NEW YORK * SHARJAH

Ordering Information
Quantity sales: Special discounts are available on quantity purchases by corporations, associations, and others. For details, contact the publisher at the address below.

Publisher's Cataloging-in-Publication data
Mi, Alexy
Perhaps It Was Fate

ISBN 9781643788555 (Paperback)
ISBN 9781645754787 (Hardback)
ISBN 9781645754794 (ePub e-book)

Library of Congress Control Number: 2021905629

www.austinmacauley.com/us

First Published (2021)
Austin Macauley Publishers LLC
40 Wall Street, 33rd Floor, Suite 3302
New York, NY 10005
USA

mail-usa@austinmacauley.com
+1 (646) 5125767

First, I thank God for being alive. I am truly grateful for each day you've granted me and all the blessings you've placed at my feet.

To my Dad, words cannot describe the love and gratitude I have for you. Thank you sincerely for everything that you do for me, my siblings, and our children. You are the glue that keeps us together.

To my daughters, I am so proud of your accomplishments!

To my family, I couldn't have picked a better group of folks.

To my girlfriends, here we go again!

To my poker peeps, see ya at the book signing.

To my sweetheart, I did it!

Innermost—of a woman
An indescribable love
It's what she gives; and he cannot steal
The true meaning of
Love-joy

–   Alexy Mi

Chapter 1

God Created Man

It was November 23, 2012, when my husband delivered the best sermon of his career, *Praise is the Way I Say Thanks*. Not his best because I assisted in pulling this pre-thanksgiving sermon together but because for the first time as pastor and twenty minutes after closing his Bible, shouts, cries, and praises unto the Lord still rang out over the sanctuary. Even some of the choir members were unable to maintain their composure as they danced and shouted, much to DeMarcus's delight. Naturally, as his biggest supporter, I too was up on my feet waving my hands in agreement of the preached word brought forth. My husband glanced over and smiled at me. I smiled back.

"Praise Him!" he then shouted, only seconds before dropping his cloth and allowing the Holy Spirit to take over and move him into a celebratory dance of worship across the pulpit. The spirit was high in the sanctuary and once DeMarcus regrouped, his right-hand and left-hand Deacons, Deacons Collins and Moyler assisted him to his office. Deacon Swift grabbed his Bible and empty cider glass. Minister Jamal "Jay" Wright, DeMarcus's best friend since their seminary days and ministry confidant, stepped to the podium and opened the doors of the church for invitation and prayer.

It was routine for me after morning worship service to gather our children from the nursery then race across the lawn to start the bread so that it would be piping hot from the oven when DeMarcus arrived home. But on this day, I wanted to personally encourage my pastor-husband, and after fellowshipping with a few of the members, I headed toward his office. I was greeted by Deacon Andrew Davis sitting guard outside of DeMarcus's office.

"Good afternoon, Bro. Davis. How are you?"

"I'm blessed, Sister Rosilyn." He rose to his feet to give me a hug.

"Pastor's changing into some fresh clothes right now, but he should be just about ready to come out in a few."

Negro, please, is what came to mind; I knew what he was doing. Yes, I saw the Authorized Personnel Only sign affixed to the door—but if anyone was authorized it had to be me. I'm the pastor's wife. But still on a spirit-filled high and instead of losing my Christian cool, I playfully winked at him then shared having seen the pastor in the buff on a few occasions. Bro. Davis attempted to block my entrance by stepping in my path. I knew he was only following orders, but I was insistent on seeing my husband and forcefully brushed past his lint ball covered, nicotine smelling—outdated suit coat wearing, Humpty Dumpty looking azz.

Entering the foyer, gospel music played softly overhead. As I neared the office, voices and laughter rang out. Smiling too as I pushed the semi-closed door open and peeked inside, my presence seemed to have startled Deacons Collins and Moyler who were sitting at the table engaged in lively conversation. I acknowledged them both.

"Pastor gagagaave aaa fine sermon," Deacon Moyler stuttered.

"Yes, he did," Deacon Collins seconded.

"Pastors in in in the shower," Deacon Moyler blurted, oddly shifting his eyes over to Deacon Collins.

"Thanks for helping the pastor today, but I'll take it from here," I told them, referring to drying his back and helping him change into a fresh shirt and a comfortable pair of slacks.

"Oh, tha that gives me so much ja ja ja joy, helping my, my pastor," Deacon Moyler admitted. Deacon Collins agreed and assured me that my husband wouldn't be kept any longer than necessary. As much as I wanted to be the first to congratulate him on his powerful sermon, the thought of partaking any further in a meaningless, long and drawn out conversation with Deacon Moyler made me cringe. My patience had started to wear then and that was reason enough for me to leave.

Truly a sweet older gentleman, Deacon Moyler was one of the few men DeMarcus trusted and was undoubtedly faithful in serving his pastor. Deacon Collins, on the other hand, was the complete opposite; in his mid-thirties, a sexy, high yellow brother with soft, babyface features. He was sinfully gorgeous, and he knew it! Tagged *'eye candy of the church'* for being the center of several ruckuses involving available and not so available women seeking affection, DeMarcus had twice expressed concerns over the huge distraction his pimp daddy, nonchalant behaviors stirred up. But looks aren't everything and although his immaculately groomed facial hair drew attention to his juicy, perfectly rounded lips and even though his chiseled physique underneath layers of clothing made even my knees buckle, his arrogance was annoying and a major turn off.

Realizing that DeMarcus was in good hands, I returned my purse to my forearm and waved goodbye. Humming along with the hymn playing overhead, all was alright in my world as I proceeded toward the door. Extending out my arm to twist the doorknob, it turned. I stepped back to allow the persons' entry and was thrown off guard when Evonne waltzed in. Our eyes locked. She appeared to be just as miffed to see me as I was her. With a fake smile planted on her face, she greets me by my first name as if we were first cousins or something. Immediately, my peace turned to pissed. I was beyond agitated when I informed her that her husband was not in the pastor's office.

"My soon to be ex-husband, good!" she laughed. "That would be a violation of the EPO."

"What exactly is it that you need then? Is there anything I can help you with?" I asked as my right hand found my waistline and simultaneously my neck shifted to the left. My tone was rough, perhaps flat out rude. Aware of my demeanor, I attempted to dredge up a semi-cocked smile of my own.

What should have been an immediate 'no' turned into a slight roll of her neck, squinting of her eyes, and a sigh that almost compelled me into apologizing for asking such an inappropriate line of questions. *But hecky to the naw, naw!* And while she stood dazed and comatose in what appeared to be formulating a verbal response in her mind, I too began contemplating my next action; an ole' school beat down! Snapping back into reality, she cockily informed me of her responsibilities of delivering the pastor's dry cleaning each Sunday after worship service.

"The mother board puts them in on Monday afternoon and I pick them up early Saturday morning."

Her words put me in fighting mode. I was beyond livid. It became a true struggle to keep my calm. Surely, at this point, she could sense my rage but yet, tall she stood while staring me right on the eyeball and blinking her long, fake extended lashes as to ask, "Now What, Huh?"

"My husband is dressing right now, so I'll take this back. Thanks, Evonne," I said before snatching the garments from her arm.

"Oh, and next time, give his suits to one of the Deacons before worship. That way, Pastor will have them when he's done, and you won't be inconvenienced or rushed."

I watched her *no girdle wearing, giggly behind* fade into the cluster of people exiting through the back door. Thoughts of tackling her from behind and pounding her face into the wall and then into the floor came to mind, but that ain't no way for a pastor's wife to act.

Closing my eyes and taking a deep breath before re-entering the office, when I opened the door, I was forced to do a double-take. I was greeted by DeMarcus's backside; he was fully nude. He must have just stepped out of the shower because shortly thereafter, Deacon Collins picked up a towel and began drying his back. Deacon Moyler who was seated at the table buffing DeMarcus's shoes, never looked up.

"Evonne?" DeMarcus called out before reaching for another terry cloth towel and wrapping it around his waist.

"No, it's your wife. Deacons, will you please excuse us?" Laying the garment bag over a chair and slamming my Bible and purse down on the table, I made my way toward DeMarcus.

The abrupt silence spoke volumes. Deacon's Moyler and Collins scurried out of the room in a hurry—as if someone had announced the building was on fire. Picking up the towel Deacon Collins inadvertently dropped, DeMarcus wrapped it around his neck then leaned back on the edge of his desk. He extended out his arms and motioned me toward him, but I was in a fury.

"Hey, sweetie. Did you enjoy the sermon?" DeMarcus grabbed for my left arm, but I snatched it away.

"Is there something I need to know, DeMarcus? You're standing here nude and calling out for Evonne. I was damn near frisked trying to get back here to see you but then she comes strolling through the door like this is her own personal office. If Collins dries your back, then what the hell is Evonne supposed to do for you? Huh? Tell me what's going on?"

DeMarcus's smile disappeared. Rounding his desk, he took a seat at the conference table and stared into my eyes. He shook his head as if disappointed.

"If what I'm hearing is correct, you're accusing me of funny business with Evonne."

"What's the heifer running to your office for? And why did your Dummy and Flunky turn white as ghosts when I walked back through the door? Even your crippled azz security guard Davis tried blocking my entry. I'm your wife and I am demanding to know what the hell is going on!"

DeMarcus rarely argued with me, but I was fuming mad. I screamed from the top of my lungs and could care less if anyone heard me. Beneath the robe and away from the pulpit, their Pastor DeMarcus was human. His life issues are no different from anyone else's. I crossed my arms awaiting his reply. He insisted I calm down and demanded that I stop with what he called 'ridiculous accusations.'

"You know she helps the mothers," he spoke nonchalantly. "The only reason she's allowed in my office is to deliver my suits. Now if that's a problem for you…"

"What?" I snapped.

"If that's a problem for you then you just need to get over it. I'm their pastor and people enjoy doing things for me. You're just going to have to accept it."

No, he didn't. Yes, he did.

"DeMarcus, I do have a problem with that floozy being in your office wanting to provide personal services for you. Now get real, she's a tramp and you know it. It doesn't look right, and I don't like it. Make it the last time she enters this office!"

"What doesn't look right, her being an attractive woman? You didn't have any problems with her when she was at our house cooking your food when you were on bed rest. Come on, honey, Darryl and Wayne are in here all the time. Everybody loves the pastor babe. Some things you've just got to accept."

"I don't like it, I'm not accepting it, and I better not catch her in your office again. And look at you. You were completely naked before wrapping up in that towel."

"Are you jealous?"

"Of a short skirt wearing, big busted skank? No. But there's no reason for any woman, other than your wife, to be in this office, especially when you're getting dressed."

DeMarcus pulled me between his legs and kissed my forehead.

"It's not your call, but OK. If it bothers you that much, I'll have it put in the church bulletin that no one other than my wife and my Deacons are allowed in this office."

I hated when DeMarcus dismissed my concerns and tried making everything better with a kiss on my forehead. I also hated feeling like I was in a one-sided conversation, but I meant what I said and said what I meant and could see doing bodily harm to someone if it wasn't adhered to. When DeMarcus finished dressing, we walked to the nursery to gather our children, DeMarya aged three and a half and DeMarcus Jr. aka 'Lil D,' twenty-two months. Holding hands as we walked across the church grounds and to our home, before we entered, he pulled me into another tight hug. DeMarcus assured me of his love.

"My vow to love and cherish you came from my heart. I meant it then and I mean it even more today. I would never hurt or harm you. I love you, Rosilyn, you and only you."

Wednesday night Bible study was shortened so that we could get on the road and arrive in Louisville before midnight. DeMarcus was tired, so I gladly agreed to drive the eighty-three miles on I-64 toward my parents' house for a much-needed family getaway. Ma was standing in the doorway when we pulled into the driveway and before I could put the gear in PARK, she had loosened Lil D's seatbelt and removed the entire car seat. Although DeMarcus was barely awake from his nap, I thanked him with a kiss on the lips for putting his pastoral responsibilities aside to spend the Thanksgiving holiday with my family.

"I know I haven't been much help around the house or with the kids. And I do realize how stressed you've been not being able to spend time with your family. You deserve this break and I needed one too. Maybe if we're lucky, we can sneak off to have some one-on-one time. Catch a movie or something."

I loved the idea of going out on a date with my husband. It had been at least two years since we'd done something together—as a couple—other than grocery shopped or attended a church-related event. DeMarcus truly deserved this time off. In my opinion, he worked way too hard taking care of others and never took any time to care for his family or himself.

DeMarcus scooped up DeMarya from her car seat and once in the house, laid her down in my old bedroom. Afterward, he and my dad went off the radar, but I knew where to find them; stretched out on the recliners in the den talking, watching college football game updates, and gearing up to down as many beers as possible.

Ma had sat a now fully awake Lil D on the kitchen island to remove his jacket and shoes. While they played, I picked up where Ma had left off in the kitchen—mixing, picking, and stirring food; things I loved doing as a teenager. Around 2 a.m., after pulling my last pie from the oven, I joined my husband in the guest bedroom. He was snoring heavily when I slid underneath the comforter. However, feeling somewhat frisky, I curled my body underneath his and asked if he was asleep.

"I was. But why do you ask?" DeMarcus chuckled and turned over to face me. He grabbed the back of my neck and pressed his lips onto mine. One soft kiss led to another, then another, and then another. His hands caressed my face; his touch was gentle. He loved me so passionately that my entire body quivered in pleasure. He held me tight and loved me long and when our breathing returned to normal, he wrapped me even tighter in his arms. For twenty minutes or better, I rubbed and watched his face as he slept. Twice, he smiled which made me smile too. Oh, how I love my husband.

Being a pastor had proven to be truly a twenty-four hour, non-stop, seven days a week job for DeMarcus but he never complained. All hours of the day and night, he was getting pulled to various locations for various reasons and his cell phone seemed to never stop ringing or buzzing. And on this night, DeMarcus's unusually loud snoring was evidence of his extreme fatigue and in wanting to ensure that his rest went uninterrupted, I reached for his cellphone laying on the nightstand to put it on silent. Simply touching the phone, the once dark screen illuminated to blue—drawing my attention to a missed call from ED. I shook my head in frustration knowing that despite us being out of town, his dependent Deacons had already begun calling. I changed his setting then returned his cellphone to the nightstand.

At 6:25 sharp, the smell of potatoes and onions frying in the kitchen woke me. For as long as I could remember, Ma had always gotten up at the crack of dawn to prepare a breakfast smorgasbord for her houseguests and insisted on fixing everything herself. After grabbing my robe from the edge of the bed and then peeping in on Lil D and DeMarya who were still sleeping like angels, I joined Ma in the kitchen. I greeted her with a big kiss and an even bigger hug from behind. Ma let out a sigh.

"Why are you in my kitchen? Go back to bed honey," she said, tossing her left hand up in the air and shooing me away.

"I'll get the kids up and feed them when I'm done cooking. You've got at least another hour or two before *Little* and *Diddle* are up and running through this house. So, go on now! You won't be nothing but in my way."

In truth, I was physically exhausted—hadn't gotten much sleep for having to listen to the snoring orchestra starring DeMarcus the entire night and closing my eyes for another hour or so would be an answered prayer. Accepting Ma's offer, I kissed her cheek again and returned to the bedroom. Closing the bedroom door woke DeMarcus. He sat up, rubbed his eyes, yawned, and then reached for his cellphone to check the time. Prepared to snuggle a lot longer with my hubby, I slid underneath the comforter and laid my head upon his chest. I kissed his shoulder blade a few times before sliding my hand inside his boxers. DeMarcus smelled musky but my love-joy wanted another deep massage and therefore, I was hardly bothered by his stench. Lifting my right knee with plans to straddle the donkey, I was a bit shaken when DeMarcus pushed me off him. He looked upset. Although his tone was low, the anger in his voice spoke volumes when he asked if I had messed with his phone.

"I put it on silent, so it wouldn't wake you, babe. Oh, and by the way, Ed called. I hope everything is OK at the church."

"You checked my phone?" DeMarcus sounded upset.

"Excuse me?" I responded, then reaching up to turn on the headboard lamp to see the facial expression behind the question.

"Did you check my phone?" he asked again with more anger in his tone.

"I put it on silent but what's the big deal?"

"Never mind, Roz, I knew to expect this out of you." Still clutching his phone, he tossed back the comforter and sat on the edge of the bed.

"Expected what? For me to silence your phone so those non-thinking for themselves Deacons of yours wouldn't disturb us on our first day of our family vacation. Or you expected me to search through your phone?"

"Why are you so paranoid? Yesterday when we stopped to gas up and to get snacks, you accused the young store clerk of flirting with me. And now you're searching through my phone, for what? What do you expect to find?"

"Listen, I wasn't meddling through your phone, OK! To change it to mute I had to first clear the screen. It was Ed from the church. Now had it been Stephanie, Gina, or Evonne, I probably would have dialed them back and asked what the hell they wanted with you, but it wasn't, so chill." *So much for getting me some.*

As he did every morning before getting out of bed, DeMarcus kissed my forehead and gently rubbed my chin with his forefinger. Having successfully killed my mood for intimacy, I plopped my back against the headboard and watched him dress for his morning run.

"I really should come with you. Having babies hasn't been too kind to my figure."

"You still look good to me," he said with an unsettling chuckle.

"What's with the chuckle?" I tossed a pillow at him but missed.

"I've heard you say that at least a dozen times, but you never seem to take the time to put on your running shoes and join me."

Although he was right, I was offended. DeMarcus knew the reason we hadn't run together was because we had no one to watch our small children. However, getting back in shape was a personal goal of mine and at that very moment, I decided that after tucking the kids in at night and while DeMarcus was closed off in his study, to walk a mile or two around the church's walking trail.

"Well, my New Year's Resolution won't be to lose weight, but to shift my gut to my butt. I know what men like in a woman. I'll get my old body back, just watch."

DeMarcus threw his towel over his shoulder and placed his cell phone in his jacket pocket. From the bedroom window, I watched as he did a series of squats and stretches on Ma's porch in preparation for his run. Setting the timer on his watch as he walked down the driveway, when he reached the end of the road, he removed his cell phone from his pocket.

Chapter 2
Giving Thanks

It felt good returning to our home in Lexington after being off the spiritual grid for three consecutive days. Immediately upon walking through the front door, we return to our normal routines—resuming our lives as we knew it. Tending to the kids between preparing dinner and washing our dirty laundry, it didn't upset me when DeMarcus refused to help calm things down and closed himself off in his study. He never asked for much other than to be left alone while preparing his sermons and surely, he had a ton of work to catch up on. So, after mixing up his favorite drink of apple cider with a splash of rum concoction, I sat the cup down on his desk and left him to his work.

When I finished with my chores and eventually winning the battle of having the kids in the bed by ten o'clock, I let out a huge sigh. I was beyond exhausted—my back hurt but was very grateful to have the rest of the night to myself. So, after securing my hair on the top of my head with DeMarya's yellow scrunchy and tossing the clothes I was wearing inside the bathroom hamper, I prepared my mind to enjoy and soak my worn-down body in my favorite soothing raspberry oil bubble bath. I tested the temperature with my toe; the water was perfect. I plugged in my earbuds and powered on my MP3. Nineties old school jams got my head to slightly bop but I wanted a mellow tone and selected tunes sung by Toni Braxton. Slowly I lowered my body into the water. Lying completely back, I allowed the water to rest underneath my chin.

With my head comfortably resting on my spa bath pillow, my mind started to wander.

The clock on the wall was nearing midnight when I finally lifted the tub stopper and pulled out the earbuds. Stepping out of the tub, I allowed the natural air to dry my body. I brushed my teeth then wrapped my body in my favorite pink bathrobe. As I was walking toward the bedroom, the light shining from beneath the study door caught my eye. I peeked inside and smiled seeing DeMarcus still going strong on his computer. I cleared my throat; it startled him. He must have been deep into his work because he nearly jumped out of his skin seeing my smiling face in the doorway. I giggled then apologized. My hubby looked exhausted and being the good wifey that I was, decided to give him a soothing shoulder massage. But when I walked toward him, he let out a long yawn then logged off the computer.

"Were you finished?"

"Not quite but I am ready for bed." DeMarcus spun around in his chair and pulled me between his legs. I smiled when he told me I smelled good.

Awakened by DeMarya's whining the next morning, having overslept threw us all off track. DeMarya was irritable and wanted to be packed around. An overly energized Lil D, aka Junior, was making a game out of leaping from the couch to the coffee table to the ottoman and back, refusing to sit down and eat his breakfast until his dad buttered and sliced his pancakes. But instead of helping with the mayhem in the kitchen or saying good morning for that matter, DeMarcus ignored us all and escaped into the shower. *How could he not hear his son calling his name or my yelling for help when the glass bowl of scrambled eggs slipped out of my hand?* However, when his cell phone rang, he scurried from the bathroom like a roach surprised by a beaming light would, just to get it.

Thank goodness for church daycares and the people with patience working in them. My kids were wired, and I was tired and having somewhere to drop them off for a few hours was a welcomed break.

Entering the sanctuary, the record-setting attendance for Sunday school was a shocker. At least sixty-five adult members filled the lower level pews. It was the first time I'd seen the sanctuary filled to capacity—ever—at this early hour but then I was reminded that Minister Jamal Wright was teaching the lessons for the month. Jamal was a fresh, much younger face around the church with an energetic teaching style; a style totally opposite from old, senile, dry, and boring Sister Bertha Mae Clark who was out due to having hip replacement surgery.

After greeting many of the members, I took an end seat on the second-row pew and retrieved my notepad and Bible from my bag. Digging deeper inside my bag for a highlighter, my head was still down when someone's hands covered my eyes. I guessed a few names then recognized the perfume. Turning around, I was extremely excited to see my best friend Kim, a skinnier Kim, standing behind me.

"O.M.G! You look great! How much have you lost?"

"Twenty-two pounds and counting," she excitedly shared before placing her purse on the pew then stepping into the aisle to do a complete spin-about to model her new size twelve waistline.

Although Kim and I talked twice a week, it had been almost three months since her job granted her a full weekend off and she attended church. We hugged and caught up on as much as possible before being distracted by Evonne's entrance into the sanctuary. Our eyes searched her up and down as she strolled in with confidence wearing a shorter than short, too cold for wearing in early-December forty-eight degree weather, mini-skirt and skimpy blouse.

"Ooooh, that blouse would appreciate another one, two, or three buttons at the top," Kim whispered in my ear. "And I bet if she sneezed, the seam on the back of her skirt would split even higher."

Ignoring our chuckles, Evonne inserted her lanky body between Kim and me. Placing her left hand on her hip, she apologized for interrupting our conversation.

"But I have the pastor's suit. Who did you say to give it to?"

"Find a Deacon, honey," I responded with a disgusted tone and facial expression.

"Evonne, are you aware that your breasts are hanging out? Your rose tattoo is not what any of us desire to see first thing this morning."

If looks could kill, morning worship would have been preempted for a memorial service held in my honor. Perhaps I could have phrased my words a tab bit differently to lessen the sting of my abrasiveness. Or I could have offered her my shawl to wrap up in or suggest that she rummage through the lost and found for a neck scarf or sweater, but I didn't. Instead, I crossed my arms and watched her lower lip tremble as she appeared to be thinking heavy of an appropriate comeback. But in my mind, I'm thinking, 'Evonne is sleazy, not crazy. She knows better than to disrespect me, the pastor's wife.'

Evonne stood tall and unapologetic about the forty-eight triple D's protruding beyond her blouse. She ignored my question and broke the awkward silence by asking again who she should hand DeMarcus's suit. I pointed her in the direction of Deacon Davis who was standing near the back door.

DeMarcus's sermon wasn't his best—in fact, it may have been his worst. He appeared physically exhausted and a few times, slurred his words. At one point, Kim and I chuckled—giving one another the side-eye when for the third time, he repeated the same passage from the Bible and notes from his tablet, but I immediately grew concerned when his movement across the pulpit became oddly slowed. Kim joked that his mug had been filled with gin instead of cider—nudging my arm with her elbow to draw my attention to how quickly he was chugging down the contents and substantiating her claim by pointing toward the podium as he held onto it so very tightly. But when services ended and Jamal announced the cancellation of his meeting with his associate ministers and Deacons, I knew for certain something was wrong.

Walking home, DeMarcus complained of a sore throat and aching muscles. After helping him undress and get comfortable in our bed, I gave him a couple of extra-strength aspirin and a cup of warm cider, minus the rum, to wash them down. Only a few minutes had passed when Sister Kiser and Sister Johnson of the nurse's guild came knocking on the door. As pleasantly as I could, I attempted to shoo them away by telling them that the pastor needed rest, but my notion was discredited. Adamant about caring for their pastor, I guess for them an invite wasn't required because before I could tell them that he was in the bed and resting, they brushed past me as if I wasn't standing there.

At DeMarcus's side, Sister Johnson grabbed my hand then DeMarcus's hand and led a powerful prayer for a miraculous healing. While holding DeMarcus's other hand, Sister Kiser expressed concern of how warm it felt then removed a thermometer from her purse. Hearing that his temperature registered at 102.5 prompted Sister Johnson to jump up and fumble through my linen closet for towels. When she returned, my eyes grew as wide as oranges when in her hands were two aqua blue—from a set of eight, soaking wet towels we received seven years ago as a wedding gift from my now deceased Aunt May.

There were plenty of fresh and neatly folded towels sitting on the lower two shelves for her to choose from but instead, her meddling azz went to the top shelf and searched deep in the back of the closet for these. My blood pressure rose seeing one of my too beautiful to use towels placed around DeMarcus's neck and the other placed across his chest. To me, they were a keepsake. I never intended on ever using these towels which was the sole purpose of hiding the eloquently hand-embroidered and laced-trimmed towels still in its original gift box and wrapped in a beautiful, oversized white and gold bow from DeMarcus. But by the smirk on her face, I surmised that she had selected those towels on purpose. *But why,* I wondered? *Just being ornery,* I concluded. But instead of speaking on my frustrations, I remained silent.

Thirty minutes had passed when Sister Kiser concluded that DeMarcus had the flu. Sister Johnson seconded the conclusion and prescribed plenty of liquids and bed rest. However, three hours later when his symptoms worsened, and his temperature reached 104 degrees, I drove him to the emergency room where he was immediately admitted and diagnosed as having pneumococcal pneumonia.

Ma arrived early the next morning to watch the kids so that I could be at my husbands' side. But as word spread of his hospitalization, everything started to become unbelievably crazy. By noon, folks began calling his hospital room to the point I was forced to unplug the phone from the wall. I eventually had to turn off his cell phone because they started blowing that up as well. One would have believed that DeMarcus had passed on with the array of visitors and flowers starting to line the walls of his room. After a while, it became almost sickening—the fact that even during an illness, folks surrounded him like he reigned supreme and wasn't just an ordinary man lying in a hospital bed. If only his faithful followers knew that at the sight of needles he breaks out in hives or at the sight of blood, he faints.

But credit must be given to his mother board for taking excellent care of me as well. Not only did they cook and delivered food so that I didn't have to ingest the bland tasting hospital entrees, but Sister Harlow arranged for me to have a nice couch bed instead of the community reclining chair to sleep on and demanded that all his room calls be rerouted to the receptionist's desk.

"Just tell them that the pastor needs his rest; it's a part of his recovery. Anybody that loves the pastor will understand that."

DeMarcus was released from the hospital after a three-day stay. Once home and comfortably resting in our bed, I used his study to prepare a quick lesson for Bible study. No, I wasn't one for the limelight nor did I feel as if I was the best person for the task, but I was next in rotation to teach my lesson as part of the month-long series dedicated to empowering women.

DeMarcus insisted I fulfill my obligation.

The classroom fit snug the thirty-two women aged sixteen to sixty who came out. In my recollection, Wednesday night Bible study attendance had never been this large, but I was smart enough to piece together the reason. Each wide-eyed and straight-backed person had expectations of hearing firsthand, the details of whether the information stirred up and blowing through town was true—that DeMarcus's quick release from the hospital was due to an incurable illness and his request to die at home.

"Good evening all," I began. "I am so glad you came out tonight and I hope that you are ready to be empowered by tonight's lesson entitled, 'Who's Watching You?'" They applauded my title. *Kiss azzes.*

"I promise to not keep you long as many of you are aware that I have a sick husband at home."

"Heal him, Lord," I heard someone say.

The room was quiet. And as I looked at each member on my right and to my left, their eyes were fixated on me as if I was about to elaborate further. I smiled, divulging nothing.

"Ladies, who's watching you? Who's watching you when you wake up in the morning? And who's watching you when you walk through the doors of your job or school? Ask yourself, what do they see? Are your children waking up in a loving home, an argument free home? Are they waking up to drugs and alcohol sitting on the kitchen table and being told that drugs and alcohol is bad for them? I am just being real. Can I be real with you, Sistas?"

Their shouts and applause pumped me up. And as many nodded their heads in agreement, I felt confident to continue. I had their full attention.

"Are your children being taught the importance of school? Are you satisfied with your tenth-grade education? If not, are you encouraging your child to finish high school and pursue a college degree? Oh, it's all in the Bible. Let us look at Proverbs. Proverbs 1:5 says, A wise man will hear, and will increase learning; and a man of understanding shall attain unto wise counsels. Proverbs 22:6 says, Train up a child in the way he should go: and when he is old, he will not depart from it. I'm not saying anything you beautiful women don't already know but sometimes we need a refresher course, a reminder. Let me get off the subject here for a moment, but I promise to bring what I say back around to the topic. You see, last week, I think I may have offended someone. As a matter of fact, I know I did and that sista is here tonight. I'm not going to call her out by name but what I am about to say is…"

I paused. Glancing over the room and seeing each woman on the edge of their seats waiting for me to complete my sentence made me chuckle. They too erupted into laughter.

"Yaw thought I was getting ready to apologize to the sista, didn't you? But no! The truth hurts sometimes but it doesn't mean that I don't still love her."

"Yes, Yes. Preach it!" co-signed Sister Frances.

"I wasn't watching her breasts, her breasts were watching me," I joked. "I had to bring this to her attention because some things are just not right! Not in the house of the Lord! I don't want to see breasts hanging outside yaws brassieres; it's inappropriate! I don't come to church to see breasts, butts, or prints, do you? I come for the word and the word alone. If I want to see breasts, butts, or prints, I'll go to the mall—out into the world! If you just got to be hoochie, be hoochie in the night clubs, but not in church! It's a problem when folks wear their hookerish attire into the house of God without an ounce of shame or embarrassment about it. And for those of you twisting up your lips and mouths—before you even think it, the Bible verse about *come as you are*, doesn't mean come in exposing your crack and cleavage. So, no, I'm not apologizing. I said it to help the sista out, not to hurt her. And right now, I'm telling all you sisters that it's not your breasts that gives you power, oh, no. It's how we carry ourselves, it's the goals we set and are on track of meeting that gives us power. It's the positive thoughts to uplift ourselves and others that give us power. It's our ability to step out on faith, to be independent and not codependent that gives us power. Are you hearing me? It's increasing our knowledge and doing what's right versus what is liked that gives us power. It is empowering to be different. It is empowering to know that you've been or

24

have made a positive impact in the life of another. So again, I ask ya', who's watching you? What are they seeing?"

"Say it!" shouted 60-year-old Sister Georgetta.

After quoting a few more scripture, I encouraged them to always be READY:

R—Respectful in Appearance and All Your Ways.
E—Encouraged; Shake off Negativity and Believe You Can Achieve.
A—Articulate; Speak Life and Speak with Purpose.
D—Determined; Never Quit and Never Doubt God's Power.
Y—Young Minded; Optimistic and Willing to Learn.

At the end of my lesson, the women hovered over me like vultures declaring their prey.

Many of them thanked me for the encouraging message while others wanted to know more about DeMarcus's current condition. After stating several times that he's recovering from pneumonia, I was on the verge of verbally exploding when Jamal stepped in and got their attention. His announcement that someone's car alarm was going off caused them all to grab their purses and bags and rush out the door.

Jamal walked me across the yard to ensure my safety. But it struck me as odd when he declined my invite inside to visit with DeMarcus who was the topic of discussion as we walked.

However, in hindsight, Jamal hadn't been coming around as often anymore and was barely attending church services. But I didn't pry. I simply thanked him for walking me home and wished him a goodnight.

After locking the door, I ran to the bedroom and snuggled beneath my husband. DeMarcus looked better and mentioned he was feeling better. I was about to ask him if he needed anything but was stopped mid-sentence. He stated he was fine but wanted to know more about my lesson. With the biggest smile I could muster up, I proudly highlighted what I believed were my most profound points of the message and bragged about Sister Johnson's remark of my lesson being the best in the series thus far.

"They received me well and I don't think that it's because I'm your wife."

"You've got a lot of potential, babe," he replied, causing my smile to become even bigger.

"Now that DeMarya, Faye is a little older, would you object to me going back to work? Being with the women tonight, made me realize just how much I miss working with adults. I mean, I love my family, but I also miss engaging in adult conversation."

DeMarcus smiled. He already had it figured out. "Create a new women's ministry. You can call it, M.O.Ms Ministry."

He must be on heavy medication. I sprung up from my relaxed position to stare him in the eyes.

"M.O.Ms stands for Mom's Only Meetings. It can be a meeting where only mothers get together and leave their kids at home. You can discuss women's topics such as keeping in shape or share beauty tips with them. Yaw can take a field trip, get dressed up and go to a play or to a movie. The Deacons can gas up the church van and drive yaw anywhere you want to go. Sisterhood outings and fellowshipping doesn't that sound like fun?"

It was obvious to me that DeMarcus's medication was taking effect. He knew exactly how I felt about social gatherings beyond the normal worship service with his congregation; I dreaded it! I couldn't stand any of them and in truth believe they simply tolerated me.

Two weeks before Christmas, I was offered and accepted, with DeMarcus's approval, of course, a position as an administrative coordinator at the Women's Crisis Center. It was only thirty-five hours per week, Monday through Friday with the option of working from home on certain days. On the surface, DeMarcus appeared happy too, but I sensed he was somewhat unsettled with me gaining independence. Without a doubt, I had spoiled him rotten by catering to his every need, but he had spoiled me too. But in taking heed to one of his favorite phrases, "Either you're rolling along or strolling alone," I was anxious and optimistic about the next chapter in my life.

My day as a working woman began early on January 3, 2014. Excited and nervous about my first day, I took DeMarcus's advice and wore the form-fitting black and white dress he and the kids gave me as a Christmas present with my favorite pair of knee-high, black boots. Kissing me on the forehead, he slid a twenty-dollar bill in my hand and wished me well.

Arriving at the center, Geo Scott, my manager, greeted me at the door and graciously assisted in carrying a tiny box of framed family photos and other whatnots for my desk. After showing me to my new office, Geo gave me a tour of the facility and introduced me to several employees in our path. At the end of the tour, I excused myself briefly to grab a notepad and pen from my office then rejoined Geo in the hallway. I followed him into his first meeting of the morning.

"Good morning, team. Please help me in welcoming Rosilyn Jackson. She's our new administrative coordinator overseeing the training unit and newly hired counselors. She comes with a ton of experience and I am sure she will be an asset for our center."

"Thank you," I said, smiling and waving to those waving and smiling back at me.

Geo's meeting lasted two hours and, in that time, I learned a lot. He praised his team for a successful 2013 and touched on upcoming department changes and his expectations for 2014. The rapport with his team was awesome and it was evident that he was highly respected. As everyone filed out of the boardroom, Geo followed me into my office and sat in the chair opposite me. He asked if I had any questions.

"Well, kinda. You mentioned that I have a ton of experience. I'm not sure if you saw my application, but the experience I listed was of mentoring youth." I was puzzled by his smile and chuckle.

"And an honest woman too. Yes, I reviewed your application and concluded that anyone who survived mentoring youth and did so for a number of years had to be tough. It takes patience and a caring person to get through to such an unstable bunch. When I reviewed the applications, I was seeking someone who has patience and someone who can listen to our clients because nearly all of them are one conversation away from breaking. I wasn't looking for anyone with a degree in sociology or previous social work experience. I wanted to take a chance on someone fresh, someone who would bring something new."

His words made absolute sense as I nodded my head in agreement and thanked him a second time for the opportunity. Geo pulled his chair around the desk and turned on the computer. After linking me to the internal email system, he explained the various databases I had access to and outlined my responsibilities in depth. All was going well, that is, until his broad shoulder brushed against mine making me a tad bit uncomfortable. And if that wasn't enough of a distraction, the scent of his body musk sent chills up my spine.

Shifting to the right of my chair to put distance between us, inconspicuously I glanced his way and thoroughly checked him out. Geo wasn't a half-bad looking guy. His sideburns were in alignment with his well-manicured mustache and when he smiled, his not so thick, not so thin shapely lips uncovered two rows of braces corrected, pearly whites. But it didn't take long to realize that I had assumed wrong; Geo wasn't pushing up on me at all. He was simply training me and over the course of the day when our conversations could have taken a left turn, not once did he say or ask anything inappropriate. Perhaps he caught a glimpse of the 24-carat, sixteen diamonds—double banded ring on my finger shouting, 'married woman.'

Arriving home, a little past five and opening the door, I stood in awe of my immaculately cleaned house. Before I could comment, DeMarcus led me into the kitchen where dinner was waiting on the table. Other than needing a sprinkle of salt, a dash of pepper, and chopped onions, the hamburger surprise wasn't too bad. I served myself seconds. And after stacking the dishwasher, I grabbed my husband and gave him a long, passionate kiss to show my gratitude and appreciation. The kids were fussy so after their bath, I read them a story until they drifted off to sleep. With the house quiet, I joined DeMarcus on the couch and shared the details of my day. He did the same. He pissed me off when revealing that church members were responsible for cleaning the house.

"Since you're working now, they wanted to help us out. Sister Maggie and her crew have managed to pull together a schedule so that someone will be here twice a week."

"Thanks, but no, thanks. I can do my own cleaning."

"I know you can, babe, but it's just the church's way of showing how much they love us. Don't block our blessing."

Blessing, my foot! DeMarcus was spoiled and although I often joked about hiring maid services, it was said with the hope of encouraging him to do more around the house. I didn't want those nosey people rummaging through my stuff—not my laundry, not my den, not even in my kitchen. Besides, there wasn't that much to clean anyway.

In mid-June, the center realigned its departments and the four divisions became two. Without applying for the job, I was blessed with a promotion to manager, overseeing the Department of Intervention. Geo and I were now equals.

On the home front, things were wonderful in my marriage. DeMarcus's sermons were getting better and I was happier than I'd ever been. I had made a slew of new friends, was thoroughly enjoying my job, losing weight, and pampering myself with weekly shopping sprees at the mall. Tuesdays were set aside for family time and on the last Friday of the month, DeMarcus and I closed off the world to have a date night. I loved my husband so much and could truly see God blessing our marriage and making it stronger. Well, that was until the September trip to Chicago, the crisis center mandated I attend along with Geo. Except for DeMarcus's hospitalization and the weekend Ma begged to babysit her grandchildren, I had never spent more than a day away from my family. DeMarcus didn't ask much about the trip but was overly inquisitive about my relationship with Geo which I found cute—seeing for the first time, his jealous side.

"You've heard me talk about Geo. I interviewed with him; he was once my manager but now my counterpart. It's just a business trip, sweetie."

In a roundabout way, I felt that DeMarcus trusted me, but I didn't push the subject or him. I had never given him a reason to doubt my faithfulness, but then again, never had I been placed in that type of situation.

Day one in Chicago was spent shopping in the mall at a store called Zaria's. Packed with fashions never seen in Lexington or Louisville, everything I touched I wanted! Geo compared me to a bratty kid in a toy store, but I was shopping on a rush of adrenaline and had to have it all. My closets back home were already filled with designer clothes, shoes, and handbags—many still with tags and never worn. But the clothes at Zaria's were marked at an incredibly low-price, no sane woman would pass up.

"Join me for dinner. I heard about an awesome restaurant on the first floor that serves soul food," asked Geo upon our return to the hotel.

I was exhausted but also hungry and after placing my bags of goodies in my suitcase, we rode the elevator down to the first floor and found two open seats at the bar. The smell of deep-fried chicken, sweet potatoes, and collard greens made my stomach growl.

"Smells like my momma's kitchen," I said.

"See that cherry cobbler?" Geo pointed to the picture on the menu. "That's what I want. I haven't had a cherry cobbler since Granny Sue passed. That was over three years ago."

"It looks fattening."

"It is, but we can work it off later on the dance floor," Geo chuckled.

"The live band starts at nine o'clock."

"Dance? After my food digests, the only thing I'm gonna want to do is crawl into bed."

The hostess took our drink order. Geo ordered rum and coke and I boldly ordered the same.

He laughed. "You look like a wine cooler chick to me."

"What happens in Chicago stays in Chicago," I blurted. "So tonight, let this be our secret. My husband would have a heart attack if he knew that I was sitting in a bar. And knowing that I actually ordered an adult beverage, he'd fall over and die."

We ordered our food and just as Geo said he was gonna do, he ordered the cherry cobbler. Insistent that I try it, he sliced a tiny piece with his fork and told me to open my mouth.

It was delicious. So delicious, I ordered my own slice to snack on later.

It must have been the adult beverages I drank that jump-started my fatigued engine, because from nine o'clock when the band began playing to ten-thirty when they took their first break, we danced, laughed, drank, and danced even more. I couldn't recall another time that I'd had more fun. Not even the '80s themed disco party the church held two years prior could top this night.

It was well after midnight when we stumbled to our rooms. Geo opened my door for me then walked across the hall to his room. Removing my calling card from my purse, I plopped down on the bed and dialed DeMarcus.

"Hey, babe, it's me. How are you? Have my little darlings been asking about me?" The background was noisy. I asked where he was.

"Hey, I'm good. You're up late," he yelled.

"And, so are you? What's all that noise?"

"Ahhh, it's just the television. The mothers came by earlier to clean the house and mentioned that the men were getting together, ordering chicken wings and watching the major league baseball games. They wouldn't take no for an answer and insisted I join them. I'm glad I did. How was your meeting?"

"Who's watching my children?"

"They're fine. Enjoy yourself, honey. Hey, I've got to go. Besides, I can hardly hear you for all the noise. Call me again tomorrow."

I was angry but in no condition to argue. My head was spinning and so was the room. I dimmed the lights and propped up my pillows to watch television. The room was cold but at this point, I didn't have the energy to roll out of bed to adjust the thermostat. I needed to brush my teeth but felt nauseated. Hoping I'd feel better by lying still for at least an hour, I closed my eyes only to rise seven hours later to the television watching me and to the worst headache ever. Making matters worse, I had overslept and had less than an hour to shower and dress before my first meeting. Luckily, Geo saved me a seat and after tossing my purse underneath the table, I used my two remaining minutes to pour a cup of coffee and grab one of the three remaining pastries.

"You look like hell," he laughed.

During our first break, I went into the hallway and called the house. Hearing from DeMarcus that the kids missed me, brought a tear to my eyes. I immediately grew homesick.

"What are your plans for today?"

"I'll probably go for a run," DeMarcus replied, moments before instructing me to either hold the line or call back later while he answered the knock at the door. Screaming through the phone, I demanded to know who it was.

"The help," he replied. The phone line went dead.

Yes, it angered me to be hung up on, but I was mostly disappointed in DeMarcus for refusing to honor my request to keep his church folk out of our house.

"Don't worry about things you can't change," Geo whispered, after allowing me to vent about what had ticked me off so early.

"This could be a really fun, stress-free trip if you allowed it to be."

Geo was right but in my gut was uneasiness. I was uncomfortable not knowing who was watching our children and it bothered me to no end that church folks—none of them I trusted, was given total access to the most intimate details of our lives and possessions.

"He's a man," responded Geo. "Women are the nurturers and men, well, we're just men. Women don't want another woman washing her undergarments, but a man can care less. We do things differently but trust me, he's not going to let anybody hurt your kids or let another woman go through your closet and play dress-up in your clothes. And just as I am trying to get you to do, your husband is out enjoying his freedom and doing things he ordinarily wouldn't do if you were at home."

Our meeting ended at five and by six-fifteen, I had slipped into a pair of jeans and had tied my hair into a tail. *Slumming,* Geo called it. I called it *relaxing.*

Dinner again was in the first-floor restaurant but instead of dancing to the live band afterward, we went sightseeing. Geo was a comedian in his own right, refreshing from a more serious personality on the job. And as we walked and talked, I was blown away to learn that he's a veteran of the U.S. Army with nearly twenty-two years of active service. He also shared being a bachelor.

"You're funny and have a great personality. I can't believe you're single. When we get back, I know some ladies at the church who would love to meet someone like you."

Geo laughed. "Thanks, but no, thanks. I'm single by choice. I date, but I'm not looking to be in a committed relationship."

"So, you're a player? You like a variety of women?"

"I'm not a player. I just haven't found a woman worthy of settling down with."

"That's why you need to come with me to church. I'll introduce you to Kim, Kim Spears. She's thirty, single, and has a bachelor's degree in business administration. She's a really nice woman."

He laughed at my persistence.

"I'm serious, so stop laughing. She's a good girl and my best friend. She's deep into the church and a very attractive woman. Kim doesn't smoke or do drugs. She lives alone and doesn't have any children."

"And she's probably a freak like the last woman I met claiming to be deep into the church. She was deep alright; deep in debt and trying to go deep in my pockets to support her deep drinking habit. Going to church doesn't make a person any more a devoted Christian than a light-skinned person wearing green contacts makes them biracial. People be 'fronting and if you pay close attention and stare long enough, you'll see them for who they truly are. I'm sorry if my words offend you. I know it's not all church women."

"Actually, I am offended by you thinking that I'd introduce you to just anybody. I met Kim over twenty years ago through her brother Jeff and we clicked immediately because she was so down to earth. Kim's not a gold digger, she holds down her own. She has her own place, her own car, and makes good money on her job."

"And so do both my sisters. I see them on Sunday mornings wearing their holy hats and carrying their Bibles. They step out looking all Christianly but believe me, by two in the afternoon when the church bell sounds and the doors swing open, my oldest sister is headed towards the east side of town looking for her weed man and my baby sister is headed to her weekend gig—pole dancer at the club over in Arlington. So just because a person goes to church and makes good money doesn't automatically mean that they have good sense. We've all got issues."

"Kim's not like that. She's the sweetest person I know." Geo smiled.

"Thanks, but no, thanks."

Chapter 3

Eye of The Sparrow

DeMarcus was geared up for the pastor's summit being held this year in Washington D.C. Being selected to speak on the topic: *Building Better Relationships Within the Church* was a great honor for DeMarcus and the support and love shown by twenty-six members of his congregation accompanying him, was emotionally overwhelming to us both. Leaving Wednesday morning for the day and a half bus ride, the members were expected to arrive Friday at noon. After delivering our children to Ma early Thursday morning, DeMarcus and I boarded a 2:00 p.m. first-class flight out of Louisville.

Arriving at the hotel, my first thought was that the brochure hadn't done this place true justice. White lilies in white oblong vases with a hint of copper lined the greenery decorated walls in the unusually spacious registration area. The marble desktops matched the marble floor and the white chairs and couches trimmed in various gold patterns were positioned near the marble waterfall. Our suite was equally as gorgeous; similar to the penthouse suites I'd seen in magazines and often fantasized about staying in. It was more like a luxurious condo than a five-star hotel room and large enough that had Ma and the kids come along, we'd still have ample space and privacy housing them on the other side of the dining area.

After unpacking our clothes and placing them in the antique dresser, I was hoping to relax on the couch and have a nice romantic night in with my husband until a knock on the door interrupted my plans.

"Paster Jackson? I'm Paster Perkins from Houston, Texas, how yer doing? It's nice to finally meet you. I saw yer and yer lovely wife checking in and thought befo'e you got too comfy, I'd let yaws know that many of us pasters are gathering in the Wyatt Room 'bout seven. There's plenty of food, so don't yer go worrying 'bout ordering out. And yer lovely wife here can join the other wives if she wanna. They'll be just across the hall there in the Willona Room fellowshipping and doing what they do best." I chuckled at his southern drawl.

DeMarcus appeared excited about mingling with the other pastors and after texting the information to his Deacons he showered then changed into fresh clothing. I really didn't want to come across as anti-social able so instead of telling him that I'd rather pluck hairs from my big toe than to socialize with the other wives, I claimed wanting to check on the kids as my reason for staying behind. By six forty-five, DeMarcus was out the door but by eight-thirty, my stomach was growling for grease, so I wandered down to the Willona Room to fix myself a plate. At least 350 women filled the room, many of them dressed to the nine in their formal wear, big fancy hats, and sparkling shoes. Admiring their attire from the steam table, I quickly noticed the eyes looking me over too—as if in disapproval of my decision to wear blue jeans and flats. *At least my doo was curled and together.*

Feeling extremely underdressed and totally out of place, I shrugged off their mean mugs and decided it was best to keep it moving once I piled up my plate. But after a brief conversation with Lynn Mitchell of Memphis Tennessee who too was in jeans, I accepted the invitation to join her and others at a nearby table. Listening in on their conversations, these women were a lively group, especially Denise Hudson of North Carolina who I spotted filling her cup with Bourbon she had stashed deep down in an oversized purse.

"How long have you been a pastor's wife?" Denise asked.

"About six years." I shoved a fork full of creamy mashed potatoes in my mouth.

"You've survived five, so good for you," she remarked.

Apologizing for being so short with my answer, I introduced myself as First Lady Rosilyn Jackson.

"Be careful how you use first lady, sweetie," said a meddlesome voice from across the table. "Calling yourself a first lady sounds ridiculous and implies that he has a second and possibly a third."

"I don't think so, but thanks for the heads-up."

This one's odd came to mind as I politely rolled my eyes then looked down at my baked chicken leg in hopes she'd find someone else to talk crazy too. It didn't work; she kept right on talking—sharing her thoughts on what a suitable name for a pastor's wife should be. I was hungry and not in the least bit interested in engaging in conversation on what name I wanted to be called. Rolling my eyes in the back of my head a second time, I hadn't noticed the woman to my immediate left.

"I'm glad it's you now and not me," she said.

"Hi, I'm Shannon Mills."

"Hello, I'm Hungry Rosilyn." We laughed.

"This is my first summit and so far, it's exactly what I thought it would be…boring! A bunch of rich old ladies in big flowery hats ranting and raving about their bad azz children and grandchildren, telling lie, after lie, after fat azz lie to one another. Excuse me for cussing, but I'm just keeping it real."

I liked Shannon instantly. To me, there was nothing more refreshing and comical than a brutally honest woman. Others would have considered her way of thinking and approach *ghettofied*, but it did my heart good in meeting someone who wasn't afraid to verbalize her thoughts. Her candidness made me laugh so hard, I dropped my fork, but there was another wrapped in my napkin. While I continued eating, Shannon continued speaking her mind. And when looking up and seeing that everyone's attention had shifted onto us, she grabbed her drink and motioned me towards the door. Placing my dinner roll on top of my slice of chess pie, I followed her into the lobby. Claiming a sofa opposite the registration area, we both let out a huge sigh, grateful to have escaped the noise and the bull crap.

"That's going to be us in about thirty years."

"That'll be you," she replied. "I love my fiancée' but I have serious doubts if I'm cut out for being a pastor's wife."

"It's a job and it isn't always easy, but it does come with many privileges. For instance, our church pays for everything. I mean the house we live in, the car, this trip. And my husband gets a handsome salary on top of that. But what really trips me out, are the people who go out of their way to kiss his butt. They treat him like he's royalty."

"I remember living like a royal family," Shannon admitted.

"My mom's first husband was a pastor and we had the best of everything. Everywhere we went people wanted to feed us, do this for us, and do that for us. We were rotten kids and didn't want for anything. People smiled in our faces and pretended as if they were always so happy to see us. I can remember spending the night over peoples' houses and not having any fun. I couldn't wrestle and do the stuff like the other kids because the pastor's child wasn't to be roughed up, just adored. And it wasn't until I became a teenager that I realized all they were doing was putting on a show. Every one of them was fake and phony."

Shannon was right on the money, speaking on things as if summarizing my own life. I understood every word that fell from her mouth and shook my head in agreement.

"Just like those women in there, they're faking too—telling the woman in the red dress that her shoes were pretty. I looked down to see her shoes for myself—they were uglier than ugly, not to mention too small. Her arch was higher than her forehead and the sides were rolling over."

Laughing hard, I nearly choked on my pie.

"They're going to talk about her like a dog when she leaves the table," Shannon joked.

"That's church folks," I replied, trying to muffle my laughter. Relaxed, I rested my neck on the armrest of the couch and stretched out my legs.

"But one of the few things I like about being a pastor's wife is that no matter what I do, ain't nobody gonna say anything about it. And no matter what I say, I'm always right. Not once has anybody ever disagreed with any of my suggestions and when I walk into a room, everybody—even the women begin offering me their chair. And each year, not only do they make a big-to-do over my husbands' birthday, but they give me gifts and money too on mine."

"I know the routine and that's how they end up with all the control—they sneaky like that. I want to be able to plan a party and invite who I want to invite. I can think back to at least four church parties held for my mom and my stepdad. It was all church folk, none of our family members, their co-workers, or good friends got to attend because none of them knew about it. It's like we had no life other than the church life. Church folks were always around."

"I know what you mean. I recently accepted a job to escape having to see church folk all day, every day. I needed some normalcy. And believe it or not, it feels good being around skanks, crack heads, and thieves. They keep it real and don't pretend to be anything they're not."

Shannon continued sharing family horror stories which to me were quite comical. I too shared pleasant and not so pleasant stories with her that now— years later, seemed comical as well. We laughed and joked for hours then

37

noticed the time was approaching 1 a.m. Saying our farewells, we agreed to meet for breakfast in the morning.

"It is morning," she joked. "I'll see you back down here at ten."

Riding up the elevator, I chuckled to myself as I began to prepare a speech for when DeMarcus grilled me on where I'd been. Opening the door and believing that he was asleep, I quietly tiptoed across the living room and into the bedroom only to find an undisturbed bed. I checked the entire suite and found no signs of him. Using the room phone to ring his cell phone, I became outraged when he didn't answer. I paced the floor wondering where he was and what he could possibly be doing at this early morning hour. After preparing for bed, the last thing I recall was flipping through channels and settling for a cooking show. At four in the morning, the bedroom door opening woke me. Sitting up, I turned on the lamp and demanded to know where he'd been.

"Go back to bed," DeMarcus said, laughing all the way to the bathroom. His speech was slurred, and his pupils appeared to be dilated. He refused to answer my question and seemingly was avoiding coming into the bedroom. Hearing the shower turn on, I ran to the door and damn near beat it down. All sorts of thoughts raced through my mind but at that exact moment, I demanded to know the reason for his early morning shower.

"DeMarcus! Unlock this door!"

He flung the door open wide and asked if I felt better.

Hell, naw, I didn't feel better!

"Where have you been?"

"I've been with a bunch of men." DeMarcus laughed and extended out his arms. Standing in only a towel, he looked from side to side as if witnesses were present to confirm his story.

"I've been playing corn hoe, spades, and basketball. For your information, I'm taking a shower because I'm musky and I smell."

"You expect me to believe you played basketball in your flats? Who do you think you're talking to, your son?"

"Stop with all the screaming; I was fellowshipping, alright! What else could I have been doing?"

"At four o'clock in the morning, what gym was still open? Don't lie, DeMarcus, who were you with?"

"Don't you think that as a pastor, I deserve to have a little fun? For as long as you've known me, when have I ever stepped out and did what I wanted to do? Never! When I'm not at church, I'm in our house working on my next lesson. And when my lesson is done, I spend the rest of my time being a good father to my kids and an attentive husband to you. I enjoyed being stress-free and care-free tonight, so give me a break! I've been back all of ten minutes and all you've managed to do is give me an even bigger headache and scream yourself hoarse."

DeMarcus pushed me out of the bathroom and slammed the door in my face. After his shower, he got into the bed and for the first time since being married, turned his back on me. Lying with his face towards the door, I attempted to make amends by wrapping my arm around him only to be shrugged off. Yes, he was upset with me but never had there been anything we couldn't talk through. It was obvious he had forgotten the pact we made early in our marriage to never go to bed upset because each time I tried apologizing for my actions, the angrier he became.

"I've had enough of your stuff, get off of me!" He smacked my hand and pushed it away. Throughout the morning I tossed and turned, even faked sniffling to get his attention but he was unmoved. His insensitivity puzzled me—it hurt me. We laid side by side, yet a great distance existed. Eventually giving up, I too turned away and hugged my pillow.

As quickly as I drifted off, even quicker arrived the morning. DeMarcus had to shake me to wake me. I must have been in a deep sleep because surprisingly he had already shaved and dressed.

"Breakfast starts at nine. I'd like for us to go together." DeMarcus disappeared into the living area.

No good morning, no kiss on the forehead or lips, no I love you, baby, nothing. And yet his punk azz expected me to sit alongside him at a table pretending that all was well. *Oh, heck, no. I don't think so.* So, springing from the bed, I marched into the living area determined to resolve our issues. Turning the corner, what I heard stopped me in my tracks. DeMarcus was laughing and whispering. "I had a good time too. Yeah, we will again, soon," I heard him say.

My heavy breathing must have alerted him of my presence because when he turned around and looked up, he ended the conversation.

"Who was that? And don't tell me it was nobody. Who were you telling you had a good time?"

"Now you're meddling in my conversations. Will you ever stop?"

"No, who'd you have a good time with last night? I have a right to know!"

"Stop it!" DeMarcus demanded. He brushed past me and went to retrieve his wallet and key fob from the dresser.

"Don't walk away from me? Where are you going? To call the winch back? Who is it, DeMarcus? Who were you whispering to on the phone?"

I followed him into the kitchen then into the bedroom. With each step he took, I was on his heels. I followed him onto the patio furious and angry. I was like a crazy woman—ticked off and visualizing pushing him over the railing when something grabbed a hold of me causing me to inhale and visually observe him. Something about him was different. DeMarcus walked toward the bathroom with such a cocky arrogance, that he must have thought that responding to me was an option rather than a requirement. I stood in the doorway of the bathroom and watched him wash and rewash his face. DeMarcus ignored my presence yet gave full attention to his uneven sideburns and a newly discovered razor bump underneath his chin. I lowered my tone and asked again if we could talk.

"Talk about what? What is it that you just need to know right damn now? Maybe I was telling Deacon Moyler that I had fun last night playing basketball. Or maybe I was whispering so I wouldn't wake you. Do you see how you're acting? It's embarrassing and I'm sick of it. You're paranoid and you sound ridiculous. Here I am, a pastor, trying to get folks to heaven but living in my own personal hell on earth with you."

What the…? He must be smoking crack.

"Embarrassing? Embarrassing is you, a married man coming in off the streets at four something in the morning."

"Get dressed!" he shouted, leaving me in the doorway to stew in my own misery.

Little Flock of Waverly members were widespread throughout the huge ballroom. When DeMarcus and I entered, they surrounded him as if he was the President of the United States.

Everyone wanted to shake his hand, hug on him, and shower him with words of encouragement and support. DeMarcus ate it up too, leaving me behind like dried dirt falling from beneath his shoe.

"Good morning, Pastor. We love you, Pastor. God bless you, Pastor," I heard at least seventy-two times. But this morning, I didn't love Pastor or like Pastor. Pastor was a bastard and I hated everything about him.

I was taking a seat when Sister Gloria called my name and grabbed my wrist. Although still in a funky-foul mood, I faked a smile and pretended to be happy to see her. Whispering in my ear that she loved me, I cringed when she kissed my cheek. *Why on earth would a woman plant a wet kiss on another woman's cheek?* Pulling away and taking my seat, Sister Gloria plopped down next to me like a fly at an outdoor picnic, annoying and wouldn't buzz off. She was overly friendly and rambling on about absolutely nothing, causing me to become leery of her pleasantries. *Was she with DeMarcus last night?* I closed my eyes to shrug off the vision of her and DeMarcus entwined in adult entertainment.

Well into her sixties, Gloria was a snazzy dresser and had the energy of a twenty-four-year-old. Her body was toned, and she didn't mind showing off her slender legs and perfectly rounded ankles. She wore twelve-inch heels like she was born with them attached to her feet, keeping perfect rhythm as she walked. I hardly doubted if having relations with a man half her age would cause her any shame and luring a man of my husbands' caliber, huh, most definitely would be right up her alley. But then I noticed a flock of other women hugging and kissing on my husband—none was he turning away. Not even Evonne who looked doubly skanktified and showing off her dried up rose tattoo boob to the world. I gave myself a headache trying to figure out which skank ho' he was with the previous night; it could have been any number of them.

"Hey Rosilyn." The voice was familiar. It was Shannon. Standing up to hug her, she introduced me to her fiancée Nate. She remarked that I looked stressed.

"Just tired."

"You were tired last night. Now you look like you have the weight of the world on your shoulders."

I faked a smile then pointed Nate in the direction of DeMarcus who was mixing and mingling at the opposite end of the room.

"What time did your man get in last night?" I twisted my lips after stating the time of DeMarcus's arrival.

"Nate was waiting for me when I got to the room. He said they wrapped up around eleven."

Shannon must have read my facial expression because she grabbed my hand and assured me that everything would be OK. "We'll talk later. But in the meantime, keep your head up." We hugged and once again I was alone.

Very little was said from the time breakfast ended and we returned to our room. DeMarcus disappeared into the living area and I, after grabbing the cordless phone, escaped onto the patio to call Ma. Hearing my kids' voices in the background made me want to catch the next flight out to be with them, but it wouldn't look right—me not being there to support my own husband. *Would it matter to DeMarcus if I left?* He wasn't talking to me anyway.

The view from our room was magnificent. The stillness of the dew filled skies was calming. From where I sat on the balcony, I could see the beautifully constructed buildings and the colorful leaves blowing from an array of trees. The noise from the cars below wasn't a distraction as I placed my feet on the ledge and closed my eyes. My mind was blank, and that's how I wanted it. No thoughts of anything to dredge up pain or anger. I focused on nothing; something I learned at the Crisis Center to help reduce stress. But then DeMarcus called my name and I was forced back into reality.

"I'm going down to window shop. Would you like to come along?"

"Window shop? No." But I did want to go shopping and after grabbing my purse from behind the bedroom door, with the sweetest of smiles, I asked for a limit. He knew that shopping was my weakness but instead of answering, he held the door open and followed me out.

DeMarcus wasn't any fun to shop with, but I did manage to rationalize the need for a new dress and pumps.

"How would it look for us to show up not matching? This purple dress is a great match to your purple tie. And you want me to look good, don't you?"

"Frivolous spending, Roz. You need a new dress like I need a new suit. This credit card is for emergencies only. You know like if the car breaks down and you have to call a tow truck, something like that. Shopping ain't no emergency situation."

"Just once can you do something special for me and not let it become a major issue? And do you really think that the other husbands are telling their wives they can't shop? What man doesn't want to spoil his wife especially when they're out of town? Geez, you act like I'm not worthy of a few stinking dollars."

Returning from our brief outing, DeMarcus went into the den to download his sermon onto his new tablet and I went into the bedroom and laid my new outfit and accessories across the bed. Aware of DeMarcus's inability to keep track of time while in the bathroom, I decided to shower first to allow myself extra pampering. I was surprised when he joined me and washed my entire body. The cascading water bouncing from his back wet my hair, but I didn't mind.

All that mattered at this point was the much-needed attention I was receiving. He kissed me passionately a thousand times and before I knew it, we were rolling around in the sheets. Yes, 6 p.m. was approaching but we chose to remain connected and entangled. *Besides, Baptist churches never start anything on time anyway*. DeMarcus continued to love on me until his body exploded. He felt different inside of me. He held me differently and I liked it. I liked my husband again.

Arriving at the summit late, DeMarcus made me feel like I was the most beautiful woman in the world. Several times he complimented me in my new outfit, even French-kissed me twice in public—something he stopped doing after we married. Folks stared at us, some even smiled. I was on a high and it made everything that had gone wrong seem so much better. Even skanky wanky Evonne with her boobs popping out of her blouse couldn't upset me. Calling her out by name, she appeared shocked by my hug and complement of her attire. I lied but so what.

I was in a great mood.

DeMarcus was the best speaker of the night. Not because he was the keynote speaker but because he spoke with so much power and conviction—something, in my opinion, the other pastors lacked. And he looked good too; styling and profiling in a double-breasted charcoal gray suit, silver and purple tie, and a *blinging* tie clip that I purchased. His shoes were shined to perfection and the tiny bifocals on the tip of his nose gave him a distinguished look as he sat in the makeshift pulpit.

When the service concluded, it was one great big celebration. I saw an old family friend from Louisville and several other familiar faces from many, many, moons ago. With so many people in the room, I thought it was impossible to run into Shannon, but I did and this time, we exchanged numbers.

It was approaching 10 p.m. when DeMarcus and I returned to our room. I was barely undressed when he began pawing all over me. I didn't resist. He loved me passionately and held me throughout the night. The next morning, he ordered my breakfast and served it to me in bed. And on the entire flight back to Louisville, he and I sat arm in arm. After scooping up our kids from my parents' home, we drove back to Lexington smiling and grinning at one another. This was the best trip ever!

Chapter 4

And the Truth Shall Set You Free

All week long, I found myself rushing home during my lunch hour to check the mailbox in hopes of beating DeMarcus to the credit card bill. Maybe I had been overly antsy since returning from the summit but after his big-to-do over frivolous spending and using the card for only emergencies, retrieving the bill was the only way to destroy all evidence of my Chicago shopping spree. It arrived on the 25th of September and had it not been for being a happily married woman, I would have planted a wet, appreciatory kiss on the lips of the carrier who had just saved my neck. I thanked him with a smile instead.

Returning to the center, the majority of the workforce were gathered in the large waiting area watching the Kentucky Wildcats play basketball. After acknowledging my return to Geo who too was fixated on the 64-inch screen, I headed towards my office to review the statement in private.

Six hundred, six-fifty, is what I guesstimated my damage to be. Per the statement, payment of sixty-nine dollars was due and the remaining balance was $1,428. *What the hell?*

"This has to be a mistake," I said aloud, certain that the limit on the card was $5,000.

Reviewing the statement further, page two revealed several large ticket item purchases and numerous hundred-dollar cash withdrawals. Zooming in on an eight hundred and fifty-nine-dollar purchase from Wright Jewelers and a two-hundred twelve-dollar payment to the electric company, I was speechless. Continuing to inspect the statement and piecing together several Monday and Wednesday noonday purchases from not-so shabby restaurants, I grew curious about whom he was entertaining. *I wasn't eating steaks and receiving nice gifts, so who was?* Hearing Geo's voice in the hallway, I was certain that he would stop by my office, so I quickly dried my eyes and tossed the statement underneath a binder.

"What's going on?" Geo entered my office without knocking. His smile disappeared, perhaps seeing the pain, confusion, and anguish on my face. Geo took a seat and grabbed my hand. He asked again, "What's going on?"

"It's a personal issue, it'll be OK, though. Really, I'm fine."

"You were fine just a moment ago. Something must have happened within the last five minutes."

I needed someone to talk to and at that present moment, Geo was all I had. Removing the statement from beneath the binder, I placed it in front of him and watched his facial expression.

I asked him to share his thoughts.

"Wow." He looked up at me.

"I think you've spent a lot of money eating out, shopping for clothes and jewelry."

"Come on, Geo. The only time I used this card is when we were in Chicago. Look at it," I said, hovering over his shoulder and pointing out the questionable expenses.

"These charges are for restaurants I've never stepped foot in and this recent purchase of jewelry, other than the aluminum necklace the kids gave me for Mother's Day, I haven't received anything that expensive."

His unwillingness to look me in the eye made me uneasy. Geo was always overly opinionated but this time, he chose not to be. *Man code?* I pleaded with him to be straight up—tell me his thoughts even if it wasn't what I wanted to hear. Geo struggled to piece together his words.

"Well," he said, after clearing his throat.

"What I believe doesn't matter. But clearly, your husband has had a lot of emergencies he hasn't told you about. Only he can explain these charges. But if it turns out to be what you think it is, how are you going to handle it?"

How was I supposed to approach DeMarcus without revealing my own purposes for confiscating the mail? And besides, I just promised to stop allowing my insecurities to lead me into accusing him of every little thing that didn't add up—in my mind. *What if the expenditures were legit?*

It took a couple of days to get my nerves up and a story together before confronting DeMarcus. And as expected, he went ballistic—accusing me of being petty for rummaging through his mail. Amid his hissy fit, he deliberately smashed my favorite ceramic vase onto the floor. It may have been done to frighten me, but I was neither frightened nor deterred from getting my answers.

"Whose water bill did you pay, huh? The last I knew; the church paid all our utilities. And what did you purchase from Wright Jewelers? It's got to be some bimbo you're supporting 'cause you sho' haven't given me nothing that sparkles lately. You're busted DeMarcus, so fess up! Holy man of God stop lying and tell the truth!"

"Why do you go through my things? Not once have I looked through your purse, your briefcase, or your mail. I'm entitled to a little privacy just as you are. What I do outside of this house is none of your business and I will be damned if you're gonna badger me over things not pertaining to you."

What? I know I didn't hear what I thought I heard him say. He must have bumped his head prior to me arriving home because obviously, a screw was loose—him talking to me that-a-way. Adamant still about getting my answers, I stayed on his heels as he went from room to room, attempting to do what he does best which was walk away to avoid a confrontation.

"How long has it been going on, DeMarcus?"

Again, I was ignored. To detain him, I reached for his arm but grabbed his shirt. It ripped. He laughed in my face as if it was a joke and with the straightest of faces, told me to get help. His remark pissed me off. Words can't accurately describe the rage that was boiling within me. I was cussing and fighting mad! DeMarcus grabbed my wrists and pushed me onto the couch.

"Stop with the craziness! Damn it, Rosilyn. You know I have meetings away from the church with the leadership. Sometimes I pay for their lunch and then sometimes they pay for mine. And the diamond earrings, necklace, and matching bracelet were to be a birthday gift for you but now you've spoiled the surprise. Are you happy now?"

Whatever. "When it was purchased, my birthday was more than three weeks away so you're a bold-faced liar," I screamed, calling him out for knowing him to be the biggest procrastinator ever. Never in his life had he done anything in advance—he was always right on time or straight up late. So, why'd he think he could pull that cockamamie story over on me?

Nice try, but I ain't buying it!

"OK, then show me the bracelet and earrings. Put 'em in my hand 'cause, I want to see them. You can't, can ya'? Because it's around the arm and neck or some other woman, you bastard! And did you pay her water bill too? Tell the truth, DeMarcus, don't lie!"

With an iron in my right hand and a lamp in my left, DeMarcus was cornered. What he found humorous was a mystery to me, but with his hands raised, he conceded and asked for a truce. He led me into the kitchen and pulled out two chairs.

"I learned of an individuals' water being shut off. When I directed them to the finance committee for assistance, they expressed being totally humiliated if others knew of their personal situation. I understood that and took it upon myself to help this individual and used my own credit card to have their services restored instead of writing a check from the church's account. Now, don't you feel stupid?"

DeMarcus sat back in his chair with his arms folded, staring at me as if waiting for some sort of reaction or apology but that wasn't going to happen. I did feel a little stupid, but no way was I going to admit it to him. However, realizing that I had his attention, I asked for clarity on another matter.

"You know, as your wife, I shouldn't be excluded from what's going on with you. If anything, I should be the first one you confide in, not Ed, not the Deacons, but me. I know you were upset when you said that what you do outside this house isn't any of my business, but you're wrong. Everything about you is my business and that just may be one of the many problems in this marriage, you trying to take care of everything on your own."

DeMarcus chuckled and grabbed at his beard. His eyes shifted to the ceiling giving me the impression that I was wasting his time. Being ignored always pissed me off and deep down, I believed that today he was doing it on purpose. But nonetheless, he remained seated and pretended to listen while I continued speaking from my heart.

"Are you done?" he interrupted. His tone was cocky. "Because if you are, I need you to pay very close attention to me now. First, before anything else, I am the pastor. When people come to me in confidence, what we discuss is not to be discussed with a third party which includes you. I should be able to be loyal to my flock and be loyal to you without it causing disruption in our home. Second, when I am at home with you and the kids, I'm husband and daddy. That's the time when we bond as a family. Mixing the two causes problems and in order to keep my focus on what I'm supposed to keep the focus on, that's just how it has to be. And you always make reference to being my wife.

48

I know who you are, I married you and lie next to you each night. But for things to improve in our marriage, you have to trust me, stop doubting me, and for goodness sakes, stop tripping. Just be my wife! Be a supportive wife and let me worry about everything else. You or the kids want for anything. Everything you ask for; don't I provide it? Let me do my job as husband and pastor, please. Your jealousy and all your accusations have placed a wedge between us and sometimes I…" DeMarcus paused.

"You what?"

DeMarcus sighed then scooted his chair closer to mine. Gripping my hands with his cold hands, he looked at me on the pupils then completed his thought.

"Just know that your behavior is unbecoming of a first lady and it's very unattractive to me. Get it together if you want this marriage!"

DeMarcus pushed back his chair and rose to his feet. He didn't wait around to hear my response—which I was having great difficulty in forming. He left me alone at the table like a child just punished and instructed not to move. Absorbing his words, a little longer, I wasn't quite sure if I had just been dished an ultimatum—shape up or ship out, or if he was simply providing insight of how immature he perceived me as being. For the most part, all appeared calm. Most importantly, I didn't have to explain my usage of the credit card.

Geo's extended weekend officially ended on Monday night and as we carpooled to a Tuesday morning conference, I filled him in on the details of my weekend. Slamming on his brakes, he nearly tossed me out the front window.

"He said what to you? Are you listening to yourself? I don't know your husband but already I don't like him. I'm single because I want to be but if I had a wife, a wife like you, there's no way I'd try to control her like he's doing you."

"It's not about control. DeMarcus just doesn't believe in bringing his work issues home or taking home issues to work. He's always shielded me from the pulpit."

"The pulpit, the bank account, and everything else it seems like by your own admission. What kind of man tells his wife not to worry about what he does outside the house? A controlling man, that's who. Hey, you're my coworker and I think you're a'ight, so all I'm going to advise you to do is open your eyes. It's none of my business, but I've played those games before and he's controlling you and he's doing it by babbling the Bible."

Laughing nearly made me wet my pants. Geo's remark brought back memories of what Ma always said was the easiest way to shut somebody up; "Quote something from the Bible."

I always believed that there was a ring of truth in her ideology, but DeMarcus wasn't one to pull scripture from the Bible and twist it for his own purposes. If anything, he was caught up into becoming an unblemished pastor and had high expectations of me being the typical token pastor's wife.

"When was the last time he did something special for you?"

"He splurged a little on me while in D.C. and he's planning something special for my birthday. He does what most husbands do which is quite a lot, actually. Where are you going with this?"

Arriving at our destination and pulling into the parking lot, Geo was quiet. He removed the key from the ignition and slid back his seat. Turning to face me, his deep stare made me uneasy. I cracked the window and pretended to be people watching. When he called my name, I turned to face him. Staring into my eyes, Geo spoke slowly when complimenting me on being a beautiful and intelligent woman. I blushed when he told me I was the type of woman a good man is looking for. Stating also that he knew nothing more about my home life than what I confided with him, Geo grabbed my hand and called me *foolish*.

"He's playing with your mind and you refuse to remove the blinders. He tells you what he wants you to know and that's good enough for you. Marriage brings two people together as one, but you've given him complete power and control over your mind; that's not good. When you stood before the minister, you both vowed to love, honor, and obey each other. I'm certain he didn't say anything about control. He's made you weak. He has you believing that you're inferior to him and that's not right or true. If something were to happen to him could you make it on your own? Never give up your independence to a man."

I listened to Geo but didn't respond. His opinion was simply that, his opinion and it didn't matter what he or anyone else thought about my marriage. He apologized for anything said which may have hurt my feelings but reiterated being a friend with my best interest at heart. I faked a smile and changed the subject, suggesting we go inside and sign in. Looking down at my watch, "Yep, it's about that time. Let's go in and get our seats."

The conference was informative and thankfully the topic Geo and I discussed driving back to the center and not my personal matters. However, he did offer to buy me lunch, but I declined. Kim was in town and bringing lunch to the office.

I was overly excited about meeting up with Kim being that two months had passed since we last saw each other since she moved, yet again, to another county—this time a job promotion. We had tons to catch up on and if I knew Kim, she had some juicy and interesting stories to tell, unlike myself.

When Kim arrived, I was paged to the reception area and gladly assisted in carrying our lunch to my office. Kim's tiny frame was even smaller. She was almost diva-ish; *if that's even a word,* clacking down the hallway in black, high-heeled boots. Dressed in black jeans and a low-cut black leather jacket, the rhinestone, flip-up shades polished her look. Kim's hair was flattened and fell midway past her shoulders. It swayed as she walked.

"Work it, Kim, you look great," I said behind my closed door.

"Thank you, my dear, thank you. I've never felt better. I tell ya', people take breathing for granted. The more pounds I shed, the better I breathe."

"Well, you look like a million-dollar '*breathing*' bucks. How are you doing it?"

Kim described her daily, early morning workout and jotted down some of the exotic foods she swore ate body fat. She listed various health drinks lining her refrigerator and proudly admitted to taking a weekly enema. As she talked, I listened in amazement to her newfound confidence. She was alive and living healthy. I was somewhat envious…and hungry.

"And see, I can even cross my legs now. And the men, whew! There's just so many to choose from," she laughed.

Kim never had a problem meeting men. Her flawless skin, dimpled cheeks, and hazel eyes were natural, attention-getting attributes. And prior to turning thirty-two and the dramatic weight loss, her rounded derriere was a rare, highly sought-after commodity.

"I'm happy for you. Just watch, in six months, you're going to be asking me where I've disappeared to 'cause I'll be so skinny. Chasing the kids through the house is my daily workout. And I hardly ever get a chance to eat for feeding them and DeMarcus."

"How is DeMarcus? The last time we talked, you mentioned a speaking engagement in Washington."

I shared the details of our trip and stated being grateful that it was over. Kim appeared pleased to hear that DeMarcus and his message were well received.

"His sermons are much better," I added. Kim laughed, understanding that I wasn't criticizing him, just merely acknowledging his effort to implement a few changes that in our opinion, would keep a growing congregation growing.

"Speak with power. Start out strong and finish strong," was my suggestion.

"Keep your sermon under twenty minutes. Anything beyond that will have me contemplating an escape," joked Kim.

We laughed recalling the time when she, I, and the handful of people still awake were focused more on the unzipped pants of the packing Associate Pastor Wallace instead of the Honorary Pastor Dr. Bradford Mikesell who we paid handsomely to preach from our pulpit.

"He lost me two minutes after approaching the podium," laughed Kim.

Kim was right. Pastor Mikesell was ancient in age, dragged his words, and ranted on and on about a bunch of old people none of us knew. His sermon was hardly a sermon—an opening scripture followed by a long, drawn-out, old hymn, another scripture then a round of participatory fillers. "Tell three people how good God has been to you. Cross the aisle and tell three more people…" he would say, followed by another scripture or two.

"On my Sundays off, there's a nice church right outside of Shelbyville I like to visit. You've got to come visit me and check it out. The eye candy in the pulpit is to die for," she squealed. "Even the men on canes are fine. And the pastor…girl, he's a combination of Denzel and Ricky Martin from 44th Street."

"Pulpit men and boring. DeMarcus is a prime example. It's always Bible, Bible, Bible, or meeting, after meeting, after meeting. It's OK for me, but I can see you now getting ready to bring the New Year in right at the club then getting mad when your man has other plans which entail attending an 11 p.m. New Year's Eve worship service. And you like to drink. Other than Sister Florida, what other pastor's wife do you know that gets skully?"

"All of them," replied Kim.

"How else would pastors know the names of all the top-rated wines and malt liquors unless they were stocking their own shelves? And walking into this church, you'd think you were at a fashion show, a twenty-five and over club, or a matchmaking convention. I've met a gazillion people there but the one I have my eyes on, his name is Shawn. He's thirty-six years old and so so so so sexy! I love me some Shawn and would fight another woman over him if I had to."

"Well, hopefully, it won't come to that. Are yaw dating or still getting to know each other?"

"We're mating," she laughed.

"I can't exactly call it dating being-that he has a wife. I know, I know," she said in response to my bugged eyes and mouth dropping.

"I ain't proud of myself for giving him the best sex of his life but he approached me when I was weak, real weak. I couldn't say no."

"You're going to hell!" I yelled.

"Hello," grinned Geo, inviting himself into my office and into our conversation. His eyes were fixated on Kim who, with the biggest of smiles, sat back in her chair and seductively crossed her left leg over her right.

"You must be Geo? Rosilyn has told me quite a lot about you. You weren't lying girl," Kim said, cutting her eyes at me.

Embarrassed and speechless, I lowered my head and laughed when realizing she only knew of his name from the badge he wore. Geo's grin grew wider. He handed me a binder. "Here's the new training manual. If you don't mind, can you review it before it's circulated?"

Nodding my head and grabbing the binder from his hand, I expected him to leave but he didn't. With a half-cocked smile, Geo sat on the edge of my desk and grabbed at his chin while staring Kim up and down. In response, Kim dipped her finger inside her yogurt cup and after placing it in her mouth moaned, "Ummm."

Uncomfortable in my own seat watching their flirtatious exchanges, I purposely slammed the binder down on the table to get their attention. Geo removed a business card from his wallet and handed it to Kim. She jotted her number on the back of the card and handed it back to him.

Batting her eyes, she whispered, "The ball is in your court. If interested, give me a call."

Geo left my office with swagger in his step. Kim sat back in her chair and began swinging her crossed leg back and forth. Holding up her hand and admiring her fresh set of acrylic nails, she smirked when I questioned, "What was that?"

"It's called an appetizer and with any luck, I'll soon be served the main course." Kim laughed hysterically.

"Didn't you just tell me that you were dating someone at the church? Wasn't his name, Shawn?"

"No, I said that I was having sex with someone. I'm not dating anyone. There is a difference."

A part of me wanted to blast her for sounding so ridiculous, but instead, I smiled and shook my head in disbelief. It was only a few months earlier that she was crying on the phone, expressing her frustrations of the night club riff-raff who after treating her to a drink then sexing her up, wanted little or nothing else to do with her. But by her recent actions, she seemed to have lowered her own standards—seeing nothing wrong with sexing married men or sliding her real phone number to random strangers for that matter. That worried me.

"See, how God works?" I chuckled, before handing her the *Adult Depression* Binder Geo had just asked me to review.

"You've got problems and instead of trying to talk it over with you, you take this book home and call me if you have any questions."

Kim laughed and sat the binder down on my desk.

"No, you read it. It has your name all over it. If I have any questions, I'll be sure to ask Geo. I'm about ten inches sure he has the answers for everything. Get a life!" Kim advised.

"I have a life. My life is full being a wife, mom, and a working woman."

"I won't knock ya'. Maybe one day that'll be me but right now I feel good, I look good, and dang it, I'ma be naughty because naughty is good."

"Kim, how do you expect to find a good man with that kind of attitude? What's gotten into you?"

"A whole lot of life, that's what. You call DeMarcus boring? You two were made for each other. When was the last time you went out and got your hair done? When was the last time you bought yourself some clothes?"

"About a month ago but what does that have to do with anything?"

"OK, let me rephrase that. When was the last time, you wore a shirt that exposed a shoulder? Roz, you're a young woman dressing like and acting like an old lady. Loosen up! Showing a little skin makes me feel sexy. And before your ancient butt says it, no, I don't do it for men, though I do like the attention. I like to dress sexy because it makes me feel good."

Realizing that Kim and I weren't going to see eye to eye on this matter, after shoving the last forkful of salad down my throat, I looked at my watch and lied about needing to prepare for a meeting. Kim helped tidy up my desk and after giving each other a nice long hug, we headed out the door. Geo must have heard the clicking of her heels and dropped what he was doing to meet us in the hallway.

"It was very nice meeting you."

"Likewise," Kim replied, winking her eye and showing her full set of pearly whites.

When I returned to my office, Geo was seated at my desk. Had it been any other time, I would have thought he wanted to discuss center matters but this time, he was smiling from ear to ear and I knew why.

"She's a hot mess I know." I plopped down in my chair and threw my hands up in the air.

"And yes, that's my friend, Kim, I wanted to introduce you to. I apologize for her behavior. I don't know what's gotten into her."

"You can't apologize for her behavior. She put it out there and knew exactly what she was doing. But the reason I'm here is to apologize to you for getting carried away. Never in a million years would I want to be anything less than professional around you. That's not the side of me I would want you or any other co-worker to see."

"What side? Your human side?"

"No, the dog in me."

His straight-faced response was unexpected and caused me to lift my brow. Never had I heard a man confess to being a dog, only hearing him call a woman a female dog, or boast about the women he's dogged.

"So, you're gonna call her?" My facial expression changed from inquisitive to quite confused.

"I plan on it. Would that be a problem for you?"

"Before today, I thought you two would be great for each other. But—"

"What's changed?" he asked, interrupting my thought.

I rested my forehead on my desk. I didn't have a migraine at that exact moment but could certainly feel one stirring up.

"I guess nothing's changed," I said, lifting my head and again raising my brow. "If you two are attracted to each other, good luck."

"Rosilyn, are you sure you're OK with me hooking up with Kim?"

"If you're interested in dating her, go for it. What yaw do is none of my business."

Geo smiled.

"I detect jealousy. I'm flattered."

"It's not jealousy, its confusion. This new way of hooking up, I guess yaw threw me for a loop."

"You've lived a sheltered life," he laughed. "You view things differently than a whole bunch of other folk but it's all good. It's like I told you the other day, say what you mean and mean what you say. Somewhere in this big ole' world, you have to do something for you—make your mark. Me, I'm single by choice and just so happened to have met a confident, outgoing, and sexy woman. She made it known that she wanted to connect; she threw the bone and I caught it. We're adults. People don't sugar coat what's on their minds anymore. Personally, I prefer a woman who's upfront about what she wants, and your friend was."

"Don't get me wrong, I love Kim like a sister, but she was ho-ish. I can't believe that you or any man would be attracted to someone just pushing it out there like that."

"It's not ho-ish, it's being straight forward and flirtatious. Remember that shirt you bought in Chicago?" Geo asked.

"The one I told you was ugly and was hanging on the wrong rack? It caught your eye and you picked it up. Well, it's the same thing here. She put herself out there to be noticed and she was."

"I'll never understand it, but thank God, I'm married and don't have to worry about that."

"Married people aren't dead, they're married. Men look at attractive women just as women look at handsome men, married and unmarried. Even in the church, girls as young as twelve years old are running around showing their ham hocks and breasts. And where do they get it from? Their momma's and their auntie's, that's who. Every woman knows that men get turned on when a woman flashes a little skin."

"Yeah, but a person can be sexy without showing their skin too."

"That's a matter of opinion," he laughed and repeated. "For instance, look at Big Shirley. I'm not attracted to plus-sized women but she's very sexy in pumps and lipstick. Even when she wears those short dresses, she shows just enough of her knee to keep me wondering about the whole leg. And Jackie, have you ever seen her arms? She normally wears a jacket to cover them up, but her arms are sexy. Men notice stuff like that."

"You're just horny." I laughed.

"I may be, but did you notice how little of an effort it took to get Kim's number? It's just as easy to get the number of another. But what I'm saying to you is, take an interest in yourself and stop being so afraid to do something out of the ordinary. Yes, you're married but that doesn't make you an old maid. We don't have a policy against women wearing open-toed shoes around here. Red toenail polish would give that nice red dress you're wearing a whole new look. And consider letting a curl dangle in your face; take off that plastic hairband. Better yet, clip it back and show off your smooth skin. You have a natural arch to your eyebrows and a little blush wouldn't hurt your high cheekbones. Wear colored gloss on your lips, you're beautiful Rosilyn. Why are you afraid to flaunt what you're working with?"

I thanked Geo for the compliments then wondered if his other remarks were a cut-down or reality spoken in a harsh tone.

"Try it. I bet you'll feel better about yourself. You've got all the qualities of a supermodel. You encourage women every day to go out and do something different. Now it's time to take your own advice?"

Geo's words stayed with me throughout the day and during Bible study the next night, I found myself observing the countless women who in one way or the other were working their own style. The majority of the teenagers were wearing name-brand jeans, rhinestone shirts, and lots of bangles. The twenty to thirty-five age group appeared to be focused more on simple comfort— designer boots, ear, and neck accessories. Even the fifty and over age group had their own style going; three to six-inch heels and a basic color suit coat.

All my life, people had commented on my pretty face but none of that meant anything to me. But Geo's words were encouraging. I was more than just DeMarcus's wife. It was time to make a change.

Chapter 5

Seasons Change

Other than for his early morning jog, DeMarcus rarely left the house before 3 p.m. on Saturdays so on an impulse, I scheduled myself an appointment at the Perk it Up Hair and Nail Salon, a place recommended by a coworker. Visiting an actual beauty salon was a rarity for me as my good grade of hair had always been easy to style and maintain on my own. I was excited about being pampered a little bit even if it was just having someone to massage my scalp. When I entered the salon, I gave the receptionist my name and was immediately escorted to the back.

Brief was my wait before a woman approached me and introduced herself as Rhonda.

"Hello. I will be your stylist today," she said with a welcoming tone. Showing me to her chair, my eyes shifted to the multitude of family photos outlining her mirror. Without her pointing them out, I knew who her offspring were. Their familial traits were strong, slanted eyes, pug nose, and dimpled chins.

Rhonda was a talkative lady and within ten minutes, I knew all five of her children by name. I talked about my children and even mentioned being the wife of a pastor but listening to her go on and on about her life, I realized just how boring my life was. This petite woman and grandmother of six once worked as a mortician and for the past twelve years has rode a Harley Davidson in an all women's biker club. *Whodathunkit?* She looked great to be in her mid-forties.

Overhearing other conversations, what didn't make me laugh made me cringe. Women were loose at the lips—boasting about their men, their jobs, and all sorts of subjects that, in my opinion, ought not to be shared in a public venue among strangers. But I kept right on listening while Rhonda played in my hair. She did so for a while then asked what style I desired.

"You have a lot of breakage. Have you ever considered wearing a short doo? You have a nice grade of hair and going short will lengthen your neck."

Clipping of my ends was something I expected but having my hair cut above my neck as Rhonda suggested seemed to be extreme. But after handing me a photo album of styles to look through, I began imagining myself sporting a shorter hairdo. In each of the before photos with long hair, the after photos at a shorter length was gorgeous. I figured if they could look that good, so could I. So, when Rhonda returned, I instructed her to 'cutaway.'

I was tickled to death to hear the pitter-patter of tiny feet racing to the door to greet me.

No sooner than I turned the knob, "Mommy, Mommy," DeMarya screamed, grabbing my legs and holding on tight. Junior came running too but halted to examine the woman resembling his mother but with much shorter hair. His lips poked out and shortly thereafter, he burst into tears. Scooping down to pick them both up, I assured them that everything was going to be OK as we walked towards the kitchen. DeMarya rested her head on my shoulder. Junior fought to be loosed from my grip. I laughed all the way to the kitchen, that is, until seeing DeMarcus who immediately began yelling and demanding to know of my whereabouts. He looked at my hairdo. From his facial expression, I sensed disapproval.

"What the hell were you thinking? Why would you let someone do this to you? You look like a boy. Rosilyn, why would you want to embarrass me or yourself by wearing your hair in that stupid-looking style?" He circled around me and stared at my head. I pushed his hand away when he tugged at a waved layer of hair spritzed into place.

Why my hair was such an issue for him was baffling to me and had it not been for my daughter still hanging onto my shoulder, I would have blasted back at him in a not-so-lady like manner. When DeMarcus and I first met, my hair was just as short—and he loved running his fingers through it. So why

59

was he tripping now? At the least, he could have held his tongue or lied and said that it looked a'ight. But he kept right on shouting, caring not that his tone was frightening the kids.

"I can't believe you allowed someone to whack off all of your hair. Did you even go to a salon or did you get it done in an alley? It's ugly and I hate it! We didn't discuss this and I'm not happy with it."

"Happy with what? My decision to want to look nice. It's my head and my hair. I wanted a fresh new look for my birthday so what's the big fricken deal? Why must you be so cruel?"

He followed me into DeMarya's bedroom when I laid her down to nap. Junior was antsy as well, so I popped a DVD inside his television to keep him occupied. DeMarcus followed me back into the kitchen and resumed with his wave of insults.

"You're the only person who doesn't like my cut. I like it too so really, what is your deal?"

"I don't care what other people say, you are my wife and you represent me. You look like a bald-headed boy and I'm very disappointed. As a matter of fact, go buy a wig! I don't want to have to look at it."

Controlling is what Geo would call DeMarcus's behavior and perhaps it was, but my hair had been cut and there was nothing I could do about it. Not that I would if I could—I loved my hair; it was cool on my neck and it made me look at least, five years younger.

For another half hour, I was forced to listen to his cheap shots and ugly remarks. My refusal to react or respond infuriated him to the point that he left the house, slamming the door hard behind him.

After checking on the kids, I grabbed the house phone and went out onto the back porch for air. Dialing Kim first but reaching her voicemail, I then decided to call Ma to tell her about the birthday present to myself. I sensed by her silence that she too wasn't happy to learn that I did the unthinkable—cut the long, curly locks, the inherited Hall family grade of hair that my great, great, great, great grandmother passed down to us.

Since my teenage years, all the elders in my family ever talked about were the family members who were cursed for simply having their ends clipped. Supposedly, an Aunt Virginia died two days after cutting the long locks that fell below her buttocks to above her shoulder. And as if it were yesterday, I could still vividly see the family photo of about seventeen cousins and aunts whose hair and ponytails hung well beyond their tailbone. Ma listened while I described my cut in detail and when I was done, she changed the subject and asked about the kids.

The next morning, DeMarcus rose earlier than normal and warmed a pot of oatmeal and scrambled eggs for the kids. He kissed my forehead then darted across the yard to the church. I truly wanted to sleep through Sunday school as my body was fatigued but doing so would have caused another argument. After the kids ate breakfast, we jumped into our Sunday morning routine.

I loved my hairdo when it was first cut, but on day two, it was even more gorgeous.

The make-up I applied to my eyes, lips, and cheeks was flawless. I wasn't one to wear long dangling earrings but what a difference my looped accessories made. My face appeared to be longer, not rounded and swollen and for a reason, I can't explain, they brought out the gray in my eyes.

Years ago, Kim suggested that I be bold and toss the pantyhose. In my opinion, a woman without pantyhose was tacky and no different from a busty woman wearing a t-shirt without a brassiere. However, after trying on my new pumps, my shaven and well-greased legs looked quite sexy, so I proceeded in sliding on my one-piece, above the knee fitted dress over my head, and retrieved a clutch purse from my closet to match my fit.

Had I taken another moment to style and profile in the mirror, the kids and I would've been late for Sunday school. But we arrived on time and almost immediately upon walking through the door, all eyes fell upon me. I received at least a dozen compliments from the time I dropped the kids off in the nursery to when I entered the sanctuary which was only twenty to thirty steps away. I smiled at each of them as if it was no big deal but seeing the reaction on many of their faces and hearing that multitude of *ooohs* and *ahhhs*, there was no denying I looked good.

Snickering and Amen's filled the sanctuary when Sister Evonne approached the floor podium and opened her Bible. After a year of teaching the youth, it shouldn't have bothered anyone that the education director deemed her qualified to teach at another level.

Since joining the church, I'd never seen Evonne's boobs covered nor her skirt at an acceptable length, but on this day, she looked nice, very nice. And although she looked the part of a holier than thou spiritual leader, she didn't look as good as me.

Sitting on the second pew when DeMarcus entered the sanctuary, Deacon Collins nearly clipped DeMarcus's heels to get to me and comment on my new look. I appreciated his comment but lowered my head to hide my smile. DeMarcus sat to my right.

"What are you wearing?" he asked. "You're not only embarrassing yourself, but me and the kids. Go home and change out of that slut suit immediately!"

I looked over my shoulder in hopes that no one on the pew behind us overheard. Looking to his right, I was relieved that Deacon Collins hadn't heard him either. In less than sixty seconds, DeMarcus had successfully crushed my spirits. I wanted to cry but didn't. I ignored him. I lowered my head and fumbled through the pages of my Bible.

When Evonne took to the mic, DeMarcus's demeanor quickly changed. His once slouched posture became erect and the look of chagrin upon his face became warm and welcoming. I noticed too how uncomfortable he became—unloosing his tie after Evonne called out his name to express her personal gratitude for the opportunity to address his flock. But DeMarcus wasn't uncomfortable too long—he enjoyed receiving the accolades. Nodding his head as if it was no big deal and at the same time, giving her a half-cocked smile.

Seconds into her lesson, the microphone began to echo and crackle. When Brandon's attempt to correct the audio issues failed, DeMarcus motioned for her to take the podium in the pulpit—the pulpit I am barred from entering and the one his firstborn child received a spanking for when running through it. I chuckled, but my level of pisstivity was high. Chuckling once more, DeMarcus shushed me. Embarrassed I was, hearing the laughter of those surrounding us who found humor in me being corrected. I pretended to not be phased.

I felt my chest tightening. And when the room began to spin, I considered resting on the couch in DeMarcus's office for a short while but remained on the pew. Knowing that the dizziness stemmed from my elevated blood pressure, I closed my eyes and attempted to block out everything. But that was difficult to do with Evonne still yelping and hopping from subject to subject in her lesson like a frog from pad to pad. DeMarcus nudged me; he thought I was asleep. I cut my eyes at him and then stared off into the pulpit, thinking about my upcoming birthday. I thought about how nice it would be taking a road trip to Louisville and a few days away from DeMarcus to de-stress and clear my mind.

At 10:50 a.m., I folded my arms and raised my left brow in hopes of sending Evonne the *wrap-it-up-signal,* but she never looked my way. Had I not been angry at DeMarcus, I would have alerted him of the time—him being such a stickler for the promptness in starting morning worship, but I didn't. *Hell, he was wearing a watch and should have noticed the time himself.*

Looking around the sanctuary and observing several members with crossed arms and looks of boredom on their faces was comical. However, when folks started tiptoeing out, I looked up to watch Evonne's facial expression but caught a glimpse of the sparkling necklace draped around her neck. A matching bracelet dangled from her wrist. At the end of her lesson, DeMarcus joined her in the pulpit and grabbed the microphone. He edified her for a lesson well done.

"And this won't be the last time you hear from Sister Evonne. She's agreed to take on the new M.O.M's Ministry beginning in January. M.O.Ms is a mother's only meeting. She's going to be teaching topics to benefit all mothers of the church and I believe a few sisterhood outings are in the plans. Let's encourage our Sista," he said, turning to me to be the next one to do so.

That punk azz! Needless to say, I was beyond pissed but didn't allow my frustrations to show. Instead, I faked a smile and made my way toward Evonne and into DeMarcus's pulpit for the first time ever. He attempted to reroute my path, but I bumped him aside. He appeared annoyed, but I didn't care. However, after giving Evonne a few words of encouragement, DeMarcus quickly grabbed her by the hand and assisted her to the floor and out of the pulpit to be received by others. But not before I caught a better glimpse of her matching ensemble. It was similar to the set DeMarcus described purchasing for me.

DeMarcus was sitting at his desk reading over his notes for morning worship when I stormed through his office doors. Deacons Moyler and Collins were also inside and about to take a seat when I apologized for interrupting then asked for privacy to speak to my husband. I was madder than hell and wanted answers. Deacon Moyler exited first. As Deacon Collins passed by, he again complimented my new look then whispered in my ear that I was too beautiful to be wearing a frown.

"What can I do for you, Roz? And I thought I asked you to go take off that slutty dress."

"If you don't like what I'm wearing, well close your eyes. Everyone else seems to like my new look so I've decided I'm not taking it off. But that's not why I am here. How are you going to ask me to head a ministry then give it to Evonne? And everyone knows that if they ain't preaching, introducing the guest preacher, or reading scripture, they are not to stand in your pulpit. Why is it that you allowed Evonne to teach from the very pulpit you spanked DeMarya for running through? Something's going on with you and Evonne and I want to know now what it is!"

"I don't have time to argue this morning over your petty and frivolous issues; I have a message to review. But what you can do is leave my office right now, go home and take a chill pill and while you're there, put on some decent clothes."

"Well, if you're not going to be honest about what's going on, I'll pull it out of Evonne."

"You will do no such thing. Have you lost your mind?" DeMarcus rounded his desk and stood in my face.

"We will talk this over later, but you better check yourself. Don't you ever step out of line and deliberately set out to put me in a negative light. Not with church members, family members, or anyone. Have I made myself clear?"

On any other day, my response would have been, *Yes DeMarcus* but I remained still—toe to toe with a man I so much wanted to bash upside the head with the granite bulldog paperweight on his desk and underneath the palm of my right hand. I had never been known to be a violent person—always managed to keep myself and my emotions in check but DeMarcus was bringing out the worst in me. He was turning me into someone ugly.

"Yep, we'll talk later. See you at home… Pastor," I slurred with sarcasm.

Whipping my neck and rolling my eyes with an attitude, I flung my hand in his face and turned my back to him. Walking toward the door, I didn't care to see his facial expression but hoped like hell I had gotten underneath his skin like he had gotten underneath mine.

Throughout morning worship, I stared at Evonne as she gazed starry-eyed at DeMarcus. After a while, I concluded that there was nothing for DeMarcus and I to discuss later as her body language and their visual interactions confirmed what I needed to know. Unbeknownst to me, while Evonne watched DeMarcus and I watched Evonne, Deacon Moyler was watching me. He must have seen me wipe away a tear because before a second could fall, he had placed a couple of tissues on my leg. I thanked him then looked up again at DeMarcus, pretending to be focused on the sermon.

My tears had nothing to do with anything related to DeMarcus's message but rather my coming to the realization that what others were saying to me about my marriage and my husband were true. In his defense, DeMarcus wasn't a perfect man but never had I imagined him being a Sugar Daddy to another woman. He had always been a quiet person; a man of very few words and the thought of him sharing his thoughts, a smile or anything with another woman hurt me to the core. It pained me as well, seeing Evonne on the receiving end of my husbands' affection.

It was four hours after morning worship had ended when DeMarcus decided to come home. After slamming the front door and finding me in the middle of bathing the kids, he shouted loud, and in my face, that Evonne or anything related to her was not a topic open for discussion. I truly didn't have the energy to follow behind to argue with him and after putting the kids to bed, I grabbed a pillow and blanket from the hallway closet and made myself a comfortable pallet on the living room couch.

Driving the kids to the daycare the next morning, I decided to use a sick day and returned to the house. DeMarcus appeared surprised by my return but didn't ask for an explanation. Instead, I sought an explanation as to why he was pacing through the house and peeping out various windows. I was ignored. However, at 9:05 when hearing a knock at the door, it was damn near a rat race to open it. Evonne stood in the doorway. Her huge smile disappeared when I stepped from behind DeMarcus.

"Good morning, Sister Jackson," she said. I didn't respond.

"DeMarcus, I mean, the pastor has been counseling me. If today is not a good time, I can come back."

"So, you've been coming on a regular basis to my house? How long has it been Evonne?" I wanted to smack her ruby red lips but Robbi, my alter ego was in my ear and whispering for me to behave.

"Damn it, Rosilyn! Not now, OK. I counsel from the house often, not just to women but men as well."

DeMarcus pointed her in the direction of his study. He followed behind her and I followed behind him.

"This is a confidential matter, do you mind?"

"Yes, I mind a whole hell of a lot. How dare you bring your whore into our house?"

Instructing Evonne to take a seat, DeMarcus excused himself and manhandled me out of his study. He pushed me in the back; I rolled my ankle. Falling into the wall to brace myself, I hit the side of my head on the edge of the bookcase. I grabbed for my head, but DeMarcus grabbed my wrists and dragged me down the hall and into our bedroom. I feared what was about to occur. He paced the floor back and forth with his hands on his hips. A few seconds later, he approached me and in a low and authoritative tone, told me our marriage was over.

"You've embarrassed me for the last time. This woman is here for counseling, nothing else and now you've got her thinking that I'm a bad husband and that my wife is crazy. I don't know what it is with you, but if you want to keep the kids, get it together!"

Accepting responsibility for losing control and second-guessing whether I could have handled things any better, I found myself dismissing DeMarcus's actions although I had been totally humiliated and disrespected. But what made matters worse was being stripped of all power—down to nothing in the presence of the very woman whom he obviously had an attraction to. I didn't deserve this, none of this! And as I sat on the edge of the bed replaying his words over and over again in my head, I couldn't control my tears. My thoughts were all over the place—it was all so crazy. But even crazier was the counseling session which lasted less than ten minutes.

Slow to lift the bedroom blinds when hearing his office door open and the front screen door close, I watched as they talked on the porch but couldn't clearly hear their conversation.

DeMarcus appeared to be calm as a cucumber, smiling and talking as if to be doing so with a dear old friend. Evonne was giddy—nodding her head and laughing at his every word. It seemed that after saying goodbye they wanted to hug but refrained from doing so. DeMarcus returned to the bedroom and with the straightest of faces, admitted that he didn't love me anymore.

"And it's not about being with other women, we're just not compatible. You don't believe in the same things I believe in and you don't respect me as your husband. And I'm tired of fighting with you. I want a peaceful home, a home filled with love. That's just not us anymore. And without going into a long and drawn out discussion over this, let's just agree to do what we have-to-do for the sake of the kids and at the first of the year, I'll have everything worked out as it relates to our divorce. I'm going for a run."

DeMarcus tossed a towel over his shoulder and left the room without allowing me to speak my thoughts. In truth, I didn't have any thoughts about the matter for being either numb, in shock, or both. I questioned whether I really loved DeMarcus or simply tolerated the man who fathered my children. Either way, it was a done deal. DeMarcus had spoken.

Tuesday morning was an awful morning, but I forced myself out of bed and into the shower. After drying off, I took a few extra moments to pamper myself and covered my entire body in coconut lotion. Deciding to wear an outfit I purchased while in Chicago, I searched the closet for my favorite pair of boots and found a purse to match. DeMarcus pretended to be asleep, but I continued preparing myself for work as if in the room alone. Entering the bathroom for better lighting, after brushing my teeth, I ran my fingers through my hair and removed my makeup case from the drawer. DeMarcus was sitting up when I returned to the bedroom. He watched me apply a dibble-dabble of the perfume that supposedly drove him wild on my neck, breast, and wrist.

"What's the perfume for? You're only going to work."

A flash of responses cluttered my brain, but I said nothing and let my silence speak for itself. *Funny, that's something I picked up from him.*

While sitting in the center's parking lot, I closed my eyes and prayed that my day would be busy. So busy, I wouldn't be able to think about anything else, particularly my home issues. Walking through the lobby, my new hairdo became the morning buzz. Even Mexican Mike left his security post for a better view. He touched my hair and smiled.

"I like, I like," he remarked.

"Personally, I think you looked better with longer hair but you're rocking that short style, Ms. Ma'am," said Shirley, the receptionist.

Geo entered my office moments later and stood at the edge of my desk. With his mouth hung wide, he circled my chair and glanced me over. When I could no longer stand his silence, I erupted into laughter.

"Well, either you like it, or you don't. It shouldn't take you that fricken long to decide." Being silly, I covered my head with my steno pad.

"It's gorgeous but it's all gone. I mean, a woman's long hair is her glory, but I am simply stunned at how beautiful you are without it."

I took that as a compliment.

"You said to do something for myself, well, this is a birthday present to me, from me."

Geo went on and on about my transformation and even complimented my wardrobe selection. I blushed at his comments, even more so at the one he slid in about how if I wasn't a married woman, the things he'd like to do to me.

"Speaking of which, have you talked to Kim? I've been trying to reach her all weekend, but she hasn't returned any of my calls."

"She's in Tennessee for training. We hung out Friday night; I'm surprised she didn't tell you." Geo continued looking me over. He asked what my husband thought about my new look.

It wasn't the topic I wanted to discuss but because he asked, I downplayed DeMarcus's reaction but then sprung on him the details of my impending divorce. Geo listened as I quoted DeMarcus, lowering his head and shaking it several times in disbelief. Sharing the specifics of my ordeal was hard but keeping my composure and my emotions in check was harder. And during our conversation, I broke down. Geo grabbed my hands and rubbed my palms.

"I am so sorry to hear what you're going through. It hurts right now but it'll get better, trust me. Losing someone through death or divorce is painful but it's not the end of the world. Go on and get your cry out Rosilyn and when you finish, hold your head up high. Other than marrying a loser, you've done nothing wrong. You're a strong and beautiful queen who deserves to be treated as such. Now I'm not what you'd call a spiritual-spiritual person, but I do believe in God and I know that God works in ways that are often a mystery to us. With all you've been through and still going through, has it crossed your mind that just maybe, the demise of your marriage is a blessing in disguise?"

Chapter 6

Renew Your Mind

"Happy Birthday, to me! Today I turned the big three-five and though it was probably all just in my mind, I felt like this was the day of purpose for me; the day I was supposed to make a statement for my life. Something about this birthday felt strange; a good strange. I woke up happy—happy to be alive, happy to be a mother, and despite the troubles plaguing my marriage, I was happy being DeMarcus's wife, for had it not been for the hell he'd put me through the last few months, my prayers for strength and sanity would not have been answered. That's what it was, strength to endure my storm. Thank you, Lord!"

When DeMarcus and I were dating, I was convinced that he was the sweet in my Kool-Aid. And once we married, his kiss is what jump-started my heart. There was absolutely nothing I wouldn't do for him. His needs were placed before my own and even on the rare occasions when something he said or did was amiss, I trusted his judgment and supported him wholeheartedly. But on this day, October 1, 2015, I've chosen to step out on faith and to trust in the sign that hangs on Ma's front door: *Put God before everything and put everything in His hands.*

Yes, I was crushed that my marriage was ending and yes, I was hurt beyond words discovering that DeMarcus had played for a fool for so many years. And yes, it scared me to wonder what my life and my kids' lives would be like without him, but I refused to cry about it. And if DeMarcus expected me to beg and plead with him to keep our family intact, *Hell, naw, that wasn't happening!*

DeMarcus pretended to be asleep when I eased out of the bedroom to tend to our fussy son who was whining from his bed and calling my name. He didn't join us in the kitchen either after I sent DeMarya to knock on the door—twice—to let him know that his breakfast was ready.

If he wanted special attention, he wasn't getting it. If he expected to be served breakfast in bed, that wasn't gonna happen either. If he was tired and not ready to get up, well, that was swell too. Keeping his distance meant a reprieve from having my day ruined by his negative behavior. Considering being dead as a reason DeMarcus had yet to get up, I chuckled behind the thought of me being so lucky. Perhaps he was sleeping in; still I didn't care. I was so fed up with his crap that searching for a pulse, a rise and fall of his chest, or peeping in the bedroom to see if he'd changed sleeping positions wasn't of importance; my sanity was. And eating, I packed an overnight bag for me and the kids and without cleaning a single dish or leaving a note, jumped in the car and drove to Louisville.

As always, Ma was more excited to see the grandkids than me and I was alright with that. But when Dad pulled me in for a long welcoming hug, unbeknownst to him, it was very much needed. It felt good being home and among my family who unselfishly gave of their time to join in on my birthday celebration and to shower me with their love, gifts, and birthday wishes. Several family members asked about DeMarcus; where he was and if he was coming. But I smiled and dismissed his absence as having important church related engagements back home.

But in all honesty, I didn't want him around and was glad that he wasn't.

You wouldn't know when entering the house that a birthday party was taking place, but the two long tables of food and humongous birthday cake sure made up for the lack of balloons and other celebratory decorations. Fried chicken, fried okra, oxtail stew, macaroni and cheese, and a green bean casserole—many of my favorites were in the kitchen waiting for me, each dish specially prepared by Ma. After dinner, everyone gathered in the basement to watch and video me opening my gifts. Dad always liked for me to open his present first and so I did and inside my beautiful birthday card was four one-hundred-dollar bills. Second, I opened a present from my color-blind Aunt Terry who surprised us all in matching a hot pink, long-sleeved shirt and belt with a pair of black leggings and black and silver pumps. But Ma's gift was best—a fully charged cell phone wrapped in a tiny red bow.

"You call us old for still watching movies on the VCR, but I think you're the only person in Kentucky that doesn't have a cell phone. How are you gonna reach us if something happens while on the road with them babies?"

Ma was right and several times I had thought about getting one for emergency purposes only, but DeMarcus would always say we couldn't afford the extra expense. And I never pushed the issue because everyone I knew that had a cell phone was mesmerized by them; unable to hold one-on-one conversations or digest their food for being interrupted by it ringing or dinging. The first person I called was Kim. She too was excited and happy about me finally entering the twenty-first century.

It wasn't until the last guest had left the house that I was able to put everything back into its original place. Ma volunteered to bathe the kids, so I sat in the kitchen entering numbers into my new phone. As I crawled into bed and began reflecting on my wonderful day, I realized that I hadn't heard from DeMarcus. He hadn't called the house phone to wish me a happy birthday or check to see if we'd made it safe. *Maybe he was dead?* I dialed his cell phone. He answered on the first ring.

"So, I guess you weren't going to call?" I snapped.

He asked who I was.

"Who do you want it to be?" I asked with sarcasm, knowing damn well he recognized my voice.

"That's a trick question," he laughed.

I laughed too and was grateful that he was in a much better mood.

"Were you busy?"

"Never too busy for you."

Bull, I thought but didn't say aloud.

"No, who is this?" he again asked, seeming anxious to get the conversation started.

"It's your wife! Who do you want it to be?"

Silence covered the phone, but I could hear him breathing.

"Whose number are you calling from?"

"It's my number. Ma gave me a cell phone as a birthday gift. Did you forget about my birthday?"

"Why did she get you a cell phone? If I thought you needed a phone, I would have gotten you one!"

"It's just a cell phone, DeMarcus, damn! And it's nothing you got to pay for!"

"Whatever Roz. Is that all you wanted? I've got a sermon to finish tonight and right now you're disturbing me."

Refusing him the opportunity of ruining the end of my beautiful day, I hung up on his grouchy, insensitive azz before he could hang up on me.

Rising early the next morning, the thought of sitting on the pew next to DeMarcus gave me a major migraine so, after tag-teaming with Ma in the laundry room washing up sheets and linens, I plopped down on the couch and watched cartoons with the kids and my dad. I wasn't a DeMarcus fan this day so playing the happy-in-love supportive wife wasn't of any interest to me. Nor was I interested in sitting through another one of his idiotic, bullshit sermons on loving thy neighbor, honoring God, and other topics that sound good and that he didn't abide by.

Shutting off my phone, I spent an entire stress-free Sunday in Louisville.

Walking into my office on Monday morning, balloons and a huge Happy Birthday sign of well-wishes from coworkers was taped to my walls and chairs. Other than Geo, no one in the office knew it was my birthday weekend so before I took off my jacket, I entered his office to personally thank him.

"Kim and I have already discussed it and have decided we're taking you out for dinner tomorrow night. We know your birthday was last Friday but we wanna take you out to have some adult fun, adult conversation, and if you feel like it, a much-needed adult drink. And before you come up with seventy-two reasons as to why you can't go, Kim has someone on standby if you don't have a babysitter. We're not taking no for an answer."

"What do I look like being a third wheel? Thanks, but no thanks—you two go on and have a nice dinner. I had a very nice birthday, really I did."

"Rosilyn, go out with us. I promise that you will have a good time. And you won't be a third wheel. You and Kim will be joining me and my good friend, Jay, at the restaurant."

I looked at him and laughed aloud. The thought of being set up on a blind date was totally absurd. What the heck was Kim and Geo thinking? I'm a married woman—for now, anyhow. Perhaps he invited a friend to keep me from feeling like an oddball. Nevertheless, I declined, fearing the backlash I'd receive if seen in public with another man.

"It all sounds real nice, it really does but I am still a married woman," I said with a chuckle and wiggling my ring finger.

"I honestly don't think that double dating is appropriate at this time."

"It's not double dating, well, maybe just a little, but my friend Jay is a decent guy. He's single, no kids, and searching for a good woman. I told him about you and you wanna know what his first comment was?"

Like a nut, I waited for his response.

"He told me that you sound like his blessing come true. His exact words, I swear. Kim even agrees that you need somebody in your life that's going to treat you good. Why wait until the paperwork is filed? You still have a life to live and you deserve to be happy. What's the harm in one little birthday dinner with friends?"

I thought about it and thought about it, and the more I thought about it, the more humorous it became. *People don't go on blind dates anymore, do they?* But if they did, my answer was still no, heck no, and no way. Geo was insistent, however, giving me puppy dog looks as we passed in the hallway and occasionally sticking his head in my office and asking if I'd changed my mind. He even went so far as to place a sticky note with Jay's number on my phones' receiver when I stepped away from my desk on a short break.

"He wears the same cologne I do," Geo whispered through his desk phone, reminding me of the remark I once made about how much a well-groomed, cologne wearing man turned me on.

I smiled and laughed aloud.

"He drives a Benzzzzz," he shared, recalling our conversation about the E Class being my childhood dream car.

"It's only dinner, Rosilyn. You and Kim will meet us at 6 p.m. and you'll be walking through your front door no later than 9 p.m."

"What the heck?" I shrugged my shoulders.

"Stepping outside of my comfort zone could be fun. But I'm not calling him, he can call me. I'm not desperate and I don't want him thinking that I am."

The next morning, I woke up energized and excited about my evening plans. Minding my business as I stuffed a duffle bag with clothing, a hair curler, and my favorite three-inch pumps, I didn't feel it was necessary to respond to DeMarcus's inquiry of if I was packing for a trip. And when he sarcastically asked if I was moving out, with a grin on my face and my left brow raised, I turned and replied, "Not yet."

"What's all that for?" he yelled.

"We're having our annual business meeting after work and they told us to dress casual."

"So, you weren't going to tell me?"

"Actually, I wasn't. How often do you leave the house and me in the dark about your whereabouts? It's Tuesday DeMarcus. You pick the kids up on Tuesdays because you're home and don't have a class or a church meeting. But if you do have plans, let me know and I will arrange for a babysitter."

DeMarcus looked puzzled—angry best describes his expression. Instead of asking him, I told him what I was going to do and quite honestly, it felt good taking charge.

"Where is the meeting being held and what time is it over?"

I raised my brow yet again and stared him on the eyeball. He wasn't my daddy; my daddy wouldn't talk to me that way, so after zipping my bag, I threw it over my shoulder and grabbed my car keys. Adamant to have answers, DeMarcus raced across the room and held the bedroom door closed with his left arm. I really wanted to say *none of your fricken' business,* but if I wanted to leave, I couldn't continue to ignore him. I guesstimated being home around 9ish.

"Is this really a business meeting? I mean, you're in casual clothes already. What's the reason for the extra clothes and shoes?"

"Really, DeMarcus? What's in your gym bag, extra boxers? Soap, toothbrush, toothpaste? You're the one with a two day a week job and places to go five nights a week. Stop with the one hundred questions, OK. You said this marriage is over so stop with the interrogation and you won't have to worry about me interrogating you ever again."

He grabbed my purse, I snatched it back. He grabbed my arm and I froze.

"As long as you live in this house, don't ever twist your lips and get smart with me like that again. When I ask you a question, I expect an answer. Regardless of what you're going through, I am still the head of this household. You are my dependent, my wife, and you do as I say do, not what you want to do. If this rinky-dinky job is the reason for your disobedience and jacked up attitude, then we may have to think about vacating that position. I run this household here; you, and everything up in here."

"Yes, Sir DeMarcus, it's your castle. If you're done, I need to go so I'm not late for my rinky-dinky job."

Just as he was wondering what had gotten into me, I too was wondering what pill he swallowed making him delusional and believing that he ran me. Nonetheless, a goodbye kiss was *null and void* so after readjusting my purse and work bag over my shoulder, I warmed the car and prepared my mind for work.

The Crisis Center was busy and luckily for me, made time fly by quickly. By noon, Kim had everything planned out and had texted that she'd be picking me up at four-thirty, so we could beautify ourselves at her place. Although I was nervous and considering backing out, recalling DeMarcus's early morning actions made me more determined to maintain the upper hand.

Kim was in awe of my cut and with her special styling gel, created a whole new, punk rockish hairstyle. She suggested a lighter lip color and facial foundation then pulled out her make-up arsenal and worked a miracle.

"Eyeliner, foundation, and lipstick are all you needed. Sometimes women can put way too much color on their eyes and cheeks and start looking like a clown. Go simple. I like the natural look myself."

Arriving at Dugan's Steakhouse at exactly five forty-five, Geo joined us on the inside and alerted the hostess of our dinner reservation. Escorted to a corner booth near an unoccupied party room, I was grateful for not seeing any familiar faces after thoroughly scanning the room.

"Good. Your friend came to his senses and decided not to get tangled up with a married woman, huh?"

"No, he's on his way. He texted me about five minutes ago."

Suddenly becoming dizzy perhaps having a panic attack, I gracefully excused myself and headed for the ladies' room; Kim followed behind. Resting the back of my head against the wall, she dabbed my forehead with a wet paper towel and assured me I'd be fine.

"What am I doing here? It's wrong, it's wrong, it's wrong!"

"You're having a belated birthday dinner. Honey, you're reading too much into this. Geo and I wanted to do something special for you, but you're in control of what happens at the table. If you and Jay decide to be phone buddies, that's on you. If you choose to be cordial and leave the conversation at the table, that's on you too. You're not obligated to do anything other than to sit down, look pretty, and eat. We've been friends way too long, and you should know that I'd never put you in any situation that would cause you harm. Come on now, stop making yourself sick."

Needing another moment to regroup, I closed my eyes to focus on controlling my breathing. I imagined being in a quiet place and the only sounds heard were of birds chirping in nearby trees. Kim rubbed my back; it was soothing. She assured me that Jay's expectations were none other than to join us for dinner and once convincing myself that everything was going to be fine and over in a few short hours, I rechecked my make-up and prepared myself to return to the table. Rounding the corner, Kim and I paused when spotting Geo shake the hand of a gentleman removing his coat.

"I guess that's Jay," smiled Kim.

"Let's go have a seat and get this party started."

Slowly dragging behind Kim, "*here goes nothing,*" I mumbled, placing a grin on my face as if excited about what was to come. Approaching the table, Geo stood and assisted Kim into the booth. Jay stood up as well.

"Jay, this is Rosilyn. Rosilyn, this is Jay." Geo smiled after the introduction.

Everything in the room began to spin. The room had become extremely warm and I was in urgent need of oxygen. My knees locked—I was too nervous to move. I was grateful to have tinkled only moments before because had I not there would have been a puddle at my feet. Geo asked if I was alright. I looked at Kim, she looked at me. Geo looked at Jay who erupted into laughter.

"Ah, man!" Jay said.

It was Jay, Jamal, DeMarcus's best friend since childhood. I was ashamed and embarrassed. My first time at almost cheating and I was cold-busted.

"Hello, Roz." Jamal grabbed my hand and assisted me in the booth.

I said nothing, just lowered my head to hold onto my last shred of human dignity. I wanted to scream that it wasn't me—that Rosilyn wasn't my real name but it was too late. And as I scooted around in the booth and locked eyes with Kim, she too erupted into a loud, attention-getting laughter.

"It's OK, Roz, really," Jamal said, lowering his head to hide his smile.

Geo asked a second time if I was OK, clueless to the situation at hand.

"No, I'm not OK. Your friend, Jay, is my husbands' best friend, Jamal!"

"Oh, snap!" Geo joined in on the laughter.

Their laughter continued for several minutes but it did help ease some of the tension. My only problem now was keeping him from telling DeMarcus.

"Lighten up. It is what it is," Jamal said.

"And just how am I to do that? I've basically been busted having dinner with another man, although this really isn't a date. I'm sure you can't wait to tell your homeboy, DeMarcus."

"Why would I do that? And anyway, DeMarcus and I aren't as close as we used to be. Now's not the time to get into that, but what I can say is that there are some relationships not even worthy of trying to salvage."

"OK, but you two have been through so much together. What happened?"

I wanted to know everything and although he asked if we could discuss it later, I continued until he opened up and shared a little more.

"There were situations occurring that the leadership should have been informed about but weren't. And when certain things came to light and folks started to ask questions, DeMarcus got defensive and tried throwing people off by claiming to be under attack by the enemy. He insisted on handling matters on his own. Who's going to argue with the pastor, huh? As his friend, I reminded him that his job was to focus on his sermons and our role was to handle the other business, but he wasn't hearing me. He's the pastor of the church and all the decisions to be made were his, he said. I can't follow leadership like that. I haven't placed membership elsewhere but surely, you've noticed that Greg and Pat have left and that neither Rudy nor Mark has been serving."

"Actually, I have. I just thought that it was hard for them to get out—them being older. And then with Eddie working second shift…"

Jamal laughed and shared that more were considering leaving.

"He doesn't understand that we want our pastor to preach, that's all. We don't need him to sign off on financial documents or be responsible for the bank deposits. We've got trustees for that, but he insisted on controlling everything."

"Baptist Bully," I called DeMarcus.

"Exactly, and he doesn't trust anyone. Pretty soon, it's going to be just him and a whole new pulpit of leaders or shall I say, followers."

"So what role is Evonne going to fill? Assistant pastor, education director, or youth director?"

Jamal took a sip of water. He didn't respond immediately which let me know that he was aware of the situation I was alluding to.

"Hey, no more church talk," interrupted Geo. "It's time to place our order."

"A steak cooked well, not burnt, a baked potato, double butter, chives, but no sour cream. And you can also bring the lady a side salad with egg, bacon bits, no tomatoes and a container of ranch dressing on the side, if I recall it correctly," Jamal said, then turning to me for approval. I nodded my head and smiled. It was flattering—his recollection of the meal I ordered nearly five years ago when he, I, and DeMarcus dined at a fancy restaurant when attending an out of town convention.

Chapter 7
Kill, Steal, And Destroy

Thanksgiving had come and gone and for the sake of appearances and perceptions, DeMarcus and I pretended we were the happiest couple. Nothing in our marriage or home life had improved, in fact, things were much worse. Conversations, *if I can call them that*, almost always turned into arguments and having to basically tiptoe through the house so he wouldn't be disturbed made us feel more like unwelcome guests than his family. When DeMarcus was home, it wasn't unusual for him to close himself off to do *only he knew what* within the confines of his study while I cooked, cleaned, and was the primary playmate for our kids. And though we slept in the same bed, intimacy between us was rare and in my opinion, only occurred when one of us was having a naughty fantasy about someone else and found convenience in turning to the half-clothed flesh at our side. It wasn't love, it was sex and because we no longer shared a passion or connection, it wasn't at all satisfying.

Christmas was a week away and though it was not a topic we'd discussed; majority of my paychecks were being saved for when DeMarcus determined that it was time for us to part ways. A small portion of my earnings went toward a layaway of clothing and toys for the kids and an even smaller portion while shopping and in somewhat of the Christmas spirit of giving, on a few whatnots for my friends and close relatives. I purchased DeMarcus a gift too; a red, white, and blue bowtie I saw in a discounted defect bin of sorts. It wasn't anything he would wear but it was a gift—a kind gesture on my behalf. And something I could give to him in the off chance that he decided to be kind and purchase me a gift also.

On December 23rd, the entire congregation was excited about the full line of Christmas activities scheduled to begin in the auditorium immediately after morning worship. Starting things off was the 3rd Annual Youth Christmas Play followed by the 4th Annual Gospel Explosion at 5 p.m. My role in the planning of the events this year was minimal, order the props for the play and keep it under $300. That was fine with me being that DeMarya was starring in her first play and chances were great I'd miss her performance if bound by doing my usual behind the scenes work. Everything else was the responsibility of the music ministry.

DeMarcus was on his best behavior, but I could see right through it. And for the time being, I too tucked all our issues underneath the pew and played along just to get along—smiling and grinning—the whole nine.

Days prior to the play, Kim confirmed her attendance but seeing her waltz in with Geo on her arm was a wonderful surprise.

"Thanks for coming, it's nice to see you," I greeted Geo with a hug then turned and introduced him to DeMarcus who from out of nowhere appeared and stood at my side.

"Honey, this is Geo, my co-worker, and Kim's new boo."

Geo extended out his arm to shake DeMarcus's hand. Although DeMarcus did the same, the look on his face was unwelcoming.

"So, you work with my wife? I wasn't aware that any men worked at the Women's Crisis Center. She must think very highly of you to have introduced you to her best friend." DeMarcus glanced at me as if I'd kept it a secret.

"It's nice seeing you again too DeMarcus," Kim said with a scowl. Grabbing Geo's arm, she hurried off to find a good seat.

"You never mentioned introducing him and Kim," DeMarcus said, in a tone totally unacceptable for what was to take place in the sanctuary.

"It may have just slipped my mind but what does it matter anyway? Your one and only daughter is about to perform in her first production, so stop with the foolishness! Nothing is more important than that. I just wish Ma could have come down to see her."

I wrapped my arm around his waist, but DeMarcus brushed it off and walked away. I was embarrassed, to say the least, by his refusal to return the affection. And had it not been for the slew of visitors coming through the door I felt obligated to greet, the church would have witnessed the pastor being called a few *not-so-nice Christianly* names.

DeMarcus was missing in action for most of the play and whether he was watching it on the monitor in his office or from the balcony for a better view I wasn't sure, but I felt abandoned. It wasn't until the second half that he appeared giving no explanation of his whereabouts or whether he'd missed any of DeMarya's speaking parts. Extending out my arm to reach for his, again, he pushed me away. Angry, and on the verge of tears, I decided not to pacify his actions nor give him the satisfaction of knowing he'd rattled my nerves.

At the end of the play, DeMarcus was called onto the stage to give the final remarks. He thanked the members, the parents and guests for their support. He thanked the music ministry and volunteers for their time and talents as well. After thanking the youth ministry leaders for writing the script and assembling the awesome performers, he called each cast member by name.

When DeMarya's name was called, she darted across the stage and high-fived her dad. It warmed my heart.

"And Sister Evonne, please come to the front. I want to personally thank you for your vision and commitment. Working with the youth is never easy but I appreciate your diligence, and this couldn't have happened had you not stepped up and took this on."

Then, in front of God and everybody in the room, DeMarcus hugged Evonne and kissed her forehead. I was too pissed and too numb to swallow my own saliva. When DeMarcus called my name, I was immobile.

"And let's give a round of applause to my wife. Come on up honey and give a few words. Without her, I don't know what I'd do."

His face was blurry to me. Still seated on the pew, I could feel my blood pressure spiking. My mind was racing and had I tried to speak, it would have come out as jibba-jabba with all the thoughts I was having simultaneously. He called my name a second time and still, I sat. Perhaps it was God protecting him because had I been able to stand or even move for that matter, I may have committed domestic assault and battery all-up-in the pulpit.

"I guess my honey is still mad at me, oh, well," he said, causing those still in the room to laugh at his dark sarcasm and blatant disrespect.

After the closing prayer, Geo and Kim reappeared at my side. I tried covering up my pain and complete humiliation with a smile but failed. Rising to my feet, a tear rolled down my face. Kim dabbed it away with a tissue but didn't say a word. Geo was also silent however, the look upon his face told a story of outrage.

"Did you two see my little angel?" I asked.

"Yes, and she was just as fantastic and beautiful as her mom," a familiar voice remarked from behind me. It was Jamal.

"Hello, stranger." I was happy to see him.

"A personal invitation would have been nice but when I heard through the grapevine that DeMarya had a leading role, there was no way I was going to miss it. She was the best one." Jamal and I hadn't spoken since my birthday dinner, though I had been thinking about him. Giving the reason for not contacting him as it being too awkward for me—his close relationship with DeMarcus, he winked his eye and stated understanding. But on the real, it was more so my personal belief that a real woman doesn't chase after a man; she waits to be pursued.

"We appreciate your support," I said to Jamal before excusing myself to retrieve DeMarya from the nursery so I could present her with a beautiful flower bouquet sent from Ma.

When I returned to the sanctuary, I was glad that Geo, Kim, and Jamal were still conversing.

"JJ," DeMarya screamed as she ran and jumped into Jamal's arms. He was just as excited to see her too and made a big to-do about her being the big star of the play; much to her delight. Removing a crisp $2 bill from his wallet, he placed it in her hand. One would have thought, he'd given her a princess's crown; her eyes grew so wide.

Seeing DeMarcus approaching from the corner of my eye, I purposely turned my back to him with hopes he'd go elsewhere and leave me alone to mingle with my guests. He didn't and quite noticeable was the shift in the atmosphere when he snatched DeMarya from Jamal's grip.

"I knew you'd be back?" DeMarcus spoke with arrogance.

To break the awkwardness, I invited the trio to stay for the Gospel Explosion, pointing out the group Heaven's Vocals from Memphis Tennessee was our featured attraction. Kim and Geo declined due to having dinner reservations, but Jamal proudly shared his intentions to stay and see his first cousin Audrey sang with one of the participating choirs. Waving goodbye to Kim and Geo, my hope was to continue my conversation with Jamal, but DeMarcus dominated our space with a brand-new conversation of his own. Eventually, I gave in and left Jamal listening to DeMarcus's line of bull crap. I took DeMarya to the kitchen for cake and punch.

It had been a long day, but everyone was hyped about the Gospel Explosion. The group Worship Him, Yes! opened the concert and by their third selection, the spirit was so high, I don't believe there was anyone who hadn't shed a tear or shouted at that point. The vocalists ministered through song, touching my heart like no one had ever before. It was as if every song sang was just for me. Momentarily forgetting my issues, the spirit took hold and control. Someone handed me a box of tissues, but I tossed them aside. Another person offered me a fan, but I waved them away. A third person tried escorting me back to my seat, but I was unmovable.

What I needed I wasn't quite sure, but without a doubt, it wasn't anything a human could provide.

Tears flowed from my eyes and a few times when I couldn't speak, I waved my hands. I praised His name and it felt good! The spirit was so high that even after the vocalists finished their selections, true worshippers continued shouting praises. I was grateful to be in the midst.

Then DeMarcus grabbed my arm.

"The nursery sent word that DeMarya is in there cutting up. They have at least 30 kids and say she's the rowdiest one. Take her home and get her ready for bed."

The Gospel Explosion was getting better and better and I didn't want to miss hearing the featured attraction we worked so hard to get. Reaching the nursery, DeMarya was indeed surviving on tired energy so after feeding her a bologna sandwich and a cup of milk, I took her to the potty and returned to the auditorium. Praying that she'd fall asleep in my arms was wishful dreaming. Fatigued and antsy, she wouldn't sit still. DeMarcus again demanded I take her home.

"She's not going to act right, she's disrupting the show!"

I was still on a spiritual high, but the devil was lurking and fighting hard to steal my joy by interrupting my worship. The evil in me, Lyn, wanted to kick him in the face with my new spiked-heel pump for again, blatantly disrespecting me in public and for being a complete azz in general. But I put my daughters' needs before my own and to the house, we went. I couldn't get DeMarya's pajamas on fast enough as for when her head hit the pillow, she was out like a light. Twenty minutes later, my cell phone rang. It was Jamal.

"How are you?"

"Tired. Exhausted. Uplifted. Did I say, tired?"

"I saw you leave out the side door and was just calling to see if you made it home safe."

"We did, thank you. I looked around and when I didn't see you, I assumed you had already left. Did you get to see your cousin?"

"Yes, I did. She was the soloist who sang *God Said Set it Free.*"

"I remember that song and I remember the woman singing it. She was a petite woman with a large voice, right?"

"That was her," he laughed. After a brief pause, Jamal stated it was nice to see me. Once I laid the children down and closed their bedroom doors, finishing my household chores suddenly became unimportant. I plopped down on the living room couch to continue my conversation.

"I really wanted to contact you," he continued. "But I didn't want to press the issue. Just thought I'd let you know that in case you were wondering."

"Actually, I was hoping to hear from you but thought that you were probably feeling guilty about moving in on your best friends' wife," I chuckled.

"Don't get me started. I don't know who DeMarcus is anymore and personally, our parting of ways has been for the best. I was very disturbed by his behavior though, and how he so nonchalantly belittled you in front of everyone tonight. And like a fool, after the play I let him talk me into following him back to his office where I was forced to listen as he talked about himself, what he's doing, and how he's turning things around in the church. It was all about him. Not once did he ask how I was doing or where I was worshipping, nothing. But when I complimented you and your new hairstyle, well, his words weren't nice. You deserve much better than him. What are you still hanging on for?"

I understood Jamal's concerns but what was I to do? Anyhow, I wasn't too bothered with DeMarcus's negative comments or his need to boost his own ego. I had already concluded that DeMarcus was jealous of me, jealous that at the age of thirty-five, I was still hot, and he was not. Life was taking its toll on him as evidence of his once muscular physique now turned to flab visibly revealed. And he was undoubtedly stressed over the receding hairline drastically changing his appearance—recalling his primping time in the bathroom mirror to be twice as long as mine. Perhaps he was going through a midlife crisis. Maybe he was just being a butt—but who cared?

"I won't pressure you, but if you ever need someone to talk to other than Kim, you can call me. I've always liked you Roz, and I kind of hate admitting this now, but you've always deserved better than DeMarcus. In hindsight, you were a better friend to me than I was to you. I knew he was a jerk, but he was your husband and my friend. Not to use being young as an excuse, but neither of us took anything about life seriously. I didn't have a wife or a child, so I was free to do as I pleased. Over time, DeMarcus should have matured but I see now that he hasn't. Becoming a pastor has gone to his head, I'm sure you've noticed. It's like he's forgotten that being a pastor is more than preaching the word but living the word. He used to be my boy but he's so arrogant and conceited, I can't stand being around him. And aside from all of that, it sickens me how he mistreats you."

Peeking out the living room window for DeMarcus who I expected to walk through the door at any given moment, when I didn't see any signs of him, I returned to the comforts of the couch.

"You don't know half of what I go through. Maybe it's my fault for not speaking up in the beginning, but I've never felt comfortable with this pastor and first lady gig. I knew it was going to change our lives, but I didn't expect it to consume our lives. In less than a year, we went from struggling to living quite well. We moved out of a tiny two-bedroom apartment and into a three-story, four bedrooms, three-and-a-half-bath home. His thirty-two thousand a year salary is twice that now and thanks to the church, we don't even have to pay for our utilities. Some call it a blessing and, in the beginning, I believed that it was but it's ruined DeMarcus. He controls all the money and wants to control everything else. I thought that by hanging around older ministers, he would mature and grow in his calling. I won't lie, I'm not the Christian I'm supposed to be, but I do believe that when God takes over, He changes people from the inside out. I wanted that change for myself and my family. I was foolish for believing in DeMarcus. I knew all along he was full of crap. Now I'm going to hell for just being associated with him."

Jamal laughed. I laughed too, realizing how ridiculous I must have sounded as I rambled. But we both agreed that DeMarcus had always been a slickster—gifted in influencing others into seeing things his way and skilled in twisting his words to make you feel like an idiot.

Talking to Jamal truly put me at ease and soon thereafter, our conversation shifted from analyzing DeMarcus and his many flaws to what we both envisioned in our lives in terms of happiness. I had his undivided attention. He listened to me and not once belittled my thoughts. He even encouraged me to register for evening classes at the local college and complete my goal of becoming a child psychologist. He spoke passionately about the field.

Listening attentively as he shared his personal tragedy of the 1998 automobile accident that claimed the lives of his parents and younger brother, although the crash occurred over two decades ago, the crackling of his voice revealed his softer side—a side I found attractive. Aside from offering my heartfelt condolences, I allowed him to continue uninterrupted. Shortly thereafter, our topic of discussion changed yet again.

Without realizing it, I had sunk deeper into the couch, engaged in my conversation with Jamal, in the same manner, I would be if it was Kim on the other end. The house was quiet and I was stress-free and in a relaxed state of mind. Jamal suggested meeting for lunch the following day, but I graciously declined, not elaborating on a reason. Stating his understanding, I thanked him for not pressing the issue however unbeknownst to him, I was hitting myself upside the head for not having the nerve to admit being very much interested in meeting—but for other purposes.

It seemed as if we were on the phone for hours—both hinting around to having so much to do in preparation for the next day, but neither of us able nor wanting to end the conversation.

Then DeMarcus walked through the door. I froze.

"Hey, honey." He leaned over and kissed my forehead.

"I'm sorry, I'm late, but I've been at the church talking to Jamal. He's been telling me about his personal struggles and how bad things are for him right now. You know, he's my boy and he really needs someone to talk to. I'm going to follow him home, alright. I promise not to be long."

"Wait," I said. "Are you talking about Jamal Wright who we saw earlier tonight?"

"Who else? We've been in my office talking for the past hour. He's not in the right frame of mind so I'm going to follow him home and make sure he's OK. I hope to be home before midnight."

Speechless, I watched in disbelief as DeMarcus walked toward the front door. He lied to me with the straightest of faces and had the gall to blow a kiss in my direction before closing the door behind him. My legs were numb from sitting on them which prevented me from raising up to chase after his lying azz. And when I attempted to straighten out my legs, sharp pains pierced my chest. My body began to tremble as if I was cold, but it was simply my nerves causing me to shake. I placed my head between my hands to sob, but I couldn't. I was too angry to cry—devastated, having DeMarcus betray me to my face without the batting of an eye or stumbling over his words. I began focusing on my breathing and closed my eyes, totally forgetting that I was on the phone until Jamal called my name.

"I heard the bastard. Are you alright?"

I wasn't alright and surely, I didn't need to convince him otherwise. And what a stupid question to be asked! I couldn't muster up a tear. The lump in my throat made swallowing difficult, let alone getting out a word to respond. Jamal asked again if I was alright.

"I'm fine. I just wish I had a car to follow him."

"Listen to me and listen to me good. Let him go. Right now, you're upset but pull yourself together. I understand that you're hurting but think things through before you react. When he comes home, don't start an argument over where he's been because you already know he's going to lie about it. And what sense will it make stressing yourself into stroke level when we both know that the end result will be you still living under the same roof with the bastard?"

"So, what do you suggest I do?"

"Devise a plan. In order to beat a person like DeMarcus, you've got to be smarter than him. Don't throw accusations without first knowing what you're accusing him of. Be smart and be patient. Without proof, it's only suspicion. So, calm down and don't let on that you're upset or suspect anything. Until you get solid proof and have a name, keep your eyes and ears open. He's bound to slip up again."

It was well past midnight—way past my bedtime and while flipping through the cable channels I found it ironic that the only channel worthy of watching was of a televangelist preaching on midnight ramblers and how ain't nothing going on after midnight but thieving and deceiving. I turned the volume down and covered my head with the comforter. Rolling onto my left side and revisiting my own personal turmoil, I questioned whether I was emotionally capable of holding my tongue and refraining from giving DeMarcus the third degree when he walked through the door. Rolling onto my right side, I concluded that Jamal was partially right—that DeMarcus was a professional liar and my yelling and screaming would only bring stress upon myself. For my sanity, I chose to remain quiet.

At 3 a.m. having tossed and turned the majority of the morning, I forced myself up to down an anxiety pill to calm my still-rattled nerves. An hour and a half later, DeMarcus entered the bedroom. I heard him call my name, but I pretended to be in a deep sleep. I heard him call my name a second time but still, I didn't budge. When he flipped on the lights and pulled the comforter away from my face, I was livid. But when he placed his chin on my shoulder, I snapped.

"What do you want?"

"Just wanted to tell you that I'm home, go back to bed."

Biting my tongue and not losing my cool was hard. Badly I wanted to confront his lying azz and beat the truth out of him, but I promised myself and Jamal that I'd be good. As my headache resurfaced, so did my nervous shakes. Seeing me tremble, DeMarcus assumed I was cold and covered my shoulders with the comforter. I cringed when with his forefinger, he rubbed my cheek.

"You must be getting sick. Would you like me to fix you a cup of cocoa?"

At four something in the morning? Really? I didn't want any fricken cocoa; I wanted him to leave me alone! He offered to pour me a glass of ale.

"No, thank you. How is Jamal?"

DeMarcus rounded the bed and told a sad story of a messed-up man. And it was a good story too. So good, that had it not been for me talking to Jamal most of the night, I may have believed some of what DeMarcus claimed. Turning my head to look him square in the eyes, I praised his selfless act of kindness for providing midnight hour counseling to his one true friend.

"That's what pastor's do but Jamal and I go way back. He's like a brother to me so of course, I'd be there for him."

I watched as DeMarcus undressed. I listened as he mumbled on and on about the duties of a pastor and how his work is never done. He thanked me for being understanding and patient then slid underneath the comforter. Pressing his body against mine, I was sickened when he began kissing my neck. His scent was of fresh soap.

"I love you," he whispered.

I was fighting mad and had it not been for my arms entangled inside the sheets, I would have grabbed my bedside lamp and smashed it against his head. *He loves me? Bull!*

The next morning was Christmas Eve and when I finally decided to roll out of bed, the Jackson household was going haywire. Everything Lil D touched landed on the floor, DeMarya was hyped on pancake syrup and every step I took, DeMarcus was on my heels or either lurking close by. Having had enough, I slipped on my purple jeans, a blue and white University of Kentucky sweatshirt, and a pair of black and white running shoes. Covering my head with one of DeMarcus's green and yellow ball caps, I grabbed my purse and keys and sought sanity behind the steering wheel. Nowhere, in particular, did I have in mind but after checking my messages and responding to a missed text from Jamal stating he was just checking up on me, I accepted his breakfast invite and drove to the diner on the corner of Elie and Sir Williams Blvd.

I wasn't in heels or even wearing eyeliner, but the image reflecting from the overhead mirror showed a vision of natural beauty. Underneath my ball cap, my uncombed locks clutched my neck and the fragrance applied the day before still lingered on my skin. The tomboy fit I was wearing worked for me. I was comfortable and felt sexy, and the stare down and a subsequent smile on Jamal's face told me that he too approved. He greeted me with a hug. Jamal thanked me for coming.

Taking our seat, I couldn't help but notice the smile still on Jamal's face.

"What are you smiling about?" I asked.

"You look different on the weekends," he said, then burst out into attention-getting laughter.

I hit him in the shoulder with my ball cap once I caught the meaning behind his joke, but I wasn't offended. Jamal had never seen me in my natural state before and after apologizing for his colorful humor, he called me gorgeous.

We talked a little more before he summoned a waitress and ordered a coffee for him and a hot cup of cocoa with whipped cream for me. Making small talk about Christmas and the ton of money spent on gifts people wouldn't use, he asked about my Christmas day plans and what I wanted as a gift.

"A better life and for Ma to feel better," I replied.

"With Ma being under the weather, I'll be deep-frying my first turkey and making all the fixings. What are your plans? Spending Christmas with anybody special?"

"Nah." Jamal nodded his head.

"I'll be at home, probably get up and watch a football game or two. Other than that, I have no special plans and no special someone to spend it with."

I suddenly felt foolish, remembering that his parents were deceased and other than a few family members living out of town, most of the holidays he spent with us.

"Maybe I'll get an invite from DeMarcus seeing how I'm so messed up and big brotha' has to keep tabs on me."

I laughed once finally getting the joke—even followed through with my own.

"When I get home, I'll tell him I ran into you and state how stressed and depressed you looked. I'll dial your number and shove the phone in his face and insist that he invite you over to eat with us."

"Truthfully speaking, I probably wouldn't answer his call. It's like I said before, relationships and friendships end for a reason and I believe ours has run its course."

"And so has our marriage. I'm done, I'm really done." I took a sip of my hot cocoa.

"Be still," said Jamal, then reaching across the table and wiping the whipped cream from my nose. He tasted his finger.

"Ummm, delicious."

"Rosilyn, if you're done, be done. If you have doubts, take your time before making any decisions. But you do know you deserve better than what he's giving you, right? When you're ready to move on to better, I'm here."

Again, I smiled then let out a chuckle. Instantly, the room got warm. Picking up a napkin, I waved it like a fan, but it was hopeless. No, I wasn't having a hot flash, but something definitely was happening. Removing my cap, I ran my fingers through my locks. Jamal asked if I was alright; I nodded that I was but seconds after fibbing through my teeth, a heatwave seared through my entire body forcing me to sit erect. My neck was wet, and so were my undergarments. Grabbing the newspaper from the table behind me, I fanned profusely. I soon came to realize that what I was experiencing is what Kim called a cootie cry. Although DeMarcus and I shared the same bed, there was no intimacy going on. I blamed my body going into shock on Jamal's gentle touch. Yes—even touching my nose was sensual. When I glanced over at him, the half-cocked smile on his face subtly suggested that he had just accomplished some sort of conquer and defeat mission with little to no effort. Yeah, I felt foolish but quickly regrouped. And after cooling off by downing a tall glass of ice water, I chalked my *'episode'* up as having a reaction to new medication.

I expected DeMarcus to question my whereabouts since I had been gone for nearly three hours and had no bags in tow when I walked through the door, but he didn't. Surprisingly, he invited me to join him and the kids on the floor who were in an uproar over a board game. I declined and proceeded into the bathroom to wash my face and brush my teeth. My sweatshirt was no longer fabric softener fresh and my jeans, well…they were sticky. Feeling yucky, I changed into a fresh tank top and gym shorts then added my smelly clothing to the laundry for washing.

When their game was over, DeMarcus placed a movie in their DVD player then pitched a tent using my best guest room linens. I had started picking the collard greens for dinner when I felt DeMarcus staring at me. He didn't say a word, but I sensed there was something he wanted to discuss. Leaving the greens to soak in the sink, I retrieved the sweet potatoes from the pantry and sat them on the island. Only two were peeled before DeMarcus's awkwardness drove me into the living room. Seconds later, I felt his presence over my shoulder. His lurking around was annoying and my gut feeling had me curious as to what he wanted. *Perhaps he wanted to confess his adulterous behavior but couldn't find the right words? Or did he want to share something with me but didn't quite know how?* Whatever it was, I needed him to spit it out and stop fricken stalking me.

It took four minutes exactly before he followed me into the bedroom. Closing the door, he leaned against it and said nothing. It was evident more now than before that something was weighing heavy on his mind, but I wanted my alone time. I didn't care to share my breathing space with him, much less engage in conversation. DeMarcus approached me with a frightening glare in his eye. Believing that his unusual behavior was related to him finally making a decision about our future as a family unit, *'get it out already'* is what I was about to scream when he knelt down on his knees and parted my legs. He slid his body between my thighs then pulled at my elastic waistband. *Gawd! He wanted sex. Shit!*

He was slow to pull my shorts down over my hips. Begrudgingly, I removed my tank top and when it hit the floor, I reached around to unsnap my brassiere. I had no desire anywhere in my body to be loved-on by DeMarcus. The very thought of his slimy hands and tainted lips touching any part of my skin sickened me. And I really didn't want him inside of me either but since it was already in progress, I prayed that he'd be quick going in and even quicker coming out. Flinging my brassiere across the floor, I was stunned when with all his might, he knocked me back onto the bed.

"Matching panties and bra," he yelled. He hovered over my body with his own.

DeMarcus grabbed my throat and I closed my eyes, initially believing he was living out a once expressed desire to engage in rough sex. His grip was tight and getting tighter. I asked him to loosen his grip, but his eyes were dark and his hand, unmovable. Struggling to wiggle free, his bare hand forced me to remain on my back.

"Who have you been with?" DeMarcus showed no signs of letting up or allowing me to breathe.

"Up," I managed to whisper, panicked and still fighting to be loosed.

"You walked out of here smelling like perfume and wearing matching undergarments. Where did you go? Is it Geo from work you're sleeping with?"

My life flashed before my eyes. I was frightened and couldn't speak. As I gasped for air, tears rolled from the corners of my eyes. Eventually loosening his grip of my neck, my movements were still being restricted with his knee which was pressing down into my pelvis. The pain was excruciating.

"Is it Geo? Or is it some other piss poor punk you met on that sorry azz job?"

"No," I cried.

"Who is it then? I swear you're not getting up until you tell me who it is!"

"Nobody, DeMarcus, get off me. Please, DeMarcus, get up!"

Removing his knee, I was slow in rolling over to my side but managed to sit erect on the edge of the bed. Reaching down for my clothing, DeMarcus grabbed me up by my hair and asked where I thought I was going. Loud was my scream when pushed into the wall. Unable to gain my bearings, he again grabbed my hair and with great force, smacked my face. Hitting the window with my arm caused the glass to shatter. My face was numb and burning with sting.

Knowing that if I wanted to survive, I had to fight back, I was quick to grab items within my reach which were my bedside lamp and a six-inch pump that lay on the floor. I felt equipped for battle. DeMarcus laughed. He called me weak and pathetic. But when he lunged toward me to strike again, he gave me the opportunity to prove just how strong I was. The lamp shattered on the first blow across his head. There was no blood, but his yell assured me that it hurt. He took a step back and stared at me in disbelief. In my mind, I was inviting him to come closer as my fancy footwork—shuffling from side to side as if in a real boxing ring made me feel like I was preparing for another bout. I encouraged him to step into my newfound energy. And as a rush of adrenaline shot through me, with my fists alone, I believed I could beat him to a pulp and have him begging me for mercy.

Fighting back felt good and when Mr. Badazz crossed my imaginary line of no return, I beat him to his knees with my fists and his belt buckle I saw hanging over the closet door. I swatted it at his head and was successful. Welts formed on his face immediately. I was pleased that his face was now stinging in a comparable manner as mine was only moments before. What propelled me to remove a picture frame from the wall and fling it like a Frisbee towards his face is still a mystery, but I did and hit my target. Now sporting a two-inch gash just above his right brow compliments of the frame's edge, when drops of blood stained his once spotless white shirt, DeMarcus cursed and threatened to kill me.

"Come on, punk," I mumbled, still skating around the room like a heavyweight boxer daring my opponent to step into my space. Grabbing my pink, Italian, silk hair scarf to wipe away his blood was a decision that sent me into another level of kick-butt mold. *How dare he? That was my good scarf!*

What happened next, neither of us saw coming—my left hand successfully snatching the scarf from his hand as simultaneously my right fist connecting with his jaw. The sound reminded me of a clean smack across a baby's butt. DeMarcus was angered.

DeMarcus charged at me and slammed my body into the wall with such force, the glass frame of my African Queen picture shattered. But I bounced back. I was in good shape, in fact, my newfound energy assured me I'd be victorious in this fight. DeMarcus was breathing heavy but with my second wind, I fought him like I would a chick on the streets guilty of stealing my purse. He air-boxed but all my punches connected. At one point he pinned me down, but I was stronger and much quicker, and came out on top.

His nails were rounded, mine were pointed. The marks I left on his face resembled railroad tracks; nice, neat, and parallel. DeMarcus wasn't giving up though and his determination to gain the upper hand was becoming quite comical. He was clearly a man defeated and a man unable to accept the azz-whooping his wife was handing him.

We tussled on the bed then hit the floor. My strength overpowered his and I had obviously worn him down. But I showed no mercy once spotting, and then grabbing one of my favorite pair of work heels and using the flat surface to assault his face like he did with his open palm to mine. DeMarcus attempted to grab it from me but didn't have the energy to do so. I had raised my right arm and was just about to dot him in the eye with the pointed heel when I heard DeMarya call my name. I paused.

Looking down at DeMarcus, he appeared to be rejoicing about his life being spared. His bloodshot eyes and severely bruised face sent chills through my body and with certainty, would frighten our kids. When DeMarya called my name a second time and twisted the doorknob, I knew then that I had to set him free. But before letting DeMarcus up, I had the final say.

"My momma taught me the fundamentals of womanhood, but my daddy taught me how to fight. If you ever think about raising your hand to me again, remember today. This is your only warning. The next time might not work out so well for you!"

Chapter 8

Honor Thy Mother

Christmas morning wasn't the same without the entire family together, but we survived.

The kids were so focused on opening the multitude of gifts underneath the tree that DeMarcus's absence appeared to not be a factor. After all the gifts were unwrapped, we ate breakfast and then curled up on the couch to watch one of DeMarya's new movies. Midway through the movie Lil D fell asleep and when it ended, I placed him in my bed and sent DeMarya to her room to assemble her new doll collection.

One of DeMarcus's biggest pet peeves was picking up Christmas wrappings covering the floor. For some reason, he believed that moving the wrapping disturbed the memory of the holiday. But DeMarcus wasn't home, and my living room looked like a cyclone had hit a toy store, so I wasted no time in hanging their clothes, placing their toys in their room, or stuffing the colorful, torn to shreds holiday paper into a large hefty bag. A few times throughout the morning, I did wonder how DeMarcus was spending his Christmas, but that was short-lived.

It was the eve of New Year's Eve—a whole six days since the fight and DeMarcus had yet to resurface or check in on the kids or me. Truth be told, having him gone was lovely and other than neglecting his fatherly duties of totting the kids back and forth and assisting Lil' D with potty training, living as if I was single wasn't half bad. I wasn't expecting an apology or for him to ask to meet to discuss any sort of reconciliation, so it wasn't a real surprise when he didn't. His selfish azz was probably enjoying being away from me just as much as I was him.

As excited as I was to leave my issues in 2015 and focus on 2016, I couldn't push past feeling moody and sluggish. Perhaps it was learning of Ma's hospitalization and having no way of getting to her. It may have been too, depression causing me to claim ill children as the reason for missing work the first week of the new year. Geo must have shared my absence with Jamal because when he called, he was greatly concerned.

"I'm good, but things have been so crazy," I said, before sharing a tidbit of my horrific week with him.

Jamal didn't ask a lot of questions, but he did put my mind at ease with his words. He seemed to understand my worries and concerns about Ma and offered to lend me his 2004 Camry. Within the hour, he was parking it in my driveway. Jamal handed me the key but we both agreed that inviting him in could be catastrophic if, in the off chance, DeMarcus returned to the house. So, after jumping into the car with his friend who had driven behind him, he called my phone and wished me safe travels. Before hanging up, Jamal expressed his excitement about preaching the New Year's Eve message at Mount Olive. Though I couldn't make any promises, I told him that if Ma was feeling better, I'd do my best to attend.

"Why didn't you tell me?" I questioned my dad once arriving in Louisville and learning that Ma was being monitored for having a mild heart attack, not being treated for asthma as I initially was led to believe. It was probably at her suggestion that I didn't know the truth, but I felt awful imagining all that Dad had to endure alone. Dad looked exhausted and graciously accepted my offer to stay home and rest. After sliding my cousin, Sassy, a twenty-dollar bill to babysit, I hurried out the door for the hospital. Ma smiled when I entered her room.

"I figured you'd find out. I would have called and told you myself, but I just didn't want anybody worrying about me."

"Of course, I'm gonna worry. You're my Ma and I love you. I'm more hurt that you didn't let me know how serious this is."

"Don't worry about me, child. I know you've got your own issues. Has DeMarcus come home yet?"

I looked at Ma but didn't answer. *How did she know he left?*

"Momma knows everything, so stop looking silly," Ma laughed.

Not being there when Ma needed me the most weighed heavy on me but as the nurses and physicians made their rounds, it eased my mind meeting the compassionate team assigned to her room. When Nurse Kathy, the dayshift nurse entered and asked if I was her daughter, Rosilyn, I smiled. It warmed my heart to know Ma had been talking about me. After having her vital signs checked, Ma confessed to receiving a call from DeMarcus.

"He told me that you hit him in the head with a lamp. He also told me that you cheated on him and he couldn't understand why you felt the need to go outside your marriage. I just listened and let him have his say. And I'm not gonna ask you what happened either, but honey just make sure you take care of them babies."

"Ma, DeMarcus lied to you. He's the one who's been cheating. I had breakfast with a mutual friend just one time and he went berserk. I've never cheated on him, Ma, I promise."

"Why haven't you?"

My tongue was tied. I couldn't believe Ma asked me that or would condone my partaking in that sort of behavior. And as I attempted to process her words, she batted her eyes and patiently awaited my response, but I didn't have one. I shrugged my shoulders and shook my head.

"I knew he was a dirty, no-good bastard from the beginning," Ma continued.

"But it wouldn't have been right for me to talk you out of marrying him 'cause I ain't for getting into grown folks' business. Yaw have been faking being happy for years and when he didn't come down for your birthday, I knew then something was wrong. You two are just playing house. When the love is gone, you find yourself simply tolerating one another. And when you start tolerating one another, everything the other person does will get on your last nerve. Life is too short to be stressed and unhappy, Rosilyn. If another man makes you happy, go for it. Even I went astray one, two, maybe three or four times, but don't tell your daddy. They were the best times of my life too," Ma chuckled.

If I was a heart patient, I would have needed oxygen listening to Ma speak of being a freak back in her day. I laughed so hard my eyes began to water. Ma was laughing too and set off one of the many machines she was connected to.

"What I am trying to tell you honey is, do what you feel is right. Marriages end every day. If you feel like it's worth saving, then try to save it. If it's not, keep your head up, your eyes and ears open. Start getting your affairs in order and don't let anybody know what you're doing."

"But I don't know where to start, Ma. And even if I wanted the marriage, DeMarcus doesn't. I always believed my marriage would last forever. I never pictured my family being split apart."

"Silly girl." Ma shook her head.

"Start at the bank. Then find out where he keeps his prized possessions? You can't be my child acting so gullible. You best wizen up and quick! When my first husband and I called it quits, you best believe that I had already withdrawn every dime from our joint account and tore out a few blank checks from an account he thought he was keeping from me. And even after withdrawing $26,000, the judge still made him split the remaining assets with me fifty-fifty. Then when I married your daddy," she laughed.

I laughed too.

"Do you remember when your daddy accused the heating company representative of stealing his collection of rare coins? Well, twenty-eight years ago the collection was appraised at eighty-four hundred dollars. All I'm going to say is that it wasn't the representative, OK, but to this day he still swears that it was. So, get busy taking care of your business, baby. And remember, some things you just gotta take to your grave. I hope you're listening, Roz, because momma's serious. DeMarcus isn't going to play nice so don't let him make a fool out of you. When you go home, you get to cleaning the house and I don't mean pulling out the vacuum. Do you hear me?"

I grinned then reached for her hand. "I hear you, Ma, but no more talk about DeMarcus. How are you feeling?"

"I'm in God's hands baby, so no need to worry about me. Hurry home and get to taking care of your business. You're his wife so whatever you end up doing now, it'll be OK. There's nothing the law can do to you, so remember that."

Throughout the night, Ma was carefree in sharing details from her past and current marriage. Some were horror stories that gave me the chills, the others were comical and made me view mom in a different light—a human light. She was by far not an angel, but for the first time in my life, I realized just how much she loved and sacrificed for my protection. Initially, it was awkward seeing my Ma all tubed up and in a hospital bed, but I found joy assisting her to the bathroom even though she didn't need assistance. And I was honored to hold the cup of water up to her lips as she swallowed her medication.

The morning came too soon but it had been a great night with Ma. By 7 a.m., she had eaten her breakfast and at eight, Dad and my kids were walking through the door. It took a moment for the kids to warm up to Ma who was normally energetic, but they eventually adjusted to the new surroundings. Dad looked refreshed and exclaimed to have slept well. I laughed, then shared how little sleep I got with Ma being chattier than ever—a great indicator, per her physician, that she was well enough to recover at home.

Hearing Jamal preach wasn't really a big deal to me, but Ma insisted we get on the road and head back to Lexington. Dad agreed with Ma and assured me that she would be in good hands now that his sister, my Auntie, was flying in from Houston, Texas that afternoon to help. After loving all over Ma a few moments longer, I told her I loved her to the moon and back and made her promise to call me once she got home and settled in. Ma blew a kiss at me and winked. She told me to go home and take care of business.

Pulling into my driveway, I had only about an hour to get us ready for church. Unlocking the front door, DeMarya bolted past me and before I could close and lock the door, "Daddy's here!" she yelled. My stomach was in knots. I dreaded seeing him. DeMarcus entered the living room and took Lil D from my arms.

"I came to get some clothes. I'll get the rest of my things later if you don't mind."

"Fine with me," I replied, walking around the couch for a clear path to the bedroom.

DeMarcus followed behind—appearing annoyed that I hadn't asked how he was doing?

"Here it is," I said, removing a form-fitting black, tan, and brown dress from the closet.

"It's too cold for that short dress," he remarked. "But I guess being a single woman you can wear those types of things."

I sensed he was fishing for an argument, but I wasn't biting. He followed me into the bathroom then back into the bedroom until I finally gave in and acknowledged his presence.

"DeMarcus, you walked out on us. If you're moving your things out, OK. I'm not gonna beg you to stay if that's what you're waiting for. And I didn't ask how you were doing because, by the looks of that expensive new suit you're wearing, you are doing quite well. Oh, the kids and I are fine and the car in the driveway, I borrowed it from a friend. We are just now getting in from seeing Ma, she was in the hospital. And this dress, well it's the only one that fits. I've lost another ten pounds and all my other dresses are way too big. Wanna know anything else?"

"Yes, can I spend time with the kids today? I'll have them home by eight tonight, I promise."

I started to cuss him out for being foolish in thinking that I'd approve of him taking my kids around his new winch, but I caught myself and against my better judgment, agreed. Without a doubt, they'd end up in the church nursery, but I trusted the caregivers and knew that they would enjoy playing with the other kids. Neither of them was appropriately dressed for church but nonetheless, they were dressed and after washing their faces, I sent them on their way.

Walking through the doors of another church, I felt like a liberated woman. Today I was Rosilyn, not the pastor's wife with the responsibility of being flawless before the people. As I checked out my surroundings, several faces looked familiar, but they just smiled and kept it moving. All but one, Geo.

"Where's Kim?" I asked, taking a seat next to him.

"Out of town again," he replied with a grimace.

"But I don't mind her going away because welcoming her home is always so much fun."

I bumped him with my arm. Jokingly, reminding him that we were in the house of the Lord.

When Jamal entered the sanctuary through a side door, I smiled. He was runway-model fine in his dark gray suit, light gray shirt, and pink tie. He had yet to see me, but my eyes were fixated on him, especially after watching a young woman—twenty-ish, rub his back before going in for a non-churchlike hug.

"Don't be jealous," Geo whispered.

"All he talks about is you."

I denied being jealous though it looked like every female there for worship was dressed to impress…in less and wanted so very much for their pastor to

100

see their God-given curvaceous gifts. It was near the end of his sermon when Jamal looked my way. He smiled, I smiled, and Geo erupted in laughter.

"I just don't understand why yaw won't just do the damn thing. You want him and he wants you. Whatchaw waiting on?"

"Hush, Geo!"

Jamal bypassed several folks lined up at the podium to encourage him to make his way to me. He pulled me in for a hug and I was like melted butter in his arms.

"Thank you for coming," he said, as if I had made his day.

"Don't leave just yet, OK. Wait here and I'll be back in less than ten minutes."

Hell, no, I wasn't going anywhere especially after making me feel like the most important person in the room. Suddenly, it didn't matter to me that women were swarming around him like bees on a hive because, at the end of the service, I was gonna be his honey. Geo waited with me while I waited for Jamal. And when Jamal was loosed, he greeted me with a huge hug and shared a few words with Geo. Jamal escorted me out into the parking lot. He again thanked me for coming and suggested we take a drive. Interestingly, the drive led us to his apartment complex. *Slick.*

Jamal placed frozen lasagna in the oven and while it baked, we talked as if we were long lost siblings. A few times I wanted to lean in and kiss his sexy lips but for fear of being too aggressive, I held back. While I mixed a salad, he set the table and filled two long-stemmed glasses with wine. After eating, Jamal lit two aroma scented candles and led me back into the living room where soft jazz was playing. For a half-hour, we danced and laughed—laughed and danced. The room was warm, perhaps because of the wine but I smiled, thoroughly enjoying his company and being in his arms.

When Jamal asked if I needed anything, I responded with a kiss. Pressing his lips onto mine, his lips were soft and his tongue, fat and warm. He kissed me slow and with passion—something I wasn't used to. His fingers ran through my locks; my head fell back. Jamal kissed my neck and nibbled on my earlobe. He didn't stop me from removing his tie, nor did he object to my tugging at his belt. Everything was happening so fast. Then, Jamal grabbed my hands.

"Wait," Jamal whispered, as he led me to the couch. He removed his shirt then laid me flat on my back. Instructing me to remain still, he examined my body with his eyes then lifted my left leg and placed it over his shoulder. First lapping at my navel, Jamal smoothly made a trail down to my thighs. Playfully—yet gently, he bit the inside of my thigh causing my rear to rise. Tasting my love-joy as if it was his personal dessert, loudly, I moaned.

Jamal lifted my dress over my head. I unsnapped my brassiere. His touch was amazing—this man handled me like fragile glass. And as I lay naked on his couch, my insides were doing its own dance. My entire body ached so-so-so good. I closed my eyes and attempted to suppress my pants and moans but when he widened my legs even further and slid in between them, words that had no clear meaning rang out. Wonderfully proportioned he was as gently he gripped my rear and grinded inside my love-joy. He moaned, and I moaned—neither caring whether his neighbors heard us. Reaching extreme pleasure simultaneously, once catching our breath, Jamal lay to my side with his right arm wrapped around my waist. He held me tight. Cuddling for what seemed to be only minutes but was actually an hour, I was tempted by his request to stay and cuddle a little longer but explained needing to hurry home.

"It felt right being with you," I replied.

I could only smile as I didn't have the exact words to describe just how wonderful I felt.

He loved me so good I wanted to cry tears of joy.

The drive back to the church was fast, despite neither of us having much to say. I prayed that his silence was not due to any feelings of guilt on his part because there surely wasn't any on mine. In fact, Jamal gave me exactly what I needed and had me contemplating wanting to ask about our next get together.

Chances were great that DeMarcus would return the kids earlier than discussed so as soon as I walked through the front door, I tossed my purse onto the couch and headed straight for his study. Rummaging through his desk drawers, I was in search of the tiniest piece of financial information or…anything. I was nervous but determined to get what I needed to begin making provisions for me and my children's future. I was also nervous about what I could find that may cause me heartache.

DeMarcus's desk was full of papers, bits and pieces of sermons and college course notes. Underneath his desk calendar, was a listing of church leader contact numbers and email addresses. There were also business cards, but in my opinion, nothing worthy of investigating. Imitating what I'd seen on television, I checked underneath his lamp, his favorite coffee mug, and his computer keyboard for clues, keys—stuff, but came up empty. But I knew the man and was certain that every facet of his personal life was tucked away in that office somewhere.

After several minutes of searching, I started to believe that DeMarcus was either three steps ahead of me or on the up and up, until stumbling upon a receipt for five hundred dollars. Dated November 17, the receipt was made out to Lanier and Associates. Initially suspecting that it was money spent on another woman, I then recalled a dermatology appointment I scheduled for him during that month. But in thinking about it further, five hundred dollars seemed overly excessive for an initial office visit fee and a tiny bottle of fungus foot cream, so I placed the receipt in my back pocket to investigate later.

The more I dug around the bolder I became. Unopened credit card statements seemed to call my name and to satisfy my curiosity, a few of them I tore open. For the most part, the expenses were minor and consistent; a deli sandwich purchase here, a gasoline fill-up there, along with other minor purchases not amounting much to anything.

There was no rhyme or reason to the arrangement of books on his shelf. Various versions of Bibles were mixed between books of assorted topics and authors. Even one of DeMarya's books had found its way into his study. One by one I flipped through the pages of various books. Midway down the shelf, from between two books, fell two pictures. The first was of DeMarcus and a woman I had never seen in my life, hugged up like a happy couple on a couch unfamiliar to me. The second picture wasn't a surprise at all; it was of Evonne flaunting her over-sized breasts in a tiny, tiny T-shirt. Observing the T-shirt more closely, I recognized it as being one of the two monogrammed T-shirts I purchased for DeMarcus two Christmas' prior. Truthfully, I wasn't hurt. Seeing this photo put an end to my speculation of how close these so-called siblings in the ministry really were.

Tossing the photos aside, I continued flipping through the remainder of the books and came up empty. I searched each shoebox, looked beneath his desk, and searched his closet high and low and found nothing. His jacket and pants pockets were evidence-free as well. In his file cabinet I reviewed past cell phone bills and jotted down numbers standing out the most; inbound and outbound calls lasting between five and fifteen minutes and the frequency. Fumbling further, I discovered an unmarked brown envelope containing several explicit pictures of Evonne.

Continuing my search, inside an old black wallet contained a code to a locker of some sort. In a smaller pocket of the same wallet, I found a tiny piece of folded paper which read: Hot_Pastor2008 and FDJackson. I laughed aloud but my heart was pumping fast as I raced over to the computer and logged in. Entering Hot_Pastor2008 as the username and FDJackson as the password, I nearly soaked my pants when I gained access. Aware that time was not on my side, I did a quick search of his desktop files. Most were church or school-related, but one folder cleverly named, College Miscellaneous, held all the evidence I needed. It contained more pictures of women—not all of them black like me or of Evonne. They were pictures taken with a digital camera, uploaded and saved. By right-clicking on each picture, the properties revealed that the pictures dated back to 2005 to as recent as last month. Yes, DeMarcus did own a digital camera. He kept it in a locked desk drawer at the church.

The College Miscellaneous file proved to be a goldmine. Not only did it hold a host of evidence for future use, it included a document listing his credit card account numbers as well as email accounts and their passwords. BanGitboy123 was his Yahoo username and theHoly1 gave me access to his church email account. FD_Jackson was the password for all accounts.

Opening his Yahoo account, I alphabetized the sender's name to have an order of the conversations. The first email I opened was from Evonne, EDelight0804.

"Hey, babe," she began, followed by an accounting of her days' events. Each email shed light on their two-year on-again, off-again relationship. Her emails always ended with an expression of love and a multitude of emoji symbols. There was no denying that she was an important factor in his life and he was in hers.

DeMarcus had never been much of a talker but the words he typed were profound and to the point. He expressed being in absolute awe of her appearance, bulging breasts and all. I also learned that it was at his request that she wore a particular outfit; dresses, mini-skirts, and low-cut blouses. At times, he even specified whether she was to wear sheer pantyhose or nothing at all.

I had always heard folks talk about the mistress getting better than the wife, but never did I believe it to be true. But in an instant message, dated April 23, was proof that my role as his wife meant nothing more to him than the ink on the paper, we signed our names to.

Evonne wrote that her husband's inability to provide a comfortable lifestyle was the reason she wanted out of the marriage. Fancy clothing, a new car every three years, and a monthly spending allotment is what she felt entitled to and was strong in her stance to not settle for anything less. In response, DeMarcus vowed to take over where Mr. Delaney fell short. He promised to take care of her in exchange for being taken care of.

"I'm just not being fulfilled," he wrote.

"Something is missing in my life and I think it's you."

Replying with a big, yellow smiley, she joked about taking her husband out with a gun and hiding his body so that they could be together.

"Don't think things like that," he replied.

"Should something tragic happen to him, you would be consumed with guilt."

"What about Rosilyn? Do you love her?"

"I'll put it like this. She's good to my kids and I love the way my clothes smell when she takes them out of the dryer. Oh, and being served breakfast in bed is the best! But to answer your question, I have a strong *like* for her. About a month ago though, I could have taken my gun down from the attic, shot and tossed her azz in the woods. Like you, I want out, but I've got to plan my next move. As pastor, I've got a lot at stake."

Reading his words hurt. I was unaware of there being a gun in our house but even more so shocked by his nonchalant and carefree admission to his mistress of his thoughts of harming me. In my gut was worry, so I decided to print off the message for safekeeping. The paper jammed. Seconds after removing the tray to loosen the jam, car lights shined across the wall alerting me of their arrival. Nervous and panicked by the printers blinking lights, I turned off the monitor and forcefully pulled at the jam. Hearing the kids running up the walkway, I yanked the surge protector from the wall, not knowing what else to do. By the time DeMarcus turned the doorknob, I was at the front door to greet them.

"I slept in your bed, I missed you so much," I told DeMarya, picking her up and giving her a huge bear hug.

"I missed you too, Mommy!"

As if all was well, DeMarcus began sharing details of their outing, but I was uninterested. I wanted him to leave so I could continue reading through his emails, but he threw a fork in my plans when asking to stay over.

Reluctantly I agreed and offered him the couch. It was awkward having him in the house and me feeling restricted to the bedroom. So, to pass the time, I called Ma who I was pleased to hear was feeling one hundred percent better. But she expressed concern about me. Ma reminded me of our earlier conversation and was adamant about getting my affairs in order.

"Tomorrow is not promised, Rosilyn. I love you and I love my grandkids. Get busy now ensuring that you and those babies are taken care of. Please be careful my daughter and be smart. If he questions you, play dumb about everything and admit nothing."

Early morning on New Year's Day, I woke up full of energy and with hopes of getting to the mall before the crowds to partake in their first of the year clearance sales—leaving the responsibility on DeMarcus to feed breakfast to the kids. I was in the midst of humming a happy tune and enjoying being all soaped up in my new body wash when the shower curtain pulled back and there stood DeMarcus. He raised his right brow as if pleased by what he saw then asked if he could join me.

"Whatever," I replied, returning to the rush of hot water that was soothing to my body.

Placing his chin on my shoulder and gently kissing my neck, DeMarcus chuckled when I politely asked him to back up. Filling the squeegee with soap, he then began washing my back. I jerked away.

"Thanks, but no, thanks. I've already scrubbed my back with the shower brush."

Perceiving my actions as playing hard to get, DeMarcus wasn't taking my 'no' for an answer and purposely dropped the squeegee. Bending down to retrieve it, somehow his hand found its way to my love-joy. I smacked his hand away when he attempted to part my legs.

"Go away, damn! I'm running late already," I screamed.

"See, I try showing you affection but you're rejecting me like always. That's why our marriage ain't going to work because you don't know how to respond to your husband."

Had I not been so annoyed, I would have laughed at his idiotic remarks, but I didn't. Instead, I took a deep breath then turned around to face him.

"If that's what you think, DeMarcus, but we have other issues unrelated to me fulfilling your need to squirt one."

"Where you get that word from, your new boyfriend?" he asked, as if I had picked up on someone else's tagline.

"You know I don't have a boyfriend so don't start in on me with that crap. But I haven't asked you, nor do I care about where you've been laying your head or your stick at, now have I?" I pushed back the shower curtain and snatched my towel from the rack. Soap still covered my body but that was minor. I wanted space from DeMarcus and went to dry off in the bedroom.

DeMarcus followed me into the bedroom continuing to fuss about how I never meet his needs. I wasn't in the mood to argue but just as I was about to lose my cool, my cell phone rang. My dad was on the other end and he didn't sound well. DeMarcus was still yapping in the background, now annoyed that I was avoiding him to talk on the phone. I could barely hear my dad, so I stepped partially into my closet and asked Dad how he was doing.

"Baby, Ma left us this morning. If you can get here sometime today, I'm gonna need your help."

"Need my help?" *What was he talking about?*

"Shut up, DeMarcus, damn, this is an important call. Daddy, where's Ma? Is she alright?"

"Ma passed on..." he shared after a brief pause.

"Just a moment ago. She wasn't in any pain, her doctor said. I kinda think she knew she was going home."

His words were clear although I had to hold onto the wall to catch my breath and digest the horrific news.

"You ain't got nothing to say?" DeMarcus yelled.

"I'm telling you that I want to have sex with my wife and you're ignoring me—taking calls while I'm trying to talk to you."

"That was my dad on the phone. Mom passed away." Tears flowed down my face.

"So, I guess you expect me to cry too. That's bullshit! I should come before your Momma, your Daddy, before everybody!"

I expected him to comfort me, but he didn't. I expected him to tend to our crying children, but he didn't do that either. DeMarcus walked out on me— offering not a word of comfort or a raggedy dollar bill for gas. Instead, he put on his sweatsuit, jumped in his car and drove away. Too distraught to make him my focus, I crammed some clothing inside a bag and got on the road.

January 1, 2016 was the worst day of my life. Ma was gone from this world forever. The lady who taught me to laugh and view life as being one big joke. The woman who cared for me and pampered me even in my adulthood—I'd never see again. I was vulnerable. I needed her insight on what to do next in my life as it related to DeMarcus and the kids. How was I supposed to make it without my Ma?

The day before Ma's viewing, Kim, Geo, and Jamal drove to Louisville and treated me to dinner though Dad's refrigerator was overflowing with food delivered by friends and family. A break from the kids and stress of the situation was truly needed and that's exactly what they provided. Kim was careful in not asking about DeMarcus and Jamal who I informed of DeMarcus's behavior, did all he could to comfort me.

"He's a punk. Everyone that loves her is here and that's all that matters," remarked Jamal.

"You love me?" I asked, believing to have caught him on a slip of words.

"Yes, I do love you and I'm not ashamed to admit it. It's just a jacked-up situation right now but I plan on making you my girl and making every day of your life special."

Whoa! His reply left me speechless. I could admit to having feelings for Jamal; however, I wouldn't go as far as to call it love.

After dinner, Jamal invited me to his hotel room where a simple kiss turned into three hours of passionate intimacy. He felt so good inside of me and the second go-around was even better than the first. Jamal touched every part of me that needed to be touched. He comforted my heart, body, and soul simply by staring into my eyes. Jamal gave me his best and I gave him what I had. When morning came, Jamal never left my side. From the time my family entered through the church doors for the funeral to the time Ma's body was lowered into the ground, he was my support.

Although it was hard, I returned to work after a three-day leave of bereavement and jumped right back into my caseload. Flowers from the Crisis Center lined my desk and bookcase and at lunchtime, a special 'just because' bouquet from Jamal was delivered. It came with a message letting me know he was thinking of me and when I was ready, give him a call. I was digging on him, a lot, but not quite ready to start up a new relationship before my marriage to DeMarcus was officially over. If Jamal was willing to wait for me, good! If not, I wasn't going to be foolish by destroying an awesome, on-the-low physical relationship that made me twitch and giggle every time he crossed my mind.

Chapter 9
Joy Comes in The Morning

Fearing DeMarcus would clean out his inbox or change his password if under duress, I slipped and admitted to knowing of his many deceptions, I printed the most damaging emails for my own purposes should he ever tried denying any of it. Three long weeks it took me to review the three hundred plus emails from both accounts, and what I learned was an eye-opener. For many years—as long as he's been the pastor, DeMarcus had blatantly lied to everyone; to me, the church leadership, and members of the congregation.

DeMarcus was on some sort of power trip and as I reflected back, it began right after he was asked to head the finance office for the Empowered Brotherhood of Lexington Council, a four-year-old organization of Baptist leaders in Lexington and surrounding counties. His wardrobe changed and soon thereafter, so did his perception of people. Under his leadership, church membership began to dwindle, and several members grew suspicious when highly thought of ministry leaders were stripped of their position; Jamal being one of the many. It was a complete shock learning through an instant message conversation dated November 2010, that DeMarcus had also revamped the finance office, appointing Evonne the CFO without a nickel's worth of financial accounting experience. And even more shocking was his authorization for her to put aside four hundred dollars per week—before funds were reconciled, for her personal expenses.

"We're a team, you and me. Take care of me and I will most certainly take care of you." I was frightened by his written admission of embezzlement because had it ever been discovered; I too would be guilty by association. I wanted to confide everything I knew with Kim, but she would have shared it with Geo and he would have speed-dialed and shared his version with Jamal. I couldn't risk others finding out, so I told no one.

A great portion of my Monday morning was spent reading and printing off emails then copying and pasting photos from his personal folder into a folder on my desktop. Around ten, I logged out of his accounts to focus on my own assignments. Deciding to take an early lunch, when standing up from my chair, I was spooked to see Geo standing in the doorway.

"How long have you been standing there?"

"You have company," he said with a devilish smile.

My heart fluttered at the thought of seeing Jamal. But it wasn't him, it was Sister Harlow. She helped herself to a seat.

"Hello, Sister, we've been missing you and I thought I'd make a personal appearance to see if you were alright. Pastor announced to the congregation that you've been away caring for your father, but I know there's something else going on. I saw those scratches on his face. Whatever it is, you can tell me, baby."

I lowered my head to laugh and to keep from being disrespectful. I assured her that all was well.

"My dad is doing as well as expected. Thanks for asking."

"Well, the church's anniversary is in three weeks and we've got something big planned for Pastor Jackson and I'm going to need your help. First," she continued, "We're putting together a slideshow and I'll need pictures from his childhood up to this present year. This year's theme is: *Honoring a True Man of God*, and I think it's only appropriate that you be at his side. Your appearance just may put an end to all the rumors circulating about the two of you divorcing. Oh, and I'll need a family photo. The last photo we have of you, well, your hair was longer, and that little boy hadn't been born. And when you talk to your husband tonight, tell him to send me an updated listing of his awards and memberships. No one seems to know where Sister Angie put the old programs or how to reach her in Iraq. You'll talk to him tonight, won't you?"

As Sister Harlow rambled on, not once did she take a breather to allow me to respond. Smoothly changing the subject from pictures to questioning my reason for working instead of raising my own children, I held my tongue instead of speaking my mind. However, when she so boldly remarked about DeMarcus's salary being more than sufficient to care for his family, I gripped my chair and imagined that it was her throat. Having endured enough of her meddlesome inquiries, I cleared my throat and showed her to the door.

"It sure has been good seeing you. I'll have those pictures for you in the next few days, OK. Have a great day and thanks again for stopping by." *The nerve of some people!*

Thanks to Sister Harlow, the migraine from the previous night had resurfaced. Making matters worse, Geo returned and begged me to cover his afternoon counseling session. His request couldn't have happened on a worse day—I was in a foul mood and quite honestly, wanted to stay in a foul mood.

My attempts to hold a productive session was a complete failure with everyone's attention focused on the breaking news story—Regina Whitehead, a former client jailed for clubbing her abusive husband to a near-death.

"She said she was going to fix his azz," Ann Marie informed the group.

"The only thing I fault her for, is not killing him," remarked Joanne.

"I would have bashed his head in with the club then shot him to put him out of his misery."

"Now, now. That's not nice. Come on, folks, let's get focused."

"I know it's not nice, but what he was doing to her wasn't nice. I bet any one of yaw a hundred bucks that she was fighting for her life. He was probably drunk and beating up on her. A bat was conveniently lying around so she picked it up and tried cracking a home run with his head," Sharri jokes.

Everyone laughed. I too found a tiny bit of humor in the way Regina turned her horrific tragedy into a personal triumph.

"The beating is over," another person commented.

I continued to listen as the women spoke on stories once shared by Regina. The consensus overwhelmingly concluded that she had reached her breaking point and in the only way she knew how, tried putting an end to it. As others shared their personal stories, I watched in astonishment the eight-strong women before me who in the presence of their abusers openly admitted to being helplessly weak. Every story was a tearjerker and at the end of our session, everyone had at least wiped away one tear.

Returning to my office emotionally drained, I was a tad bit perturbed at the women who willingly endured such turmoil for the sake of love and shelter. Then something hit me like a ton of bricks; I was one of them.

DeMarcus eventually wiggled his way back into the house and yes, into the bedroom. It was only for the sake of my children that I disguised my true hatred for him by putting on a *happy-mommy* face. It was disheartening when realizing how their lives had also been affected by our fights, arguments—even his moving out. They needed normalcy and so did I. I wanted to enjoy life again, whatever that entailed so I returned—not retired my boxing gloves to its box, figuratively speaking, and declared an inner personal truce. But that was short-lived. DeMarcus was just as heartless and demanding as ever. He acted as though I was the lucky one, as if I should have been rejoicing for having him back in my life or something, but no! I was not.

"I'm not too much worried about what people say, but I am a pastor and until we come to some sort of resolve, we've got to set a good example for our kids and the congregation. People have been asking where you've been and to keep down speculations, I've told them that you're in Louisville on the weekends helping your father. You know I don't like to lie, Rosilyn, but the last thing I need is to have my flock thinking negatively of me especially when I'm trying so hard to lead them down the right paths in life. So, what I need you to do is stop being Raggedy Rosilyn from the streets and step back into your first lady role. You're still an extension of me so act accordingly."

I laughed at his foolishness. "So, you're telling me to act like a first lady, so people won't question whether we're human and having marital problems?"

"What I am trying to get across to you is that you have certain responsibilities—first one being to have my back. We don't have to see eye to eye on everything but as the head of this house, I make the decisions for us. You battle me on everything and through every situation. That's not what a first lady does. Remember, you only hold this position because of me. You're nothing without me."

"I'm better without you," I screamed, totally offended by his latter remark.

"You know what I meant, and that's a part of the problem too. Everything is either a smart response or words designed to start an argument. Just do as I say, damn! That's another thing I hate about you, your mouth. I take good care of you and these kids—none of you want for anything. All I ask from you, is to be shown a little appreciation and respect!"

"Yes, Paaaaastor. Let me take off your shoes and rub your feet, Paaaaastor. Can I cook you something to eat, Paaaaastor? Is that what the winch you were staying with did for you? Huh?"

"There you go again, shut your beaker! You don't know who I stayed with or whether I stayed in a hotel. Always assuming you know what you're talking about when you really don't know jack! And that's another one of your many faults. When you talk you make us both look stupid so shut the hell up! And if it was another woman, you'd best believe that she'd…"

He paused. I begged him to continue.

"She'd be prettier, have bigger breasts or nicer knees. She'd have long, wavy hair?"

"What DeMarcus? She'd kiss your dusty butt? What?"

DeMarcus sat back in his chair and crossed his arms appearing to be waiting for me to fall out onto the floor as DeMarya would do when she doesn't get her way. I was pissed but I wasn't going to be ignored and calmly walked over to him and stared him in the eyeball.

"Listen, it really doesn't matter anymore what you think about me or how you feel. But just so we're clear—for the record, you're not my ideal man either. I think you're stupid and insecure for running off the leadership you were so obviously intimidated by. They could have taught you a thing or two about how to become a better pastor because everybody agrees that your pastoring sucks. You're a weak man walking around in a strong man's robe, too stupid to realize that ain't nobody in their right mind coming Sunday after Sunday to hear your dry, boring azz, put-me-to-sleep sermons because they like hearing you preach. The older members come out of habit, and the younger members are either their children or horny, teeny boppers barely over 21 years old who think your old monkey azz is cute. And even your looks have changed.

"You're going bald at an alarming rate and everything you eat sticks to your belly. For the life of me, I don't know why you waste your time jogging. You ain't lost a pound in years and nothing about you is attractive anymore. But you're a halfway decent father, I'll give you that. But as it relates to being a good husband, it takes more than paying the bills and putting food in the refrigerator. Hell, I can do that on my own now. So, stop trying to be something that you're not. Be a better example for your children because one day, this sham gig you got going on in the pulpit, it's going to catch up with you!"

Chapter 10

Vengeance Is Mine

Running home during my lunch hour to get my cell phone I left on my nightstand, spotting Sister Harlow's car in the church lot, I figured it to be the best time to deliver the photos of DeMarcus because I had no spare time to socialize. Approaching DeMarcus's office, I was thrown off—actually shocked to find his door open and Sister Harlow at the computer because DeMarcus trusted no one in his personal space—not even Deacon Moyler who had become his new best friend. Nonetheless, I spoke and placed the envelope of photos on the desk with hopes of keeping it moving.

"About time someone came to help me," she said. "I done turned this darn thing on but it's not accepting the password."

Looking over her shoulder, it only took seconds to realize that the CAPS LOCK was on. So, after asking for the password, I depressed the key then slowly entered the password. When access was granted, her eyes lit up like a child seeing Santa Claus for the very first time.

"I volunteered to do the weekly bulletin and the church program until someone is hired," she chuckled.

"I retired over ten years ago and don't think that I've been on a real computer since."

I smiled. "Yeah, those computers are something," I said, wondering why she'd volunteer to fill in as secretary when CAPS LOCK and ENTER is clearly foreign terminology. *It's just what we need...another jacked-up program!*

"I'm hoping the pastor will look into getting LaDonna or Sister Clark to do all of his secretarial stuff, but I know with the issues you two are having, that may not be a good idea."

I should have walked away, but I didn't. Jumping across the desk and smacking the lint out of that matted, nappy looking, twisted wig on her head was a thought, but Ma's voice was clear in my right ear, telling me to bite my tongue and respect my elder. I obeyed but it wasn't easy as in my left ear, a voice similar to Ma's screamed for me to cuss out the crusty lipped, mustache wearing old bitty for simply being all up in my business. The tension in the air was obvious and though my nerves had been rattled, I took the high road and complimented the pearl necklace and earrings ensemble she wore. She smiled and thanked me.

Picking up my keys to leave, I gasped when Evonne entered then immediately exited DeMarcus's office.

"Hey," I yelled.

"What are you doing here?"

"Dee asked me to serve on the anniversary committee, so here I am. I was about to—"

"Who the hell is Dee?" I interrupted with neck-a-tude.

"Pastor, I'm sorry," she giggled.

"Dee sounds overly personal to me Evonne. My husband and I would appreciate you calling him pastor or Pastor Jackson, OK?"

I was pissed. *The nerve of that trick.* But having just put her azz in check, I placed my purse strap over my shoulder prepared to exit.

"But he told me to call him Dee." *What did she say that for?*

Turning around, Evonne had assumed a position of control; one hand on her hip and the other planted on his desk—kind of like she belonged right where she stood. Her long, lanky body stood erect in a pair of eight-inch stilettos. Sister Harlow sat quietly, shifting her eyes from Evonne to me and back as if watching a tennis match. Clearing my throat to confront the hussy, Sister Harlow must have sensed a beat down forthcoming because she didn't hesitate in rolling her chair back into the nearest corner. Evonne didn't flinch, nor did she show any signs of fear—but I didn't want her to be afraid. I wanted her to keep talking smack so my reason for blackening her eye would be justified.

"It doesn't matter to me what my husband told you to call him. He's a married man and anything other than pastor, I consider disrespectful. If you have a problem with that, then perhaps you, me, DeMarcus, and your husband need to discuss what is appropriate and what is not. You're a leader in this church but you're acting more like the church floozy. Respect yourself, respect me, and respect your pastor. You got that?"

116

Attempting to exit a third time, oh, how I prayed for her to utter something smart; giving me a reason to body slam the stiletto-ho into the floor and rake my nails across her cosmetic caped face. Beating her azz would have been solely for principle, not for anything having to do with DeMarcus.

Returning to the center, the atmosphere was an eerie somber. The waiting room was empty and the always packed to capacity break room was also vacant. Walking past Geo's office, I leaned against his door prepared to make small talk, but he quickly rounded his desk and grilled me on why I hadn't returned his call. He grabbed my arm and in doing so, frightened me. He literally pulled me down the hallway and right before opening my office door, announced I had visitors.

Introducing themselves as detectives investigating the Regina Whitehead case, for two and a half hours I was deposed. Having been the last person at the center to speak with Regina, they inquired about our last session and sought explanations of several entries of documentation in her case file. When the deposition was over, Geo was the first in my office wanting to get the full scoop. Still very much shaken, I ignored his questions and went out to the employee gazebo to get some fresh air.

It seemed to take the clock out time forever to roll around but when it did, I was the first out the door. Physically exhausted and hoping to relax on the couch when I arrived home, I hadn't quite placed two feet inside the house before DeMarcus laid into me—yelling from the top of his lungs about how I disrespected Evonne. He referred to her as his most trusted and dependable leader.

"She does exactly what I ask her to do, unlike you. Who the hell do you think you are?"

I stared in amazement at the veins pulsating over his temple. His face did a metamorphosis—man to mule in ten seconds flat. He was beyond angry and cursed me like I had deliberately poured syrup into his laptop. DeMarcus paced the floor expressing his disappointment. He stated his many regrets for marrying me.

"You're a hindrance to me fulfilling my calling."

I lowered my head. No, not to cry but to sigh. Having gone down this road before, I knew there was nothing I could say or do to change the situation and adding my input would have escalated matters into something much uglier. While he ranted, I stood in the doorway mentally drained and physically exhausted. I so badly wanted to shower and rest my feet, but I allowed him to angrily vent all that was on his mind. I was grateful when he'd worn himself out and locked himself inside his study. It was then that I dropped my purse and my work bag and went in search of my kids.

Lil D and DeMarya were watching a DVD when I peeked inside their room acknowledging my presence. Neither of them raced to jump into my arms or appeared happy to see me, but I didn't mind. Their preoccupation allowed me to enjoy a moment of much needed alone time.

The pot roast DeMarcus cooked was in a pan on top of the stove, but I wasn't hungry. However, after showering, I warmed a cup of leftover soup and got comfortable underneath a fresh set of linen. Turning the television on for sound, I covered my head to shield my eyes from the light. In a matter of minutes, my fatigued body shut down and I drifted off into la-la land.

Approximately two hours later, noises heard from the outside woke me. From the window, I saw DeMarcus backing out the driveway. He waited until he was completely out of the driveway to turn on the headlights which pissed me off. He was creeping off to be with skanky Evonne—I was certain of it. Slipping on my house shoes to check on my kids, I was surprised to find them already tucked into bed.

DeMarcus's behaviors had worsened. Clearly, he had no conscious of how his actions affected me or the kids, but nonetheless, just as he demanded respect for being the pastor, I decided to put my foot down and demand respect for simply being me. It was no secret he stopped loving me a long, long, time ago, but I refused to live another day under his roof being treated as if I didn't exist.

Leaving the kids room and walking past his study, the computer's blue screen fading to dim caught my attention. Suspecting DeMarcus had used it prior to his departure, touching the spacebar gave me immediate access to his email account left open. Moments later, an instant messenger box appeared. Curious of his last communication, I browsed the history file.

"It's all been taken care of," DeMarcus assured Evonne, whose concern was of upcoming trip expenses.

"I haven't purchased the traveler's checks yet, but I will on Thursday. And if I don't, you'll still be able to shop until you drop."

Piecing together bits and pieces of their communication, it only took a short while to realize that the trip they were taking was the Bahamas Cruise

DeMarcus purchased a year prior for us. I was crushed. It was hard stopping the tears streaming down my face. Devastated doesn't accurately describe my true emotion but I was tired of being hurt and lied to and declared this action to be the final straw. I wiped away my tears and vowed to move forward with my life. Shutting down DeMarcus's computer, I had just exited his study when through the front door he re-appeared. In one hand, he held a grocery bag of small items. In the other hand, he was carrying a 2-liter of ginger-ale.

"What are you doing out of bed? You didn't eat dinner and you didn't drink your tea. I thought maybe your stomach was upset so I went to get you some clear liquids. Here, let me help you get back into the bed."

No words could I muster up. And if my face looked lifeless, it was only because I was in disbelief.

"Why was he pretending to care about me when in three days, he and his mistress will be relaxing in lawn chairs and enjoying mixed drinks through a straw?" I asked Jamal, who after two days finally returned my call.

"It's called a guilty conscience. We all do it."

"So, I guess that's why you are pretending to be happy to hear from me? I've called you a thousand times in the past few days; I know you saw my number. You were ignoring me, but that's OK. All men are full of crap."

"Not all men, I've been busy, Rosilyn. The pastor's convention DeMarcus has you believing he's attending at the end of the week, well, that's the one I'm preparing for and will be attending. It's a big deal; can't go half-stepping when I'm on the program for God."

"Whatever."

"Don't whatever me," Jamal chuckled. "But seriously, what are you going to do?"

"What can I do? I mean, DeMarcus can be standing next to Evonne with luggage in his hands and deny that they are going on a trip together. I'm tired, Jamal. Mentally, I'm tired."

"But how tired, Roz? I know it's not going to make a whole lot of sense to you right now but consider this. What if God arranged for this trip to take place at this very moment so that while he's gone, you can take steps for moving on with your life? I'm not gonna preach to you but what if…just what if DeMarcus is the mountain in your path to a happier tomorrow? What if it was God's plan to put him on that boat and send him far enough away so that he wouldn't be in your way or hinder your progress? You've got a lot of things on your plate to take care of and a short time to do it in."

"What about her? Why does she get to enjoy the trip I was supposed to be taking?"

"Forget about Evonne," Jamal shouted. "This isn't about her. It's not even about DeMarcus. It's about you. It's about God answering your prayers and giving you exactly what you need to initiate your next move. You've got a decent job and I'm sure your credit is good. Think about renting a tiny apartment close to where you work. I'll get the truck and even help you move in."

"You just want some of my chocolate," I giggled.

"That has crossed my mind but first things first. We've got time to work on our situation. Right now, it's all about you and your kids. Whatever you decide, I've got your back, OK?"

Driving a different path home to avoid the rush hour freeway traffic, red and blue balloons waving from a huge iron gate grabbed my attention. Out of curiosity, I followed the trail of balloons inside the Cul de Sac and stopped at 13201 Larimore Circle where an Open House sign was planted curbside. Pulling into the driveway with intentions to quickly snatch a description of the amenities and drive away, I got trapped. Blocking me in was a beautiful black on black, 2014 Corvette Convertible.

"Four bedrooms, two full baths, a large finished basement, and a two-car garage. Hi, I'm Fred with Butler Properties. Let me show you inside," he said. His smile was sexy.

Having not a penny to my name to put down on this home or any other home, I too faked a smile and pretended to be an interested buyer. Knowing that it was only a matter of time before DeMarcus and I would be parting ways, I expressed an interest while silently praying for a miracle.

Entering the front door, I was blown away by the spacious living area with a fireplace. From the doorway, the large backyard was visible through the undressed sliding doors of the kitchen that too, was spacious and beautifully equipped with updated appliances. The bedrooms were small, but large enough to hold the few possessions I foresaw DeMarcus allowing us to take. And what didn't fit, I could see being easily stored in the finished basement. I knew better than to get my hopes up though. And with Fred ignoring my inquiries about the price, I figured he was waiting until the end of the tour to drop the financial bombshell. Making our way back to the living room, I thanked Fred for his time and proceeded toward the door.

"Wait!" Fred grabbed my arm and handed me his business card.

"Are you in a hurry?"

Fred was more than attentive throughout the tour, clutching my waistline with his big, strong hands while guiding me from bedroom to bedroom. And when entering the master bath, through the mirror, I watched his dark mysterious eyes adoring my backside and perusing my entire frame. He smiled with approval. Fred made no apologies for causing my knees to buckle when placing his chin on my shoulder and grabbing my waistline—then pointing in the direction of the den with the huge bay window. His scent was unfamiliar but effective in arousing my sensual areas.

Unbeknownst to Fred, I had been checking him out too. Sexy was his walk. His tall slender build was pure muscle—not a row of fat was visible through his well-fitting, white button-down oxford. Watching the sway of his dreadlocks hanging midway down his back and comfortably over his broad shoulders, I stereotyped his persona as being a roughneck—somewhat thuggish. However, his well-groomed facial hair told a different story—of a sensual man, a professional man all about his business.

"This property won't be here long. For what they're asking, someone's gonna snatch it up to rent it out."

"Well, if they do, that means that God had something better for me," I laughed.

"I believe in God too. It may not be this house he wants to bless you with, it could be me."

I stopped in my tracks and smiled—he couldn't see my face. I was contemplating a response but sometimes I believe folks ought to just leave things as they are—especially when it can lead to trouble.

Folks huddled around me like football players surrounding their quarterback calling out plays to offer condolences and hugs of comfort. It had been a short six weeks since losing Ma and though the majority of the people hugging me I couldn't stand, their expressions of sympathy were appreciated. As if I was her child, Sister Johnson wrapped me in her arms.

"I know it hurts baby, but your Ma is no longer suffering. Go on and cry, honey. It's OK.

"And when you finish, understand that she truly is in a much better place. She's pain-free and living in glory. Can you imagine being in the presence of God? Baby, if your Ma had a choice to come back, she wouldn't. But she loved you more than you'll ever know so treasure your memories, OK. When I lost my mom over twenty years ago, I thought my world was ending but God showed me that it was only the beginning. He's still good, yes, He is! Trust and believe that when you call on Him, He will answer."

I felt like a baby and cried like one too. The pain of Ma's death was still so very fresh and with all the craziness prior to and presently, I had been too preoccupied to cry. Sister Johnson allowed me to sob in her arms, and in doing so, made me realize that in being strong for others, I was deprived of grieving for myself. Her arms were like my Ma's—soothing and comforting. When she began humming a hymn, I felt an instant release.

"That's enough, that's enough." DeMarcus snatched me from Sister Johnson's grip.

"She's alright," he told her while shooing away those who had formed a prayer circle around us. By the arm, DeMarcus escorted me to a pew and ordered me to take a seat. If looks could have sparked a flame, DeMarcus would have been a roasted beef frank right smack dab in the center of the sanctuary from all the evil stares. He totally humiliated me, but I was glad that others got to witness his ugly side.

"Good morning, Saints. These are the last days that the Lord has given to us, so let us rejoice and be praising Him."

The majority of us knew what she meant to say but it didn't stop the congregation from laughing hysterically at the twenty-something woman jacking up elementary scripture.

"After worship," she continued looking confused by the laughter, "Pastor wants to meet with all the men and Minister Delaney wants the culinary ministry to meet her in the large classroom."

"Who are all these new people?" I whispered to Deacon Moyler.

His laugh made me chuckle.

"Seriously, who are they?"

"She's the new receptionist and well, you know Minister Delaney."

"Evonne?"

"Yep, but I ain't got nothing good to say about it so I'm not saying nothing else."

"Moving up in the ranks, huh? It was only a few weeks ago that she gave her initial sermon."

"Sister Rosilyn, I ain't got nothing to do with it, OK."

Chapter 11

Enlarge My Territory

Leading up to the night that DeMarcus and Minister Skanky Boobs were scheduled to board a plane and fly into their four-day lust-filled vacation of naughty pleasures, DeMarcus played the role of an attentive husband and to keep the peace, I played along. However, it was difficult playing ignorant to their body language and obvious attempts to avoid interacting with one another. In passing, their faces glowed. But confirmation for me—and perhaps others was during Wednesday night Bible study when Evonne approached the podium to teach. Watching DeMarcus enter the sanctuary and take a seat to my right, when he wrapped his arm around my shoulder, her disposition went from holy to helly. She stared at me as if I was the other woman. His display of affection was for appearance sake only—I know, but witnessing her come unglued and made to feel like the church skank she was, was nothing short of priceless.

How to be a better Christian was the title of her lesson and after stomaching a wretched twenty minutes of the horribly tied together bullshit, I excused myself telling DeMarcus I felt ill. My plans were to grab the kids then head home to rest but instead of exiting the back door, I entered DeMarcus's office for a bottle of spring water. Flipping the light switch, a garment bag hanging from his closet door frightened me. Taking a closer look, the bag was monogrammed with the initials E.D. It reeked of a woman's spray perfume.

Laughing it off, I proceeded toward the mini fridge. Kneeling to retrieve a beverage, I nearly tripped over two boxes of recently purchased women's pumps that had yet to be placed in her suitcase. Stunned by her boldness and DeMarcus's care-free and nonchalant attitude, had I not been so concerned with getting caught, I would have ripped all her clothing to shreds and broken the heels to those expensive shoes.

"Take the high road," Ma would say…but if only she was here.

Kneeling down to retrieve my beverage underneath his desk, I spotted two black duffle bags. Curious of the contents, I unzipped the first bag. The contents inside belonged to DeMarcus. With being caught no longer a factor, piece by piece I removed each item. New boxers, new cologne, and a pair of leopard print thongs were among the contents packed for travel. I laughed to myself but there truly wasn't a damn thing funny.

Unzipping the second bag, more signs of a shopping spree was evident as a variety of neatly folded designer tops and coordinating shorts—things I hadn't seen DeMarcus wear since becoming pastor-fied. Toward the bottom of the second bag was a brown envelope. Their passports and official documents were my first thoughts but when peeling back the flap, my hands began shaking as my mouth flew open. In my hands were twenty-six stacks of one-hundred-dollar bills, each wrapped in a two-thousand-dollar band. I nervously reburied the envelope deep inside the bag and grabbed my purse to leave.

I had only taken two steps when taking the money crossed my mind. And after a brief conversation with myself and answering my own question of, *what would Ma do?* I quickly secured my findings—placing stacks in my purse, brassiere, and panties. Shaking and sweating profusely, I neatly refolded the envelope and tip-toed towards the door. Sliding out of his office when the coast was clear, I quickly gathered my kids from the nursery and darted across the yard for home.

By the time DeMarcus walked through the door, the kids and I were in bed. He appeared to be in a good mood and apparently a frisky one too. Twice, I pushed him away, but he kept tugging at my pajama pants. It seemed like the more I rejected him and the nastier became my remarks, the more insistent he was to be with me. Reluctantly, I parted my legs. DeMarcus dove right in. There was no intimacy, just sex. In truth, it took longer for him to persuade me into submitting to him than it did for him to explode, but I wasn't mad. I was grateful it was over.

"So quick?" I asked with sarcasm.

"You sound disappointed?"

"Not at all, but I am curious to know what made you want to be intimate with me. I don't mean anything to you. From your own mouth, you said you weren't attracted to me, remember? You treat me like I'm nothing. I hope you don't think that being inside of me makes everything better."

"That wasn't my intent, damn! Can a man just want to be with his wife?"

"Oh, really, now I'm your wife. If that meant anything to you, you'd treat me better. And why am I not attending the pastor's convention with you? Patricia is going with her husband and Valerie is going with Kenneth. Do you realize that this will be the first time I didn't accompany you on a trip?"

"Who'd watch the kids? And I didn't think you had any time left on your job. I'll take you on the next trip, OK?"

"It's not too late to request the week off. A mini vacation would be good for me right now. And Dad, he can watch the kids, Auntie is there with him. We can leave from Louisville like the last time."

"I said the next trip! I've got a lot of meetings to attend this week so this trip I'm taking alone."

"It's always what you want, isn't it? You come in here demanding sex and now you're dictating when I can and can't travel with you."

"It's because of reasons such as this," he screamed.

"You nag and nag and it's never about anything. Keep your azz home and be productive. Quit trying to keep tabs on me! And it wasn't that I wanted to have sex... I was just doing your azz a favor. You walk around here tight-lipped and always in a foul mood, I figured you needed a little bit but don't worry, that was the last time, for sure."

"You were doing me a favor?" I laughed then rubbed my eyes to make sure I wasn't dreaming.

"Yes, a favor. Do you know how many women offer their bodies to me daily? At least ten. But what do I do? I come home to your ungrateful azz! And for what? To be turned down and bitched at."

"Sounds like you're unhappy DeMarcus. Are you leaving me?" He hesitated.

"If you're talking about this house, no! I'm not leaving anything. This house is for the pastor and his family but if you think you can make it without me, do what you feel you need to do. But we're not discussing this tonight. Deacon Moyler will be here shortly to drive me to the airport and I don't want to leave stressed."

Relaxing in my bed and underneath my queen-sized comforter felt good but it was nearing midnight and I was having great difficulty falling asleep. For hours, my eyes roamed the ceiling and every noise heard inside and outside the house caused me to jump. Perhaps it was from the guilt of stealing the money. It could have also been my fear of a recurring nightmare coming true; DeMarcus planning my demise while faking being at the pastor's Summit.

Around 2 a.m. the phone rang disturbing my much-needed rest. I hadn't checked the caller I.D. but cringed at the thought of answering to someone needing prayer from their pastor for their hurt or dying loved one. I didn't want anyone to know that the kids and I were alone in our great big house, so I let it roll to voicemail. The phone rang twice more before I finally picked it up. It was DeMarcus.

"Hello!" I screamed.

"Why are you calling so early? You know me and the kids are asleep."

"This is important," he said. I heard urgency in his voice.

"Look in the bottom of my closet for a brown envelope. Get up now!" he ordered.

"It should be on the lower right-hand side."

I made sure he heard me hit the nightstand as I jumped to my feet. I put the receiver near the door and let him hear it squeak as I opened it.

"No, I don't see an envelope. What am I looking for? Maybe it fell out of the envelope."

"Just look for an envelope," he demanded.

"I ain't got time for games damn it! Look on the other side and if it's not there, go look in my trunk."

I did as instructed, *tee-he-heeing* the whole way. I was nervous but felt vindicated.

Getting revenge was so sweet!

DeMarcus never let on or said what he was missing, but I pretended to be just as concerned as he was—even more so when he blurted out the code to the church door and told me where to locate the emergency keys to his office.

"I don't know what all this is for but you're scaring me. What is it, DeMarcus?"

Entering his office, all signs of travel had been removed. As instructed, I looked in his closet, personal bathroom, and in the conference room. I even pretended to look underneath the couch pillows.

"I don't see an envelope, honey. Is it your hotel confirmation or something? Are you having trouble checking in?"

DeMarcus didn't reply. He hung up the phone without saying goodbye. In the wee hours of the morning, I should have been afraid of walking back across the yard alone, but I was not. Nor did I fear the howling winds or rattling of the trash cans as my laughter kept me company. I was thrilled to know that his vacation had been successfully ruined.

The next morning after dropping the kids off at daycare, I jumped on the highway en route to work. I must have looked like crap for Geo to make a special trip to the kitchen to bring me a cup of coffee. It was black.

"Where's the cream and sugar? It's just like a man to jack up a freshly brewed cup of coffee."

"You look sleep-deprived. You and Jamal have a late night?"

"No." He stared at me as if I had said something wrong.

"You stayed over last night, didn't you?" Geo asked, then quickly changed the subject.

He asked about my dad.

"Sorry, it wasn't me but I'm not stupid. He hardly returns my calls or responds to my texts. That's OK, though. His loss will soon be someone else's gain."

Geo didn't admit or deny knowing anything about Jamal's new interest, but his facial expression revealed having knowledge of something. Silence filled the room. Sitting across the table from Geo—neither of us knowing what else to say, to break the awkwardness, I asked him to hand me two sugar packets and sweetened my cup of coffee.

Following Geo and other managers to the conference room for the morning meeting, when Earlene, our administrative assistant announced that it had been cancelled, we all scattered like roaches under a spotlight. When I got to my office, I rested my head on my desk. Geo must have returned to his office too and alerted Jamal of his slip of the tongue, because moments later my phone rang. Jamal was on the other end apologizing.

"No need to apologize my friend. I understand, you're a man and yaw do, what yaw do. I'll be fine, don't worry. And thanks for letting me use your car. Dad's putting Ma's old car in the shop tomorrow for some minor repair so when he drives down to pick up my kids at the end of the week, I'll ride back with him to pick it up. Dad's mechanic, Mohamed, promised to have it ready by Saturday evening."

"If you can wait until the middle of the week, I volunteer to drive you and the kids down and save your dad a trip. I really would like to spend time with you."

Jamal sounded sincere but knowing that he too had been loving on another woman, I had lost all romantic interest.

"Why are you giving me the cold shoulder? And don't compare me with most men; I'm not most men. Just because one man has hurt you it doesn't mean that I will too. I've been straight up with you Rosilyn. I told you that I've been busy preparing for the conference and that's the honest truth."

"So, who was at your house last night?" Jamal was silent.

"Yeah right, have a wonderful day, OK."

Hanging up the phone, I was hoping to pout and rest my head on my desk for a while longer without any interruption but like clockwork, Geo burst in. He plopped down in the chair ready to play catch-up.

"Kim's flying in tonight and I have something big I want to ask her. Tell me what you think of this." Geo was excited and fidgeting in the chair. Believing it was a proposal, my eyes grew wide and my mouth flung open.

He laughed then clarified what I was thinking.

"She's always on the road and when she gets home, it's always in the wee hours of the morning. I try to give my baby her space to unwind, but it's always later the next day when I get to see her. I'm thinking about asking her to move in with me. That way, she can have a hot bath and a nice hot meal waiting for her. Besides, she's paying for an apartment that she hardly gets to relax in. Moving in with me, she'll be pampered and be able to stack her money. What do you think she'll say?"

"Damn, it's like that? I mean, you've known each other what…less than a year?"

"I ain't saying I'm in love, it's just that things are going good and by moving in together, we can kind of get a feel for what the future could look like if we decided to step things up a notch. You know, live the life before I make her my wife."

"I'm happy for you and to answer your question, I think she may say yes. Why not? Every woman wants to be more than a booty call. Asking her to move in, to me, is a sign that you're serious about the relationship. Treat her good Geo. She's my girl and she deserves true happiness."

Geo was pumped up when he left my office. I hadn't talked to Kim in a while to get her take on Geo, but knowing her as well as I did, I was certain she'd jump at the opportunity to be financially supported and spoiled.

My cell phone rang.

"Good morning, Roz. Look, I need a huge favor from you. My credit cards are maxed out and I need you to put at least $1,000 or better in our joint account."

"Where do you expect me to get that type of money, DeMarcus? Besides, the last I checked, we had over $3,000 in that account. Did you spend it all? And what do you need that much money for? Your hotel stays, and food is paid for isn't it?"

"Stop flapping your lips and deposit the money into the account, please. Damn! Just do as I say and do it now! I need it within the next hour."

His demands made me laugh. Oh, how I wish we were on a webcam so I could see the anguish on his face—him begging me for something I had always been deprived of, money. DeMarcus had apparently lost his mind but by no means had I lost mine. Yes, he was aware of my savings account that I used to pay for minor household expenses. But I also had another personal savings account—under my maiden name, that I had managed to save about $2,300 for a rainy day—my rainy day, not his storm. But it would be an icy day in hell before I willingly forked over a penny from either account to support the flunky and floozy vacay.

"I'm sorry, I'm stressed. Please, babe. Just do this for me, OK?" His tone was different.

Now I'm his baby. Huh!

"Babe," I said with a chuckle.

"If I had it, I would but I don't. But you still haven't come clean on what you did with all of our money. That's what I want to know. Do you have a drug problem? If so, we can get you help."

I covered the receiver to laugh. But quickly, my laughter turned to concern when his stance changed from determination to desperation. His words were slow and direct. The manner in which he spoke sent chills through my body.

"You've never been anything more to me than the mother of my kids. It was only at the advice of my mentor that I married you. If it wasn't for those kids, you'd be on the next bus back to Louisville. I hate you with every fiber of my being. And every time I see you, I wish you death."

DeMarcus ended the call having the last word. I feared what seeing him again would bring.

Too tired to cook the next evening, I ordered Chinese fried rice for dinner. After eating, I started a DVD for the kids with hopes they'd retire early so that I could do the same. Resting on the couch, I was on the verge of falling into a deep sleep when someone knocked on the door.

Had it not been for Lil D running towards it screaming, "Daddy," the knocks would have gone unanswered. *Hell, I wasn't expecting anyone.* I had only opened the door midway when Sister Harlow and her big hips squeezed in and past me. She helped herself to a seat on the couch.

"It's been years since I last was in this house. You and the pastor are doing quite well."

"How can I help you today, Sister?" I asked loudly to draw her eyeballs back into the living room where she sat. I truly wasn't in the mood for socializing and nor was I for the full line of meddlesome questions I knew was forthcoming. Sister Harlow reached into her purse and handed me the envelope containing photos of DeMarcus.

"You two were so happy once. But what I see in your eyes now tell a different story. You want to know why I am the way I am?" she asked, twisting her body to comfortably fit into the couch's dip and continuing on. "Because nobody respects a weak azz woman, pardon my French—they'll run right over you if you let them. When my husband was alive and serving as the pastor, I went through a similar situation too. And just like my husband, bless his poor soul, Pastor Jackson has grown accustomed to living what people perceive as the good life."

"How's that?"

"He's conceited and takes for granted the beautiful wife at his side and the little people who believe he's the smartest and best dad in the world. He's not the same pastor we voted in…how many years ago? Instead of uplifting God, he's uplifting himself and focusing more on dressing super sharp and playing the part of the distinguished pastor. He preaches a good sermon from time to time I must admit, but I recognize the signs. But lately, when I watch your husband, all I can do is shake my head. You know, at one time we had some good, honest, and decent folk handling the business of the church. Now what do we have? A handful of title crazed butt kissers that bow down to him every time he snaps his finger. And I'm not just talking about the ones in the pulpit wearing suits and ties either. We've got a few floor ho's, pottitutes, and troublemakers amongst us holy and righteous folk."

131

"Pottitutes?"

"Yes, pottitutes. Young and dumb women chasing after old men for their money. We have a congregation full of them, baby. These women are out for themselves and don't care anything about these old men pissing in them; they'll do anything for a dollar. Anyhow, open your eyes and see what's going on. Women love men in authoritative positions. From the pastor, to his associates, to the Deacons, and even VJ, RJ, you know who I'm talking about—that cute young thing in charge of maintenance at the church. If they wear a title in the church and can clean up real nice in a suit and tie, you best believe some hot tailed hussy is chasing after him."

I laughed.

"My husband was in his late 60s—he was half-blind, hairline had receded all the way back to damn near his neck and had gotten so damn fat that after walking eight steps, he'd be asking for his oxygen tank. But that didn't stop them heifers from calling my house all day and all night. Once, one of them winches got bold and knocked on my door. He pretended not to know who she was, but I was standing behind him and heard her ask why he hadn't shown up. Hell, I invited her in."

"I bet she was sweating like a Ho' in church sitting on the front pew, wasn't she?"

"Baby, Ho's don't sweat no more. They sit on the pews, in the choir stand, even in the pulpit and throw their hands up in praise just like me and you do. But anyhow, Henry kept saying that he didn't know who she was. The woman was so spaced-out, she tried convincing me that she was there to sell bottled perfumes. So, when I asked to see her bottles, of course, there weren't any. She eventually came clean and admitted that he had been giving her money. Henry claimed the money came from the church and it was to help her get caught up on her small bills but when I offered her twenty dollars for the truth, she spilled her guts. That's how I found out about their Saturday noonday meetings, sex for a few dollars. There was another time too when I had to stand up in church and call a few people out by name. I told them to stop running up to my husband and kissing all over him. You best believe that it didn't go over well, but they all got the message."

It was difficult containing my laughter visualizing the daytime storyline dramas she described. And while I could relate to the situations, I pretended to be dumbfounded.

"Vengeance is the Lord's," I said, portraying an act of innocence.

"Yes, it is, my dear, but the devil took it to a new level. Folks sometimes forget that God is in control and try fixing things on their own—I did. See, I already knew that God was gonna get him for bringing all that foolishness into His house, but I had to get my husband for bringing the drama, the drugs, and the foolishness into mine. His actions affected me and our kids mentally and physically. He damaged our reputations and our future. Now, I didn't give him forty years of my life just to lose it all over some dumb stuff. So, in sharing this, all I am telling you is—if you really want your husband to act right, you're going to have to do some things that'll make him and even you uncomfortable. Men are like children. Sometimes you've got to manipulate the situation to make it work in your favor. Break him down if you have too. Place him in a position where he's going to need you. It'll be hard work, but I promise it will pay off in the end. It definitely got my husband to acting right."

"Did he ever apologize for what he did to you?"

"He did. It was while he was in the hospital and our family had been called in to say goodbye. I can only guess that before he died, he felt the need to clear his conscience. It was bittersweet, but nonetheless, it was an apology. And since he was dying anyway, why not forgive him?" She laughed and shrugged her shoulders.

"I do sometimes wonder about DeMarcus's working relationship with Evonne. Every time he sneezes, she's there with a tissue. And you witnessed her attitude when I corrected her for calling my husband, Dee. Four hundred people on the church roll and she's the only one who doesn't feel it's appropriate to call him pastor."

"The little flings on the side, don't worry about them, baby. Women will come and go just as quick as the money does. And don't worry about Evonne either. From what I hear, her husband has cut her off completely and has her making her own car note and paying every single one of her credit card bills. She's only smiling at your husband for his money and whatever else she thinks she can get him to do for her. If and when he says no and cuts her off, she'll be on to the next sucker. I know about women like her. But remember what I say." Sister Harlow grabbed her purse and rose to her feet.

"In order to change some things, you've got to take action to change them. Even kids learn to steer clear of a hot stove after touching it the first time. Understand what I am saying? Break him down!"

Chapter 12

Amazing Grace

Before I could even finish brushing my teeth, DeMarcus had rung my cell phone twice—stressing me out with his demands of placing money in our joint account. I offered up $100 stating that I was certain I could borrow it from Kim, but that amount wasn't sufficient for his needs. DeMarcus was desperate for cash—so desperate, he promised to pay all the NSF fees if I wrote a hot check and overdrew funds from the one personal account he knew about.

"The childcare expenses, our family health and dental coverage, and my student loan payments are automatically paid from that account. And have you forgotten about their trip to Disney World in a couple of days? The last payment of $500 comes out tomorrow."

"Damn their trip!" he yelled, using their young ages to rationalize forfeiting the $1,050 already paid toward the package deal total.

"You make triple what I do, DeMarcus. Where's all your money? Whoever you're taking care of must be a gem for you to have depleted all of your family's savings."

"And that's another reason why I want out of this marriage, you're selfish! Everything always has to be about you. But that's OK. When I get back, there's gonna be major changes. I've got something for your azz!"

I'd be fibbing if I denied being worried. At this point, DeMarcus was desperate, and momma always said that desperate people did unimaginable things. Fearing for my safety, I texted his verbal threat to Jamal, Geo, and Kim. *If anything happens to me, DeMarcus did it! LOL.*

"That's nothing to laugh about," Jamal quickly responded via phone call. "Where are you?"

"At home, getting the kids dressed for daycare and myself for work. We just got off the phone and he's madder than hell because I won't send him any money. He's yet to explain where our savings has disappeared to but expects me to send him what I've saved up. Now I do stupid things every now and again but I'm far from stupid. He's not gonna force me into giving him any of my money."

"Rosilyn, why do you keep allowing him to stress you out? Pack up the kids and move out; you are more than welcome to stay with me. No one has to know, not Geo, no one. A threat against your life is a serious matter, take it seriously!"

Jamal was right and after digesting his comparison of my situation to that of the clients I assist, my search for an apartment began. My entire morning was dedicated to searching online and through the newspapers. Several listings were in my price range but none in an area suitable for my kids. I removed Fred's business card from my wallet. I inquired about the property on Larimore Circle and learned that it was going to be placed on the public foreclosure listing. To me, this meant that the bank wanted a quick sale of the property and would possibly consider settling for less. Prayerful that the selling price would be close to the amount of DeMarcus's money I had stashed away, I expressed my interest and agreed to meet Fred on Monday morning to discuss the financials.

It was 12:45 on a Friday afternoon when my dad arrived to pick up the kids. At least a year and a half had passed since his last visit to Lexington but having him in my home again was a true treat. Insisting that he rest up before heading back to Louisville, it was my pleasure fixing him a warm turkey, tomato, and mayo sandwich. And Dad appreciated it too—commenting that it was almost as good as the ones Ma used to make.

"Everything is different now without Ma," he said.

I nodded in agreement and commented on how much I missed her.

"Where are my little ones?" Dad asked, seemingly revived once downing the sandwich.

"They're still at daycare. We can get them in a little while but first, I need to talk to you about something."

I managed to hold back my tears as I nervously explained my marital situation to Dad, whose facial expression revealed pain and worry. Hearing of how his grandkids and I had been mistreated by DeMarcus brought tears to his eyes.

"But don't worry, Daddy. I'm planning on moving out and things are looking like they're finally coming together. I've found this house..."

"Of course, you've got to move out. Whatever you need me to do," he said.

"I've never liked him anyway. He was never good enough for you."

I chuckled but then my laughter produced tears.

"I've been looking for a place to live, Dad, and I think I found one."

"Why don't you come home? I know you can find a nice job in Louisville and you can save up your money for a good little place nearby."

"I like it here. I have a decent job and there's a good chance I'll be considered for a promotion soon. I've registered for college already and my job has offered to reimburse all the expenses if I pass my classes with a C or better. By next fall, I'll be within four classes of having my bachelor's degree. I know DeMarcus isn't the greatest person, but he is their father and they need him. I'd hate to move away and deprive the kids of spending quality time with him."

"Well, honey, I'd rather you come home but if you want to stay here..."

"I do, and I found a nice home that's near my job. The thing is, it's in foreclosure and could be sold next week. The realtor says I've gotta move quickly and let him know something by this coming Monday. The only thing I need from you is, well, for you to put it in your name. That'll keep DeMarcus from trying to take it from me and the kids before the divorce is final. I have some money saved, but if you will sign the paperwork...please, Daddy, please," I begged.

"For you, Rosilyn, anything."

Dad and I were getting in the car en route to pick up the kids when my phone rang. It was Fred calling to reschedule our Monday appointment.

"What about today then?" I asked with hope.

Fred was available and within the hour, Dad and I were doing a walkthrough. Though he never verbally admitted it, I sensed Dad liked the house and the purchase price.

While Dad sat reviewing the paperwork and calculating figures, I escaped into the master bedroom and closed my eyes to pray. I was only alone a few minutes when Fred joined me. He grabbed my waist and whispered in my ear.

"What brought you back?"

"The house brought me back," I replied, politely removing his hands and shunning his advances. Rejoining my dad in the kitchen, when everything that could be completed was, Fred phoned his contacts and arranged an early Monday morning meeting with the bankers to complete the process and sign the last of the required documents. The asking price was $48,500. I wanted to breakdance, but maintained my composure. However, once I sat behind the steering wheel, tears of joy flowed from my eyes. Staring into the heavens and basking in the moment, I thanked God for my blessing. I also thanked Dad for signing the dotted line on my behalf.

"Merry Christmas, happy birthday, and happy college graduation. Don't worry about a thing, baby. I'll wire the money to the bank first thing Monday morning. You're doing the right thing and I know Ma would be pleased too."

It was then that I covered my eyes and completely broke down. Not only had Dad signed for me, but he was also gifting the money to me.

By 5:30, Dad, the kids and I were on the road headed to Louisville. Arriving an hour and a half later, once we pulled into his driveway, Dad began making preparations to rent a cargo trailer so that I could transport items from their garage to furnish the house. Glancing over the items, some were in good condition but none of it was what I envisioned sitting in my new living room. Graciously declining his offer, I fibbed about already having beds and other household furniture in the lay-a-way. However, unbeknownst to Dad, as I was driving, I was also devising a plan to furnish each room of the house with the bulk of DeMarcus's love money.

It was difficult returning to my parents' house and not hearing Ma's voice or smelling fresh collards cooking on the stove. It was even harder chasing after DeMarya who ran from room to room in search of her granny. In every room I entered, Ma's presence was felt. And in every room I exited, I felt her absence. It was then that my mind shifted to Dad who I sensed was lonely and grieving silently. After forty-plus years together surely, he missed her goodnight kisses and maybe even her voice fussing at him about the volume of the television. Appearances are deceiving but Dad seemed to be doing fairly well. Most days he said he kept busy fiddling on an automobile that hadn't worked since I was a teenager.

The next morning, Auntie was removing sausage links from the skillet when Dad entered through the back door. It was always an honor to fix his plate and after doing so, I poured him a tall glass of iced cold milk.

"And this is for you." Dad handed me the wire transfer confirmation.

The moment was surreal. Standing in the middle of the kitchen, Auntie grabbed my hands and together we cried tears of joy. Pretending that the purchase was no big deal, Dad shrugged his shoulders and walked with his plate into the living room. When he was out of sight, Auntie shared his comment about how doing this for me gave him so much pleasure.

"It's about to rain," Dad yelled from the next room.

"It's about time you get on the road little lady to avoid the severe weather they're predicting."

Auntie agreed and after kissing my kids and making them pinky swear, they'd tell Snow White and Minnie Mouse hello from me, I jumped in Ma's old car headed back to Lexington.

As always, Dad stood at the edge of the walkway wishing me safe travels.

"Wait, until you get home before pulling out that cell phone," he yelled back, possibly seeing my head down as I dug around the bottom of my purse for it. But I was anxious to share my good news with somebody—anybody I could reach. When Kim didn't answer, I assumed she was spending time with Geo. And when Jamal didn't answer, I tossed my phone in the passenger seat and jammed the radio.

Exiting ramp 15 towards home, my first stop was at a furniture warehouse to do some impulse shopping. Momma always told me to shop around—don't settle for the first price of anything but today, I wasn't searching for deals, I had a wad of money stashed away—DeMarcus's money and the price was not an issue. I fell in love with almost everything on the showcase floor and at the end of my impulse shopping spree, except for office furniture, items for every room of my new house was placed on hold.

Leaving the furniture store, my cell phone rang.

"What's up, peoples?" I answered, expecting it to be Kim or Jamal. It wasn't. It was DeMarcus asking of my whereabouts.

"I just got off the highway. Remember, the kids are in Louisville? They're going to Disney World with Auntie and their cousin this week. Where are you?"

DeMarcus didn't disclose his location but stated needing a ride from the airport. To avoid an argument, I agreed to pick him up at the stated time and let him know where I'd be parked. As if truly interested, I asked about his trip.

"It was just a trip, damn!"

"OK," I mumbled in response to his short and smart reply.

I felt a sense of peace walking into the house and knowing that for at least the next six hours, I had it all to myself. But instead of resting, my intent to do a little light cleaning turned into completely rearranging the living room. Deciding to replace the figurines on the mantle with greenery, candles, and photos, I went to the garage in search of boxes. Filling one box after the other with whatnots and other items I subsequently decided to transport to my new house, by the time I loaded Ma's car and Jamal's car down, three hours had disappeared.

Tired and hungry, I placed a call to Austin's Rib Shack. Moments after receiving and eating my steak cooked well—not burnt, baked potato with butter and chives, and apple-walnut garden salad, comfortably situated on the couch I surfed through several television channels and settled on watching a scary movie. An hour and a half later, I cleaned up my mess and headed out the door for the airport.

Twenty minutes I waited before dialing DeMarcus's cell phone which rolled to his voicemail. Physically exhausted and anxious to return home to shower and sleep, I decided to glance over at the huge screen displaying arrival and departure times and was angered by his inconsideration to notify me of the one-hour delay. Napping while I waited, when DeMarcus finally approached the car, he tossed his bags in the backseat and in a smug tone, informed me that we needed to talk.

"Do we have to do this tonight? You've got to be tired. I know I am?"

"I don't want to do this anymore," he continued. "I don't want to argue about it, but I want out of this marriage and I think it's only right that you and the kids move out of the house. Move in with your dad, I'll pay for the U-Haul. But it's over, Roz, I want a divorce. I'll have my lawyer draw up the paperwork and make sure you get a fair amount in child support. And I'll—"

"Sure DeMarcus, whatever you want." I interrupted his speech.

"I'll find someplace for me and the kids to live, but I'm not going back to Louisville. I like my job and if we stay here, you can spend time with the kids when you choose to. Just because we're divorcing doesn't mean your relationship with them ends. They need you."

My reply must have angered him; his breathing grew heavy and I swear to feeling heat radiating from his body.

Walking inside the house, the redecorated living room angered him as well. He stood in the middle of the living room with his hands on his hips, looking around and shaking his head. Sensing an altercation brewing, I walked towards the bedroom. Once inside, I propped my pillows against the headboard. DeMarcus followed behind—mumbling something but I didn't ask him to speak up. He undressed, dimmed the light, and crawled into bed. Although the room was dark, the moons glare shining through the window made visible his t-shirt tan and what appeared to be a medium-sized bruise on his shoulder.

"How'd you hurt your shoulder?"

"Don't worry about that." DeMarcus turned to face me.

"The problem with you is," he began.

"Is that you're too needy. You'll always be dependent on someone to take care of you. The woman I need in my life is someone who wants something out of life and that's not you. You're happy with having the simple basics but I'm not. I want more out of my life and that goes for my kids as well. At this point in our marriage, we should be living on easy-street. We should be connected in mind and soul, but we're not and you're the blame. You fight me on every issue, you question every one of my decisions, and as it relates to our growth, you contribute to nothing! You've never supported me in this ministry and you've never done anything I've asked you to do…like working to finish your degree. If you want to be somebody in this life you've got to have that piece of paper. Instead, you're content with being the wife of Pastor Jackson but I am tired of carrying you. The majority of the time, you are an embarrassment to me, with that raggedy mouth—always so full of negativity and smart azz remarks. What I envisioned us doing was working side by side and building an empire of our own, but you have managed to destroy each and every brick I've brought forth. You're not who I need you to be, and I won't continue to allow you to keep me from getting what is rightfully mine. I mean it this time Rosilyn, this marriage is over but until I have worked things out or I'm ready for people to know we're divorcing, you just keep smiling and keep your mouth shut. Keep my kids clean and basically, you stay out of my way. Oh, and no matter what people ask you, think before speaking especially if it's related to me or our family. I don't need my image diminished when I've worked so hard to gain people's trust and respect."

This fool is crazy. That's it—just crazy. He spoke what was on his mind, laid his head on the pillow and had no problem resting his eyes with a guilt-free conscience. As for me, having slept with one eye open the entire night and jumping each time DeMarcus moved, I knew that waking up for church in the morning I would be a walking zombie or an irritated grouch, at best.

DeMarcus slept like a baby and rose with the chickens, stretching, yawning, and passing gas—disregarding my presence. I faked being asleep but as he circled around the bed, I watched him walk out with his cell phone. Hearing his voice and the study door close, I wondered who he had called at such an early hour. After taking a shower, DeMarcus prepared breakfast. The aroma of bacon and cinnamon toast filled the entire house. And that's all he left too—an aroma. The bastard was too ornery to leave a toast crumb or a smidgen of grits for me on the stirring spoon.

Sitting alone at the island in the kitchen, I pondered over incidents which may have led to the tensions between DeMarcus and me. I tried to piece together time frames of when he stopped loving me and of when I stopped caring. Had I bruised his ego? Had I really stopped being supportive and encouraging? Had I given up on our dreams?

It may have been fatigue that had me talking to myself—trying to make sense of it all, but after replaying situations over and over in my mind, I concluded that it was DeMarcus, not me, who had changed. It was his need to control everything, including me, opposed to working together as a team that threw us off course. And it was he who disrespected me in public and so lovingly apologetic in private. Recalling the many months of his lies, hurtful remarks, and being made a complete fool of—in conjunction with the previous nights' conversation, pissed me off again!

Watching from the kitchen window as DeMarcus walked across the lawn and over to the church for a meeting with his leadership, I returned to the bedroom and rummaged through his belongings. In his pants' pockets was a taxi receipt and loose change. Tucked away in his closet was one of the two duffle bags. Unzipping it quickly, the stench of dirty clothes and even dirtier underwear in need of urgent washing caused me to gasp. Continuing my search, I learned that room 620 of the Paradise Island Harbour Resort is where they stayed. The occupants: DeMarcus and Evonne Jackson.

Pressing past my pain, I dug further inside the bag and discovered a $400 ATM withdrawal receipt dated two days prior to their return. Curious to know where he obtained the funds, I logged onto the computer and discovered a $1,000 wire transfer from EBLC to our personal checking account. Prior to that transfer, there was a $2,500 transaction the month before and other

141

sporadic transfers received on various dates. But what was EBLC? Evonne, something, something, culinary? Something, something, Baptist Church?

Making my way into the shower, I only had forty-five minutes to wash and blow dry my hair, fix my face, and dress before morning worship church began. I managed to do it all with ten minutes to spare. Entering the sanctuary through the side door, I was heading for DeMarcus's office when Evonne exits. At her side was Dora Jones-Cooke, wife of Pastor Darryl Cooke, guest speaker of the morning.

"Good morning, Evonne," I said, throwing her for a loop. I complimented her attire; a one-piece slinky dress perfectly hugging her body. She nearly ripped the lace trim trying to pull it below her knees. Her accessories were red—a perfect match to her now Burgundy doo.

As if we had been friends all our lives, I hugged Dora and made a big-to-do about seeing her again. DeMarcus would have been delighted to know that I invited her into the kitchen and talked over coffee and fresh fruit. In past gatherings, Dora and I were just cordial but today, she was very talkative.

"So, how have you been doing? Missed seeing you two at the summit."

"Oh, well," I said, not really sure what to say.

"Can't make everything…you know how it is with small children."

"And how long has Evonne been with your church? The way she was carrying on in the office, one would think she's taking over."

"I'm not sure what to say to that," I chuckled.

"She's helpful to DeMarcus and he trusts her."

"But do you trust her?" Dora asked, putting me on the spot. *I hated being put on the spot.*

Dora sat her coffee mug onto the table and awaited my response.

Again, I laughed. "She's done nothing that would warrant me not trusting her. Do you know of anything?" I asked Dora, placing her on the spot.

"Just keep your eyes open, honey." Dora sipped from her cup.

"I've been a wife for twenty-eight years and a woman knows another woman and can sense when something's funny. People don't respect people anymore or what they're trying to have. They'll smile in your face as long as you're standing at their side and be tugging on your mans' belt buckle the moment you leave the room."

"I'll keep a lookout, thanks."

Entering the sanctuary, the second, third, and fourth rows were packed with men uniformly dressed—making quite a presence.

"OK," I said, turning and smiling at Dora.

"Are these your Deacons?"

"No, they're members of the EBLC. They always show up to support the anniversaries of those in their membership. EBLC: Empowered Brotherhood of Lexington Council. The voice of the community," Dora said looking perplexed that I didn't recognize the most prestigious African American group in which my husband was a member. Nonetheless, I welcomed each of them, downplaying my lack of knowledge.

"Nice turnout," I said to change the subject while observing folks being ushered to folded chairs placed in the aisle.

It was times like these when I enjoyed being the pastor's wife; seeing familiar faces, being in the midst when the full choir sang in unison, and of course, celebrating the man of God. But things were different, the church and my marriage were different. Though I smiled and embraced folks with warm hugs of love, my heart was full of resentment and hatred. And when casting my eyes upon DeMarcus who stepped into the pulpit in a white double-breasted suit with red accessories, I was outraged!

"Doesn't he look nice?" whispered Dora.

I smiled then reached in my purse for my notepad.

All eyes were fixated on Evonne's and DeMarcus' matching attire. Side by side in the pulpit, they stood greeting the guests—looking like two peppermint sticks. Remaining silent and in my seat was hard, but keeping my composure was harder. I was embarrassed—perhaps paranoid, and unable to shake the feeling that everyone was looking at me and whispering. Returning to my seat after placing my offering in the collection plate, my eyes may have been shifted in the direction of the pulpit but my mind was elsewhere.

Thoughts of serving DeMarcus the same level of humiliation he had no issues serving me, became my sole focus.

Chapter 13

Truth Revealed

Arriving fifteen minutes early to work, all appeared gracious for the two dozen assorted doughnuts and eight cups of freshly brewed coffee I placed on the break room table. Grabbing a cup for myself, I started down the hallway toward my office but was summoned by Geo into his. No words were immediately exchanged but the expression upon his face was of pure dismay. I took a seat then sipped from my cup. In a solemn tone, he asked about my weekend.

"Better than yours apparently! What's going on?"

Placing my cup on the edge of his desk, I sat back in the chair and gave him my full attention. Geo shook his head and clenched his fists. He hesitated before informing me that Kim declined his offer to become roommates.

"I'm good to that woman and for all I do, she said, 'No.' What woman would turn down all I have to offer? She said she wanted a good man and here I am. It was because of her that I stopped running the streets. I even blocked the phone numbers of females who were longtime friends for her. I spoil her rotten! I take her where she wants to go and don't mind spending every penny in my pocket on her, because she's my girl. And every time we're together, I show her how much I care but now it's like she's pulling back, like she's tired of me."

Geo took a breath then asked if I thought it was another dude. He sat on the edge of his chair tapping his fingertips together awaiting a reply, but I didn't have one and nor did I want any further involvement in the woes of their relationship. Since introducing him and Kim, my relationship with her had also changed. Our two to three conversations per week were more like two to three times a month, if that often. And if she did have a secret lover and I knew about, I wouldn't betray her trust by divulging that info to Geo. His poor little heart would be crushed.

"I wouldn't give up so easy Geo. Kim's crazy about you, she's told me so several times. Moving in with somebody means giving up a piece of yourself and all your privacy. It just may be that you're ready to step things up and she's not."

I tried to be encouraging but no matter what I said, Geo had a rebuttal. Clearly, he sought definitive answers and not my opinion. Clueless as to what more I could say or possibly do, I offered to call Kim to get her take on things. Geo looked hopeful.

"Give me a hug," I said, rounding his desk. Like a child, I rubbed his back and assured him that everything would be alright. The hug lasted all of eight seconds, however, when I pulled back—out of the embrace, I turned and spotted DeMarcus in the doorway. I stood there speechless. Momentarily, my heart stopped. Caught off guard, I turned towards Geo, but he was too distraught with his own situation to recognize the one I had created for myself.

"Sorry to interrupt you two." DeMarcus handed me a newspaper.

"I've circled a few apartments I thought you might be interested in. If you get started this morning, you'll probably have two or three to look at by the end of the day. Get back to work though," he said with a smirk on his face and eyeing Geo as he exited.

"I'm sorry, Rosilyn. He looked pissed—I know what he's thinking."

"Oh, well," I said, shrugging my shoulders and shaking my head, not really caring what DeMarcus thought.

"Had he asked what was going on I may have told him the truth. But I've got my own issues and can't waste time worrying about his issues."

"I can see that. What's up with him bringing you a paper? Pastor or not, that's still your home and ain't no court in this world going to let you and your kids struggle while he lives happily ever after and mortgage-free. Get a restraining order, Rosilyn. Get it today! At the least, an order can give you up to six months to make provisions on securing a new place. They may even give you longer."

"I'm not worried," I smiled.

"I've found us a place and plan to clean up a little bit today and start moving my stuff in tomorrow. I just haven't told DeMarcus."

Joyful about my news, Geo momentarily pushed aside his issues to hone in on mine. Question after question he asked of how it came to be. Vaguely but to his satisfaction, I shared what I wanted him to know and kept the rest a mystery.

"It's not much, just a little house in need of a lot of work but it's mine and I can move in at any time. Other than purchasing office furniture and having the utilities turned on in my name, all I need is a welcome mat."

Having wasted the first hour of the day in Geo's office, I was anxious to get to my office and attend to my personal business. Turning on the computer and waiting for it to boot, I affixed a stamp to the envelope addressed to the EBLC and placed it in the outgoing mailbox. Ken the courier arrived around 10:10 and crammed my mail amongst the other mail in his big blue bag.

For a moment my heart pounded from nervousness, but it wasn't enough to reconsider bringing to light, DeMarcus's accounting practices to the attention of the head honcho and others trusting him with their finances. When Ken was no longer in my view, my nervousness subsided. I felt avenged. "One down," I uttered.

It was around noon when Geo entered my office, insistent on accompanying me to the bank and to the house. Against my better judgment, I agreed and allowed him to tag along.

Turning into the subdivision, he was full of compliments about the neighborhood I'd chosen. One inhale and an exhale later, he boldly asked how I would be able to afford the rent on the salary I get from the center.

"Child support and if that stops, my daddy," I chuckled.

Geo helped me unload boxes from my vehicle and when we finished, I gave him a tour of the entire house. However, there was little time to talk and being determined to accomplish something—anything, I led him into the kitchen where we washed the cupboards and scrubbed the grease splattered walls. Geo sanitized the bathroom while I washed down the bedroom windows and doors. Cleaning while listening to R&B music saved on his cell phone, after a short two hours, we put away the supplies and headed back to the office. I thanked him by paying for lunch.

Everyone was way too preoccupied with their cases and personal conversations to notice our return. Having no afternoon group session scheduled, my free time was spent contacting the various utility companies and having services connected in my name. By 4:00, I was out the door again to sign their documents. At 5:15, I was depositing $3,000 of DeMarcus's love money into my personal bank account to pay the $80 service fee securing a next day delivery of my furniture.

DeMarcus was exiting the house carrying two black trash bags as I walked up the paving.

I wasn't surprised that he didn't acknowledge my presence nor was I shocked when he failed to apologize for hitting my left knee with one of the bags. I laughed and shook my head behind his immature behaviors, then proceeded through the front door. I stopped in my tracks. A mountain of my belongings had been tossed in the center of the living room floor. I didn't ask him why; I didn't ask him anything. Instead of arguing, I took a deep breath and retrieved boxes from the garage, stuffing in them what I could. Nine trips it took back and forth to load the boxes and five trash bags of the kids and my clothing and shoes in the car, but I did it—all while DeMarcus watched. When I was done, he handed me a key.

"I found you and the kids a place over on 22nd Street. The deposit and first two months' rent have already been paid. It's ready for immediate move-in."

I found pure joy in handing the key back. Smiling hard, I thanked him for his concern and stunned him with my wonderful news.

"Thanks for looking out for us though. Dad helped me get a new place and I know we'll be fine."

"Where's it at? And how much is it going to cost me?"

"Other than paying support for your children, I think I can manage the bills with what I make."

"So that punk at your job is going to be taking care of you? You must think I'm stupid! I knew something was going on between yaw. Do what you want to do but keep him away from my kids."

"Don't start, DeMarcus! He's just my co-worker and you know it. But when I do start dating again," I said, rolling my eyes and neck, "That part of my life won't be any of your business. You're putting your family out. And you're the one who filed for divorce. Get real, DeMarcus! When I walk out of this door, it's for good and I'll be damned if you're gonna control what I do in my own home. This is what you wanted, so deal with it!"

Seeing the frustration mounting up in DeMarcus of my newfound independence, I thought it was best to leave his property before the situation escalated into yelling or a physical altercation. Hopeful that for the sake of our children our relationship would be cordial, it didn't take me long to conclude that with DeMarcus, cordial was impossible. As I walked toward the car, DeMarcus called me everything but my mother-given name. I laughed and in response yelled back, "Now that you've got what you wanted, can you handle what you got?"

Mixed emotions consumed me as I unloaded the car. Standing in the center of my empty living room, what should have been a happy moment for me— celebrating my freedom, wasn't. I missed my kids and I felt alone. *Alone is good,* I tried convincing myself before deciding to keep busy and decorate the bathroom.

A little past 10 o'clock and not having a bed or couch to sleep on, I grabbed my newly purchased laptop and an outfit for work the next day and drove to a nearby hotel. It wasn't the greatest hotel in the city—in fact, the outside grounds were much nicer than the inside living quarters. The curtains, barely hanging, were dingy and reeked of cigarette smoke and the putty patched bathroom walls gave me the creeps. If that wasn't enough, the multi-color, multi-pattern bedspread failed to hide the numerous spots and questionable stains I was quick to notice after reading the cleaning check-off list placed underneath three stale pieces of peppermint.

Quite cozy sitting at the equally as nasty desk, I passed the time browsing the internet and researching the area where I had moved. Out of habit, I logged into DeMarcus's accounts and viewed the newer messages. I was expecting to see the usual *'I wish I was with you'* email from Evonne or one in which she thanked DeMarcus for something he'd done or purchased for her but was sidetracked by an incoming email from G. Wesley. The subject line read: *Hello Rev and Ev.*

Opening the attachments gave me a glimpse of their Bahamas vacation. In the first photo, DeMarcus was wearing swim trunks and carrying a joyous Evonne who too was in her swim attire; the tiniest of tiny, two-piece bathing suit. The second photo was of them lip-locked in a passionate smooch. The last photo was of their shoulder blade tattoos. DeMarcus had a set of praying hands and Evonne's tattoo was an arrow shot through a heart. Inside the heart was the letter 'D.' I wasn't hurt or jealous, I was angry. I deleted the email.

Several days had passed since I had last spoken to DeMarcus and after literally being tossed out of the marital home, I had come to grips with our separation. Not once since pulling out of the driveway had he attempted to contact me, make certain that I indeed had a decent place for his children to stay, or offer up anything such as money or a canned good. But on the fifth day, a Wednesday night and after receiving three nasty grams via text, I dialed his phone hoping to put an end to his harassment.

"Keep it up here!" he answered.

"Until the divorce papers are signed and the ink is dry, if you want anything from me, you better stop embarrassing me and do what a pastor's wife is expected to do. Where were you tonight? Screwing around with your new lover? And when are my kids coming back? You sent them away so you could get your freak on all over town, I know you did. You're a horrible mother and personally, I don't think you're fit to care for them."

I almost cussed but caught myself. I laughed at his insecurities and his thoughts of being a better parent than me. I knew, and he also knew that being a full-time daddy would not only cramp his style but deprive him of his ho-ish freedoms. Concluding that his tantrum stemmed from my absence from Bible study, I informed him that our children were expected to return on Saturday but purposely kept him guessing about the rest.

"My sole focus now is to make sure my kids are happy. In the meantime, I'm gonna do me and if I so happen to meet another man, oh, well. I don't consider you or any other man more important than my kids but if you truly feel I'm unfit to care for them, pursue full custody. It's a brand new me and I look forward to dating, going out for a drink or two and hanging out with my new friends. We can share custody—you keep the kids January through May and I'll keep them June through December. We can alternate the holidays if you like. DeMarcus, it's all about the children, right?"

I know I sounded like a crazy woman, but I was pulling a ropey dope—testing his bark. And now having planted a seed in his mind of me being on a manhunt, there was no way he'd pursue full custody of our kids especially if it meant me gaining a little more freedom.

The conversation was quickly spiraling out of control but before I could end it, he reminded me of my role and responsibilities as his wife—despite the impending divorce. I could hear the frustration in his tone as I responded with short 'yes's and no's,' to his very long list of demands.

"We'll be there with bells on Sunday," I spoke with sarcasm.

The stress of the conversation led me out of the house and into the cheap wine aisle of a nearby liquor store. After returning to the house and popping the cork off the bottle, I carried the raspberry and melon concoction to my bedroom then grabbed my laptop from my nightstand. Propping my back against the headboard then downing a few gulps of the best-tasting off-brand, never heard of before, thirst-quenching adult beverage I'd ever had, I logged into my computer then created my first personal email account as WillowDee.

Copying photos from DeMarcus's private folder to place them into a folder on my desktop, I laughed aloud from the tons of crazy ideas that crossed my mind. Remembering being shown how to send photos as an attachment, I blocked my cell phone number and forwarded the full-body shot of Evonne in her birthday suit to Ashton, Sister Harlow's fifteen-year-old grandson. For nothing more than sheer evil, I attached a message which read:

For a youngster, you've got a body like a grown man. If you like what you see and want to see it in person, give me a call.

How this would play out, I wasn't for sure but what I did know—and with certainty was that by the end of the night, all of Ashton's school buddies and youth ministry friends would see it and know that Little Flock's Minister Evonne Delaney was an ole' school freak. I knew it was a low-down and dirty prank to play, but it gave me great pleasure anticipating the ruckus and humiliation this would cause. Chugging down a little more of my new favorite beverage, my focus shifted to DeMarcus who, in my opinion, was the blame for all the turmoil. In getting him back, I knew I had to be extremely careful because the stakes were high. My attack against him was personal. And whatever I decided to do—in terms of breaking him down, I had to ensure that nothing pointed back in my direction.

Resizing the May 2014 photo of DeMarcus and Evonne embraced in an intimate moment, I pasted it into a word document and after a little creativity, produced a flier soliciting interested parties to join them for a swinger's night out, recalling the strippers, swingers, and Saturday Night Sinners sermon DeMarcus preached two months prior. I could hardly contain my laughter when inserting their actual phone numbers at the bottom of the flier and adding the disclaimer:

Not responsible for STDs. BYOC, Bring Your Own Contraceptives.

I was pleased with my creativity.

After placing, '*For Your Congregation*' in the subject line, I attached the flier and sent it to everyone in his address book. The list included seven associate pastors of churches we frequently fellowshipped with and four members of the EBLC.

To familiarize myself more with swinging, I searched the world-wide-web and was led to a Swingers-Over-Forty site. Seconds later, I was directed to their membership page and with a huge smile, signed DeMarcus up to receive a yearly subscription. Bombarded by various pop ups of nude African American men, for kicks and giggles, I also signed him up to receive a yearly subscription of Down-Low Bro magazine, using the church's credit card information to secure payment and address for delivery.

To further link the expenditures and with Mother's Day the upcoming Sunday, I used the same credit card to purchase three bouquets of roses. The first bouquet I addressed to me. *Happy Mother's Day, I love you,* the card was to read. The second one addressed to Sister Harlow would read: *Happy Mother's Day. Thanks for all you do*! And the last bouquet addressed to Evonne would read: *To the love of my life. Flowers Just Because. Yours Truly, D.* Requesting a delivery time of noon-ish on Saturday, I knew that one of the nosey mother board members would receive the deliveries and read beyond the name on the envelope. Pleased with the damage I had stirred up; I closed my laptop and my eyes for the night.

Chapter 14

The Light in Darkness

With moving into my new home and everything else going on, sending out invitations to the senior mothers to remind them of their annual pre-Mother's Day brunch totally slipped my mind. Every year since being the first lady, I've graciously assisted DeMarcus in pulling this event together honoring basically the women who took care of him. This was his way of giving back—or rather, looking good in the eyes of the church for hosting an event solely honoring the aged and faithful. For this event, DeMarcus would charge the culinary ministry with preparing a meal so huge, little else besides their plates, cutlery, and cups would fit on the table. Afterward, he'd present each woman with a red, white, and yellow rose, symbolizing a beautiful heart, purity, and unmatched love, respectively. However, the big-to-do of the brunch was taking individual pictures with their pastor.

It was Friday night—way too late to send the invitations but early enough to apologize to DeMarcus for forgetting and inform him of my intent to call each woman personally and work through the night decorating the fellowship hall. Most importantly, I wanted to assure him that the food catered would be tasteful and meet his expectations, so I dialed Sundee Lee's Soul Food Restaurant. Having used them in the past for other church-related events, I knew that her crew would come through quickly and in a hurry—accompanied by a hefty fee for the last-minute request. But I wasn't troubled by the fee.

I planned on charging it to DeMarcus anyhow.

By 10:15, my three attempts to reach DeMarcus via home and cell phone were unsuccessful. Knowing he wasn't one to retire early on the weekend, I fell into a slightly mild depression suspecting that enjoying the company of another woman kept him from answering my calls. Shrugging off my thoughts and attempting to refocus my energy, when my curiosity wouldn't allow me to rest, I grabbed my purse and jumped in my car.

Approaching the church grounds, out of habit, I veered towards the house. Noticing both the living room and bedroom lights on and DeMarcus's car in the driveway, I continued towards the property but then quickly applied my brakes. Having second thoughts, I questioned whether showing up was a good idea.

It may have been my imagination or perhaps my bang that swayed across my face, but from where I sat idling, I swear I saw a woman's silhouette through the living room curtain. I contemplated using my key and busting up his freaky deaky party and ripping to shreds whoever was up in my ex-house with my soon to be ex-husband, but I quickly regrouped. I was better than that and kept it moving. Putting my car in reverse, I purposely parked on the far side of the church to avoid detection.

Walking through the sanctuary and retrieving two boxes of decorations from the upstairs storage closet, one by one I carried them down the steps and placed them in a chair outside the fellowship hall. Ready to start decorating, when I opened the door and flicked on the light, I expected to see a room in disarray. I let out a puzzling sigh seeing that the room had been eloquently decorated. Three long tables placed in the center of the room were covered with white, draped, table linen and teal accessories. Fresh gardenia flowers in tall, clear vases laced with silver and teal bows were placed on every other table and those in between were nicely decorated with floating water candle vases surrounded in greenery. Initially grateful for the work being completed, my gratefulness turned to anger knowing that DeMarcus had replaced me.

"Get over it. It's over. He's moved on and so should you," I said aloud, along with a few other things to keep me from getting more worked up. But I failed—I was heated, felt cheated and unneeded. And while pacing the floor talking to myself, I wondered if the woman who decorated the fellowship hall was redecorating my old house as well.

Crossing the hallway for the women's restroom, I couldn't help myself from peeking out the blinds and over towards the house. Just as I did, the living room light dimmed, and seconds later, so did the bedroom light. A part of me wanted to karate kick the door down and kick some azzes but I wasn't prepared to battle nor wanting to be jailed for trespassing or assault. In my gut, I sensed it was Evonne's skank azz who was rolling around in my old bed as if it were her own.

Feeling the onset of a panic attack, I leaned my back against the baby changing table affixed to the wall. Holding my head in my hands, I closed my eyes until my breathing returned to normal and the dizziness subsided. Exiting the bathroom then retrieving the extra set of keys to DeMarcus's office from his not-so-secret hiding spot, I entered his office and turned on the computer. He must have been proofing his personalized message: *A Message from the pastor* for the Mother's Day booklet, because when I logged in, jumping off the screen was his face plastered within the text.

Perusing through the booklet, comical best describes the handful of members and ministry leaders who purchased the $5, quarter of a page ads and the $10, half page, black and white ads wishing their loved ones, moms, and mother figures a Happy Mother's Day. But they weren't being stingy with their money, no. It was at the request of DeMarcus—stating cost as the reason, that no photo other than the First Family photo was to be printed in color. But this year and to my surprise, there was no family photo—just DeMarcus sitting on the edge of his desk, posing as if he was important. He was *Cat Daddy* sharp in the white on white suit and pink tie I bought for him two Easters prior. His desire to roll solo angered me a tiny bit. It was embarrassing knowing that I had been purposely excluded from the booklet. The more I tried calming my nerves the madder I became. Then creating my own pages came to mind.

Removing the clip art and text boxes from the music ministry's ad, from his personal email account I inserted a photo from DeMarcus's recent vacation; the one of Evonne sitting in his lap. I changed the caption to read: *Happy Mother's Day from Pastor Jackson and Associate Pastor Delaney: The Dynamic Duo*. Limited to printing only 22 copies before the color copier jammed, the ones successfully folded and stapled were mixed amongst the others in the box awaiting distribution.

Printing other personal photos from his file, by the time I reached the sanctuary I had strategically planned where each one would be placed. The first photo—a selfie taken by Evonne sitting up in a bed with DeMarcus visibly asleep in the background I placed on page 666 of Associate Pastor Henry Coleman's big letter Bible. Henry was everything all rolled into one: free labor, a yes man, and an overly generous tither—which probably was the reason he wasn't shuffled out the door like the other Associates when DeMarcus reorganized his pulpit. A little on the slow side however oddly intelligent, at one time, he and DeMarcus had grown so close, I thought he had become the new confidant; Jamal's replacement. But somewhere, somehow, there was a misunderstanding of sorts creating obvious tensions. Maybe it was a minor disagreement over preaching time DeMarcus rarely gave or perhaps a major argument over Evonne's sudden rise from pew member to associate minister. Who knows?

A second photo I slid in the pianists' hymn book. It was a semi-nude pic snapped of Evonne in DeMarcus's favorite necktie. I laughed aloud visualizing Jared's reaction to seeing his beloved pastor's involvement with the woman he so highly despised. It was just last summer during an open church meeting when the discussion of the expectations of a leader and members outside the church walls turned sour.

"If you're gay, everyone doesn't need to know it. A man in leadership wears a suit, not sequin T-shirts and he doesn't switch when he walks. Oh, and honey is a word used to describe what you want on your breakfast biscuit, not a term of endearment used by a man towards a man," Evonne barked, staring Jared dead on the eyeballs—all but calling him out by name.

No one mumbled a single word. Quietly, the leadership sat awaiting a reaction from Jared who simply lowered his head in humiliation after pretending to not be bothered by her remarks and waving her off with his hand. But her words toward him, they hurt me. 'What a bitch!' I thought as I stared her down with pure hatred and disgust when she waltzed from her seat and over to the water cooler and back. Crossing her legs, she attempted to move on to the next topic until I spoke up.

"Wait just a minute," I interrupted. "If what you say is true, then it goes both ways. I don't believe tearing someone down for being something you personally perceive as beneath you is being productive. If that's the case, what needs to be discussed next is how some of you," giving emphasis on *you* and staring down my nose at Evonne as she did Jared, "can sit up in the pulpit acting like a real woman of God but looking and acting more like a professional woman of the streets. To me, uncovered tattoos, exposed cleavage, and thighs ain't appropriate for a church leader. But it seems like some folks have talked a good game with their mouth and have gotten away with being common and worldly; or is that not the only thing they're doing with their mouth?"

DeMarcus was quick to intervene, shushing the chucklers and ending the sidebar conversations in hopes of getting the meeting back on track. And although Jared chose to not stand up for himself, I knew he appreciated me having his back.

I slid the third photo—a vacation pic of DeMarcus and Evonne in their swimwear and holding hands underneath the peppermint in the usher's visitor card basket. I wasn't sure who but knew that somebody was gonna see it then run to show another somebody. And lastly, the fourth photo—another vacay photo of the two in matching *I belong to him and her shirts*, I placed underneath the white sheets in the Nurse's Aide section. A senior mother, if not Sister Alice, would gather up the sheets before morning worship service unaware of the photo on the pew. Having done all of this, I was satisfied with what DeMarcus had coming.

After locking up the church, I sat in my car toying with the idea of sliding a photo or two in Evonne's husbands' mailbox. Before long, I was doing just that—parked two blocks away and attempting to fit into an unfamiliar neighborhood oddly active for this late hour. Within yards of the house, I inconspicuously stood behind a bush to check out my surroundings.

Noticing the porch light on and the front door ajar, I boldly walked up the walkway and knocked. After knocking a third time and receiving no response, I let myself in.

"I'll be right out, Evonne, just got to scrub this grime off me. I'm glad you stopped by," a man's voice yelled out.

I heard the shower curtain being pulled back then a rush of water streaming from the showerhead. I took a seat on the couch and placed my purse in my lap. Nervously I awaited his arrival. Only seconds had passed though, when I decided to give myself a quick tour of the house. Believing by his new song selection that time was on my side, I tiptoed into the bedroom and fumbled through the closets. There was no sign of a woman's presence anywhere.

When the sound of rushing water subsided, and the lyrics of his latest R&B tune became a soft hum, I froze. I was no longer interested in speaking with Evonne's husband. Quickly sliding one of the pics underneath his wallet on the dresser, I placed my purse strap over my shoulder with plans of vacating the premises. In doing so, my keys fell to the floor. Quickly retrieving them, when I lifted my head, I was spooked by a semi-naked man demanding to know what I was doing in his home.

"I, I, wasn't stealing," I blurted.

"Just leaving this photo for you and, and… I promise, I don't want no trouble, so I'll be leaving now."

He blocked my exit and I panicked. He nudged me into a corner—between the bed and his dresser, frightening me even more. Glancing at the photo, he tossed it onto the bed and laughed. He acknowledged knowing about their affair and stated not caring.

"I thought you looked familiar," he said showing all nine of his tobacco-stained teeth.

"You're the wife."

Scanning my body with his eyes made my skin crawl. I begged for him to keep his distance and allow me to inch around him to leave, but he laughed at my pleas.

"You're in my bedroom," I was reminded.

"And I can only come up with two reasons why that would be so. You already said you weren't here to steal which leads me to the only other reason you came by—to get back at your husband. A sister as fine as yourself wanna get with Big Willy? *Hee-he-he,* I ain't mad at ya', girl. Come on over here."

He dropped his towel and moved closer in my space. Although fresh from the shower, his breath and pores reeked of hard liquor. Leaping onto the bed in an attempt to escape, I was pulled down by my legs. His body was heavy as literally, he sat on my stomach. Fighting to be freed, I was eventually successful in pushing him onto the floor. Springing to my feet, again, he was just as quick and blocked the doorway and my exit. To him, our tussling was a game, but I was fighting for my life.

Promising to give me what he thought I came for, Mr. Delaney, Big Willy, Willy D, Yellow teeth, whatever his name, slurred his lewd intentions upon my capture. Spotting then grabbing a pocket knife from his dresser, I thought he'd take me seriously and back away, but he didn't. And what felt like an hour of threatening to slice his face, his arm, and if I could, his manhood was only a long, horrifying couple of minutes.

"That blade won't cut an orange," he said, but I couldn't tell. It was my only weapon and so far, was what kept him at bay. My arm had grown tired, but I continued pointing it at him and was almost successful in clearing a pathway to the doorway when he lunged at me. Reacting to his sudden movement caused me to lose my footing and the knife when I stumbled over the bath towel in the middle of the floor. Jerked up by the arm and flung onto the bed, we fought and tussled until we both landed on the floor. His head hit the floor hard. But despite his drunkenness, his strength surprisingly overpowered mine.

Binding together my wrists with his left hand, with his right hand he tugged at and unzipped my pants. Turning my head towards the door, I screamed from the top of my lungs in hopes of someone—anyone hearing me. It was then that from the corner of my eye I spotted the knife underneath the chair and pretended to surrender. I allowed him to lift my shirt midway before asking for a pillow to prop my head. I was surprised that he fell for it…the pillow thing, but he did. And when he turned his body and reached up for the pillow, I managed to scoot my body back just enough to grab the knife. Clutching it tightly, I turned with quickness and jabbed it into his chest. He didn't flinch, just stared at me in disbelief. It wasn't until I removed my hand and blood spattered everywhere that I realized the magnitude of the situation.

Perhaps shock prevented him from speaking or coming after me when on my elbows, I crawled from beneath him. I needed to get out of there and once on my feet, I grabbed my purse and keys. I was slowing inching backward—towards the door, keeping my eyes on him when his eyes shifted up from his chest unto me. Although wounded, he rose to his feet and attempted to pursue me and in doing so, entangled his feet in the bath towel falling face-first to the floor. His grunt was faint when the knife lodged even deeper inside his chest. It was a horrific sight; witnessing this in real life but even more so, being involved.

As he lay still on the floor, I wanted to check his pulse but stood numb and in silence. Uncertain of whether he was breathing, my initial thought was to help him; roll him onto his side but then fear led me into the living room. Assuming that since no one had come to my aid my screams were unheard, I looked back into the bedroom and begged his forgiveness. Wiping my prints from the doorknob with the sleeve of my jacket and turning the porch light off with my left elbow, I lowered the screen door handle with my purse strap then exited through the front door.

After a long sleepless night and paranoia, holding my children in my arms the next morning made everything that was terribly wrong, feel somewhat better. Dad took notice of my bloodshot eyes which I jokingly chalked up to being the long hours I spent washing walls with strong cleaning supplies, but only I knew the truth.

Guessing that Dad was tired from the drive, it didn't take much convincing for him to rest up in the den and in front of a 64-inch television until I returned from the Mother's Day brunch. I was grateful too that Auntie and Tay-Tay, her great-grandchild came along. The kids had their cousin to play with and I knew that Auntie would make sure everyone was fed.

Pulling into the church lot around 10ish, it was hard taking my eyes off VJ, the high-yellow, stocky build, ridiculously sexy, goatee wearing brother washing the church van. He knew his azz was fine too—showing off his nice firm abs as he approached the car.

"What are you doing here so early?" he asked. "You forget something?"

Staring him directly on the eyeball to avoid being sidetracked by the baby fine hair covering his chest that ran down below his navel and into his unbuttoned, stone-washed jeans, I cleared my throat and shared being there to receive the food delivery.

"Food for the Amarant wedding reception? That's not until 4:00 this evening. If it's for the Mother's Day brunch, well, the pastor called everybody last night and said it was being held at the all-you-can-eat buffet on Ralston Street. I'm surprised you didn't know that," he laughed.

"Minister Evonne and a few of the others left about an hour ago with table decorations and whatnots."

Watching his strong hands wring out a wet towel, "You're looking mighty pretty Sister Rosilyn," snapped me back to reality.

Instead of engaging in small talk, I thanked him for the information, smiled and excused myself. Driving across the lot, I parked my car in the driveway of my ex-house then approached my ex-door. Before I could knock, DeMarcus had flung the interior door open and was posted up behind the locked storm glass door with his arms folded across his chest. He appeared angered to see me—this I concluded from his squinted eyes and swollen jaws.

"The kids are back," I said.

"Is that why you're on my doorstep? Well, where are they?" he asked, unlocking the storm door and stepping onto the porch in his boxers. He looked over my shoulder and towards the car.

"They're at the house, DeMarcus, with my dad. Just let me know when you want to see them and…"

DeMarcus laughed. He looked me up and down as if I was on his doorstep begging for a crumb.

"Why are you really here, Roz? You don't live here anymore, remember? I bet you're here to see if someone's inside. Am I right?"

His laugh sent a sharp pain through my left butt cheek.

"I was coming to help out with the Mother's Day brunch but was just informed of your plans to host it elsewhere this year. Arrangements were made to have the food catered and had you answered your phone last night, I could have told you that."

"I don't have to answer my phone if I don't want to. Look-a-here, I think you're confused about this, this separation thing. All I need you to do until everything is finalized is to show up and pretend to be a loving and supportive wife. It ain't nobody's business as to what's going on between us, and if anyone asks, change the subject. I really think this is best until its official, you know. You do you and I'll do me—it's that simple. And as for you just showing up on my doorstep, I'm not breaking down your door to see who's behind it so give me that same respect. Unless you've got my kids and I have invited the three of you over, call or text me when you need something. I ain't trying to be mean Roz. I just feel that this is an amicable solution for us both. See you tomorrow."

DeMarcus closed the door in my face. Thoughts of kicking it in with my foot seemed appropriate but that's exactly what he expected me to do—make a fool out of myself. *Wrong answer!* He'd successfully touched my last good nerve, but I wasn't giving him the satisfaction of knowing that.

Mother's Day 2016, I woke up sad and with feelings of emptiness. Had it not been for the toys Lil D kept dropping onto my hardwood floors and DeMarya squabbling with her cousin in her bedroom, I probably would have stayed in bed with my head covered the entire morning. The previous night was an awful night. I heard the voices of my neighbors to the right arguing and jumped every time I thought I heard someone call my name. Dad had settled down in the den—this I knew by the television's loud volume. I was grateful he decided to stay another night with this being our first Mother's Day without Ma, neither one of us wanted to be alone.

Walking into the kitchen, Dad had a wonderful breakfast awaiting me on the stove along with a bouquet of assorted flowers on the counter. It didn't bother me that everyone else had eaten or that my steak, eggs, and toast were cold. My heart was heavy, and my thoughts were cluttered. Physically exhausted and mentally on edge, a true gift would have been if they all just disappeared and left me to sort through my issues. Closing my eyes to pray over my meal, I became distracted by the voices outside my door. I peeped out the window.

"There she is," Dad said, summonsing me out to be introduced to my neighbors.

"Tony and Lisa, this is my daughter Rosilyn."

The last thing I wanted to do was to socialize but for the sake of being a friendly neighbor, I affixed a welcoming smile upon my face and appeared interested in getting to know them better. While Dad and Tony discussed the neighborhood, Lisa and I discussed our children. And although our conversation was brief, I learned that Lisa managed a storage facility second shift and Tony was the stay-at-home parent for their three-month-old son, Antonio Junior. Lisa's teenage daughter, Ree-Ree, provided neighborhood babysitting services.

Seemingly a nice couple, I wasn't offended when Lisa excused herself to dress for church as I too needed to shower and get dressed.

Kim was the first person I saw when entering the sanctuary. I wasn't aware she was in town, but it was certainly good to see her. She hugged me and asked how I was doing—this being my first motherless Mother's Day. Shrugging my shoulders, I replied that I was good, "considering."

"And how are you? It's been nearly a month since we last talked. So much has happened, you're gonna have to spend the night at the house so we can catch up."

"DeMarcus told me about your new place. Good for you. I'm happy that things are starting to look up for you."

"DeMarcus? You mean Geo? Where is he anyway?"

"He swore he was coming," Kim said, looking perplexed. Seconds later she clutched her cell phone and fumbled through it as if checking for a missed call or text message.

Barely surviving on tired energy, when morning worship began, DeMarcus called me to the front to assist him in presenting a rose to the mothers in the congregation. I faked a smile and took my place at his side.

Fifty or more women nearly toppled over one another when instructed by DeMarcus to make their way toward the front for their rose. The line reminded

161

me of a cheese line; no one was giving up their spot or allowing anyone to jump ahead of them—not even the elderly. Some ran while others walked quickly as if there wouldn't be enough to go around.

As he always did, DeMarcus made a big-to-do about this day, stating the appropriateness of pausing worship to honor our mothers in the church house. And when everyone seemed to have simmered down, one by one I began handing him a rose which he personally presented to each mother; followed by a hug and a brief pleasantry.

"And lastly," he said. "Everyone knows that my wife recently lost her mom. Losing a loved one is never easy but we all must understand that death is a part of life. Baby, I know it's been hard—it's been hard for us all. But I wanted to tell you in front of the entire congregation that in my eyes, you are the greatest mother ever."

Mother what? I could read through his bull-crap!

The congregation applauded as if I had done something spectacular. DeMarcus was laying it on thick, but I played along anyhow. Handing me a dozen red roses and a gift card for a full body massage, the congregation erupted into cheers when I touched his face and planted a soft kiss on his lips. Making my way back to my seat, Deacon Hall approached the pulpit with a special announcement.

"We're not through yet. Pastor's been so busy, he almost forgot about the roses in his office. From the back door, Deacon Moyler entered carrying two bouquets and Deacon Collins carried a third. Wide-eyed and sitting on the edge of my seat, I smiled at DeMarcus who too was smiling as he returned to the podium."

"To my lovely wife," he said.

"These are just for being you." Deacon Collins handed me my bouquet.

"And to Mother Harlow, has she not been holding it down in the office?" he said with enthusiasm.

"I didn't have to ask her for help, she just stepped right in and took over. She's responsible for printing these lovely programs. Love you, Mother Harlow and I thank you for all you do. Happy Mother's Day."

Deacon Moyler walked the bouquet to her pew.

"And this one is for…" DeMarcus paused.

"Evonne?"

It was obvious that he too was caught off guard but nonetheless, he smiled as she walked across the pulpit to collect her bouquet. Members shrugged their shoulders and nodded their heads.

"These are from the leadership, we say, thank you. You've worked so tirelessly behind the scenes and we all just wanted to honor you for being so faithful. Can I get an AMEN?"

As if it was scripted, instantaneously, folks throughout the sanctuary began whispering amongst themselves. My best guess was that someone had obtained a *'special edition'* program and found its contents more interesting than the information being shared from the pulpit. Pretending to be distracted by the noise, I looked over my shoulder and was amazed to see everyone, including Kim, staring at me as if I had a third eye on my forehead or something, but I knew the real reason they were staring. So, after smiling back at them, I focused my attention on the activities in the pulpit.

"In honor of our mothers, turn your Bibles to Ephesians 6: 1-3 and read along with me," said Associate Minister Henry Coleman. He placed his Bible on the podium and began flipping through the pages. Finally reaching the scripture, or so I thought, when he paused, looked back at DeMarcus and then over to Evonne, I knew exactly why. A tiny smile formed on my face as I rose to my feet with my Bible in hand. Upon Henry's face was disgust. However, instead of letting on, Minister Coleman led us in reciting the congregational scripture then closed his Bible.

Clutching it tightly as he returned to his seat, he loosened his necktie and loudly cleared his throat.

The sanctuary was unbelievably loud and it didn't stop when Jared began playing the piano either. The rowdiness reminded me of being in the stands of a high school pep rally than being inside a holy temple with worshippers. When the choir members rose to their feet and began singing its first selection, it seemed to calm folks down a tad bit. It was one of DeMarcus's favorite songs and unfazed by the noise, he too rose to his feet and began waving his hands. Shortly thereafter, ministry leaders in the pulpit, as well as a few lay members, joined him in worshipping our Lord through song.

In my opinion, Jared was the best piano player in Kentucky. Excellent in selecting songs to compliment the message of the day, he was awesome as well in setting the atmosphere for every aspect of worship—whether it was a fast-paced celebratory selection, or a softer selection designed to bring reflection. At the end of the first song, Jared played right into the second selection. Watching as he turned the page of his hymnal, all eyes shifted towards him when the music abruptly stopped.

Jared nearly fell off the piano bench when he jumped away from the piano and shouted, "Oh Lord!"

Something had definitely caught him by surprise too and to call his reaction simply less than comical would be a true understatement. To over dramatize—become a drama queen/drama momma was totally in character for Jared, but the high-pitched squeal and the sashay as he returned to the piano is what got folks to speculate about the cause. But only he and I knew the truth. In unison, people—to include myself, laughed aloud. Jared quickly regrouped and resumed playing. Jared's over-the-top enthusiasm had indeed affected the atmosphere and when DeMarcus approached the pulpit, he disguised his bewilderment with a chuckle. When he opened his mouth to speak, the sanctuary grew quiet.

"When I woke up this morning, I knew it was going to be a good day. I knew walking into this sanctuary that there would be an atmosphere of love and joy. I am very excited about this day. You see, today is the day when the world recognizes momma, big momma, little momma, my momma, and your momma. Amen."

Folks' eyes were glued to DeMarcus as if he was about to perform a magic trick from the pulpit—and they didn't want to miss it. He had everyone's attention and although in some cases that was the norm, it was unusually odd—even to me, that none of the leadership were in position. The ushers weren't ushering, nor were the designated Deacons at their posts. But Sister Harlow rising from her pew and calling Ministers Maloney and Coleman out of the pulpit and behind closed doors caused a rash of whispers from the congregation and concern to DeMarcus. He looked at me, but I shrugged my shoulders and pretended to not know what was going on. But seconds later when Minister Maloney returned to the pulpit and Deacon Moyler took his post at the back door, DeMarcus appeared to be at ease and continued with his message. However, he rushed through his Mother's Day message and after shouting out a few bars of a song entitled, "A Momma's Love for Her Child," he signaled for Evonne to conduct the benediction.

When morning worship was dismissed, I grabbed my purse and turned around in search of Kim. I was miffed by her rushing off without saying goodbye, but figured she had a good reason for doing so, Geo.

As Kim raced out the door, it was like everyone else raced toward me. At least twenty-five women had flocked around me like I had promised them something immediately after service. A few of those gathered around me began whispering amongst themselves while others stood around with peculiar smiles upon their faces. But the bolder ones—the troublemakers stood with their arms crossed, waiting patiently as though I was holding a press conference. Nearly stumbling over one another to get to me, a few of them shouted out their questions while others awaited my response.

"Why you not in the pictures with the pastor?" one asked, while another had the audacity to ask why he'd given flowers to Evonne knowing that Evonne was childless. Smiling at those who meant well and ignoring the ones who were obviously attempting to stir up trouble, after wishing each of them a wonderful Mother's Day I begged their pardon. I was almost through DeMarcus's office door when I was greeted then stopped by Brother Davis. He was nervous in telling me that the pastor asked not to be disturbed by anyone.

"Pastor needed to meet with some people and I know you're not just anybody, but he…"

"Don't worry, Brother Davis, he's handling church business," I said with a smile.

"Please, wish your wife a wonderful Mother's Day from me, OK."

Chapter 15

Reaping and Sowing

It was another sleepless night and as I laid in the bed looking at the ceiling, visions of Mr. Delaney and the blood spewing from his chest consumed my thoughts. Ever so vivid were the events of when I entered his house, fought to keep from being raped, and protected myself against my attacker with a knife. The constant flashbacks were horrific.

Convincing myself to get up and keep busy, every hour on the hour was spent searching news channels for coverage of a break-in and assault only to discover nothing. Mr. Delaney knew who I was despite his drunkenness. And believing that at any moment, the police or the S.W.A.T team with big automatic machine guns would bust down my door to arrest little ole' me, sent me into a deep state of paranoia. I had never seen the inside of a jail cell and it truly wasn't on my list of things to do in my future.

Persuading myself to get dressed, after dropping the kids off at their new daycare center, I stopped for coffee and headed into the building though I really wanted to use a sick day. Swallowing two aspirin before entering the building, I convinced myself that everything was going to be fine and put on a happy face. It was still early yet and with the hallways quiet, I took the opportunity to close my eyes and collect my thoughts behind closed doors. At 8:08, Geo's entrance disrupted my peace.

"You look awful," Geo said, plopping down in a chair.

"Good morning to you too," I said, removing lip gloss from my purse remembering that I hadn't fixed my morning face.

"Lip gloss ain't gonna fix that. Did Mother's Day stress you out? Party too hard, what?"

"I'm just tired. The kids are back and I'm still fixing up the house. It's hard being a single mother and running a household. I missed you yesterday," I blurted, shifting the focus off me.

"What did I miss?"

"Church, you fool! Kim said that you two were meeting up yesterday. I looked around but didn't see you."

"Kim lied to you. As a matter of fact, Kim's one big liar! I haven't talked to her in over three weeks and why she'd tell you that, I don't know. She hasn't returned any of my calls or texts and honestly, I don't care if I ever talk to her again."

I laughed. "Aww, you're just bitter. You don't really mean that. Kim probably got scared when you asked her to give up her freedom."

"Whatever the reason, I'm not chasing her down. But one thing's for certain, she's not gonna find another brother like me. I gave her the world, but I guess that wasn't enough. Next!"

"I'm sorry to hear that G, you two made a good couple. I guess that's what people said about me and DeMarcus too. But things change. And sometimes, we never fully understand the reasons why they changed."

"What's up with you and Jamal? I thought you two were working on something."

"Jamal is the typical man who says he wants something but does nothing to get it. Yeah, he and my soon-to-be-ex were friends, but he expressed an interest in me. We got together a few times and that was that. Maybe I'm not his type. Maybe he just wanted a sip of my cocoa—not the whole cup. Really, I don't know what happened, but I've got too much going on to let him stress me. We cool though, I guess. Hold that thought," I told Geo, swirling around in my chair to answer the desk phone. It was DeMarcus—the last person I wanted to hear from.

"Good morning. I didn't get a chance to thank you for the roses."

DeMarcus was straight to the point. He asked if I had been running my mouth to anyone or if I'd been questioned about our marriage, or heard rumors negative in nature about him or his leadership.

Responding that no one had, I questioned why anyone would.

"Just something someone said," he vaguely replied.

"Apparently, a lay member is upset about something and now she's spreading malicious rumors, being petty."

"You know, ain't nobody gonna be bold enough and say anything negative to me because they know I'll bring it right to you. What's the rumor about, may I ask? If it's about Evonne getting flowers, it's nothing to get bent out of shape over. I didn't. Those who serve, deserve to be recognized."

"That's all I was calling for." DeMarcus ended the call.

Geo was deep into my conversation when I spun my chair back around. He appeared to be waiting on a full rundown of my conversation with DeMarcus but instead of allowing him to get all-up-in my business, I offered to treat him to lunch as an early birthday present. Taking me up on the offer, by noon we were walking into Damon's, a new barbeque restaurant he'd chosen.

Barbeque chicken or beef ribs with two sides and a drink was their lunch special. After placing our order, we got deep into a conversation about relationships. Sharing that living alone and doing things on my own was challenging, I admitted to enjoying the single life and had no urgency for a mate whether it be Jamal or someone else. Geo on the other hand, obviously bruised and still angered by being dumped, verbalized his plans to be the player he used to be.

"Women don't want to be loved; they want to be dogged. Yaw love being on an emotional roller coaster."

I disagreed but no matter what I said, I couldn't change his mindset so eventually, I stopped trying and stared down at the sloppy, mouthwatering spare ribs, baked macaroni, and collard greens with a hunk of fat on my plate. Licking the sauce off my fingertips and wiping the corners of my mouth with my tongue, I pretended like it was no big deal when Jamal appeared. Removing my purse from the chair to my right and hanging it on the back of my chair, I invited him to have a seat.

"It's good seeing you," he said, taking my right hand and kissing it.

"Hand sanitizer, please, somebody!" I yelled, looking around the room.

"Everybody got jokes," he said, shaking his head.

"I don't know where your lips have been, and I don't want nobody's cooties!" Geo chuckled then excused himself.

Jamal grabbed one of my ribs and put it in his mouth before I could snatch it back. He moaned in delight.

"Oh, this is good. So, is this what I gotta do to get to see you? You haven't returned my calls or responded to any of my text messages. If it's another man, I understand. If you're ticked off at me, you shouldn't be. I've been busy with seminary classes and working ten hours a day. But I have been trying to reach you, for real."

I knew that he had and for no other reason than going through what I was going through, there was no real-good reason I could give for not responding.

Dressed from head to toe in all black and sporting a fresh, closely shaven and well-trimmed goatee, I was completely turned on. The scent of his cologne was driving me wild as well, but it wasn't until his shoulder brushed against my shoulder that internally, I melted. I laughed it off then informed him of my new residence.

"Yeah, I heard it through the grapevine. I'm still waiting for my invite but in the meantime, do you have everything you need? I mean a bed, sofa, and table?"

"I'm straight, thank goodness for having a few bucks stashed away though. DeMarcus packed our clothes and the kids' toys and sent us on our way. God has blessed me though, so yeah, we're in good shape."

Jamal dropped his napkin. "Are you kidding me? When I last talked to DeMarcus, he made it seem as if you left on your own. His words exactly were that when he came home, everything but the living room furniture was removed."

"And you believed him? You knew almost everything that was going on, come on now Jamal."

"So, do you think he's still kicking it with Evonne?"

"Do I think?" I repeated, cocking my head to the side and stopping short of divulging what I knew and how I came to know it.

"If it's not her, it's someone else. What else can make a married man lose his mind, disrespect his wife, and with a clear conscience, sit his wife and their kids out on the curb?"

Engaged in the conversation with Jamal, I had almost forgotten that I was on lunch break until a giddy Geo returned to the table. He had a devilish grin upon his face.

"See that chick over there?" He pointed toward the huge bay window.

"She's 28 years old and looking for a man to take care of. I gave her my digits and in four to five hours, that halter top she's barely wearing will be hanging on my bedroom door knob."

Jamal shook his head.

"Be careful what you ask for. You heard about that man they found over in Hillview Estates the other night, didn't you? Some woman pierced his heart with a knife and left him to bleed to death in his own home. Boobalicious Boneka over there may be who the police are searching for," he laughed.

"What man?" I asked. My heart skipped a beat. I dabbed my forehead with my paper towel as suddenly, the room got uncomfortably warm.

"They haven't released a name yet, but they want to question the woman a neighbor saw going in and coming out of the house. It's nobody famous so I doubt if we hear much more about it."

"Well," I said, rising to my feet and looking at my watch.

"We need to get back Geo. Good seeing you, Jamal." Jamal stood up as well and pulled me in for a hug. He told me he'd call me later.

"So answer your phone!"

I promised to answer and waved goodbye. I nearly trampled over Geo to get outside for air.

Back at my desk, I searched the internet and the local news sources for recent murders. Locating the article, my blood pressure escalated at the description of the woman they sought to question; petite in build, wearing a red hooded shirt and denim jeans. A witness said the woman drove away in a dark, four-door Toyota or Ford. Although the description was vague and fit a gazillion people, it didn't make me less nervous or jittery. Nor did it have me considering turning myself in. It was an accident!

Twisting off the top of my bottled water then taking a long sip, I flung my feet up on the desk and prayed that Geo wouldn't invade my space while I tried to relax and collect my thoughts. *Wishful thinking.* No sooner than I had laid back my head, he walked in to inform me of a gentleman requesting to see me. Taking a moment to check my hairdo and lipstick, I proceeded toward the lobby and introduced myself. The gentleman was petite with a rugged-edge shave. He wore dark pants and a suit coat to match. Believing he was a detective coming for me, my knees buckled and slowed became my footsteps.

"Mrs. Jackson?"

"Yes, how can I help you?"

"You've been served."

I watched the gentleman walk away and could feel the eyes of Geo and others upon me.

Grateful that it was not who I thought it was didn't lessen the humiliation of being served divorce papers on my job.

"No, he didn't!" screamed Geo. "He just doesn't know when to stop, does he?"

Reviewing the contents in private, it wasn't a shocker that DeMarcus was seeking full custody of the kids, a waiver of paying child support, and the 2014 Range Rover initially purchased for me but kept for himself. Had it not been utterly ridiculous, I would have laughed at the redundant piece of paper characterizing my many years as his wife and mother to his children as meaningless. But I knew what he was doing—having absorbed the stories told by women of the center of the tactics men use when trying to gain or maintain control. Refusing to consume myself with his nonsense, I placed the letter in my purse to deal with later.

May 19, 2016 had proven to be another stressful day. After warming up leftovers from the day before of a crockpot roast, sweet potatoes, and cabbage, I crawled into the tent with my kids and played cards, dolls, and a big momma monster until we wore ourselves down. Still very much in need of a distraction from all my personal issues, after filling my glass with my new favorite raspberry and melon concoction, I dimmed the lights and plopped down on the couch. Grabbing the universal remote that was on the coffee table, I powered on my cd system and played a cd I borrowed months back from Geo. The volume was low. Checking my cell phone for missed calls, I smiled seeing that both were from Jamal.

"I'm sorry I missed your call, I was playing with the kids. If this is not a good time, you can call me back."

"I want to see you. I need to see you. Just tell me where you are and we can…"

"My kids are home, Jamal. They're still asking about DeMarcus. I don't want to confuse them anymore than what they already are. You can understand that, can't you?"

"We need to talk, Rosilyn. And as much as I'd like to make this a personal visit, there's something I need to share with you but not over the phone."

I gave Jamal my address and hurried into the shower to saturate my body in a new black orchard scented body wash. Slipping on my purple, silk shirt and matching shorts pajama set, I brushed my hair over to the side. Hearing Tony and Lisa who were enjoying the night air on their front porch, I decided

171

it was best to text Jamal and ask him to pull into the garage when he arrived. He arrived at 11:17 pm and after giving him a brief tour of the house with the exception of the bedrooms, we rested in the den. I offered him something to drink.

"Water, juice, or sweet tea? I'm drinking wine."

"When did you start drinking?"

"When or why did I start is the question." We laughed.

"You have a nice spot. Are you renting or buying?"

"What's with all the questions? Are you on a spy mission for DeMarcus or something?"

"No, and I apologize for asking. It's a very nice house and I'm glad that you and the kids didn't end up in a bad neighborhood."

Revealing Dad's part in securing the house and not much else, I swore him to secrecy in keeping my location private. I then asked the purpose of his visit.

"Well, I'm not exactly sure how true it is, but I heard through a friend that DeMarcus is under investigation for theft. Apparently while going through their books, the EBLC discovered that DeMarcus has been using their funds to pay his personal expenses."

I asked a lot of questions that Jamal couldn't answer and seeing me consume myself with DeMarcus's issues, he pulled me into his arms and told me not to worry. We talked for several hours and though I don't recall drifting off, I felt safe in his arms. When Jamal's cell phone rang, I lifted my head from his chest. Watching him check the screen before answering, I joked about it being his girlfriend who was probably wondering why he wasn't at home.

"Yes," he said.

"OK, OK. I'll be there when I can."

"Short answers. It must have been your woman."

Turning to face me, Jamal explained that the caller was a caseworker. "DeMarcus is in jail. They asked if I would come down and bail him out."

"Damn," I blurted, appearing shocked but internally harboring mixed emotions.

"I really don't want to have anything to do with this. I mean, he and I aren't cool like we used to be. Surely his Deacons would be willing to pool their funds together to help get him out."

Resting upon his chest a few more hours, I woke him up just moments before waking the kids. It felt natural—sending him on his way with a long hug and kiss. Jamal smiled.

Sitting in my office at my desk, the softer side of me sympathized with DeMarcus but the angry and bitter side of me laughed at the P.I.M.P (*Pathetic, Insane, Manipulative, Pastor*), who once thought he was so high and mighty, and the slickest of all slicksters. DeMarcus had never received a speeding ticket but now he's behind bars like the misguided criminals often referenced in his sermons.

Staring up at the clock, it was almost lunchtime and I had yet to hear from Jamal who only hours before, offered to spring for lunch. I was looking forward to seeing him again and even more so to hear of DeMarcus's woes, but he wasn't answering his phone. Disappointed but not wanting to appear desperate, after reaching his voicemail a second time I called in a to-go order from the Chinese restaurant up the street.

The restaurant's lobby was packed but I proceeded toward the pickup window and gave my name. Swiping my bank card to pay for my purchase, I swiped it a second time after it declined. Certain of having at least $400 in my checking account, after a third decline, I quickly removed the emergency twenty-dollar bill from the secret compartment of my wallet. After grabbing my food and reaching the car, I called the bank. Four hundred thirty-three dollars and seventy-two cents exactly was my balance. Then the automated recording stated that the account had been frozen. *Frozen? Dang it, DeMarcus!*

It hadn't occurred to me until arriving back at work that if my personal accounts were frozen, so were the kids' college accounts and their Christmas club account I had recently opened. Luckily for me, none of DeMarcus's love money had been stashed in those accounts. The remaining bundles of green were nicely tucked away in the chair cushion inside my bedroom.

Ironically, the next morning and after walking through the centers' lobby, I was greeted by two FBI agents asking to speak to me in private. Inside my office, I responded to a multitude of questions regarding my marriage, my finances, DeMarcus's finances, among other things. Despite my constant pleas to be given information, not once did they divulge the purpose of their interview or whether they'd be returning. Portraying a woman completely dumbfounded, when the interview was over, I escorted them through the lobby and out the front door. Returning to my desk, I placed a call to DeMarcus.

"Answer your phone!" I screamed. "Two detectives just left my office questioning me about your finances, my finances, everything! They had obtained my payroll history from human resources and asked me to explain every single non-work-related deposit into my bank account. Whatever the hell you've gotten involved in, it ain't got nothing to do with me and I'd appreciate it if you would tell them that. I don't want to get wrapped up into your foolishness. I've got two kids depending on me so fix your mess and keep me out of it!"

It wasn't as bad as I made it seem, but still, I didn't need detectives, police officers, process servers, or anyone else showing up on my job arousing curious minds and drawing unwanted attention to myself. It was humiliating, to say the least, but more so it made me look unstable in a place where my mental stability was a requirement.

Every move I made I felt as though I was being watched. I'd become so paranoid that I began using my turn signal and making complete stops at corners whereas I would normally slow, roll, then go. I made certain too that if ever I was pulled over, my insurance cards and transfer papers were readily available. And just for GP, I shredded all the documents with Ma's name on it to prevent a cop or someone from suspecting the car was stolen.

Everything was happening so fast. While plotting against DeMarcus, never did it occur to me that I'd too suffer the consequences of my actions. I was innocent; *well kinda*. Beneath the flawless make-up, new wardrobe, and sexy hairdo, I was literally a walking basket case.

Taking a mini vacation was ideal but I didn't want to appear defeated. I decided to stand firm through my storm.

Three whole days had come and passed over before I tried contacting DeMarcus again. And when learning from Jamal that he had been released, I figured he was focused more on remaining free than caring about the needs of his children. I knew he didn't have any money, but that was beside the point. Regardless of his situation, he needed to be reminded that although we live in separate residences, he hadn't been pardoned from his parental obligations.

Jamal and I began conversing almost daily, and through him, I learned that the theft; stealing over $20,000 from EBLC funds—far from the $1,000 I initially thought it to be was the reason for DeMarcus's arrest. Jamal expressed his doubts that DeMarcus was solely responsible for all the unaccounted funds. He partly believed DeMarcus's claim that it was his predecessor, the now deceased 89-year old—half-blind, half-deaf bookkeeper no one was gutsy enough to ask to retire.

"It's a mess," I responded. "But when you do wrong it eventually catches up to you."

And that's exactly what Sister Harlow shared when she interrupted my lunch with an unexpected visit to my workplace.

"Hello, Sister Rosilyn. Let me get straight to the point." Sister Harlow helped herself to a chair to the right of my desk.

"We all love the pastor, but there's a rumor going around about you and the kids moving out. Now, everybody has their own spin on things—about what's going on but I wanna hear it from you, so I can put the confusion to rest. So, is it true baby? If it is, was it because you discovered what he was doing and didn't want any parts of it?"

I laughed, nearly choked on my sub sandwich. Had she not been meddling in my personal business, I may have found her no-nonsense, straight to the point, arrogant disposition comical, but I didn't. She was just downright indignant, as usual.

"It is nice to see you too Sister Harlow. How have you been?"

"Listen, Sister, several of us have been asked to give depositions tomorrow afternoon about the church's finances. As far as we can tell, the books are accurate, but we want to know your side of things. We've held a meeting and folks are questioning why you're working with the salary we pay your husband? We came to a consensus that it's more than enough to live comfortably. We're yaw having money problems, baby?"

"The pastor and I were having some marital problems, but it wasn't related to money."

"Well, does he have a gambling problem or a nasty drug habit he can't shake? Child, everybody but you know about his fling with Evonne."

"Huh?" *No, that old bitty didn't go there*!

"Sister Harlow, it's been nice talking to you now get out of my office." I pointed toward the door.

"And may God bless, even you!"

Chapter 16

Enter His Courts

Watching DeMarcus waltz through the same doors I did, was a shocker. In truth, my expectations were to see him handcuffed, shackled, sporting an orange jumper, and escorted in under the accompaniment of sheriffs. Eighty-eight days exactly it had been since his re-arrest but as he walked down the aisle with only one guard at his side, he appeared thinner, well-rested, and in good spirits. Having been found guilty and sentenced to five years of probation the month prior for embezzling funds from the EBLC, DeMarcus was now on trial—the primary suspect in the murder of William Delaney.

Smiling at those yelling their support and the others who shook his hands and offered words of encouragement, DeMarcus's demeanor spoke confidence—that is until completely breaking down when spotting an older couple sitting on the bench down from me. Moved by their embrace and the tears flowing from their eyes, it became obvious they were his family. Having only heard about his family and vaguely recalling the faces of the old photos in his possession, it was hard to decipher whether the woman he clung to was his biological mother or his often talked about favorite Aunt who spoiled him rotten as a kid. DeMarcus looked in my direction but didn't acknowledge my presence.

The court was called to order at 9 a.m. sharp. Seven men and five women of various ethnicities entered through a side door and filled the juror box. Seeing this, DeMarcus again was overcome with emotions and called out, "Ma!" In zero seconds flat, the petite woman ran to embrace him while many eyes, including mine, filled with tears. DeMarcus held her tight, even after repeatedly being instructed by the bailiff to break it up. Instantaneously, members of the congregation rose to their feet and formed a circle around the room. In unison, individual prayers for DeMarcus rang out. Witnessing the power of prayer overtake the lone bailiff who eventually accepted his defeat to regain control was amazing. Overcome with emotions from my own guilt, I prayed for his forgiveness—acknowledging that his only crime against me was infidelity.

Reaching for the hand of his mom as she made her way back to her seat, I handed her a tissue and properly introduced myself. Her stare was cold and full of hatred.

"You!" she yelled. "You're the reason my Markie is here! I told him not to marry you and see what happened? He tried to make a life for you, he stole for you, and now he's going away and you are divorcing him. Where is my grandchild? You don't deserve to be her mother!"

The room was quieter than a funeral home after hours. Stunned by her outburst, I was grateful when the courtroom doors opened and through them strolled Evonne, making a grand entrance. All eyes shifted from me onto her as she walked the aisle as if it was a New York City runway in a white, pin-striped pants suit.

When Evonne embraced DeMarcus's mother, I pretended to not be bothered by the fact that they already knew each other. Instead, I fumbled around in my purse for my cell phone and sent Jamal a good morning text. Moments later, the courtroom was called to order and the judge took his seat. The first order of business was alerting the spectators of the courtroom expectations.

"This is a courtroom, not an arena. Prayer is appropriate, but this is not a church. This is not a participatory forum so if any of you choose to verbalize your thoughts, you will not be heard but you will be escorted out. Please turn off all cell phones and recording devices. If one is detected or if it interrupts our proceedings, it will be confiscated, and you will be jailed. For your protection and mine, we have cameras throughout the courtroom."

Day one and day two were basically preliminary in nature; however, day three was the worst when evidence collected from the crime scene was introduced. Reports in the media of DeMarcus's admission that the keys found on the floor of Mr. Delaney's residence were indeed his had everyone questioning how they got there. DeMarcus repeatedly and adamantly denied ever being in their home.

For forty minutes or better, everyone attentively watched DeMarcus stumble over his words when questioned about his relationship with Evonne.

He downplayed their involvement with explanations that didn't make sense. DeMarcus portrayed a picture of *guilt*—perspiring profusely, wiping his forehead dry with his sleeve, and trembling like a crack head as he sipped water from a paper cup. However, after a brief recess to regroup was granted, DeMarcus returned to the stand with a different story and demeanor.

"Initially, it was a professional working relationship. Evonne and I—things just kind of happened. At one point when my wife and I were at odds about everything, well, I would confide in Evonne and she seemed to understand my reasoning. Evonne and I were good friends; she was available when my wife was not. It wasn't a serious relationship at all. We went out together a handful of times, to dinner and once to see a movie. We weren't in love, we were friends so there wasn't any reason for me to want to kill her husband."

Shushing the spectators when their whispers became loud and distracting, the judge banged his gavel and warned that further outbursts would result in a closed session. When I was called to the stand, anyone listening for a cotton ball to drop would have heard it.

Avoiding eye contact as I walked past DeMarcus, my focus became putting one heel in front of the other to prevent being further embarrassed by falling. After swearing-in and giving my full name, questions about my private life was put on public display. Twisting the truth a bit about when I actually learned of his affair, when asked if that was the reason for our impending divorce, I stated, "well kind of."

It appeared I had the sympathy of the jury when recalling various occasions of not so happy times in our marriage. And when the questions became harder, I pretended to be blindsided about almost everything.

"When DeMarcus became the pastor, he had a lot of new responsibilities placed on him. He was always in meetings, always being asked to speak at events, and people were always inviting him to be a part of their committee or organization. It mattered to DeMarcus what people thought of him and as his wife, I had to play my role to keep this new image of him up."

"What image?" I was asked by Defense Attorney Delcour.

"The first lady image, you know...walk around with a smile on my face even when there's nothing to smile about. I greeted folks with hugs as if welcoming them into my own home. The first lady is to be visible and I was. I supported my husband in everything he did as it related to church events. Things like that."

"Why would you do that?"

"Because that's what pastor wives' do? Why would I want to make my husband look bad in front of other people?"

"That's deception, isn't it? And please explain what a first lady is? If you're the first lady, what does that make him?"

"The first lady is a name given to a pastor's wife. Like the president of the United States, his wife is the first lady. Well, DeMarcus is the pastor of a Church and I was his first lady. Pastors are just pastors. They lead the flock, I mean, its members."

"You say that as if you two are some kind of royalty. Does leading the flock make him superior? If so, please explain how?"

"We were not royalty, but people sometimes treated us like we were. DeMarcus loved having people wait on him, but not me. I didn't care to have people all up in my business and doing things for me and him that I could do just fine myself."

"Can you explain a time where someone treated your husband like royalty?"

"Sure, every Tuesday and Saturday morning someone was there to cut the grass as if DeMarcus was handicapped. And when it snowed, before it could even stick to anything, there'd be four to five men outside shoveling it up. He had somebody running his clothes to and from the cleaners and he even had grown men on standby to wax his shoes."

"But that's a benefit to you as well isn't it? I mean, you don't have to run to the cleaners or shovel snow. That makes you two a royal couple?"

"No. I said earlier that we were not a royal couple, but people treated us as such. What people didn't realize is that we fought over things such as me being a shopaholic, him being a control freak, how to best discipline our kids and what to get at the grocery store just like other couples. Folks failed to realize that the man they put high up on a pedestal was pulled from the snatch just like we all were. His feet sweat and stink just like every man does, and he must wait in the checkout line to purchase toilet paper just like you and me. Don't get me wrong, I'm not trying to knock him down in any way, but DeMarcus is human. He's not royalty. He's a decent man but he has flaws."

Before adjourning the morning session, the judge instructed the jurors to return no later than 12:45. As folks began filing out of the courtroom, Sister Harlow pulled me to the side. "When everyone else turns their back on him, he'll come-a-running back to you, just watch. You'll see. But I don't believe he murdered her husband though. Willy was into the drugs, so it could have been a deal gone wrong," she concluded. "Keep the faith," she encouraged me, then clutching and tapping my hand before complying with the bailiff's instructions to exit the courtroom.

Walking opposite of the group huddled around DeMarcus and his folks, purposely I exited down the back stairwell to avoid detection. Once reaching my car parked on the lower level B, I took a deep breath before returning a missed call from Jamal. He responded via text that he was in a meeting but asked if I would secure us a table for lunch at the Mexican restaurant two blocks down from the courthouse.

"Thank God, you don't look like what you're going through," is how I was greeted. Jamal kissed my cheek. Taking Jamal's remark as a compliment, I smiled, though I always smiled when Jamal was near.

Sexy couldn't get any sexier than Jamal but to me, looks weren't what was important to me. I knew firsthand that he was full of crap like all the other single, well dressed, good-looking brothers with a little something-something going for themselves are. But I was happy with our friendship and occasional hump and bump sessions. Jamal inquired about the proceedings.

"I hadn't talked to DeMarcus since the day I picked him up from jail. He thanked me for the ride and got out of the car."

"Perhaps he's embarrassed. After all, you two used to be so close. Yaw were as thick as thieves once upon a time," I giggled.

"But he's taken that sentiment to a whole new level."

"Literally," laughed Jamal.

"But I don't think he did it. If anything, I think Evonne may have set him up. She could have been at the house and fighting with her husband when one thing led to another and she stabbed him. And to take the blame off her, she dropped the keys on purpose. My ex is a butthole but he's not a killer. But the way those attorneys kept twisting folks up with their questions, it's hard to say which way it will go."

Changing the subject, Jamal lightened the moment when sharing that Little Flock asked him to serve as their interim pastor until a new pastor was chosen. Happy for him, I encouraged him to accept it.

"This just may be your blessing. And Little Flock needs you. Nothing personal against Minister Coleman, but if they don't find somebody soon, he's going preach the members remaining right on out the door."

"I haven't decided yet. I prayed about it—just waiting on a sign from God. It's too much going on right now and I'm not sure if I want to step into that mess. And another thing, I don't trust the leadership in place, namely Evonne and Deacon Moyler."

Jamal asked about my kids and with excitement, I shared the good news of Lil D's acceptance into pre-school in the fall and of DeMarya's enrollment into Samantha's School of Dance.

"All she wants to do, all day long, is prance around the house in her pink, fluffy tutu and tap shoes. She's scratching up my hardwood floors."

It was good to laugh and to be in Jamal's company. But looking up to see DeMarcus's mother and entourage walking through the door, my smile disappeared as I sat back in my chair.

"What are you looking at?" Jamal turned to look for himself.

Spotting me as well, the petite woman left her party and approached our table.

"When will I be able to see my grandchild?"

"Mrs. Jackson, I am more than willing to discuss a date and time for you to visit the kids. I haven't kept DeMarcus from seeing them and nor will I keep you from meeting them, but not with that attitude."

"I want to meet my granddaughter. That bastard boy isn't his! My Markie told me so!"

"Excuse me?" Quickly rising to my feet caused my hip to bump the table. My glass of water fell to the floor. Jamal too jumped up and put distance between us when I promised—not threatened, to punch her in her mouth and clear across the room for talking such nonsense.

"He said you were crazy," she shouted. "You're a crazy lady! Crazy, crazy, crazy!"

"Your son has two kids, but you're the nutcase! And with your foul attitude, I don't want you around them!"

Restrained by Jamal when I lunged toward her 4'2", 280-pound, rounded frame which was charging toward me, over her own feet she toppled over unto a frail gentleman who was attempting to restrain her. As bystanders came to their aid, Jamal grabbed my jacket and my purse and suggested we leave. Yes,

I hated having displayed such a lack of control, but she crossed my '*no cross zone*' and pushed all my '*do not push*' buttons.

Once outside, I inhaled the cool air then placed my hands, then my head on top of the parking meter. My head began to throb, and my heart was racing. I was livid—fighting livid! Asking if I was alright, Jamal laughed when I raised my head and cut my eyes at him.

"Never let them see you sweat, sweetie. I know you're under a lot of stress, but you've got to let some things roll off your back. Are you OK?"

"Why would DeMarcus lie about Lil D being his son? He's the spitting image of him."

"Who knows why he says or does what he says or does? Rosilyn, no matter what comes your way, you've got to keep a cool head. You've got to be the bigger person. Things are getting ugly and I wouldn't be surprised if he's trying to set you up."

Jamal walked me to my car and opened the door for me. Before closing it, he leaned inside the car and kissed me softly on the cheek. Jamal assured me that I would be OK and told me to keep my head up. With forty-five minutes remaining before the proceedings were to resume, I drove to the office to calm my nerves and check emails. No sooner than I sat down in my chair, my cell phone buzzed. Certain it was Geo calling for details, I purposely ignored his call knowing it would be only a matter of minutes before he burst into my office anyhow. And he did, forty seconds later but he wasn't the caller. It was DeMarcus.

"Yes, DeMarcus. How can I help you?"

Yelling and screaming obscenities, it was apparent that the fiasco at the restaurant had gotten back to him. Unable to get a word in edgewise, I held the phone to my ear and when he stopped for a breath, I chimed in.

"Believe what you want but your mother approached me; she started the argument. And why are you denying being Junior's father? How dare you, DeMarcus?"

"Shut up, just shut up! All the hell I'm going through and you just keep making things worse. She wants to see both the kids, OK? Can you make it happen or will you be too busy with your new man friend—whoever it was you were dining with?"

"Hell, no, she's too angry to be around my kids. The three of us can meet to discuss it and clear the air, but otherwise, no! I don't give a damn about her being your mother! I'm not accommodating her when she clearly hates my very existence. She was cruel, mean, and nasty toward me and I will not allow that mean-spirited woman to be around my kids!"

"And now you know why I never introduced you to her. You're a bitch! Just wait, just wait, I'll get permanent custody and you'll be begging me to see them. Keep your distance from me, Rosilyn, I mean it! Stay away!"

Disconnecting the call before I could respond was typical of DeMarcus. Raising his voice and screaming at the top of his lungs was rare and only occurred when he felt he wasn't in control of a situation. But today, he had an audience to impress so it was quite likely that his child-like behavior was to appease his mother. *The nut didn't fall far from the tree.*

Sharing only tidbits of what I wanted Geo to know, it was then that he went into counseling mode and made me realize that DeMarcus was still playing games. I listened for a couple of minutes then asked for privacy to make an important call. When Geo closed the door, I grabbed my file of emails between DeMarcus and Evonne from my drawer—all acknowledging their love for one another and placed them, along with some photos, in an envelope. Purposely waiting until one o'clock before re-entering the courtroom, when no one was around, I slid the envelope underneath the office door of Prosecutor D. Druin.

Just as I was taking a seat in the rear of the courtroom, Evonne was being called to the stand. Interesting was hearing her speak of her husband as a loving man and a great provider. Other than belonging to the same church, she denied having anything more than a working relationship with DeMarcus, though admitting to daily communications via cell phone. Adding that despite their impending divorce, she and Mr. Delaney continued to be good friends and that moving into her own apartment had nothing to do with DeMarcus. She explained that it was her soon to be ex-husbands' involvement in drugs that caused her to fear her safety. Her story sounded believable—that it could have been a drug deal gone wrong, but the more questions she was asked, the more confusing became her answers.

Separating the truth from the lies was hard but as I sat amid the mayhem, it became evident that people viewed me as stupid. No one spoke those exact words, but it showed on their faces especially watching for my reactions when Evonne crumbled under cross-examination when forced to explain specific details related to her relationship with DeMarcus.

Long before the trial began, Geo asked what my purpose in attending was to represent. And as I sat on the hard courtroom bench being publicly humiliated in front of God and the world, I found myself still unable to provide an honest reply.

The afternoon session ended around 3:00 p.m. and instead of returning to the center to work the last two hours of the day, I decided to pick the kids up early since Dad and Auntie were coming to Lexington for them—volunteering to lighten my load until the trial was over. Picking up a quick meal of Chinese special lo mein, sweet and sour chicken, and a dish of beef and broccoli for dinner, it was just as I was setting out the plates that they walked through the door. Still at the table relaxing after finishing his meal, Dad expressed having second thoughts about leaving me alone; he was concerned for my safety. He offered to stay in Lexington with me, but I convinced him that I wasn't in any danger.

Lord knows, that as happy as I was to see them, I was even happier to see them go and when they finally backed out of the driveway, I poured myself a tall glass of wine and curled into a ball on the couch in the den. No sooner than I got comfy, my cell phone rang. It was Jamal offering to bring over dinner and a movie. Sharing that I had already eaten didn't detour him from wanting to come by. He was adamant about seeing me and stated that instead of bringing dinner, he would be bringing his wonderful conversation and a movie.

When Jamal arrived, I was stretched out on the couch having downed my third glass of wine. My mind and body were in a relaxed state. Grabbing my hands and lifting me onto my feet, he pulled me into his big arms and nearly smothered me with a hug. Whispering in my ear, Jamal prayed with me and encouraged me to stay strong. He promised to always be in my corner and stated that if I ever needed him, he was just a phone call away.

Every moment I was close to Jamal, I felt different. Different as in—I could be myself. And despite my curly naps that resembled an uncombed afro, he called me 'beautiful.' I trusted Jamal enough to share my deepest feelings and thoughts. But when it came to DeMarcus, each time I brought up his name or the trial, Jamal shushed me and would say, "Not tonight."

We never got around to putting in the movie for taking a fresh bottle of wine out to the back deck where we talked and enjoyed the nice cool breeze. We were both quite buzzed and enjoying ourselves—not at all worried about disturbing the neighbors with our laughter. But when a car pulled into my driveway, we froze. Hearing the cars' engine shut off and jumping up when the lights once shining brightly on the garage door faded, I pushed Jamal into the house and asked him to wait in the den. Placing our glasses in the sink and the bottles in the trash, I proceeded through the living room and opened the front door.

"I wasn't sure if you were home, not seeing your car in the driveway," DeMarcus said, brushing past me.

"What are you doing here and how did you find me?"

"Were you hiding?" he asked, staring me on the eyeball as if he had a right to know.

"The kids are not here if that's why you've come."

"Pretty nice house you've got here." DeMarcus gave himself a tour, opening doors and inspecting how we're living.

"And you've got a flat-screen television in every room. Silk sheets on your bed, hmmm. You're doing quite nice. So, where'd you get the money for all of this?"

"I work, DeMarcus. And Dad bought most of this stuff with the money from Ma's life insurance policy. Anything else? I've told you that the kids are not here!"

I followed him closely as he walked through the kitchen and into the den. He opened the door to my makeshift office and walked over to the basement door.

"What is it that you want?" I asked, slamming the basement door for fear that Jamal may have relocated there.

DeMarcus sat on my couch and continued looking around. I sat on an island barstool separating the den from the kitchen.

"I'm here for a couple of reasons. Yes, I miss my kids. Where are they?"

"They're with my dad, next question."

"Why do you keep putting them off on him? He's too old to do your babysitting. If you don't want them, I'll take them. My parents are here, and they want to meet them so either you go get them or have your poppa bring them back."

"The kids are good for my dad and besides, Auntie's great-grandchild Nikki, moved in with them last month, so they have somebody to play with. It's just until I get things straightened out, damn! They left about an hour ago so no, I'm not asking him to turn around just so you can see them. And why now does your mother want to play Granny, meet the kids—or shall I say, DeMarya? And how dare you lie about Lil D not being your son!"

He avoided my questions and again demanded that the kids be returned.

"So, you're just gonna run free and be buck wild? And what's up with the silk sheets?" I laughed. *My reason for purchasing silk sheets was none of his business.*

"DeMarcus, the kids are not here and it's late. I'm not in the mood to play twenty questions with you. I think it's time you leave."

"What's the rush? Were you busy? Expecting somebody? If so…?"

"Just tell me what you want DeMarcus. You're not the only one stressed these days, OK."

"What do you have to be stressed about? Look at ya'—living better now than you were when we were married."

"It's just Jesus," I remarked.

"What the hell is that supposed to mean?"

"I'm just saying that despite getting put out, caring for two kids on my own, paying monthly bills I never had to pay before which includes car insurance without any help, I'm just giving Jesus his props because none of this has been easy."

"Go ahead and gloat," he said. DeMarcus's tone grew louder with every word spoken.

"Yeah I'm down on my luck right now but things are going to start looking up for me. The devil is a liar, believe that! And I ain't killed anybody—you and the whole wide world know I didn't. Where these witnesses and evidence is coming from, I don't know. But I didn't know the man like that and Evonne, man…you can believe what you want to believe but I am telling you with my hand up to God that I ain't never even kissed that woman. Just because a man talks to a woman or a woman talks to a man, people assume they're kicking it. But that wasn't the case. She was having trouble with her husband and as her pastor, I counseled her. That's all it was."

Pacing the floor, DeMarcus continued pleading his case and I pretended to be interested. And after sharing everything on his mind, he asked for a reply. All I could offer was, "Keep your head up. It'll all work out."

"Is that all you've got to say? You're a part of this too! Everything that's done happened to me had something to do with you."

"What?"

186

"First it was the money—every dime I had, went into that house, on you and the kids. Those nice clothes you wore, everything. That jewelry I bought you—none of that was fake. And I may have written a check or two that I wasn't supposed to write, but you best believe that it was for something or someone under my roof. I've spent good money on you throughout the years."

"DeMarcus, where are you going with this?"

"I'm reminding you of how good I took care of you and now it's time for you to help me out. The church has given me until the end of the month to move out of the house. Ain't that something," he laughed.

"They've already convicted and evicted me but I'm not sweating that though. The electricity has been shut off and I've had to sell the Italian curio cabinet, the dining room furniture, and other stuff just to pay for my attorney 'cause my accounts are frozen so I'm low on dough."

"I don't have any money. My accounts are frozen too."

"This is all going to be over soon. I need a place to stay—just for a few days."

I stared at him but didn't utter a word, though my thought was that cold-water faucets would be installed in hell long before his head touched any one of my pillows. He was serious too, asking a second, then a third time if I would share my space. My blood pressure was rising—I could feel the blood racing through my veins.

"We can bring the kids back home and pretend that we're a family again. Whatcha say?"

"I say no, DeMarcus! That'll just confuse them and they're already acting out. Our divorce will be final soon and it's time we both move on."

I expected him to yell and scream, which he did. And everything he ever did for me in my entire life was shouted out from the top of his lungs. Three times I asked for him to leave but each time seemed to make matters worse. He cussed me for refusing to help him in his time of need and when I grew tired of being called out of my name and threatened to call the police, he ripped my cell phone from my hands and tossed it against the wall.

Wherever Jamal was hiding, I prayed silently that he'd remain still and quiet while DeMarcus continued his rampage of cussing, fussing, and throwing my breakables. I was caught off guard, however, when he threw Lil D's storybook at my forehead. Covering my head, I dropped to the floor. DeMarcus pulled at my arms to lift me but when I refused his assistance, an angered

DeMarcus kicked me so hard on the right side of my chest with his boot, I feared my ribs were broken. Loudly and in excruciating pain, I screamed for help.

The screen door opened. Oh, how grateful I was to see Tony. DeMarcus too was surprised to see him enter and immediately began backing away from me. Proceeding towards DeMarcus, Tony didn't ask questions but with one punch, knocked DeMarcus across the living and into my wooden rack of CDs. Grabbing DeMarcus's shirt, a second punch from Tony knocked him onto his back. Pinning DeMarcus down with his three-hundred plus frame, the physical altercation turned to verbal communication. Tony was the facilitator.

"See, I don't think you crazy," he said in a calm voice.

"I just think you're a man trying to bully a woman. And I ain't one for getting into people's business, but ole' girl here, she's a'ight with me and I promised her dad that I'd look out for her and them kids and that's what I'm gonna do 'cause I don't break no promises. And I'ma make a promise to you too so listen up. The next time I see you over here and I find out that you weren't invited, it's gonna be steel in your azz and not my knee, OK. Ya' feel me? Now I'ma let you up and when I do, I need you to walk out that door and don't look back. We straight?"

DeMarcus wasn't quite steady on his feet before two squad cars; flashing lights, sirens and all, pulled up in my yard. With their weapons drawn, four officers entered the house and warned us not to move.

"Handle that girl," Tony said referring to the officers instructing us to raise our arms.

Informing them that I was the homeowner, I provided the details of what transpired which led to the physical altercation. Explaining that Tony was my neighbor responding to my pleas for help, after assessing the scene and the bruises on my face, DeMarcus was handcuffed and escorted out. I had almost forgotten about Jamal until he reappeared through the back door. He clutched me tightly in his arms.

"Where in the hell was you at, man? Have you been hiding out all this time?" Tony yelled.

"I wanted to help but he would have killed her if he'd seen me. I called the police then crawled out the basement window."

"He's right," I added. "They have a history so when DeMarcus showed up, I begged him to stay put. Things would have been much worse had my ex seen him in the house."

"Yeah, Lisa and I heard yaw outside talking and having a good time, it was all good though. I saw ol'boy park his car in your garage but when I saw another dude pull in then park and yaw stopped laughing, I told Lisa that something was about to happen. I wasn't prying or nothing, I just know that two men at the same residence at the same time with one woman is trouble. So, I listened by my window for a minute and when I heard yaw yelling then arguing, I put on my shoes and came on over. I told your pops I'd look out for you and I meant that. But yaw can't be calling the po-po and stuff. I don't need them running my license and getting all up in my business, ya' feel me?"

I laughed. Further explanation was not needed.

Jamal stayed the remainder of the night and tended to my physical injuries. We snuggled on the couch and talked well into the wee hours of the morning about various issues. His arms were warm and comforting. His words were kind, supportive, and loving. His leg rubbing against mine was soothing and although being entangled within the sheets would have been ideal, he showed me that I meant more to him than a few moments of physical intimacy.

Jamal spoke to my heart and my mind and over the course of the morning, a special bond was formed that neither of us wanted to lose. As 6:45 crept up on us, it was tempting to call in sick as he suggested, to hang-out and do nothing all day long. Had it not been for the mandatory department training taking place this day, I would have.

Returning to work after a weeklong of sporadic appearances was awkward. Feeling the stares from folks as I walked the halls didn't help much either. At that point, anyone in the center who hadn't heard about DeMarcus's trial was either unable to read or didn't keep up with the local news. His scandal was big-time news in Lexington—a prominent pastor pleading guilty to theft, stealing money from an organization he oversaw and weeks later, on trial for the murder of his mistresses' husband. But of all of this, what I dreaded the most was having my name and photos with DeMarcus used by the media as if I were an accomplice.

"Hey, girl, welcome back!" Geo entered my office.

"You've been quiet, what's going on? You look tired too. Are you OK?"

From past experiences, I knew not to share too much with Geo; his mouth ran faster than any woman I ever knew could when the gossip was good. Luckily, our conversation was brief for answering a call from Jamal. He asked if I had read the morning paper.

Dropping the phone and running to confiscate Shirley's paper from the front desk, once back in my office, I laid the paper flat on my desk and read the headlining caption: *"Pastor Facing Murder Charges Accused of Assault."* DeMarcus's mug shot was plastered all over the paper and though the writer didn't print my name, anyone that knew him knew that I was his estranged wife, the victim.

"Don't worry about it," Jamal said.

"And don't be bothered with what anyone else thinks or says. This is DeMarcus's storm. You're just getting a few of the rain droplets. Trust me, you will get through this."

Chapter 17

My Brother's Keeper

It was Wednesday, June 29th when my divorce decree arrived via the U.S. Mail. And although I knew it was forthcoming, holding the dissolution of marriage in my hands was surreal. It had been three weeks to the day since the mishap at my house and not knowing whether DeMarcus was still behind bars or out on bail was unsettling. But Jamal knew his status but wouldn't say. He chose to be tight-lipped about all things related to DeMarcus and encouraged me to focus on my future, not consume myself with thoughts of DeMarcus or of our past life.

I was grateful when a three-day weekend rolled around. An extra day of sleep is what I had planned for myself but when Dad called excited about an Independence Day carnival near his home, I decided to drive to Louisville as a surprise. I received a surprise too—from Jamal offering to accompany me. And I was so glad he came along; he was great with the kids! He played games with them and helped them to win stuffed animals and other fun toys.

He even rode the kiddie rides with DeMarya while Dad rode with Lil' D.

The carnival was awesome and exhausting, but on the ride back to Dad's house, Jamal stopped and purchased a boatload of fireworks. My children were small and other than watching the colorful array of flickers from our driveway or the church parking lot, they had never held a sparkler. But Jamal showed them how to hold them far from their bodies before safely flinging them onto the pavement when the flickering got closer to their hand. It was hard to tell who was more excited, him or the kids.

Staging the larger fireworks on the curb of Dad's driveway, Jamal gave DeMarya and Lil D the huge responsibility of choosing the order they were to be lit. They were having the time of their lives and so was Dad who several times whispered in my ear, "I think I like this fella."

Returning home and after helping tuck in the kids, I invited Jamal to stay for a nightcap. Of course, DeMarcus returning to the house still haunted me, but Jamal accepted the offer and encouraged me to not live in fear. Interestingly, there seemed to be so much to talk about as we laughed into the early morning hours. Before we knew it, we had finished off two bottles of wine. At 3 a.m., I woke to discover my head upon his shoulder. Opening my eyes a few hours later, I was wrapped in his arms.

As a rule, Jamal was to be gone before I woke the kids but on this beautiful morning, I fixed him breakfast and while he ate, made him a hearty sack lunch. In appreciation, he pulled me in for a long kiss which to my lips was beyond magical. It must have been special for him too because instead of pulling away, he kissed me again with greater passion.

On cloud ninety-nine the entire day, I wasn't upset when receiving a text from Jamal later in the day canceling our dinner plans. I was exhausted— extremely exhausted and after grilling ham and cheese sandwiches for the kids, I plopped down on the couch and rested my eyes.

Unable to sleep or find a show on television worthy of watching, to amuse myself, I logged into DeMarcus's email accounts. To my surprise, communications between him and Evonne had resumed. Ironically, the flow and tone of their conversations had changed. It was difficult to pinpoint just when the loving stopped but I certainly knew why. DeMarcus was broke— penniless, and no longer in position to pamper her.

In several emails, DeMarcus begged her to be patient but it was evident that without a steady flow of green, ole' girl was moving on. Obviously irritated, DeMarcus's words grew harsh—borderline threatening, especially when she taunted him about his inability to provide for her. Their emails were getting juicier and juicier and after a brief pause to tinkle, I returned to the den with a glass of wine and sat Indian style on the couch. I continued reading from where I left off.

From my guesstimation, they had several heated discussions ranging from the missing money, to the once private now very public intimate photos shared across the nation, to the deliberate personal attacks of both of their characters, and everything else in between. DeMarcus blamed Evonne and she blamed him.

It was comical discovering that the forty-two days they shacked up in her tiny one-room apartment was pure hell. In her own words, she called

DeMarcus 'useless.' She blasted him for not being man enough to find decent work to assist in paying the minor bills which included his own monthly fifty-dollar cell phone payment. And to add gasoline to the campfire, his weight gain angered her—alluding often to the constant stuffing of his face minus an exercise regimen being the contributing factor for his new muffin physique. In response, he referred to her as ghetto-fabulous and expressed embarrassment by her appearance, particularly the dried up rose tattoo she often exposed. Yes, the one he once thought was sexy.

Reading their emails was like reading a good novel of suspense; it kept my interest.

The next morning, feeling refreshed from a very much needed night of uninterrupted rest, I looked forward to having a productive and stress-free day. I was barely through my office door when Geo called my name and asked if we could meet. Sensing uneasiness in his voice, I figured it was somehow related to Kim, so I took a seat in the chair next to his desk. Geo probably thought that asking about my kids would throw me off, but I knew him well enough to know when something was awry and called him out on it. I asked him to share what it was that had him looking so stressed.

"Is it Kim? I don't know what's up with her either," I said, shaking my head. "Evidently she's mad at me for something. I called her three times last week and her skank azz has yet to call me back. She may be out of town though, she's always traveling. She's been hard to get in touch with lately."

Geo didn't seem interested in what I had to say, and nor did he react to the mentioning of Kim's name. Instead, he raised his brow and oddly asked if I'd spoken to DeMarcus.

"DeMarcus who?" I joked.

"Your ex-husband," he responded, failing to pick up on my comedic moment.

"I don't know if DeMarcus is even still in Lexington. For all I know, he may have moved to Washington with his folks. Why do you ask?"

"Just hadn't heard you say anything about him lately, that's all."

"So, what's really up with you? Women trouble? Kim trouble?"

"I'm straight and Kim, she's just Kim. She's the worst at returning calls but we talk at least once a week. In fact, I called her Friday to get her input on celebrating your divorce over lunch and she went ballistic. She snapped simply because I suggested it. She called the whole idea tacky."

"Ah, that's Kim just looking out for me. She probably thinks that I'm off moping and wasting away. I haven't been able to reach her to tell her just how much stress has been lifted off my shoulders. Thanks for wanting to throw me a party but you can buy me lunch one day if you just have to do something."

"And there's something else," he said. I sat back in the chair.

"Kim has a new boo. When we talked the other day, I heard a man's voice in the background. I asked if she had company and she snapped at me again. I knew it wasn't the television because they were having dialogue back and forth."

"See, there you go being paranoid. And if she did have company, what would be wrong with that? She's a grown woman and if yaw aren't dating anymore, she's free to entertain anyone she chooses. I know you have feelings for her, but it is what it is. Sorry, Geo."

"And when I ride by her place," he continued, "It's always the same car parked in one of the slots assigned to her. It even has a tenant pass hanging from the mirror."

"So, you're stalking her now? Don't do it, Geo, don't do it!" I laughed.

"Trust me when I say this, the best way to hurt your own feelings is to go searching for answers on your own. Let it go, pleeeeze! She'll realize one day that she's lost a good man in you. And if she is seeing someone else and allows him to stay at her apartment, there's nothing you can do about it."

"I think it's your old car, the one you used to drive to work before the engine blew up."

Squinting my eyes as if that would help to hear him better, "Huh? What did you say?"

"I said I think it's your old car."

"Why's it gotta be my old car? What are you saying, Geo? Come on, just say it."

"I'm sorry, Rosilyn, but I think your ex is playing house with Kim. I can almost swear to it because the back bumper is dented right where yours used to be and there's an orange and yellow Hawaiian lei around the mirror too. Sorry, sweetie."

His words stunned me. I didn't want to believe that my lifelong friend could betray me in such a manner. DeMarcus was a low life, yes, but Kim? Nah, our friendship wouldn't allow for such foolishness. And anyhow, she hated DeMarcus from the top of his balding head to the bottom of his scaly, funky feet. And DeMarcus hated the fact that Kim was alive and breathing.

Aware that if I were to have a mental meltdown, Geo's office would be the best place to do so, but I couldn't comprehend it being true, so I left his office to collect my thoughts. For the most part, Geo left me alone to sort through my emotions, however throughout the day he poked his head inside my office to check on me. A few times I gave him the thumbs up but no matter how many times I claimed to be alright and even with the many smiles I affixed to my face, I was dying on the inside. *Was Kim helping DeMarcus out or was she helping herself to him?*

At my desk and staring at the clock, I silently prayed for the noon hour to hurry up and roll around. There was plenty of work requiring my attention, but I was mentally elsewhere and working on others' issues was no longer my priority.

I was checking my emails when the receptionist rang my desk phone alerting me, I had a visitor. Usually concerned about my appearance and checking my hair and lip color before leaving my office, today was a bummer day so I walked towards the receptionist station *as-is*. There was no visitor at the front counter—just three bouquets of flowers and a dozen red long stem roses. Geo assisted in carrying them to my office and before I could remove a card from the envelope, he was asking who they were from.

"Whoever they're from you must have rocked him good," he laughed.

"They're from my dad, fool," I lied, reading clearly Jamal's name signed on the card.

When Geo left my office, I dialed Jamal twice to thank him but got his voicemail. Continuing to smell and adore my flowers, I was glad I decided to read the next card because it gave me instructions to be ready for dinner at seven o'clock.

At ten dollars an hour, I was grateful that Ree-Ree, Lisa's teenage daughter was available to babysit. And when Jamal picked me up, I personally thanked him for my flowers with a big hug and kiss which he reciprocated.

Driving down East Broadway, he turned into a lot of a restaurant I never knew existed, CC's. Proclaiming it as being the classiest soul food restaurant in the east, walking through the foyer, I saw for myself how right he was. The atmosphere was welcoming, and the staff was attentive and uniformly dressed. The menus were in leather trifold covers and not the standard copier or printed laminated sheets. My sweet tea arrived chilled and served in cocktail stemware and the greenery was real, not artificial or dusty. And last, but not least when our food was served, it arrived covered and on piping hot dinnerware. Light jazz played softly overhead and though other couples dined nearby, the only conversation I heard was the one between Jamal and me.

"OK, enough of the suspense. What's going on with you?" I asked.

"How was your day?" he asked me with a straight face.

"It started out great, went south, and now it's great again."

"Went south? Did DeMarcus call or show up?"

I shared my earlier conversation with Geo. Jamal doubted that any of what Geo spoke was true but encouraged me to view it differently if later discovering that even the tiniest piece of what he mentioned was the truth.

"He's homeless, Roz, and I know it sounds crazy, but what if when Evonne kicked him out, Kim was the only person willing to help him? Really, why did they hate each other? DeMarcus once told me that he always felt like she hated him but never knew why. What is it that the old folks used to say, *'God will send you help, but you'll never know who God will use.'* They probably talked at one point and squashed their differences. For you, I hope that's the case but if it's not, let it go anyway. But enough of that depressing subject. I've got great news to share with you."

I gave him my full attention.

"Remember when I told you that Little Flock asked me to fill in while they searched for a pastor to replace DeMarcus? Well, after much prayer and asking God to guide me in making the right decision, I've made one."

"Whatcha gonna do?" I excitedly asked when he failed to provide an immediate response.

"You said yes, I know you did!" My smile was a mile long.

"I know it doesn't make sense, but I turned them down. Things weren't coming together right—it wasn't feeling right either. But last night when we met, God revealed to me why it wasn't coming together. See, Pastor Larry at Mount Olive is having surgery in October and has decided to retire to focus on his recovery. Last night's meeting was to vote on waiving the process of searching for a new pastor because they had already decided to choose me. Pastor Larry met with the other leaders and told them God revealed me to him as his successor. Little Flock is where I wanted to be but look how God has turned it all around. I was initially willing to settle but God gave me something even greater!"

"That's great news Jamal and I know you'll be a wonderful pastor. But why are you treating me to dinner when I should be treating you? And you sent me flowers. Not one, but three bouquets?"

"Because I received a blessing today and in turn, I wanted to bless you. I was walking down the strip this morning to get a bite to eat when I saw the roses on display. The first bouquet I bought because it reminded me of you, so beautiful and full of life. The yellow flower arrangement reminded me of the yellow and white dress you wore the night of the leadership banquet in 2008, remember? And the colorful arrangement reminded me of Christmas Eve when we met for breakfast. You had on seventeen colors, plus a multicolored ball cap," he laughed.

"You were beautiful though."

Our food was served fresh and hot and it was delicious. Over dessert, we talked about everything under the sun and in no time, ten o'clock had crept up. Returning to the house, Jamal handed Ree-Ree a crisp fifty-dollar bill then helped me bathe the kids. Lil D was antsy but eventually drifted off after being read a story. I then joined Jamal in the den where we resumed our conversation.

"Roz, I've prayed about a lot of things these past few months. Some things I've had to wait on God to make happen and other things, God has told me to step out on faith for. One of those things is asking if you are willing to be my one and only. Before you speak," he said, and placing his forefinger over my lips.

"What I mean when I say that is, I want you to consider being my life partner. I know your divorce just became final and truthfully, that's what I have been waiting for. I love you. I have always loved you, and everything in my heart tells me that we are meant to be together. It may be too soon for you but I pray you will consider it."

"What makes you think you love me? And people are gonna assume..."

"Damn, what people say or think! I don't care about DeMarcus, church members, or anyone else. They don't control my heart and I won't allow them to cause me to miss out on my blessing which I know is you. I'm convinced this is God's plan for my life and I want what He has for me. What do you say?"

"You didn't answer my question. What makes you think you love me?"

"I know it's love because every night in my dreams, it's the same dream over, and over again. I can't sleep most nights because I wake up and realize it's you that's missing. I kiss and grab my pillow praying that when I open my eyes, it's you I'm holding. And I'm not just talking recent dreams, but dreams as far back as four to five years ago. When you come around my heart flutters, imagine that. Thick or skinny, long hair or short hair, I still see you as the most beautiful woman in the world. And you've always accepted me for me. I know its love because I'm willing to refrain from sexing you so that you get to know, love, and respect me. Intimacy is extra."

"Hmmm, and I thought you just weren't attracted to me that way anymore," I joked.

"My flesh says yes, but God has answered my prayers for restraint and patience. See, I believe that anything worth having is worth waiting for. I know you are my soulmate Roz; I feel it in my spirit. I want more than just a physical relationship with you and by keeping your love joy as you call it," he chuckled, "and my love toy covered up, it'll prove that our relationship is not based solely on sex. I want you to be my wife someday and I want our union to be blessed by God."

Jamal's words stayed with me throughout the night and over into the next day. And although he didn't ask me to marry him, I hoped through the passion-filled kiss reciprocated, he left my house believing I was open to considering his 'almost' proposal.

At work the next morning, Geo was quick to point out the glow on my face and questioned the source. Refusing to appease his curiosity, I winked, smiled, and continued down the hallway. Geo followed me into my office but before he could jumpstart his game of asking one-hundred questions, I asked about his weekend.

"Been stalking anybody we know?" I laughed.

"Haha, funny," Geo responded, followed by a bobblehead shake.

"For your 4-1-1, no I didn't drive through the apartment complex this weekend. For the most part, I chilled at my place and caught up on some movies I saved on my DVR."

"That's good to know because I'd be bored out of my mind sitting in a car watching for someone's door to swing open. Nah, but seriously, I'm sorry things didn't work out between you and Kim. I guess she wasn't who either of us believed she was."

"I ain't sweating Kim no more. I met a young woman Saturday at the grocery store. She's twenty-three, younger than what I like to date but she is fine, ooh she's fine! Her name is Jaylinque, but I nicknamed her J.C. She's got a kid, but the Daddy has custody of him. She's got her own place and says she's looking for a good man."

"Twenty-three? You're robbing the cradle man."

"I know, I know. But she's legal and that's all I care about. Besides, age ain't nothing but a number."

"You're almost double her age. Why you have to go messing with somebody's child? Six years ago, she was probably taking home economic classes—learning how to sew and bake a cake when your old azz was complaining about turning forty. You're probably the same age as her mother. Better yet, you may have even dated her momma in high school or played basketball with her daddy. Think about it Geo, it's just wrong."

Geo ignored my warnings and changed the subject to Jamal. I lied, telling him that I hadn't spoken to his friend in four days. And just before telling another lie, my cell phone rang. It was Kim. Initially, I was reluctant to answer having not first thought through what I was gonna say if, from her own mouth, she admitted to being in a relationship with DeMarcus. I placed my cell phone up to my ear. Instead of greeting her with the normal, "hello," I started the conversation by telling her how much I missed talking to her.

"I was wondering if you were out of the country or something and not wanting to waste your minutes calling me long distance. It's been forever and a day since our last conversation. Send a girl a text sometimes."

"It's not that," she mumbled. "I've been laying low and trying to regroup since being laid off."

"I didn't know, sorry to hear that. It seems like every company wants to do more with less these days. They've been talking about laying folks off here too." I lied again.

"What's been up? We've got so much to catch up on. The trial, the kids, you, and Geo."

"Geo's cool and we're still friends. He's a good guy but the timing wasn't right for us. I mean, I had a lot of other stuff going on and I was forced to choose between him and it."

"So, you chose 'it.' Does this 'it' have a name?" Kim paused.

"Ah, it's complicated. How are my godchildren doing?"

"We're all doing well, considering."

Kim asked if I'd heard from Jamal.

"The last time we talked was about two months. He's dating some chicken head I've heard. Anyhow, he was like my brother-in-law, in a jacked-up kind of way. It's way too many people in the world to wanna connect with someone who's practically your family, know what I mean? But tell me about this 'it.' How long have you and 'it' been kicking it?" She laughed and again avoided my question.

"We're supposed to be girls Kim, but it seems like you're keeping something from me. Are you alright? Are you in trouble?"

"If you call being pregnant trouble," she blurted.

The charade was over, and the truth was out. The news was a shocker that rendered me speechless. Geo, still ear hustling and seeing my once rosy cheeks drop, pounded my desk with his fist and tugged at my arm wanting 'real-time' details of our conversation. I congratulated Kim then asked why she sounded so sad.

"Are you not happy about bringing a life into this world?"

"It's not mine," Geo mumbled under his breath.

"I'm not trying to pry into your business, but having a baby is a really big deal. Is Geo the father?"

"No, but I don't want to talk about it because I doubt if I even keep it. The timing is all wrong."

"Kim, you keep talking about timing. What timing? And why would you not want to have this baby? You love kids?"

Her voice trembled as she gave me a long drawn out story about pressures from the child's father to terminate the pregnancy. And as I continued to piece together her storyline, her baby's daddy's likeness and thought process seemed identical to that of DeMarcus.

"There's plenty of single moms out here you know. If you've hooked up with the wrong guy, you can change that. But God doesn't make mistakes and this child shouldn't have to pay for yours. Pray about it. Listen, I'll come by after I get off work, OK."

"Please don't, but thanks for your concern. I'm not sure what time I'll be home, so we'll get together another time, I promise."

"When you're ready to talk, feel free to call me back."

"She's pregnant!" yelled Geo.

"That baby ain't mine, it ain't mine. Ain't no telling how many dudes she was fooling with but I'm not going down like that. How many months is she claiming to be? I ain't been with her since…"

"Chill, Geo, she said it isn't yours."

Discussing the conversation with Jamal over dinner, he expressed being pleased with how decently I handled the situation. He applauded my demonstration of patience and for my sincerity in offering a listening ear for when she felt ready to talk.

"You've got a heart of gold and that's one of the many reasons why I love you. I know you're hurting but still, you're willing to reach out to her. Most women would be ready to scratch up the other woman's face or throw a brick through the man's car window. But not you and I respect you even more for keeping your emotions intact. Only a strong and classy lady can do that. Roz, if you trust me," he said, rubbing my cheek with his forefinger.

"If you're willing to make DeMarcus a memory, I promise to make you the happiest woman in the world."

I hugged Jamal and though his words were of little comfort, it did my heart good knowing he viewed me as strong because I truly wasn't feeling very strong.

The next morning and just as Jamal predicted would happen, DeMarcus was once again the local headline news. Pastor *Acquitted of Murder Receives Five Years of Probation for Theft* was the news story I and other center staff watched flash across the 32-inch, flat-screen television in the break room. Feeling the stares of my co-workers who appeared to be awaiting a response or reaction from me about the verdict, I shook my head, filled my cup with coffee and returned to my office.

At my desk, I promptly responded to a missed call from Jamal. Still on a high after the non-physical yet intimate moments we shared the night before, I grinned from ear to ear when he answered. He called me 'Sweetness.' Brief in exchanging pleasantries, I placed the ball in his court as to whether he'd be eating dinner with me and the kids or if he wanted to dine out alone.

"Neither." Jamal was headed to his apartment after Bible study to pack for a business trip to Louisville the next morning. When asked to accompany him I was thrilled and quickly packed a mini suitcase. By 11:00 p.m., Jamal and I were in Louisville dropping the kids off at my dad's house. Dad was elated to see them, but they were zonked out and he too was well on his way. After tucking them into the bed, Jamal and I checked into his hotel room.

Waking the next morning, we dined in the hotel's restaurant. Jamal stared in amazement while I pigged out on fried potatoes and onions, country ham, eggs, fresh fruit, and other items Ma would routinely prepare on holiday mornings.

Paying the tab with his credit card, he then handed the card to me and told me to enjoy my day—minus a spending limit. Sending him to his meeting with a full belly and a sweet kiss, I returned to the room and waited until 9:00 a.m. before heading over to see my children. Auntie was preparing their breakfast when I arrived. After they ate, I cleaned the kitchen, then Dad, Auntie, the kids, their cousin and I loaded up the car and went to the mall to shop.

By noon, the kids were exhausted from playing in the jungle gym and Dad was full on ice cream. Auntie had shopped herself arts and crafts happy and I was excited about my new outfit purchased for Jamal's evening business meeting dinner. After dropping everyone off, I was successful in locating a beauty salon available to take me, a nappy-headed walk-in.

Around 5:30-ish when Jamal returned to the hotel room, I was ready and waiting. He complimented my hairdo and spun me around to admire my new dress. His wide stretched smile of approval made me feel like a million bucks! Changing into a suit coat and tie that coincidentally matched the color of my dress, arm in arm we walked down the corridor.

Chapter 18

Restoration

It was the first week in September when Jamal's name went up on the marquee as the pastor of Mount Olive. We must have driven past the church at least a dozen times to look at it with each time being more special than the last. Witnessing together his lifelong dream become a reality, Jamal thanked me for supporting him and helping to tighten up his installation message. Jokingly, he nicknamed me his first official church groupie. I had a nickname for him too, my Pulpit Pappy.

Over two hundred people were in attendance for his installation service. And when Jamal took to the podium, folks jumped to their feet praising and applauding. He tried keeping the services dignified, referring to himself as the old Jamal simply filling a different role, but the outbursts and praises filling the sanctuary made that impossible. Several times Jamal stepped back from the podium—waiting out the verbal and foot stomping praises only to be interrupted by another round of thunderous expressions of love. Tears of gratefulness flowed down his face.

The spirit was high in Mount Olive for sure and when the associate ministers and visiting pastors built a human fence around him, I too became emotional and cried like a baby.

"You're Awesome, Lord!" someone from the pews shouted out, bringing a more thunderous response from the attendees. The power in the room had even brought Geo to his feet to applaud the blessing he was in the midst of witnessing firsthand. Moments later, a regrouped Jamal approached the podium.

"I'm not perfect," he began.

"And it was just the other day when one of my closest friends punched me in the shoulder and told me I thought I was all of that." The congregation laughed.

"I didn't immediately respond to his remark but what it caused me to do is start reflecting on all God has blessed me with. I'm not referring to what He's done throughout my life but just within this past year and you know what, He's been good to me! I see some of yaw already twisting up your lips and noses thinking that I'm bragging and boasting about myself, but you've got it all wrong. If you listen, my testimony is giving honor and praise unto Him for using me as His vessel. I haven't always been this fine," he continued, stirring up laughter.

"In fact, I used to not even care about combing my hair or shaving my face on a regular basis, nor did I put in any effort into matching my clothes. I was about making my money and loving the honey's and the only time I acknowledged God is when somebody got shot and I thanked Him because it wasn't me."

The audience was attentive.

"Many of you are unaware that I lost my parents at an early age and was raised by two uncles who'll never attend another family function as long as they breathe. I lived in the streets for a great portion of my life, I never married, and I never fathered any kids. But today!" he shouted, "I stand in this pulpit so very grateful that He has kept me. Yes, I was sad and cried when momma left me, but it is all because of Him that I didn't lose my mind. And when my uncles were given life sentences without any consideration of thinking about future possibilities of parole, it was right after I secured my first full-time, real job and my first check was more than enough to rent myself a room. See, I could have been out on the streets, but He didn't see fit to let that happen for me. I give Him honor yaw, not as your pastor but as a once broken man who has been so richly blessed. I won't take this opportunity for granted either. I'm mindful that God giveth and He can taketh away. I asked God to mold me into the man He wanted me to be a long time ago and as I still reflect back on how good He's been to me, I can honestly tell you church that when I started to obey Him, I was promoted on my job not once, but twice. He removed the worldly girls from my life and gave me my soul mate. Yes, He's a God of a second chance, another chance, another and another chance! He's taken my desire to teach the youth and made it possible to teach the youth, children, and adults. He's even given me a podium to stand behind. Thank you, Lord! So, to my dear friend Geo who said I thought I was all of that, I am! I am a product of an All That God so All That is who I am! How can one be humble when it's evident that God is working in your life?"

The congregation and choir members again rose to their feet, each one waving and shouting, seemingly understanding his journey. Folks showered Jamal with so much love. I too was so proud of him and his breakthrough that I wanted to run up and give him a huge hug but refrained from doing so. Instead, I simply clutched my hands and smiled.

At the end of his message, a line of folks, mostly women, waited to greet him and shake his hand. In disbelief, I sat on the pew just watching the multitude of females nearly tumbling over one another to press their breast into his chest or leave their lipstick print on his cheeks.

Geo called me paranoid, but a woman knows another woman. Nonetheless, I didn't trip. Jamal was spending the night at my house and promised to pamper me with a full course breakfast in bed the next morning. I laughed at the skanks pushing up on my *almost* man.

When my turn came to congratulate him, I went in for a simple hug, but it was Jamal who embraced me long, drawing the attention of those lingering around. He stared me in the eyes, perhaps waiting for a kiss but I pulled away. I wasn't about to place my lips over the top of the colorful mixture of pastel pink, ruby red, and passionate purple lipsticks smeared all over his face and cheeks.

"See you in about an hour," I whispered.

I hurried home and put the kids in their beds and by 10:20, Jamal was walking through the door. I led him into the bathroom where a hot bubble bath was waiting. As he soaked, I sponged him down and gently massaged his temple and shoulders. After patting him dry, I applied baby oil all over his body which he found comical. Propping his feet up onto my stool, I massaged his feet and legs. From the bathroom, I led him into the bedroom and helped him get situated under a nice clean set of sheets. Entering the bed from the opposite side, I slid underneath his right arm and listened as he began reminiscing about the service.

"Tonight, it was beyond special. I've never felt so much love and I believe it all was genuine."

"It was," I replied.

"Your testimony helped somebody too. Right off, you let them know that you're not perfect, so I don't think anybody is going to expect you to be." When asked if I saw DeMarcus, I sat up.

"Yeah, he was sitting on the back pew. He waited around to talk to me too. I was walking toward my car when he called my name. He'd been drinking, but I didn't question it. I told him I was glad to see him and immediately he started giving me tips on pastoring. He even offered to help me study. Can you believe it? It was awkward hearing him talk about how he's getting back on his feet and stuff. But I was glad to hear that he's found a job working in a warehouse."

"Did he say where he was living?"

"He mentioned staying with a friend. I kind of felt sorry for him but he's a grown man. But beyond encouraging him to stay in his Word and continue believing and trusting in God, there was nothing else I had for him."

"Karma's something else," I added.

"Yep, he's the poster child example of the consequences received for blatant disobedience. But what still bothers me is when he stated that I was now the big dog and advised me not to mess up like he did. I know what he meant so I laughed it off, but I made sure to tell him that being in ministry has never been a joke to me. Never!"

With Jamal out of the country for another business trip, the five nights of not seeing him felt more like five long months. Knowing that the training for his new nine to five, executive-level position was important, I hadn't realized how much he meant to me until distance separated us. I missed his smile, his smell, and his touch. Inside, I felt that I loved him but for fear of destroying our blossoming friendship, I refrained from letting those words slip from my lips. Excited about his return on Friday, I secured Ree-Ree to babysit and scheduled myself a hair appointment.

In a conversation with Jamal while he was away, he had mentioned at least twice, winding down a busy work week at Billy E's Place when he returned. I wasn't much of a jazz fan but if that's what he wanted to do while sipping on wine, then that was alright with me. Jamal arrived at the house a little past 7 p.m. and when I opened the door, he stared me up and down. I was a vision of loveliness—I knew with certainty and he also remarked. My hair and makeup were flawless, and my new off white, one-shoulder, silver-sequined blouse was an awesome match for the fitted black jeans that appeared to be glued to my slender body.

Greeting him with a kiss, I felt his lips quivering. When he pulled back, his unreadable facial expression spooked me, but he explained it as being fatigued but otherwise stated he felt alright. On the ride to Billy E's Place, very little was spoken. Perhaps he didn't want to bore me with details of his training, but I would have listened. I missed him so much and was so happy to be at his side.

Seated at a table on the edge of the dance floor, we had the best view of the live jazz band performing. Shortly thereafter, a bottle of wine was delivered and poured into our glasses. I hadn't noticed Jamal placing the order, but apparently, he did and tipped the waiter a $100 bill. Twenty minutes later, I was escorted onto the dance floor and swept off my feet. Regardless of the rhythms that played, Jamal's pace was slow and mellow. Fatigued? Perhaps, but his deep dark eyes were focused solely on me, not the music or the other couples, just me.

When the band announced they were taking a break, we returned to our table where another chilled bottle of wine awaited us along with an appetizer of chicken wings. I laughed aloud when the waiter returned with a tiny cup of ketchup and ranch dressing mixed for me to dip them in. I realized then that Jamal had planned this night in advance.

We hadn't quite finished our wings and other appetizers when the main course of steak and lobster was served. As we dined, we talked, drank, and caught up on each other's week. The atmosphere was awesome and the thirty and over crowd were well-behaved. Several of Jamal's friends stopped by our table, but he kept their conversation brief and kept his focus on me.

The band returned a short while later and just like the first half, their tunes set a romantic, relaxing tone. Stuffed on steak, wings, lobster, and bread and a little woozy from the wine, I swear that when sitting back in my chair, I felt a stitch in my girdle panties pop. I smiled at Jamal though praying with my eyes open that he too was full and buzzed and not wanting to return to the dance floor just yet. He was—so we remained in our seats, holding hands while awaiting the next selection of tunes. Only two selections were played before there was another brief pause in the set. Attentively the audience listened as a band member dedicated their next selection for a newly engaged couple.

"Awww, how sweet!" I said to Jamal, as I turned to look over my shoulder for the couple I expected to make their way toward the front. But when Jamal grabbed my hand and knelt on one knee, before he could ask, and I could answer, the audience were on their feet applauding. Jamal removed a tiny black box from his jacket pocket.

"Will you take this journey with me? Will you let me love you forever and ever?"

"Hell, yes," I shouted!

The remainder of the night was full of slow dancing and tears. He stared into my eyes and I stared into his. Although other couples were dancing on our left and our right, in Jamal's arms it felt as if we were the only ones in the room.

As badly as I wanted to share the news of my engagement, the first two days back at work I managed to keep it a secret from Geo. However, on the third day, while retrieving my incoming mail from the front desk, Shirley grabbed my hand to inspect my shiny rock. I didn't divulge much information, just smiled and expressed being surprised by the proposal.

"But you just got divorced. How long have you known this dude?" she boldly asked.

"Years," twisting the truth of my fiancée being an old high school flame with whom I'd kept in close contact with.

"What did your husband, I mean ex-husband think of yaws friendship? The news reports made it seem like he was cheating on you, I'm just saying."

No, that black, double-chinned, four belly gut roll bitch didn't!

"You don't know me like that. And for your information…" I shouted just as Geo grabbed my arm and stopped me from dotting her eye.

"Hey, hey, hey," he laughed. "Chill."

"I don't know what she's flipping out about. The truth is the truth and it hurts sometimes, but if she didn't want anybody asking about her funky azz ring, she shouldn't be dangling it in peoples' faces."

Embarrassed by my own conduct, I tossed my hands in the air and headed toward my office to regroup. Geo trailed behind insistent on getting the story fresh off the press.

"Oh, I let that gorilla looking pig get under my skin, that's all. It's nothing, really."

He grabbed my hand and inquired about the ring. Lying about it being one of Ma's favorites, he appeared satisfied with my answer and went on to inform me of his latest love interest. I pretended to be interested in what he was saying but in truth, I couldn't stop focusing on my good news.

Jamal and I had only been engaged 93 hours, 12 minutes—not sure of the seconds when eloping crossed my mind. It seemed the most logical solution to a complicated situation and after dinner, I sprung my idea on him. Jamal was excited and shared having pondered the same.

He suggested an earlier date than my proposed date of late November.

"What are we waiting for?" he asked.

"We both want to be together and God is on our side. I can ask Reverend Crentsil to marry us in his office this coming Saturday and after worship service on Sunday, we can fly to Florida for a couple of days. And no, that won't be where I take you for our official honeymoon. I've just heard about Miami having several awesome get-a-way spots sufficient for what we're going to do until we can properly plan for a weeklong cruise."

Jamal had thought of everything. All I was required to do was show up.

Although excited about becoming his wife, I was leery of how the kids would adjust to their Uncle Jay-Jay becoming Poppa Jay and what would go through their minds when seeing him and I kiss and hug. DeMarya was a smart cookie—inquisitive and undoubtedly would quiz DeMarcus on how an uncle becomes a daddy.

I wasn't planning for a big wedding but shopping at the mall during my lunch hour and after work for the most eloquent outfits was tiring. Not to mention the numerous trips back and forth to the courthouse to first apply for a marriage license, and on two separate occasions returning to provide a second photo I.D. then proof of my divorce wore me out. Jamal hinted about saving my energy for more important things, but I was anxious and antsy and didn't want to wait until the last day to pull everything together. Geo sensed my preoccupation and questioned whether it had anything to do with Kim or DeMarcus.

"Just busy taking care of personal business," was my reply.

"I'm going out of town this weekend and I won't be back to work until next Thursday."

"It's your dad, isn't it? This is like the second time you've taken off to take care of him. Why doesn't he just move down here with you?"

I smiled. I let him believe that to be the reason for my absence.

"Kim called yesterday," he announced. "I didn't answer though. I ain't trying to hear no talk about being no kids' daddy especially when some other joker could possibly be the sperm donor. I'll call her back eventually but right now; I can care less about her or what's going on in her life. I ain't bitter, but when I was trying to do right by her, she bounced and left me wondering what I did wrong. So, nah, she can go cry on somebody else's shoulder."

"Well, don't give up on love just yet. That special person just may show up when you least expect it and when it does, you won't know how to act."

Chapter 19

Friends

On October 8, 2016, at 1:08 in the afternoon, I, Rosilyn, vowed to love, honor, and cherish Jamal, *the hell with obey,* taking his hand in the presence of God, Reverend Crentsil, his wife and a Deacon serving as witnesses and my dad who was adamant about attending. The ceremony held in Reverend Crentsil's office was short and sweet, but special. Reverend Crentsil presented us with a monetary gift of $500. The black stretch limousine waiting to transport us to the airport was a surprise gift from my dad.

It was only a few seconds after waving goodbye to everyone that Jamal pulled me in his arms and we rode off to begin our new lives together as husband and wife. We prayed together and then cried together. Magical was the moment when he kissed my lips. Reaching over and raising the privacy divider, it was then that we consummated our marriage. His rub, his kisses, and his touch made my body melt like butter—dissolving as it heated up. There was no verbal communication only physical; Jamal's moans complimented mine. Our bodies meshed together like puzzle pieces and when I could no longer tell his heartbeat from my own, I knew we were in sync. When Jamal laid his head upon my shoulder and our breathing patterns matched, I was assured that he and I were as one.

Arriving in Florida, I smiled each time Jamal introduced us as Mr. and Mrs. Wright. Jamal treated me like a Queen everywhere we went and made me feel as if I was the most important person in his world. High was the pedestal he placed me on—emotionally and physically. Jamal pampered me with full-body massages as well as intimate horse and buggy rides through downtown Miami. We dined at fancy restaurants for dinner then took long, intimate walks on the beach. With Jamal, nothing else seemed to matter other than my happiness.

And when our three-day blissful honeymoon came to an end, we were excited about returning home to share our happiness with the world.

We were checking in our luggage when Jamal excused himself to answer a private call—the first time during our honeymoon which I appreciated. When he returned, I read bad news all over his face. Before I could ask what had gone wrong, he remarked, "Some things will never change. That was DeMarcus's attorney on the phone."

"His attorney? Why is he calling you?"

"DeMarcus is in jail again. I hate to bring this to you, but it was Kim and according to his attorney, she's been beaten up really bad. For obvious reasons she hasn't called you, but this may be the last opportunity you have to reach out and help her. Baby, I know how deeply she hurt you, but she needs you. Can you put aside your issues to help someone you once cared about? I'm gonna do what I can for DeMarcus, even after everything he's done to me."

We hadn't planned on spending much time in Louisville once we got off the plane, but when we arrived at Dad's house to pick up the children, he was sitting on the front porch. Before we could get both feet out of the car, he had jumped inside and informed us that the kids were at the bowling alley celebrating their cousin's birthday.

Taking notice of the trophy cases aligned against the wall when we entered, Jamal reminisced about his younger years on his high school's bowling team. Dad too boasted of being a former bowling champion in his day and challenged Jamal to a game. I laughed out loud at the thought of watching these two lift an actual bowling ball instead of flipping their wrists and using the lightweight game system paddle they had grown accustomed to and loved.

Greeted by Auntie who appeared out of nowhere, after embracing me and Jamal, she escorted us to the party room adjacent to the concession area. It took a moment for Auntie to open the door but when she did, the flickering of candles in the dimly lit room gave away what was forthcoming. Nonetheless, Jamal and I pretended to be surprised once Auntie flipped on the lights and everyone shouted, "Congratulations!"

"Happy married, Momma," DeMarya yelled. I ran to her and Lil D and gave them both a smothering hug. The room was packed with about twenty of my closest family members and Geo. Geo was the first to shake Jamal's hand.

"Man, you didn't tell me that all of this was going on. Heck, I work with Rosilyn and she didn't say a word. I saw the rock on her finger though but didn't think much of it. I ain't mad at ya' though for keeping this a secret. Congratulations, man!"

It was after midnight when we arrived in Lexington and pulled into the driveway. And though we'd never discussed when he would be moving his things into the house, Jamal had been given keys to the house, a remote for the garage, and a section in the closet for his clothing. Jamal laughed when I offered him the entire basement and suggested he make it his man cave or office.

"I won't even go down there," I promised. "Cross my heart and hope to gain a pound if I do."

Keeping my word to Jamal, it was Monday—during my lunch hour when I went to the hospital to check in on Kim. Initially, my emotions were all over the place, but I felt stronger mentally, and believed I could show compassion in an awkward and painful situation.

'True friends will reveal themselves. So-called friends will too,' Ma would sometimes say when I was younger, and Kim and I were at odds about something silly. And although we always made it full circle and reconnected, leaving whatever we were squabbling about in the past and never looking back, I needed to show my face and prove to myself that I was indeed, a transformed woman.

I paused when entering room 709 and seeing Kim's black and blue swollen face. When she looked over at me, it was hard to decipher whether the tears rolling down her face were because she was embarrassed, happy to see me, or tears of guilt.

"You've had better days," I said, surprising her and myself when leaning over her bed rail to kiss her cheek.

"How are you feeling? And why didn't you call me?"

I folded my jacket and hung it over a chair then helped Kim to sit up. She asked how I learned of her whereabouts.

"Oh, I know people. I know things," I smiled.

"You being here, is this supposed to be a secret too? I mean, it's like I don't know you anymore; we've never kept secrets from one another, never! I miss hanging out with you, going to the mall, meeting for lunch, and yapping on the phone for hours about nothing. It's been forever and a day—it seems like. I miss that, don't you? We've both been busy but when did we get too busy for each other?"

Kim asked about my kids to break the tension-filled atmosphere. I played along and bragged about DeMarya's acceptance into an elementary school and Lil D into preschool. I joked about how old each of us were getting then figured it to be an appropriate time to ask about her child. Silent for a few moments, Kim eventually admitted to losing her child but not much else. I didn't press the issue but simply reminded her that God doesn't make mistakes, and, in every situation, there is a message to be learned.

"Yeah, I guess so," Kim responded.

"I didn't want a baby anyhow. And the father wasn't who I wanted in my life anyway. It just kinda happened you know. The message I take from all of this is that none of this was supposed to happen."

"You've got to be more careful about who you allow in your life, that's all." I clutched her hands.

"And a man who'll put his hands on a woman ain't the man you need to be with. I remember the first time DeMarcus hit me. He hit me so hard I cried like a baby. To him, my tears were a sign of weakness, but I got his azz the second time he raised his hand to me. He was purple when I got finished with him. Cuts and scratches covered his face. He never raised his hand to me again."

"You never told me that."

"Well, I guess I kept a secret from you too. But not only did he abuse me physically, we had a lot of arguments that I realize now were also abusive. DeMarcus had a way of making me feel like I was a bad mother and like I was stupid and needed him. I tried to make myself attractive to cover the pain, but he would always find fault in my hair, my clothes, and even my fragrance. I'm glad I got out. It's truly a blessing not having to live through that hell anymore."

"That's how they get control, huh?"

"Yep. DeMarcus needs help and I hope he gets it. So back to your man," I said.

"Is he in jail for doing this to you?"

Unaware of his whereabouts, Kim admitted to being afraid of returning to her apartment. I was puzzled when she refused to link the assault to her miscarriage. I was baffled by the look of panic and worry upon her face when mentioning that his actions would be considered murder in the eyes of the law.

"You're a strong woman though. But what I want to know is how did you meet him and what prompted you to let him move in? If you wanted to shack up with somebody, why didn't you accept Geo's offer?"

My words may have offended Kim, but she held strong in not divulging details about this mystery man including his name. I thought that if I kept asking, eventually she'd give up something, but she didn't and each time I asked a question about him, she'd ask about the kids or my dad.

"What's that on your finger sparkling like a fine piece of glass? Is that an engagement ring?"

Grinning from ear to ear, I proudly admitted to eloping over the weekend. Kim appeared happy, shocked, and confused all at the same time. She asked if it was anyone she knew but just as she'd been avoiding my line of questions, I avoided hers.

"Just know that I am very, very happy." I wiggled my ring finger in her face to give her a better glimpse of my bling-bling.

Feeling better about my visit than when I first approached hospital grounds, seeing her still in a depressed state tugged at my heart. Not knowing what more I could do, I reached again for Kim's hand and prayed for her a swift healing. Standing to my feet then leaning over the bed to give Kim a heartfelt hug, I apologized for having to shorten my visit then reached for my jacket. And as I turned to wave goodbye, I noticed Kim's lips trembling and tears again wailing up in her eyes.

"What's the matter?"

Kim nodded her head and replied. "It's nothing. Thank you for coming."

The sincerity upon her face was the unspoken apology I needed and at that moment, my heart was freed of animosity.

"Kim, I forgave DeMarcus a long time ago. My heart is big, I forgive you too."

I knew eventually that in moving forward with my new life, something from my past would resurface to haunt me. And I should have suspected it would be from none other than a nosey, trouble starting, sanctified sista fulfilling the role of the undercover church detective. Her name: Shelley Funkhouser, seat one, pew three. All was going well during what started out as a sisterhood meeting to discuss feeding the hungry and gifting the poor but inappropriately turned into a '*we want to know more about your session*' when her dumpster shopping azz embarrassed me. She had the audacity to ask about DeMarcus.

"Excuse me?" I whipped my neck around to stare her in the eyeball.

The room grew deadly silent.

"Sister, Funky lunk, Funk house, I'm sorry. What is it, funk what? Whatever it is," I continued, stepping to her toe to toe.

"What business is it of yours to know anything about my ex-husband or my past? I left a church that was full of troublemakers, schemers, folks thriving on keeping havoc going; I'm not doing it here. I escaped a very bad situation and my life is back on track. What my ex did was on him and it had nothing to do with me. But what I will tell you is, mind your own business because I am not the one!"

"I didn't mean anything by that, I was just…"

"You know, folks tried whispering in my ear to tell me about you before I even knew your name, but I didn't listen—I don't get wrapped up into nonsense. And just the other day, I politely walked away from another person trying to warn me about the church troublemaker slash church ho.' I knew they were talking about you but like I said, I don't get into folks KoolAid so stay out of mine. Did you know that's how people viewed you? Did you know you carried the title of church tramp? Until now, I thought you were a decent person, but I see firsthand that you are a troublemaker."

"Amen," shouted a slew of sisters.

"If it ain't about edifying your sister then you ought to keep your comments to yourself. That's what I'm about ladies. If we stick together as women, I can be someone you can rely on and you'll become someone I can rely on. It's time-up for dragging a sister through the mud. If what you got to say about your sister ain't good, don't bring it to me, I mean it!" Amen closed out the meeting.

Christmas was a month away and I knew it was inevitable keeping DeMarcus from wanting to spend time with his kids. However, in his absence, Poppa J had won over their hearts and the every now and again mention of their biological dads' whereabouts was becoming less frequent. Jamal was the best playmate. Daily, he wrestled with them and gave free pony rides throughout the house while I cooked and cleaned. He was also an educator, devoting thirty minutes or longer each night to making a game out of their schoolwork or watching an educational tape designed to have fun while they learned.

Preparing for an intimate first Christmas together, I was overwhelmed with emotions to learn that as a surprise for me, Jamal arranged for my dad, Auntie, and my little cousin, Tay-Tay to celebrate with us through the New Year; and they weren't being placed in a hotel either. Over a period of two evenings and while I was at work, Jamal and his friends worked tirelessly to totally remodel the basement with furnishings from his old apartment. Jamal had created the perfect spot for him and my dad to bond. And the most touching part of it all for me was the handcrafted sign he hung over the matching recliners which read, 'Jay and Pops.'

Christmas wasn't Jamal's favorite holiday and he kept no secrets about it. He recalled the many Christmases in his family's household as being extremely depressing.

"There were no presents given or love felt in my house," he stated, clearing his throat and attempting to fight back tears. Continuing on, my heart ached for him when he shared the promises made by his parents to buy him one special gift of his choosing were never kept and how when visiting other family members' homes and forced to watch his cousins unwrap their presents made him feel unloved and rejected. But when I suggested creating traditions of our own, his mind seemed to go wild. Stating that his family never had a real tree or one that was fully decorated, the first Wright family tradition he introduced was to purchase a live tree as a family.

The second was to celebrate Christ the entire month of December.

Picking out the perfect tree was a family affair indeed as well as memorable. DeMarya was given the task of choosing the perfect Angel to reign on high and Lil D was given the responsibility of flipping on the light switch upon Jamal's command.

By the second week of December, the tree skirt was fully covered with a multitude of presents. Jamal had gone overboard with purchasing gifts for everyone, even Ree-Ree the babysitter. I too had purchased a few gifts for my family and others but struggled to find the perfect gift for Jamal. Geo suggested a nice music system for his man cave, but he had one already. He then suggested a sports-themed refrigerator.

"It's football season, Rosilyn. Popping back the tab of a beer you got from your personalized refrigerator while watching your favorite sports team on television is a man's dream."

I considered the idea—believing it may have been something Jamal would honestly enjoy but I wanted bigger, something better. And after much thought, I settled on purchasing him a new truck. Not just any truck—I wanted a black truck for my black man and when I located one at a reasonable price, I paid a little extra to have the heated seats and floor mats monogrammed with his initials.

It was a huge relief spending the bulk of DeMarcus's money after the many months of storing it in my attic. Still having a little over $12,000 remaining, I decided to deposit it in a private rainy-day account under my newly-married name. After placing my deposit receipt in my wallet, I was only about seven steps outside of the bank inside of the mall when I felt a tap on my shoulder. Turning around, I was startled to be standing face to face with DeMarcus.

"It's been a while," he said. DeMarcus appeared overjoyed to see me. He hugged me as if we were reuniting siblings.

"How's my little man and little princess? I'd really like to see them. I'm doing better. I'm working, and I miss them more than you'll ever know."

"Hey, DeMarcus," is all I could utter. I was nervous, shaken, and wondering how long he'd been watching me.

"Out shopping, I see. What plans do you and the kids have for Christmas? Are yaw going to Louisville? What toys are they asking for? Did I tell you that I'm working now?" I nodded my head, though the awkwardness of being face to face with him gave me the creeps. He rambled on and on about his life with such enthusiasm that after a short while with an affixed smile on my face, my cheeks began to hurt.

"Look at you." He circled around me, complementing the highlights in my hair and visible weight loss. He reached for my chain and recalled the day he'd given me the heart charm to add to my necklace as if it should have been a memorable time for me as well.

"You look good, Roz. God's been good to you."

"He has," I replied.

He inquired about my job and then about my plans for my future. I laughed when he asked if I had a special person in my life.

"As a matter of fact, I do. And he's waiting for me in the parking lot. It's good seeing you, DeMarcus."

"Hold on, Roz. When can I see my kids?"

Chills shot through my body when he grabbed my arm. My mind flashed back to the not so long-ago tussle and fight.

"My cell phone number is still the same. Give me a call and we can arrange something."

I held onto a smile the best I could and at the first opportunity, pulled my arm from his grasp. His smile appeared genuine, but it did absolutely nothing for me. Hurriedly waving goodbye then turning away to blend in with the wave of mall goers, I prayed I'd never have to see him again. When DeMarcus was no longer in my view, I breathed a sigh of relief.

Stressed completely out when I walked through my front door, Jamal cradled me in his arms and allowed me to cry as I shared my opinion and feelings about the encounter. Jamal's belief was strong that DeMarcus's presence would cause a disruption in the kids' lives, but he encouraged the visitation stating the importance of reassuring the kids that their biological father hadn't abandoned them and that he still loves them.

It was two days later—early on a Saturday morning when DeMarcus called to arrange a day and time for visitation. After going around and around about various days of the week that wasn't convenient for my schedule, I invited him to join us to watch DeMarya's sixth gymnastics lesson at noon. Stating that he had nothing planned for the day, he jotted down the gymnasium address and asked that I keep his visit quiet as a surprise to the kids. In my gut, I dreaded seeing him again but felt meeting in a public facility was best and would provide witnesses in the event something was to pop off. And although Jamal assured me that I was doing the right thing and believed strongly that DeMarcus would be on his best behavior, I silently prayed that he'd be a no-show.

Lil D was the first one to see DeMarcus when he arrived and nearly stumbled over his own feet racing to greet him. Taking a seat next to me, DeMarcus and my exchange of pleasantries was cordial and brief. Aside from watching the father and son reunion, having DeMarcus in my immediate space was eerily odd. And though Lil D was happy to see his father, he preferred horsing around on the deck with the other children versus sitting in DeMarcus's lap.

Every so often, Lil D would return and sneak a peek—making certain that his dad hadn't left but in truth, I prayed that somehow, he'd persuade his daddy to follow him outside. But that didn't happen.

DeMarcus was content sitting at my side and grinning in my face. DeMarcus's conversation was all over the place—nothing at all related to the kids. His interests lay mainly in discounting rumors I may have heard during his turbulent season and building himself up, in an attempt, to regain my trust. He inquired about my finances which I chalked up as measly pennies and he even asked if I'd returned to Little Flock. But when he so boldly inquired about the last person I was intimate with, I shut his meddlesome azz down.

"I'd like to think it was me," he said, followed by a laugh. He cocked his head to the right and stared me in the eye; patiently awaiting my reply. Instead of an answer, he got a cold shoulder. Subsequently, I turned my head and my chair away from him.

"You're a beautiful woman, Roz, and I know you've got guys sniffing after you. But aside from all that, it looks like you're holding things down and doing a fantastic job caring for the kids. Listen, I kind of feel like I owe you an apology for all you've had to go through these last few months. It hasn't been easy for me either, but I survived. You got a good heart, Roz, so I know you'll forgive me but from the bottom of my heart, I beg your forgiveness because that deal with Evonne, man, it wasn't anything but lies made up by the media. Evonne and I were only friends. You know that, everybody knows that. But she tried to set me up though—making people think I killed her husband. Personally, I wouldn't be surprised if she killed him for the insurance policy. But now all jokes are on her because she hasn't seen one thin dime from any of the policies."

Totally disinterested, I crossed my arms and looked him in the eye as he told one lie after the next, after the next. He was overly dramatic—intensifying his lies through hand gestures.

He talked fast and in circles.

"How do you know so much of her business, DeMarcus?"

"Cause when I would talk to her, all kinds of crazy things would come out of her mouth, that's how. But I encouraged her to tell him the truth about what was going on in her life, and even quoted your old saying about no matter how much it's gonna hurt, speaking the truth is the only way to have a clear heart and peace within...or something like that. She treated him like dirt. I could never be attracted to someone like Evonne; she was all about herself."

DeMarcus called my name then grabbed my arm. I jerked my arm away.

"Don't be like that, Roz. Have you heard anything I've said? If not, hear this and know that I mean it from the bottom of my heart. I'm still the man you married and fell in love with seven, eight years ago. And just because we've divorced, it doesn't mean that I stopped loving you. All I'm asking for is to spend time with you and the kids occasionally. We gotta keep it together and remain friends for them. Who knows, maybe sometime soon, we can work towards reuniting our family."

I grew agitated with his presence and the craziness falling from his lips. If he knew how difficult it was to simply be cordial, he'd sit back, shut up, and stop wasting his time—and mine on hopeless possibilities. There was nothing I liked about him anymore and the feelings he proclaimed having for me, I could give a rats' azz about them. He tried telling jokes to get me to crack a grin, but I wanted him to shut up. His breath was stank, his once upon a time nicely trimmed facial hair was nappy, scratchy and gray, and his hairline had receded to the point that shaving himself bald was his only option. And although his lavender button-down shirt and freshly creased jeans were new, he was ugly to me—inside and out.

DeMarcus rubbed my cheek with his finger.

"Don't touch me, please. I thought you were here to watch your daughter."

"So, it's like that," DeMarcus laughed.

"I remember when all you wanted me to do was touch you and show you affection. You're still bitter, huh?"

"Bitter? I was never bitter. We're divorced DeMarcus so cut out trying to relive the past. Why don't you go play with Lil D? Because trying to butter me up, ain't gonna happen."

"Now the truth comes out. You're bitter because I divorced you. I did it to protect you, to protect my family. We had our ups and downs but no matter what went on, you and those kids were always first."

My squinted eyes shifted towards him, telling a story of their own. I wanted to ask what planet he lived on but held my tongue. I also wanted to ask him to recall a time in his mind that he felt he'd put the kids and me first but refrained from asking that as well. I was sooooooo beyond DeMarcus that all I could do was laugh at my own self for entertaining the fool and allowing him to get underneath my skin.

"There it is—that pretty smile I remember. You're gorgeous Roz and I miss you."

I thanked him for the compliment then pointed towards DeMarya who was up next to tumble.

"After this, I'd like to treat you and the kids to a burger? We can make this family time. It'll be more time I can spend with the kids and if we go to the park, they'll be able to swing and run free. You and I can take turns spinning each other on that wheel ride that always made me dizzy."

When DeMarya's class was over, I was the first to hug and edify her for doing such an excellent job. When spotting her daddy, I no longer existed. The joy on her face when she jumped from my arms and into his was priceless. Their reunion was a tear-jerker and watching the kids fight for his attention was evidence of how much they truly missed him. Making our way into the parking lot, DeMarya who was in DeMarcus' arms clung tightly to his neck while Lil D gripped his hand. Seeing my kids this happy made me happy, and not wanting to be a killjoy, I offered up another hour to DeMarcus and held him to his word on treating us to lunch.

It wasn't until we reached my car and had strapped the kids in that I realized that he was without a vehicle. *Imagine that, me being his chauffeur.* I didn't ask, and he didn't say, but for DeMarcus to be without his prized possession meant that it had been repossessed. A tiny part of me felt sorry for his misfortune but my memory wouldn't allow me to forget the time when Ma was ill and driving his luxury vehicle to Louisville wasn't an option.

We collected our burgers from the drive-through window and picnicked at a nearby park. Giddy were the kids about spending time with their dad but DeMarcus appeared to be more interested in spending time with me. *Aggravating.*

"Seems just like old times," he stated more than once, and I ignored with hopes that my facial expressions revealed a lack of interest in reminiscing about our past. But DeMarcus was adamant, smiling when recalling the day I gave birth to DeMarya.

"I was so happy and nervous," he began. "I remember the first time she grabbed my finger and wouldn't let go. She's always been Daddy's little girl. Look at her now, she's beautiful and getting so tall. And look at my little man.

I remember when he needed me to lift him up onto the slide but he's a big guy now and can do it all by himself. I sure miss spending time with them. I miss you too Roz."

"Well, things are different now but we're adjusting. They are happy to see you so why don't you go play with them? Go, push DeMarya on the swing or something."

"The kids are fine," he said.

"What I really want to know is how you're doing? My last apology wasn't sincere but from the bottom of my heart, I am truly sorry. I've got my head on straight now and things are looking up for me. Every night I lay in the bed and ask God to show me what it is that I need to do to get my family back. Right now is proof that God's answering my prayers because, in my dreams, I saw the four of us together. Just like this, having family time like we used to. It's OK to smile," he told me.

"I see you trying to play tough, put down your guard. It's me, DeMarcus, your one and only love. I know you still love me."

Listening to him was torture. His words were repetitive and meaningless. The sight of him was becoming even more sickening.

"I messed up, I did. But if anyone's ever had my back, it's been you. As far back as seminary school to when I became a pastor, and even through my turbulent times, you were there. You're a good person, Rosilyn, and you didn't deserve any of what I've put you through."

"Apology accepted."

DeMarcus stroked my face again with his finger. I smacked his hand although I really wanted to yank his finger out of its socket.

"You still love me, don't you?" he asked, smiling and again reaching up to touch my face.

"You're supposed to be interacting with your kids, not me. Apology accepted, damn! Stop with all the sob stories and lies. It's over, so let's move on."

"You're angry, but I understand why you've got your guard up. I hurt you but cross my heart and swear to God, I'll never put another hand on you. Through all of this, I've realized just how much I need you. God blessed me with you and I messed it up. But I'm going to do all I can to win back your heart."

"You'll be wasting your time DeMarcus."

He laughed at my words; that infuriated me. He threw his arm around my shoulder pulling me in for a sideway hug; that sickened me. No matter what I said or how I said it, he refused to accept me being done with him. Killing his spirits by acknowledging that I had remarried came to mind, but that would have either created an argument or started another round of seventy-two questions which I was unwilling to be a participant.

"My mom will be here next weekend and I was hoping that, just this once, I could stay over, and we could set out cookies for Santa like we used to do. And if anything needs to be assembled, I can do that while the kids sleep. She's excited about meeting and spending time with them, really."

I chuckled, and then burst into a *he's done lost his fricken mind* laugh.

"No, DeMarcus, we've got plans for Christmas! Listen, if you're not going to play with the kids then it's time to go."

"Chill, calm down. I realize I may be trying to rush things, but my only intent is to make things right with you, so don't snap at me. Can't you see that I love you? With everything within me, I want to show that to you."

He grabbed my hands in a calming manner, but it only raised my blood pressure. I didn't want him to love me nor did I want him in my breathing space. Grabbing my purse from underneath the picnic table I whistled for the kids and walked alone toward the car. Stating living nearby, DeMarcus asked to be dropped off at Wiley's Convenience Store located on the corner of Stokes and Irvine Road. Literally, I wanted to kick him out as soon as I pulled into the lot and applied the brakes, but I demonstrated patience for the kids' sake when he turned to tell them goodbye.

"Is a kiss out of the question?" he turned and asked me.

"Goodbye, DeMarcus," I responded, as politely as I could.

"You must really like this fella," he laughed.

"I remember when I was your one and only and you couldn't get enough of me. Whoever he is, he's found a gem in you. He must be a special man."

"Yeah, he is. Goodbye, DeMarcus."

I peeled out of the parking lot and never looked back.

Jamal was on the porch talking to Ree-Ree when I pulled into the driveway. Once I freed them from their car seats, they followed Ree-Ree over to her backyard to watch Tony deskinning catfish. Grateful, for having a few moments to calm my nerves, once inside, I kicked off my shoes and stretched out on the couch in the den. Jamal handed me a glass of wine. It was exactly what I needed.

I hadn't turned on the radio or television and nor did Jamal. Instead, he placed a pillow underneath my feet and kneeled at the foot of the couch to rub them. He attentively listened as I summarized my afternoon.

"It was awful! DeMarcus wasn't focused on spending quality time with the kids; he was trying to get closer to me. He acted like I was his girlfriend and we were squabbling or something. It was so nerve-wracking."

"Yeah, I know, but everything is going to be alright."

"You weren't there to see him or hear him, Jamal," my voice squeaked. "It was more than awful!"

"No, I wasn't there but right after you dropped him off, he called asking me for advice."

"Advice about what?" I sat up for his answer.

"He asked me to help him win back his family." Jamal shook his head.

"We've got a problem on our hands, babe. I haven't quite figured out how to address it just yet, but I will. Trust me, it'll be OK."

"Naw, we don't have a problem, DeMarcus does. Even if I hadn't married you, there's no way in the hell I'd consider taking him back. What did you tell him? Oh, God, I can't believe this!"

"I didn't advise him on anything, and for the most part, I just listened. But I did point out that your life has changed and that he needs to accept that. DeMarcus is going through what I call a mental pause."

"What?"

"Women experience menopause and break out in sweats and the chills. Well men experience mental pause—a form of memory loss, but worse," he chuckled. "See, when a man loses his memory, it's a sign that his brain juices are out of whack, not flowing like they should, and he loses all concepts of reality. But when he snaps back, even though things have changed the man expects things to be as they once were. As it relates to DeMarcus, he's on the rise after falling from his pedestal. He's been humiliated and has hit the lowest of the low. He's lost his financial security, his children, and his wife and now that he's on the upswing, he wants to recover what he lost."

"Lost, my azz! Are you kidding me? That's bull, Jamal, and you know it! He was in his right mind when his fat azz got on that plane with Evonne. And he was in his right mind when he spent all our savings on only he knows what, and put me and the kids out without knowing whether we had a place to stay or not. Damn, DeMarcus! And I mean that! If you don't tell him about us, I will!"

I shook uncontrollably from being so upset. Jamal pulled me into his chest and loved-on-me, but the damage had been done. My blood pressure became elevated and my migraine was massive. I was pissed too at Jamal for not nipping their conversation in the bud so that I wouldn't have to. Then it occurred to me that neither of us had discussed *how* and *when* we would tell DeMarcus.

"We knew there'd be consequences for our union, but never in a million years would I think that I'd be the person DeMarcus contacted for advice about anything. But before he finds out from someone else, I'll meet with him man to man. I'd never place you a situation that as your husband I should handle, remember that. When I said, '*I Do,*' that meant I accepted the responsibility of paying every bill in this house and standing in the gap to shield you and the kids from hurt, harm, and danger. You handle the woman stuff and let me take care of everything else, a'ight."

Perhaps it was the series of nightmares starring DeMarcus I had in conjunction with the frequent trips to the toilet to rid myself of the grease burger consumed the day before that assured me that on this day, Sunday, was gonna be crappy. Yesterday's migraine still lingered and with exception of the bones in my inner ear, every other bone in my body ached to the point that ingesting another pain-relieving pill may have caused an overdose.

Jamal was sweet in caring for me, however, what impressed me the most was the call placed to an Associate Minister instructing him to handle the church affairs in his absence. Yes, he put me first and for this, I loved him even more. Jamal tended to the kids--preparing their breakfast and bribing them with gifts to keep quiet while I rested. But I assured him that I was alright and sent him and the kids out the door in just enough time to make it to morning worship service.

My intentions were to at least put a roast in the oven and have the leftover sides warmed by the time they got home, but sometime during the peaceful morning, the medicine kicked in and my body shut down. It was well past five when I opened my eyes to find Jamal at my side and asking if I felt better.

"No need to get up babe, I've got everything covered. There's a bucket of chicken in the kitchen and because they were so good, they both got a new

DVD. They're in DeMarya's room so rest up and I'll go warm up the soup I got ya'."

As I prepared for work the next morning, I faked feeling better, but in reality, my stomach cramps had only subsided a tad bit, leading me to believe I was either dehydrated or suffering from food poisoning. Walking into the center, the smell of a freshly brewed pot of coffee made me nauseated but the fresh from the bakery chocolate-covered lemon filled doughnuts on the break room table seemed to be calling my name. Had Geo not commented on the two he watched me shove down my throat, I would have wrapped a third in a napkin and pretended that it was my first.

"Guess what?" Geo said, following closely on my heels and into my office. His face displayed a half-cocked smile.

"I saw Kim this weekend. I was out with my new lady friend when out of nowhere she appeared. It caught me off guard hearing her voice but looking in her eyes shut me down completely. I mean, it was nice to see her, but she looked sad. I felt sorry for her. Why? I don't know, but I couldn't enjoy my dinner or company for wondering how things were going for her."

"Well, did you talk to her?"

"I called her cell phone, but her number has been disconnected. I rode by her place and before you say it, no, I wasn't stalking her. I didn't see her car and her apartment looked vacant. But last night I found an unsigned card underneath my windshield that read: Thinking about you. It could have been from anybody but I'm hoping it was from Kim."

"The last time we spoke was the day I visited her in the hospital. Before I left her room, I let her know that as far as I am concerned, we're still friends. I left the next move in her court."

"Yeah, but something tells me that she's in trouble. Don't yaw have a mutual friend or somebody that may have her new number?"

"I don't, but if she's in trouble, she knows how to find us."

"Would you consider asking DeMarcus for her contact information? Maybe they still communicate."

I wasn't offended by his suggestion but mentioning DeMarcus's name sent sharp pains through my stomach. So sharp, that during my lunch hour I drove myself to the immediate care center.

Chapter 20

Joy to The World

It was on December 23rd when I received the call from the dealership informing me that the detailing of the truck was complete. Instead of having it delivered to our house, Tony agreed to ride with me to pick up Jamal's new SUV and volunteered to store it in his garage as opposed to parking it on the street as I initially planned to do.

Jamal and Tony had become good friends so inviting him, Lisa, and Ree-Ree over to share in our 1st Annual Celebrate Christ with Family and Friends gathering seemed most appropriate. Everything Jamal could imagine wanting to be cooked for Christmas, I purchased. And although the menu was already planned out, Tony offered to contribute a fresh pot of chicken and homemade dumplings.

"And Lisa makes the best the apple butter stuffed biscuits," he added.

"We'll bring that too."

Jamal was as content as one could be, even remarked about feeling on top of the world with his family safe, happy, and under one roof. I concurred, but as well as things were for me and my family, I couldn't stop worrying about Kim. To ease my mind, Jamal suggested that I try to locate her.

Praying as I drove to her apartment complex, I mentally prepared myself for seeing Kim with DeMarcus, but that wasn't the case. Peeking through the front window of her apartment, I was stunned to find an empty room.

"I felt sorry for Ms. Kim," a young guy approaching me from behind said.

"Ms. Kim was cool. But the day after her boyfriend beat her down, the sheriffs sat her stuff out, then a day after that, her car got towed away. If you see her, let her know that T-Baby said hello, a'ight."

From the apartment complex I drove to the hospital she was released from in search of a forwarding address. Knowing that sharing confidential information was prohibited, I flashed my crisis center badge at the front desk clerk and explained needing to reach a former patient presumed to be in danger. Without further questions, the clerk checked her database then jotted down an address.

Arriving at the Ackerman Estates Apartments Complex, I had only stood at door 3103 for a second when it opened. A young woman invited me in as if I was expected.

"I'll tell Ms. Kim that you're here," she said before disappearing.

When Kim turned the corner and saw me in the doorway, she covered her eyes and began crying. Making my way to where she stood, I placed my hands on her shoulders and whispered, *"It's OK,"*. Kim sobbed uncontrollably. Through her tears, I sensed remorse. Leading her to the couch and taking a seat, I clasped her hands with my hands and shared that she'd been weighing heavily on my mind.

"It's funny," she began. "Not even twenty minutes ago, Shayla, the girl who opened the door was in my room and asked if I believed in God. When I told her that I did, she asked why I was staying with them and not my own family. I told her a little bit about my family then, the best I could, explained how I managed to mess things up with the one person who always protected me, encouraged me, and treated me more like a sister than a good friend. That led us into another conversation about Angels. And the last two things I said to her were that we may not be able to see God but never doubt that God is real. And I let her know the importance of treating everybody good because there are real Angels on earth, we can't see who are down here making sure His people are alright. When she left my room, I got on my knees and started praying. When I stood up, it was no more than 10 or 15 seconds later that she reentered my room and stated that my Angel was here."

"God's just that good, isn't He?"

We embraced again then took our conversation to a nearby diner for privacy. Initially, Kim was tight-lipped about how things transpired between her and DeMarcus, but she eventually admitted to engaging in a short-lived affair right after the church set him out. Recalling the beating that hospitalized her, through tears she acknowledged that the child she lost was his.

"None of this was supposed to happen. I saw him coming out of a store one day and I spoke. The conversation was brief but then he asked for a ride up the road, but the road never ended. It didn't take me long to realize that he had no place to go and figured one night on my couch wouldn't hurt. But then one night became two and so on and so on and when I started pressuring him about vacating my space, he would make me feel guilty about putting him out. Before I knew it, I had become his psychiatrist, then his maid pretty much, to his closest friend and from there, well, you know. We didn't love each other—hell, we really didn't like each other. The baby surprised us both," she said sniffling and wiping away tears.

"Don't take this the wrong way, but things happen for a reason. None of us knows the plans God has for us but in my heart, I truly believe that DeMarcus's downfall is from being a devil in the pulpit. The majority of the stuff he was involved in, I had no clue about and the stuff I suspected was going on, he led me to believe it was a figment of my imagination. As for you, I strongly believe your lesson in all of this is that God has bigger plans for you. Not DeMarcus, but a man who will support you and not the other way around. A man who has his life together and has prepared himself to care for your heart, not hurt it. You will be blessed with a man wanting to marry you, and you'll be blessed with children. God's gonna bless you with your own relationship that won't have to be kept a secret. So, keep your head up and know that you're passing through a storm. Yes, I was hurt by you and DeMarcus but that was then, this is now. And one of the reasons why I can forgive you and DeMarcus is because just like you, I was going through a storm. I realized that either I had to move on or get stuck with being miserable and missing out on what God had in store for my future. And when I decided to forgive the both of you and let go of the hatred I was harboring, God released my pain and blessed me beyond words. My heart is no longer heavy, and He's placed a very special man in my life."

"Who? Jamal?"

"Yes Jamal. And we would be so honored if you would come by and eat with us tomorrow. It's an all-day celebration, breakfast at 8:00 and dinner around 6:00 with a few friends and family. Wait! Come home with me tonight!"

Jamal was chopping ingredients for his self-proclaimed, mouthwatering turkey dressing when we walked through the door. Putting down his cutlery to embrace Kim, to make her feel welcomed, he pulled up a stool and gave her the responsibility of choosing the celebratory wine selection of the night. Returning to his chopping board, Jamal talked to her as if they were dear, old

230

friends and shared how much she'd been on our minds. Watching from afar, I was amazed at how Jamal was able to keep the conversation upbeat, purposely changing the subject when Kim wanted to discuss her dark moments.

"Forget those things from the past," Jamal said.

"We love you, girl, so kick off your shoes and get comfortable. Our home is your home. We don't want you to feel bound by anything that's happened in the past because we've let it all go. Tomorrow we're celebrating Christ with our family and friends and we're gonna have an awesome time worshipping God in this house. And Kim, we would be honored if you would spend the entire holiday with us. We have plenty of room."

Kim accepted the invite and once situated in the guest room, we toured the house then returned to the spiced-filled kitchen where two freshly-poured, chilled glasses of wine awaited us—compliments of Jamal. As midnight approached, only two of the six pies had been made and there were chitterlings still to be cleaned, collard greens washed, and snap beans snapped. By 2 a.m. having boiled water for the macaroni twice only for it to be forgotten and evaporate, Jamal relieved us of our kitchen duties and escorted us into the den. Spending time with Kim was great. We laughed, cried, and laughed some more. In many ways, it felt like old times.

It seemed like I had only blinked twice before Jamal nudged my shoulder to tell me that it was time to get up. My fam' from Louisville was expected in at any time and as part of our newly created Christmastime traditions, I was responsible for preparing a hearty breakfast.

Stepping away from the hot streaming water that downed my face was hard. My body was fatigued and interestingly, my small ankles were swollen. Kim was an excellent help in the kitchen though; all but for the apple dumplings and grits, she had everything mixed and ready to serve.

It was 8:20 a.m. exactly when Dad, Auntie, Jamal's co-workers, a few members from Mount Olive and their families assembled around the table for breakfast. After Jamal blessed the food, Kim helped me set up an extra table in the den for the children to eat. The food was served piping hot. And after stuffing our faces, Jamal and some of the fellas took advantage of the fifty-four-degree weather by playing rounds of corn hole in the backyard. Those remaining inside conversed amongst themselves over freshly brewed coffee.

By 10 a.m., Auntie was ready to start preparing dinner so after clearing what was left on the tables, Kim and I washed the breakfast dishes. She wiped,

I dried, and my Auntie fried chicken that is and by three o'clock, every dish for the evening celebration was in the oven or on the stove bubbling. I could tell in Kim's eyes that she was tired, but not once did she complain. She catered to the needs of my dad and Auntie, and even gave the kids a laugh by joining them on the trampoline. Pulling her to the side after flipping herself dizzy, I handed her an early Christmas present—$1,200 from the Wright family.

My house was noisy, but it was a wonderful noise. It was chaotic, but an organized chaos. The household was warm and welcoming, full of love and the spirit of the holiday, so I didn't find it at all odd when Jamal called Lil D inside to do the honors of flipping on the lights of our Christmas tree. Everyone was pretty much doing their own thing. The younger children—still out on the back deck were content with chasing one another while the preteens and teens congregated at the bottom of the decks' steps dancing and listening to rap music. Dad, Jamal, and a few others were happily hidden in the man cave watching football highlights, stuffing their bellies with desserts, and playing '70s and '80s albums on Jamal's *mint condition* turntable.

Using their preoccupation to my advantage, I grabbed a light jacket then stepped out onto the front porch to enjoy the cool and mid-morning calming breeze. Moments later, hearing my cell phone ring interrupted my thoughts but I raced back inside the house to answer it in case it was someone calling for directions. The number was blocked but I answered it anyway. It was DeMarcus asking to see the kids. In no way was I going to allow him to interfere or ruin my Christmas Eve family and friends gathering, so to appease him, I offered a two-hour visitation on Christmas morning. I faked having an upbeat attitude about the visit then asked to be texted the hotel information of where he and his mother were staying.

Dinner was promptly served at six o'clock and except for two of Jamal's co-workers who left, everyone invited was in attendance. Spacing was limited, however, but the food was plentiful and judging by the smiles on everyone's face, no one seemed to mind. Fried chicken, baked chicken, chicken and dumplings, pork roast, beef ribs, and a honey glazed ham were the meats. The table of sides was a colorful mixture of fried corn, corn pudding, candied yams, collard greens, macaroni and cheese, broccoli casserole, and deviled eggs. Jaws were yapping and flapping—there appeared to not be a stranger in the midst.

After dinner, Lisa, Kim, and I cleaned the kitchen then joined the others in the den for karaoke. Tony brought out a deck of cards and got a spades game going while Jamal and a few of his 'pushing-forty' friends attempted to imitate their favorite NBA player using the rim he attached to the garage. Dad was having a wonderful time as well, planning a golfing outing with Geo.

When darkness fell, Jamal called everyone into the living room. Asking for Lil D and DeMarya to join him at the front of the room, their eyes lit up when they were handed a present and permission to open them. Jamal enlisted Geo's help in gifting our guests. Afterward, he called my name.

"If you didn't know already, well, this is my wife." Everyone in the room laughed.

"We've only been married for seventy-six days but I want all of you to know that she is the love of my life and I thank her for making this day so very special. For that, I'm gonna let you open up one of your gifts."

"You're silly," I chuckled, when opening the box to find an electric blanket inside.

"I know it's not what you wanted but we've gotta compromise, Sweetie. You have it so hot in here, the kids and I wake up sweating in the middle of the night because you keep the thermostat set on ninety-five."

"Whatever Jamal!" I laughed, along with the others who found humor in the subtle way he decided to bring this to my attention.

"Can I have everyone's attention, please?" I said, clearing my throat. I waited until all eyes were upon me.

"If you didn't know already, Jamal is my husband. And I want to tell the world that he's been a wonderful husband. Honey, I also want to publicly apologize for making you feel like a cooked turkey. But the only reason I do that is, so you'll understand what it feels like having a bun in the oven."

Jamal shook his head in denial and lifted his left brow. "I don't turn the heat up, you do. You have it so hot in here that some nights, I've thought about putting a window unit in DeMarya's room so that the three of us can sleep comfortably."

"Awwwww!" said Auntie, covering her mouth with her hands.

"Listen to what I'm saying, honey. A bun is in the oven, Merry Christmas."

"I left the bread in the oven? Oh, snap!" Jamal headed toward the kitchen. "There's nothing in here," he yelled back.

Hilarious best describes his inability to catch the message and when returning to the living room, he was clueless as to why everyone had laughed themselves into tears.

"What's so funny?"

"Jamal, honey, I love you, OK. Merry Christmas, baby." I placed his hands on my belly.

"I'm pregnant."

He kissed my lips several times. Through his tears, I saw joy. Someone remarked that this was the first time he'd shut up the entire day, but his silence spoke volumes as he rested his head on my shoulder while gently touching my belly.

It was late, a little past eleven when I shut down the kitchen and turned off the lights in the living room. Except for Geo and Kim who were on the back patio talking, all our houseguests had left, each one full, happy, and gifted. Watching my Auntie creep into the back with a bottle of wine and knowing the kids were in Lil D's room watching the last movie of the night, I joined Jamal in the shower where we again embraced and shared excitement over our great news.

"Today has been the greatest day of my entire life. Being asked to pastor a church doesn't come close in comparison to finding out that I am going to be a daddy. For so many years, I've just existed. I've done what I needed to do to stay out of trouble and to keep a roof over my head. When my parents died, I never imagined being anything other than alone. Yeah, I dated a few women, but I couldn't find love. But look at me now. I have a wonderful wife, two awesome step-kids who love me and call me Poppa, and every room in this house is full of people that call me their family. And tonight, you tell me that you're having my baby. Rosilyn, I never believed I'd have any of this. I knew that my God was good but all at once, I've been showered with so many blessings. My cup truly is overflowing."

Christmas morning—a crack after dawn, Jamal woke us all up and asked us to gather around the tree. While he prayed a long, but appropriate prayer to remind the kids of the true meaning of Christmas, no one noticed Geo strolling into the living room for watching the excitement on the kids' faces. When I looked over at Kim, she smiled then raised her hand and wiggled her fingers.

"Wait, wait!" I said, pointing over to Kim. Kim again held up her hand and flashed her rock. A proud and teary-eyed Geo happily announced that Kim accepted his marriage proposal. Excited for them both, I gave Kim a heartfelt congratulatory hug.

"He told me last night that he'd been praying for me," she whispered.

"He confessed his love for me and said he's been miserable without me in his life. Little did he know, I was miserable without him too and had been praying for his forgiveness for mistreating him."

"Never underestimate the power of prayer," I responded.

"Prayer changes things. Yes, prayer still works!"

"A blushing bride," remarked Auntie.

"Congratulations, you two!"

At 10:05 a.m. and just as Tony and I planned, he pulled into the driveway and honked the horn. Alerted by Geo of the arriving guest, Jamal stepped away from his breakfast plate and out onto the porch.

"It looks like Deacon Cuffee from the church."

As Jamal made his way toward the driveway, I called everyone away from the table and over to the bay window. Spotting Tony behind the wheel, Jamal laughed then complimented him on his new truck.

"This baby is beyond nice," I heard Jamal remark then laugh.

"Merry Christmas, it's yours, man. It's a present from me and Lisa."

"Yeah right, man. Whatever," Jamal laughed.

"Naw man, all jokes aside. Your wife hooked you up with this. Come on, get in."

"Bull," Jamal replied before turning around to find me a few steps away and with a huge grin on my face.

"Baby, is this me for real?"

Confirming with a nod of my head that it was, Jamal jumped inside and thoroughly checked it out.

"The seats have my initials on them, dang!!! Even the keyring is monogrammed. It's beautiful, Rosilyn, how did you…?"

I shushed him before he could ask.

Chapter 21

Confess with Your Mouth

It was nearing noon on Christmas Day when Jamal suggested I invite our neighbors over for brunch. We had more than enough and graciously, Lisa accepted. Like the day before, our table was complete with mouth-watering meats and sides. And once Auntie sat the bowl of fried potatoes and onions on the table, Jamal asked everyone to bow their heads for the blessing over the food.

I was hungry and had only shoved a forkful of potatoes in my mouth when a knock on the door pulled me away from the table. I hadn't forgotten about DeMarcus wanting to spend time with the kids but became livid by his just showing up. At his side was his mom who brushed past me and shoved a tiny bag in my hand. The bag contained an angel figurine probably purchased from the drug store up the road prior to their arrival. DeMarcus too brushed past me and waltzed into the den. He helped himself to a plate, a drink, and a seat. He reached out and shook Dad's hand then leaned over and kissed Auntie on the cheek. He nodded his head at Jamal and Geo. Seeing Kim, he nodded his head and spoke a dry, "hello."

"Merry Christmas, everybody. This is my mom, Dee. Hey kids, come meet your grandma."

His presence had caused a shift in the atmosphere, but Jamal was cordial. Being a gracious host, he welcomed them to the table.

"Auntie, it's nice seeing you again," DeMarcus said.

"It's been years since I had your fried potatoes. Rosilyn tried making them like you, but she could never seem to get them just right."

He chuckled but no one else one found humor in his joke. In fact, the harder he tried being the life of the brunch, the more annoying he became.

Cordial best describes everyone's interaction with him as he attempted to fit in. Noticing the skepticism on the faces of my guests, I suggested the kids show their dad their gifts to get him up from the table but that plan backfired. DeMarya was deeply engaged in a conversation with Grandma Dee and Lil D had crawled into DeMarcus's lap asking for assistance with an action figure requiring batteries.

It hadn't occurred to me that DeMarcus came empty-handed until Lil D asked him for his present. The room got quiet. So quiet, you could hear a mouse poot if you listened hard enough as everyone else wanted to know too. DeMarcus laughed it off and turned to ask Lisa to pass the gravy.

"Mommy's going to have a baby," I heard DeMarya say.

"I hope it's a baby sister."

My eggs fell into my lap and all eyes shifted to me. Not because I dropped my fork and my eggs, but to see my facial expression. I began to choke and reached for my glass of orange juice.

"She's having a baby and it's a bun in the oven," DeMarya repeated.

"My, my. That's good news," DeMarcus said.

"But I don't think mommy wanted you to tell me that."

DeMarcus looked up at me and smiled. But knowing him as well as I did, I was certain that he would be asking for clarity and specifics later.

"It's OK, Daddy. Poppa J and Mommy told me. And Auntie Kim is gonna be a pretty bride. Did you see Poppa J's new car, Daddy? It's got his name on the keys and the seat."

"DeMarya, finish your food," is all I could utter. Jamal was speechless too but laughed at her innocence.

"Poppa J? You acting Daddy over here Jamal?"

"We'll talk later," Jamal responded.

"'Cause right now we're having a family brunch and today ain't about nothing but celebrating Christ."

"So, you're running things up-in-here? I thought you were my boy?" DeMarcus rose to his feet.

Dad instructed him to sit down but was ignored.

"*Look-a-here*," interjected Tony. "He said he'd talk to you later. You jumping up outcha' seat makes me a little nervous and sometimes I do foolish things when I get nervous. So, sit down and respect the man up in his house."

"Better yet, DeMarcus, I'm gonna have to ask you to leave. Now if you like, we can arrange a time later in the day for you to visit the kids, but your presence has been a downer. You're ruining Christmas for everybody. I'm sure you can understand that, so Ms. Dee, DeMarcus, please follow me to the door."

DeMarcus looked like the devil, bloodshot eyes and bulging veins visible in his temple. He repeatedly refused to leave but when Geo threatened to call the police, DeMarcus agreed that doing so would be a wise choice. Kim gathered the kids and quickly shuffled them from the area and into the back. Ms. Dee grabbed her coat. Auntie located the cordless phone and dialed 9-1-1.

"I don't give a damn about yaw calling the police. Man to man, tell me how you think you can just step into my life and take over as daddy to my kids and lover to my wife?"

"She's my wife now," Jamal admitted.

"I'm sorry, you had to find out this way, but yeah, we're married. Look D, man, you're still on probation and I'd hate to see you get into more trouble so go on, grab your coat and your momma and give me a call later."

"Everything I ever owned is up in this house and I ain't leaving it!" DeMarcus demanded 'right now' answers regarding our involvement.

Lisa pulled my arm attempting to help me escape through the back door, but I pulled my arm away and ran between Jamal and DeMarcus whose argument was escalating with every second. DeMarcus was like a crazed man, but Jamal wasn't backing down. I'd never seen Jamal so angry, nor had I ever felt so helpless.

Auntie begged them to talk it out like grown men, but her words were drowned out by their loud outbursts. Harsh words were the only things exchanged until DeMarcus pushed Jamal in the chest. When Jamal pushed back, a fistfight erupted; chairs were knocked over and plates hit the floor. Tony tried breaking them apart but was unsuccessful.

Jamal showed no mercy pinning DeMarcus down in a chokehold. When DeMarcus called for a truce, Jamal loosened his grip and again demanded he leave the house.

Resurfacing from the back, Kim asked if I was OK. Nodding that I was, I ran to my husband's side and clutched his arm. Expecting DeMarcus to leave when he reached for his coat, none of us was prepared for when he turned around with the look of Satan upon his face. Dropping his coat as quickly as he picked it up, DeMarcus reached for the carving knife with his left hand then pulled Kim into his chest and placed her in a headlock with the right arm. Kim and I screamed in terror. Struggling to be loosed, DeMarcus threatened to stab her if she didn't stop fidgeting. In exchange for her release, DeMarcus demanded answers.

"She ain't got nothing to do with this. Let her go," Jamal pleaded.

"Come on, man, she doesn't deserve this," shouted Geo.

"Ain't yo azz got something better to do?" questioned Tony.

"I'll kill her, I'm serious. Yaw got me looking like a fool—like I'm the bad guy. Now, somebody's gonna tell me what the hell is going on here!"

"Tell me, right damn now!"

"You've taken life from me already DeMarcus, please don't hurt me again. If you kill me, you're going away for life. You've got four years of probation now, don't mess that up, OK. Think about your kids. They are in the next room. If you hurt me, you may never see them again and I know how much you love them. Think about what you're doing please," Kim sobbed.

"Markie, let's go," shouted his mother.

DeMarcus loosened his grip but jabbed the knife in Kim's back when she attempted to run for safety. Falling to the floor, Kim screamed my name, but it was Geo who scooped up her lethargic body and cradled her in his arms like a baby. Blood spewed from her body like a running faucet but for her sanity, Geo maintained a calm disposition. He assured her that help was on the way and she'd be fine.

"This mofo is crazy," I heard Tony say in response to the third person conversation DeMarcus began having with himself as he paced the floor with his hands on his hips.

Terrified and frightened, I helplessly watched from the kitchen as Jamal and Tony physically struggled to take possession of the knife. But it was difficult with DeMarcus, a crazed man, slicing at the air and promising to cut anyone in his path. Tony's taunting wasn't helping matters—challenging DeMarcus's manhood and calling him a wussy for fighting with a weapon versus using his fists. Jamal attempted a non-physical approach. He warned DeMarcus of the potential consequences of his actions.

In all the chaos, I didn't recall seeing Dad leave the dining room until out from nowhere he appeared carrying a nail filled 2x8. I was unable to restrain my dad as he briskly pressed by me to swing the plank at DeMarcus. Dad missed and while brandishing the knife with his right hand, DeMarcus grabbed the plank with his left, overpowering Dad. Dad lost his footing and fell hard onto the floor.

Simultaneously, the knife dropped out of DeMarcus's hand and it became an immediate body pile up to retrieve it. Tony dove first underneath the table, then DeMarcus, and then Jamal. During their scramble, the knife got pushed underneath the curio cabinet. Jamal reached for it, but DeMarcus was quicker and once the knife was in his grasp, he used his foot to kick Jamal away and into the curio cabinet. Quick upon his feet, when DeMarcus pounced on top of Jamal, the room was deathly silent. Then, in a low muffled tone, I heard Jamal ask DeMarcus, "Why?"

"Put it down," Tony demanded in an '*I dare you*' tone, waving in the air a gun that Lisa retrieved from home and handed him.

"Your knife ain't no match for this here gun so again son, I'm telling you to put it down. I can claim self-defense. From what I know about you, you can't claim jack."

"My beef ain't with you," DeMarcus yelled back at Tony, "So do what you feel you got to do."

Auntie begged and pleaded with DeMarcus to give her the knife, but it was as if he was in a trance and fixated on nothing more than getting straight answers from Jamal.

"How could you pretend to be my friend then steal everything I ever had?"

"Let me up and we'll talk about it like men," pleaded Jamal.

Jamal's attempt to be loose created another scuffle and this time, his hand was sliced deep by the sharp blade. The arguing, cussing, and yelling was already stressful enough but Tony waving the gun and threatening to shoot DeMarcus, had raised my blood pressure to a dangerous level.

Everything was happening so fast and I needed it to stop! Lisa began quoting scripture from the Bible just as Auntie fell to her knees and prayed out loud over my dad. Geo too was now coming unglued and yelling impatiently from the top of his lungs for someone to check outside to see if the ambulance had arrived.

Concerned about the amount of blood coming from Jamal's shoulder, it wasn't until I stepped around the table and saw the handle protruding from Jamal's chest that I realized he had been stabbed again. I dropped to my knees then bumped DeMarcus with my body from atop of Jamal's body. I laid my hand on Jamal's chest and screamed for him to hang on. Seconds later, two gunshots rang out. DeMarcus was hit. Grabbing his chest, DeMarcus fell face-first into the floor.

"You whaten playing and I whaten either," bragged Tony.

"You'll bleed a lil' bit but you'll be a'ight."

"Markie!" I heard DeMarcus's mom scream before she ran to his side. But I was unconcerned about DeMarcus; my focus was on Jamal who began foaming at the mouth and moaning in excruciating pain. Assuring him that help was on the way, I was a complete wreck when for a brief second, he looked into my eyes then his head fell to the side.

It seemed odd having the police arrive before the ambulance but after explaining the situation, DeMarcus was handcuffed and taken away in the first ambulance. It seemed to take forever for the second and third ambulances to arrive but when they did, Kim and Jamal were both placed on stretchers and taken away. The paramedics assessing my dad determined his injury to be a sprained wrist and after wrapping it up, provided Auntie with in-home instructions for continued care.

Anxious to get to the hospital, Lisa offered to watch the kids, so I grabbed my purse and the keys to the truck, then darted out the door. Tony jumped in the passenger seat. We rode the expressway—80 mph the entire way.

I wasn't surprised that we beat the ambulances to the hospital but to expedite the admissions process, I provided the intake clerk with Kim and Jamal's medical information. And ten minutes later when the ambulance arrived, I grabbed Jamal's hand and followed the gurney down the long hallway.

"Dry your eyes, babe, I'll be OK. We're gonna get through this, I promise. I love you."

Tearfully waving goodbye as he was rolled into surgery and I was prevented from going further, I returned to the nurse's station to inquire about Kim. Geo was there doing the same.

His shirt was stained with her blood and visibly, he was a mental basket case.

"No news is good news," I said, hoping to lift his spirits but my words were of no comfort.

Grabbing Geo's hands, I motioned for Tony to join us as I led the prayer for their speedy recovery. I thanked God for things not being any worse than they were.

Totally focused on keeping upbeat, I hadn't thought about DeMarcus until we were interrupted by a man asking if we were DeMarcus's family. Revealing a badge, Detective Macklin then asked if any of us were named Tony. Acknowledging his presence, Tony and Detective Macklin moved their conversation to the back of the waiting room.

Waiting for information on their status was nerve-wrenchingly grueling, but three hours later when Dr. HD Mills called me by name, my heart sank. I feared the worst. My heart rate increased, and my knees buckled beneath me, making it hard to stand. Thankfully, Geo and Tony were at my side.

"Your husbands' surgery was a success. He's in recovery now and in about an hour, you'll be able to visit with him."

"What about Kim Spears? Can you tell me anything about her?" Geo asked.

"I was also told that Ms. Spears is going to be fine and she too is on her way to the recovery room. I'll make sure the staff informs you when you're able to visit her as well."

What was to be an hour wait rolled into an hour and thirty minutes, then into two hours, and then into three hours. By the fourth hour, I had grown overly anxious and needed to see Jamal. It felt like we'd been forgotten— watching several doctors and nurses pass by us without making eye contact or even looking in our direction, for that matter. My nerves were shot from not knowing, and it was then that I decided to sneak to the back the next time the security doors opened. It worked!

Glancing at the boards outside of the room doors wasn't helpful in finding Jamal. It must have been for privacy protections that none of the patients' names were written on them, so I devised a new plan to inconspicuously peek inside each of the rooms until I found him. Walking toward the first door, I froze when a nurse tapped my shoulder and asked me to follow her.

We walked down a long narrow hallway which was a great distance from the waiting area. Approaching a door monitored by cameras and guarded by officers, 'what the hell' I thought when asked for identification. Oddly, they searched my purse and scanned my body with a wand. The nurse was also scanned. When clearance was given, an armed guard escorted us through the next security door.

"It's the procedure," the nurse said, seeing the perplexed look upon my face.

"Your husband, victims of domestic violence and gun crimes are kept away from the general public for purposes of anonymity and judicial reasons. We've had people under witness protection and even cold-hearted criminals kept under lock and key back here."

Entering a code then swiping her badge to gain access, she turned and informed me that my visit was restricted to ten minutes.

"But if you need anything, sweetie, push the red button on the wall, OK."

I had only taken four steps into the room before realizing the huge mistake taking place. The lights were dimmed but I could see that a handcuffed DeMarcus lay in the bed, not a recovering Jamal as I was expecting. Seeing his face nearly sent me into cardiac arrest. My knees locked—I was unable to turn around or move toward the door to exit. I was within reach of the red button but unable to extend out my arm. I stood in silence. Then I heard DeMarcus's voice.

"I've lost everything; you, my kids, my church, everything. But for everything I did that brought you to tears, and the times I struck your pretty face with my wicked hand, I apologize. Roz, from the bottom of my heart I offer my sincerest apologies."

I wanted out of his room and fast. I didn't accept his apology, nor did I want to waste another precious moment away from my husband listening to DeMarcus's lies. I pressed the button on the wall, but no one answered. I banged on the door, but no one came. DeMarcus called my name and like a child, I covered my ears.

"It's no coincidence that you were brought back to see me. I prayed to God that I'd get the chance to talk to you before I go. Roz, for my sins, my time on this earth has been cut short. There's nothing more the doctors can do for me and I've settled it in my spirit that this is my fate. But God has granted me this time with you to share some things I feel you must know. First, I didn't marry you because you were pregnant. I asked you to marry me because I was in love with you. And I know with certainty that DeMarya and Junior are my children. DeMarya is the spitting image of me and well, Lil D, he has my mannerisms. I don't know why I let my mom and others believe otherwise but I love my kids and I wish that I could have been a better father. Please tell them that I loved them very much."

"What do you mean, you loved them? You're not making any sense, DeMarcus."

"I've lost a lot of blood and I know my fate, Roz. Two doctors agree that it would be some sort of a miracle if I make it through the night. The bullet left a substantial amount of metal fragments in my heart and the powder inside of the bullet is toxic; no surgery will help. But I'm OK. We all got to leave this world one day. I'm just sorry for having hurt so many people. But He's given me this opportunity to get things right with you before I go home. So, please listen."

DeMarcus continued to speak and revealed most of what I had already known and had forgiven him for. He admitted to the adulterous relationship with Evonne and a few others in the church and confessed to stealing money from the EBLC, the church, the kids' savings account, and from me.

"You've hurt a lot of people, DeMarcus, but I forgave you a long time ago. But what made you snap? Why did any of this have to happen? You stabbed Kim, and you could have harmed your children, or me. Why, DeMarcus?"

Jealousy and envy were the reasons he gave. He apologized for hurting Kim and Jamal then asked about their condition. He choked up when explaining that the encounter with my dad was an unfortunate accident.

"This may be the last time you ever see me, so may I ask you one last thing?"

My emotions were all over the place, from hatred to anger, from compassion to love. And although DeMarcus's actions were reprehensible, my heart had softened. I didn't know what to feel and I didn't have the heart to turn away from him—a man on his death bed with one last request.

"Did you ever love me?"

"I did then and a part of me still does." My response was immediate and said with a complicated smile.

"You were my first love and even through the tough times, I loved you. Why do you think I stayed? I knew about Evonne and about our trip you took her on. I knew about the expensive jewelry you bought her, and about your matching tattoos. I also knew about the credit card you gave her and was paying off with our savings. And when I learned that you were living with Kim, I never said anything because I figured you were doing it to hurt me—through my friend, that is."

DeMarcus looked stunned—as if I had just lit a bomb underneath his bed. He shook his head and with an ashamed grin, admitted that I was always three steps ahead of him.

"There's something else," I said, taking a deep breath then clearing my throat.

"I know you didn't kill Evonne's husband."

"You believed in me, thank you!" DeMarcus smiled and attempted to sit up.

"I wasn't trying to harm him," I admitted, sobbing. "We struggled, I grabbed the thing, and it went in his chest. I wasn't trying to frame you, I promise! And the money, I... I saw it in your bag and because I was already angry about you taking Evonne on our trip, I took it. Please, DeMarcus, I beg your forgiveness too!"

DeMarcus didn't utter a word. In fact, he closed his eyes and fell back onto his pillow. Everything about clearing my conscious felt good. It was like a heavy rock had been lifted from my shoulders. Instantly, I felt released from my lies and was hopeful that on his deathbed, DeMarcus would forgive me as well. The door opened. DeMarcus's doctor entered accompanied by his nurse. Apologizing for interrupting our visit, the doctor extended out his hand and introduced himself as Dr. Frank Malone. He assumed I was Mrs. Jackson but I was quick to correct him.

"Well, Mr. Jackson," he said, looking down at his clipboard.

"I'm sure they've told you that for the remainder of your stay, you'll remain on the psyche ward and under the watch of a guard. It'll either be myself or Dr. Stone checking on you periodically to ensure you are healing properly," Dr. Malone informed him.

"He's not dying?" I questioned. Dr. Malone's words had me gasping for air.

"He told me he was dying and there is nothing more anyone can do!"

"Well, he's not dying but I have heard several people pierced with metal say that," chuckled Dr. Malone.

"Getting a tattoo is one thing but he was branded like cattle. So, he may feel like he's dying, but he's going to be just fine."

I raced out of the room in need of different air. Fumbling my way back to the emergency room, a nurse grabbed my arm and informed me that Jamal was out of recovery and asking for me. Excusing myself to freshen up, I locked myself in a hallway restroom and paced the floor. Foolish I was for allowing DeMarcus to play on my sympathy and manipulate me as he had all so well mastered. Overtaken with fear for revealing my darkest secrets, my nerves were in bunches wondering what he planned to do with the information.

My palms were sweaty and so was my forehead. I trembled profusely and literally could feel my blood pressure rising. Feeling faint and light-headed, I sat on the wobbly toilet seat and put my face in the palms of my hands. Twice, the doorknob giggled—I guess someone needed to tinkle but twice I yelled that it was occupied. When feeling as though I could stand on my own, I splashed my face with water and glanced in the mirror. My reflection revealed a vision of stress. After running my fingers through my locks, I put on a happy face in preparation of greeting my husband.

Seeing Jamal was the highlight of my day. His right shoulder was bandaged so I ran to his left side and laid my head on his chest. Quick to notice my sweaty palms and trembling, I chalked my bizarre behavior up as being overly worried about his condition. He rubbed my back and told me not to worry.

As news of the Christmas day tragedy spread and church members began arriving in droves, it took everything within me to not fall apart with things weighing so heavily on my mind. The company was good for Jamal and for me too as every time his room became filled-to-capacity, it allowed me to escape into the hallway to sort out my thoughts. All was well until spotting Sister Harlow who before asking about Jamal's or Kim's condition, pulled me aside and asked if we could talk.

"You've been through a lot, Sista," she said, forcing me into a hug.

"Oh, how good our God is. I'm so glad to hear that everyone is doing well."

"Yes, I thank God that everybody is going to pull through. Jamal may be released as early as tomorrow but Kim's gonna be here a few more days. But still, our God is good!"

"That's good, baby, real good news. But I wanted to talk to you about Brother Jackson. I just left his room and he has a very interesting story to tell."

As if I care, is what I hope my body language displayed when I shifted my weight—and neck to the side and stared at her on the eyeballs.

"I apologize, Sista Harlow, but he's the reason for all of this, so forgive me if I choose not to focus on or discuss him right now, OK. Surely, you can respect that."

"It's just that," she continued. "I recall the conversation I had with you some time ago about how to bring your husband back down to earth. I can't help but wonder if some of what Brother Jackson has gone through was, well, because of you. According to him, he says that you confessed to setting him up."

"Sista Harlow, are you talking about DeMarcus Jackson in the psych ward, bed 2?"

"Yes, I am and the only reason I wanted to talk to you is because some of what he's saying makes a whole lot of sense. Like, where did you get the money to buy your new husband that big truck? And it is possible that you planted the keys at Mr. Delaney's house when they found him dead? The police are looking for the woman a neighbor saw leaving the house, was it you? And the notes and pictures found all over the church, it's not likely that Evonne would expose herself in such a distasteful way now, is it? Woman to woman, you can tell me. Was it you?"

It was at that moment I recalled what Ma told me when she too was in her hospital bed—*that some things you gotta take to the grave,* so I thanked Sister Harlow for coming and put an end to the interrogation. Turning my back to her, "Well did you know anything about it?" she yelled from afar.

Pausing briefly and before reentering Jamal's room, underneath my breath and with a slight smirk I mumbled, *"Perhaps."*

CPSIA information can be obtained
at www.ICGtesting.com
Printed in the USA
BVHW041040200521
607796BV00005B/745